What others are saying about St. Anne's Day

"Equal parts hilarious and heartfelt. Reading *St. Anne's Day* is a blessed event!"
- Julie Long, co-author *Baby: An Owner's Manual*

"Palko's feisty protagonist fights to overcome her past to find friendship and love. *St. Anne's Day* is a fast, warm, funny, and fulfilling read."
- Judith Burnett Schneider, *co-author The Frantic Woman's Guide to Life*

"*St. Anne's Day,* is a delightfully entertaining read with something for everyone: romance, suspense, humor, intense situations, good guys, bad guys. The characters are real and the story engaging."
- Ellen Gable Hrkach, award-winning author *Emily's Hope, In Name Only & Stealing Jenny.*

ISBN 978-0-6156-6224-4

Website: janicelanepalko.com
Twitter: @janicelanepalko
Blog: thewritinglane.blogspot.com
Facebook: Writer Janice Lane Palko
Pinterest: Janice Lane Palko

To those who have loved me in the past and present and whose love will carry me into the future—my parents, husband, and children.

There is no fear in love, but perfect love casts out fear. –
1 John 4:18

St. Anne's Day

By Janice Lane Palko

Chapter 1

"Come on. Move it." Anne Lyons slapped the steering wheel, her green eyes darting to the Malibu's digital clock. She was to be there by nine. If the traffic on the Fortieth Street Bridge didn't soon move, she was going to be late on her first day.

Her shoulder muscles kinked as she berated herself for not allotting time for traffic. Anne hadn't yet mastered estimating allowances for Pittsburgh's gridlock. She sighed. The rush of air from her lips ruffled a rust-colored curl that had slipped from her headband.

The previous night's thunderstorms had chased away the sultry July air. Beneath the bridge, the Allegheny River, a shimmering glass path, coursed toward downtown Pittsburgh, which gleamed like the crystal in Macy's Bridal Registry Department.

Ahead, an orange-vested worker flipped his "Stop" sign to "Slow," waving Anne's car through. "Finally." Her nose wrinkled at the odor of hot asphalt. There were only two seasons for Western Pennsylvania roads—snow removal and pothole patching.

The clot of cars flowed over the bridge. She turned left onto Butler Street, entering the heart of Lawrenceville. Anne had never been to this section of the city before. She was amazed at how much life had been packed into so little land. Bars, restaurants, doctor's offices, banks, and repair shops were crammed together, and where they left off, row houses took over, running perpendicular from the main street, up the hill to the site of the new Children's Hospital.

Anne slowed the Malibu, reading addresses. There it was on the corner—518 Butler Street. Bold brass letters above the entry spelled out MAC'S PLACE. "Oh, great," Anne snarled, "they gave me the address of a bar. That can't be right." She'd have to call the agency to get the correct one. Anne felt the pocket of her scrubs and groaned when she realized that she had forgotten her phone at home.

A block down Butler Street, she found a parking space. She hoped no one was watching as she did hand-to-hand combat with the steering wheel, fighting to wedge her car between two others parked at the curb. Having grown up in nearby rural Westmoreland County, she'd not yet mastered on-street parking.

Anne's jaws ached from clenching her teeth. She shut off the engine, quickly gathered her file and her medical bag, and stepped out of the car. The clock on the bank flashed 9:03. She felt as if the large digital numerals were timing her. Quickly, she fed a few coins into the parking meter and bustled up the sun-drenched street.

She scanned the old brick building for a side entry to a residence but saw none. Large plate glass windows, shrouded by tan and white striped awnings, wrapped around both sides of the corner. A forest green façade trimmed in brass framed the windows and the doorway. In comparison to some of the other storefronts, the bar looked as if it had been renovated. She'd heard other nurses in the office mention Mac's Place as having good food. Anne hoped it was open this early. Perhaps someone inside could direct her to her patient.

She pulled on the brass handle of one of the double door, passing through a small vestibule and another set of doors, entering the dark, cool pub. A scent of pine, as if the floors had been freshly mopped, masked a trace of spilled liquor. In the dimness, she made out the shadowy figure of a man working behind the bar that ran the length of the far wall.

Anne crossed the scuffed plank floor, weaving between tables, the rubber soles of her tennis shoes not making a sound. She had to stand on the foot rail, leaning across the counter to find the man who had stooped below the counter.

She cleared her throat and rapped her knuckles on the top. "Excuse me . . ."

The man startled, jerking upright.

When he turned to face her, she heard her breath catch with a small squeak in her throat. Before her brain could register that he was handsome, her body reacted by sending a rush through her as potent as if she'd been given an injection of adrenaline. Thick, wavy black hair contrasted to his light eyes that were as blue as a gas flame. As she gazed into them, something ignited inside her. Something that surprised and alarmed her.

"I'm looking for a patient." She was embarrassed at how breathless her voice sounded.

The man leaned across the bar with a wide grin. "You can take care of me anytime."

Anne stepped off the rail, backing away, and laughed nervously. "No, I'm serious."

"So am I." Resting an elbow on the bar to prop up his head, he smiled wickedly.

Anne felt herself blushing. She was used to flattery. What she wasn't used to was the feeling of wanting to fall for it.

Focus, Anne. You're already late. She tucked the straying curl behind her ear and covered her uneasiness by studying the file in her arm. "Really. I'm looking for a Margaret McMaster," she said, tilting her head, reading from the file header. "They have her listed at 518 Butler Street, but that is obviously wrong. Do you know where I can find her?"

Silence.

She straightened her spine, drawing herself up to her full four-feet, eleven and three-quarters inches and demanded, "Well, do you?"

"What's the information worth to you?"

Everything. I can't lose another job. "Please," Anne said, "this is important."

"What could be more important than you and me?"

What am I a jerk magnet? Anne felt the all-too-familiar anger building in her gut, the rage that waited like a coiled cobra for the opportunity to strike back at men who reminded her of Zach. What did that counselor say that she'd been forced to meet when she

5

worked at the hospital? *Take a calming breath.* Anne inhaled deeply, trying to speak calmly. "Look, do you or don't you know where my patient lives?"

He smirked. "Oh, I know."

When he didn't volunteer any more information, Anne looked at her watch, huffing. It was already nine twenty-one. "Is there a phone I can use?"

"There might be."

"You don't understand. I'm late. I don't have time for games." Anne spun on her heels, starting for the door.

"Wait! Why, it's your lucky day," he said, as he caught up to her at the doorway, placing a hand on her shoulder.

"Don't touch me!" She jerked away.

He threw up his hands. "Whoa, sor-ry."

Seething and embarrassed that he been able to provoke her temper, she turned and pushed on the door. It opened a foot then stuck. She shoved it again, putting all her one hundred and two pounds behind it. It didn't move. She drove her shoulder against it, and as she did so, she looked up and discovered that he was holding the door in place. Out of breath, her face as red as her hair, she glowered up at him. "Let me out now!"

He smiled. "She's here."

"What?"

"I said she's here."

"Who's here?" Anne glanced around the bar.

He leaned in closer, so close she thought he might kiss her. And half of her hoped he would. But he stopped, just inches from her lips. "Your patient. Mrs. McMaster. She lives upstairs."

"What? Why didn't you tell me?"

"I was having too much fun."

Anger erupted in Anne, a mushroom cloud of rage roiling throughout her. Grimacing, she curled her fingers into a fist and swung at him.

Before she could connect with his jaw, he caught her wrist

"Let me go." She struggled to wrench herself from his powerful grasp until her fury subsided and logic took over. He was much bigger and stronger; she could not get away from him. *Perhaps if I play on his sympathies.* "Please let me go. I have a very sick patient who is waiting for me."

Still clutching her wrist tightly, he pulled her closer until she was nearly smack against his chest. Anne could see each individual black whisker of his beard.

At that moment, she decided that whoever he was, no matter how handsome he was, she hated him.

He laughed, dropping her hand. "Aren't you the little hothead."

"Hothead? Who do you think you are?"

He tilted his head, smiling smugly. "Only the person who hired you."

Chapter 2

Anne closed her eyes and softly groaned. Her temper had been the reason she'd been let go from her last job at Latrobe Hospital and had been forced to move to Pittsburgh.

Now, after attempting to punch her client, she knew she'd be fired again. She braced herself for the man to begin screaming at her and throw her out of the bar.

A smile broke over his face as he stuck his hands in his pocket. "Wow, that's some temper you got there, Slugger."

She stepped back, eyeing him warily, but all he did was grin at her. If he was going to fire her, she wanted it over quickly before she started to cry. "Look," Anne said, raising a hand, "I'll save you the trouble of phoning the agency. I'll go to the office right now and have another nurse sent over."

"You can call me Mac."

"Pardon me?"

The man thrust out a hand. "Mac, that's what everyone who works for me calls me."

Anne cautiously shook it. His hand was large and warm. "Works for you? Aren't you going to fire me?"

He raised a black eyebrow. "Do you want me to?"

"W-well, no."

"OK then. I won't." He crossed his arms in front of his chest.

Not trusting him, she squinted. "Why not?"

He shrugged. "I figure any nurse who's willing to duke it out to get to her patient is the kind of nurse I want taking care of my mother."

Anne blushed. She'd always had trouble controlling her tongue, but she'd never had trouble controlling her fists before. There was something about this man that provoked in her a physical response.

He waved an arm over his shoulder. "Come on, I'll take you to my mother."

Puzzled and grateful that he hadn't dismissed her, Anne followed. As he led her through the bar to a door in back, she readjusted her headband, trying to tame her disheveled curls.

"After you." He held the door, making a sweeping gesture with his arm. As she ascended the staircase, intuitively, she felt his eyes scrutinizing her body, appraising her backside. She wished she was wearing something more attractive than scrubs.

At the top of the stairs, she found a kitchen, with white metal cabinets and a chrome and Formica breakfast set. The smell of freshly perked coffee filled the air. The refrigerator, going through one of its cycles, softly hummed against the far wall.

Mac guided her across the yellow-speckled linoleum into a hallway painted Pepto-Bismol pink. The floor was covered in avocado sculptured carpeting. A hallway ran through the center of the apartment, with doors flanking each side. Anne noted a bathroom on the left. Its ceramic tile gleamed but in a dreadful color combination of purple and lime. The apartment was clean and neat, but the dated décor shouted that an elderly person lived there.

Mac stepped through the doorway, passing by a credenza upon which sat a three-foot tall statue of the Sacred Heart. As Anne stood behind her new employer, she eyed the statue. Her grandmother had had one similar to it when she was small. It had always given her the creeps. Jesus, looking placid, wore his heart outside his chest. It was wrapped in thorns, pierced, and bleeding.

That's what exposing your heart will get you.

"Oh, Peg, Nurse Goodbody is here."

Anne wasn't amused but was so relieved that he hadn't fired her, she thought it best to hold her tongue. Without so much as a dirty look his way, she entered the room.

10

A yellow rosebud-printed sheet lay over the sharp ridges and angles of the frail old bones of the woman sleeping in the hospital bed, which dominated the room. Depressions left in the gold carpeting revealed that the nightstand and dresser had been moved to accommodate it. The woman slept with her mouth gaping. Faint light coming from the room's lone window left deep shadows in the hollows of her sunken cheeks as she snored softly.

Anne had read over her patient's file while eating her breakfast. She knew Mrs. McMaster was nearly eighty, had a history of heart disease and had recently had triple bypass surgery. She had come home only yesterday.

The old woman's roots had gone white, but the rest of her hair was dyed a color that was a cross between Punk Rock red and flamingo pink.

"Peg, wake up," Mac said, raising his voice a notch. "Florence Nightingale is here."

Mrs. McMaster slowly opened her eyes, giving Anne a weak smile. "Don't pay any attention to him, Dear," she said, her voice sounding weak. "He's always a pain in the ass."

Anne chuckled.

"She's already discovered that," Mac said.

At least he doesn't take himself seriously either. His remark reduced the tension level; Anne felt less ill at ease.

Mac went to the bedside and rubbed his mother's spotted, veiny hand. "Mum, this is . . . Sorry. They told me your name, but I've forgotten it."

He can't remember my name, but he probably has every curve of my ass memorized. "It's Anne. Anne Lyons," she said softly as she moved closer to the old woman, gently touching her spindly arm. "I'm going to help you to get back on your feet."

Mrs. McMaster's face brightened and her skin, which had been pale while sleeping, now pinked. "What day is it?" Her lips were dry and stuck to her teeth as she spoke. Pushing with her hands and elbows, she struggled to sit up.

11

"It's Friday," Mac said as he held her shoulder to the mattress. "Hold still, let me raise the bed."

Anne noticed that he was not wearing a wedding ring.

Mrs. McMaster licked her lips as the head of the bed slowly rose. "No, I mean, what's the date?"

"July 26," Anne said. "Would you like some water, Mrs. McMaster?"

"Yes, Honey."

Anne moved to the other side of the bed and grabbed the pitcher from the nightstand. She shook it. "Is this fresh?"

"Yes," Mac said. "Went down to the banks of the Allegheny River this morning and filled it up myself."

Mrs. McMaster waved a hand at her son as she scrutinized Anne. "He's a wise guy. Ignore him. Did you say your name was Anne?"

"Yes, Anne Lyons."

"Irish?"

Anne poured her some water and helped her to drink. "Nearly all, except for one German grandparent."

"That explains the hard-headedness," Mac muttered.

Anne shot him a withering look across the bed.

Mrs. McMaster smacked her lips and handed the glass back to Anne. "You're such a pretty little thing with that red hair. I knew you had to be Irish." She looked up at her son. "Isn't she pretty?"

He patted his mother's hand. "I've got eyes, Peg."

Anne felt the heat begin in her chest, rise up her neck, spreading across her cheeks. This was going to be a challenge working here.

"Where are my glasses?" Mrs. McMaster asked.

Anne laughed. "You might not think I'm that pretty after you put them on."

"She'll think you're doubly so." Mac winked.

Anne felt her heart speed up.

As he located the trifocals on the nightstand and held them up to the light to check if they needed to be cleaned, Anne took the opportunity to study him more closely. She judged him to be six feet

12

tall. He had the perfect bone structure of a model—well-formed nose, firm jaw—but the small scar on his chin gave his face enough ruggedness to keep him from appearing pretty. His green golf shirt and pleated khakis hugged a toned body. The brighter light of his mother's room, made the contrast of his dark hair and shocking blue eyes more distinct. And more handsome. *Why did he have to be such a jerk?*

Out of the corner of his eye, Mac caught her staring at him and smiled. Anne quickly looked back at her patient.

"Do you believe it?" Mrs. McMaster said, her eyes looking three times their size behind the thick lenses. "What luck! I'm feeling better already."

"Why's that?" Mac asked. "Because you're back home with me?"

Mrs. McMaster rolled her eyes. "July 26—it's the feast of St. Anne." She folded her hands contentedly. "They send me a beautiful Irish nurse named Anne on St. Anne's feast day. It's a sign."

Mac rolled his eyes. "Be forewarned. My mother has a saint for every day, every circumstance, and every occasion."

Anne wondered if Mrs. McMaster had a saint who could change his personality. Then she remembered there already was one—St. Jude, the patron saint of hopeless causes.

"Don't laugh." The old woman glared up at her son. "When I was a young girl, I'd say the prayer, 'Dear St. Anne, get me a man as fast as you can.' The nuns at school taught us that so we'd get dates for the dances. It worked. St. Anne found me my Martin."

"Wasn't St. Anne demoted by the Pope, like St. Christopher?" Mac said.

"You're going to roast in hell," his mother warned.

He aggravates everyone.

"Well, Ladies, I know you'll be heartbroken," Mac said, "but I've got to get back to work. I'm expecting a delivery." He turned to

13

Anne. "If you need me for anything, I'll be downstairs." He patted his mother's head. "Don't do anything I wouldn't do."

She batted his hand away. "That doesn't leave much," Mrs. McMaster scoffed.

As he left the room, Anne took her turn and scrutinized his ass. The khakis were nicely filled out.

"He laughs about the saints, but they work," Mrs. McMaster said, interrupting Anne's thoughts.

"Pardon me?"

"The saints. They really work."

Not wanting to get into a theological debate, Anne changed the subject. "Mind if I ask you a few questions?"

"Knock yourself out, Honey."

Anne dragged a chair over to the bed and sat. "How have you been feeling?" She opened the file on Mrs. McMaster and prepared to take notes.

"Like death warmed over."

Anne chuckled.

"Had I known how hard this surgery was, I'd have never had it. It would have been easier to die."

"You've been through a lot, but let's not talk about dying. I'm here to help you get you well."

After Anne inquired about her general health—her appetite, bowels, energy level—and made notations, she reached into her medical bag for her stethoscope. "I'm going to examine you now, Mrs. McMaster." Anne rose and began to elevate the bed.

"Anne, Honey, call me Peg. Mrs. McMaster sounds like an old lady."

Anne smiled as she pressed her stethoscope to Peg's chest. While she listened, to the lub-dub of her overhauled heart, she observed the red incision between her slack breasts. It was healing nicely.

"Sounds good," she said, removing the stems of the stethoscope from her ears. Anne looked over the list of medications that had been prescribed for Peg. "Have you taken your medication this morning?"

"Yes, my Gerry gave them to me."

"Gerry?"

"My son. That's his real name, you know. I named him after St. Gerard, the patron saint of motherhood. Mac's just what the people in the bar call him. I hate it. Sounds like something you call a cabby or bookie. Gerard's such a beautiful name. He laughs, but if it weren't for St. Gerard, he wouldn't be here."

"Why's that?" Anne took Peg's thin wrist, searching for her pulse.

"I had Gerry when I was forty-one, which was pretty risky back in those days. My Martin and I tried for ages to have a baby, then when I thought I was too old . . . " Peg shrugged. "Don't you know I got pregnant. As they say, as long as you're in the infantry, you can always get shot. Marty was so proud of himself. All the guys in the bar ribbed him. I was so happy. And scared."

Anne recorded her heart rate. "It's natural to be frightened at that age, especially that many years ago."

"That and I'd had five miscarriages."

Anne looked up from the chart, placing her hand instinctively on her abdomen. "Oh, my! Five? That must have been terrible."

"It was, but I prayed faithfully to St. Gerard for a healthy baby. God answered my prayers." Peg smiled sweetly, the love for her son evident on her face. "He gave me a beautiful boy."

No wonder he thinks he's God's gift to women. His mother thinks he's God's gift to her.

"Do you and your husband have any children, Dear?"

"Children? Me? Oh, no. No children. No husband either."

Peg's mouth dropped open. "A lovely girl like you—not married? I don't believe it. You must have a beau then?"

Anne patted Peg's shoulder. "You sound like my mother. No beau either. I don't think I'll ever get married."

"But you'd like to?"

15

"I don't know. Sure. I guess. But I've given up hope." More than anything Anne wanted to find the right man, fall in love, and get married, but she thought it'd be easier to locate the "missing link" than to find Mr. Right.

"Don't give up. Say the St. Anne prayer, Honey. She'll find you a husband. I bet she'd find you a real dreamboat since you're named for her."

Anne snickered. "Oh, I think I'll need more help than that."

Peg grabbed her arm, her grip surprisingly strong. "Don't laugh. Say the prayer. Your day will come, Anne. Just wait. You'll see. You'll find your true love."

"True love? I think that went out of style years ago."

"Oh, no. It never goes out of style. What does St. Paul say— 'Love never fails.'"

Anne wished she could be as sure as Peg, but she'd seen and experienced too much to believe in fairy tales anymore.

"You believe in true love, don't you, Honey?"

She thought of her parents and how they seemed made for each other. "I guess I believe it can happen for some people. But today? I don't know. Times have changed. It seems rather old-fashioned."

Anne fastened the cuff around Peg's saggy upper arm, pumping it up.

"I just wish Gerry would find a nice wife before I die. Then I could go to my grave in peace."

Anne stopped pumping, the cuff slowly deflating as she pointed a finger at the old woman. "Now that's the last time I want to hear you talk about dying, Young Lady. You have a completely revamped heart. If you take care of yourself, you've got many good years yet to come."

"You're the nurse," Peg said, pursing her lips.

Anne finished taking her blood pressure, noting the figures in the file. She looked around the room. "Now, did the hospital send a basin home with you? I'd like to bathe you. We'll do this in bed for now until you get a bit stronger."

16

Peg pointed to the closet where Anne found a small tub along with other medical supplies. "Towels are in the linen closet in the bathroom."

Anne returned, an orange towel thrown over her shoulder, carrying the basin filled with hot water. With her hip, she nudged the bedroom door shut. "Ready?" Peg was so weak Anne had to help her remove her cotton gown. Her wrinkled skin hung in slack folds. As Anne started to bathe her, she noticed that Peg was softly crying.

Alarmed, Anne stopped. "Am I hurting you? Are you in pain?"

Peg shook her head. "Look at me." She sniffled, holding her hands out. "When I think of what I used to look like." She took off her glasses, wiping away huge tears.

Anne knew where Mac got his beautiful blue eyes—from his mother. But hers looked so sad now, Anne's heart went out to the old woman.

"I had great legs. Now look at them." She slapped her atrophied thighs. "You know, I entered a Betty Grable look-alike contest. That's where I met my Martin. I lost, but afterward this big, handsome lumberjack came over and said, 'I know why you didn't win. You're prettier than Betty Grable.'" She sobbed. "Now, I'm a mess."

"You're not a mess." Anne put her arm around her. "You're just depressed. It's common after heart surgery. Once we get you up and around, you'll feel much better."

After Anne had bathed and dressed her, she combed Peg's two-toned hair. "There now." Anne stepped back from the bed to survey her handiwork. "Don't you feel better?"

"A little."

The rest of the morning passed quickly as they got to know one another. Many nurses Anne knew didn't like caring for the elderly because they tended to reminisce and prattle. Anne, however, enjoyed hearing how after Peg had been widowed when Gerry was small, she took over the bar and worked in it until she was 74, when she had her first heart attack.

Near noon, Anne stood. "Now, you're going to hate me, Peg, but I need to get you out of bed."

She shook her head. "I can't. I'm too fagged out."

Anne stifled a chuckle at Peg's politically incorrect term. "I know, but it's not good to lie there. I'll help you."

Anne adjusted the bed to the proper height and helped Peg swing her legs over the side. She instructed Peg to put her arms around her neck while she supported the old woman under the arms.

"On the count of three," Anne said, "we'll stand, and I'll help you into the chair. Ready? One. Two. Three!" Anne felt Peg shift her weight onto her. She lifted and Peg struggled to rise on her wasted, wobbly legs.

"Oh, Jesus, Mary, and Joseph!" Peg cried. "I'm falling."

"No, you're not. I've got you."

"Put me back in bed. I'm too weak!"

"You're fine."

"The hell I am."

"Oh, Peg, I've got you."

"You're going to kill me!"

"What the hell is going on?" Mac shouted.

Anne looked over Peg's shoulder and saw him rush in, plop two Styrofoam boxes on the dresser, and run to his mother. He wrapped his arms around Peg's waist and began moving her back toward the bed.

"Don't put her back in bed." Anne tried to steer her the other way.

"She's too weak," Mac shouted, wrestling Anne for control of his mother.

"I know what I'm doing."

"You're going to hurt her. For God's sake, she just got out of the hospital.

"Stop playing tug of war with me," Peg cried.

"Let go of her. Now!" Anne barked, stomping her foot.

18

Startled, Mac released his mother. Anne slowly guided Peg into the seat.

Peg slumped in the chair, panting. Gerry dropped to his knees beside her. "Mum, are you OK?"

"I'm a little lightheaded."

He looked up at Anne, panic in his blue yes. "See. She's lightheaded. Should I give her some water?" Before Anne could answer, he turned to his mother. "Need some water?" He didn't wait for a reply; he dashed over and refilled her glass.

After Peg took a few sips, she looked up at the two of them and smiled feebly, obviously enjoying the attention. "It's nice to be up, even though I feel like a lily dipped in shit."

Mac frowned, staring Anne down. "I think she should be back in bed."

Anne put her hands on her hips. "She can't stay in bed forever. It's bad for circulation."

"But my God, she just got home. Take it easy on her."

"Are you a nurse?"

"While you two argue, I'm wasting away. How about my lunch?" Peg said.

"OK, OK." Mac hustled to the corner and brought over a tray. As he set it up, Anne glared at his back. He retrieved one of the boxes, set it before his mother, and opened the lid.

Anne stared in disbelief at the lunch he'd brought his mother. "Fried fish?"

Mac's jaw tensed. "What's wrong with that?"

"Nothing, if you want to kill her. She just had heart surgery. She can't eat fried foods."

But Peg had already grabbed the fork and was chewing, tartar sauce smeared on her lips.

Anne looked at Mac, her green eyes blazing. "She's on a low-fat diet."

"Who are you?" he asked. "Nurse Ratched?"

Before Anne could reply, Peg asked for a cup of coffee.

"I'll get it," Mac said, asserting his authority. He walked out of the room.

"It better be decaf," Anne cried. Not sure if he'd heard her, she followed him into the kitchen. "It has to be decaf."

He turned. "What?"

"She can't have caffeine."

"I don't have any decaf up here, and she hates decaf. Can't she have anything good?"

"We have to discuss her diet."

Mac stared at her. This time his blue eyes were icy. The scar on his chin turned white as he clenched his teeth. "We have to discuss a lot of things. In fact, before you leave here today, I want you to stop by my office."

"Fine." Anne stomped away. He's going to fire me for sure now. But I don't care. I'll move back home and work in the brewery before I let someone tell me how to take care of a patient.

Anne glanced at the Sacred Heart statue. She looked at the wounded, tortured organ displayed in the center of the statue's chest. "I don't know about you, my friend," she whispered to the statue, "but I'm protecting myself. I'll quit before he can fire me. That should fix dear old, Gerard."

Chapter 3

Mac set his paperwork aside, pushing away from the desk. He closed his eyes, feeling the heaviness of the day's problems weighing him down. Although the office's furnishings were Spartan—a desk, metal file cabinet, chair, and leather sofa that he often slept on when he stayed late in the office, it was his sanctuary from the frenetic atmosphere in the bar. But today, even here he could find no peace.

Puffing out his cheeks, he exhaled and tallied worries in his mind. First was his mother's health. Would she recover fully enough so that he could have his life back? He felt as if he were a wishbone with Peg and the bar pulling at him from one side and his old life on the other. He'd thought hiring a private duty nurse would be his solution, but that brought him to his next problem.

Anne Lyons.

What do I do about her? After she'd berated him about his mother's lunch, he'd been so angry he fully intended to fire her. He was justified, he reassured himself. After all, she'd taken a swing at him and scolded him as if he were a child. However, as the day wore on, his anger had ebbed. Now, near the time for Anne to leave, he pondered his situation. *If I fire her, what will I do with my mother?* It could take days before the agency could replace her with another suitable nurse. He couldn't manage that long. And Peg liked her too.

As he reflected, Mac was forced to acknowledge that he was partly to blame for his and Anne's rocky start. He had come on strong to her, but he hadn't done it to upset her. He was only flirting the way he did with all the beautiful women he met.

Anne's face, scarlet with anger, flashed in his memory. Oh, she was tiny but mighty. *Mighty attractive.* Even dressed in dowdy scrub pants, her round, firm ass begged to be grabbed, and from his height, the V-neck on her cotton top had bloused enough to allow him a glimpse inside her shirt at her ample breasts as they swelled out of her bra while tending to his mother. With those flaming curls and sea-green eyes, she must be accustomed to men hitting on her. *Why would she get so upset with me?*

Maybe she was involved with someone. Maybe she was a lesbian. Or maybe I'm losing my touch.

Mac's eyes flew open. *Losing my touch? No way. Women love me. She's got some kind of problem.*

He rested his elbows on the scarred mahogany desktop, massaging his temples until the picture sitting on the corner of the desk caught his eye. Picking up the brass frame, he scrutinized the grainy, black and white photo. It had been taken when he was four. With a hammy smile and bad haircut, he sat perched atop the bar between his mother and father. They looked young and vibrant. It was their last family picture.

Everyone told Mac that he was his father's spitting image. How ironic to look exactly like the man who had given him life, yet be barely able to remember him. Mac was thirty-nine now, a few years younger than his father had been when he died. Mac felt that if he didn't soon change things in his life, he'd follow his father into an early grave.

He set the frame back on the desk, slouching into the leather chair, slowly swiveling it aimlessly back and forth. Mac couldn't say that he missed his father. It's hard to miss someone you never really knew. Mostly when he thought of him, it was regret that stung Mac's heart. Regret that he'd never known the man and regret for the life his father had led. He'd fought in World War II and then had worked himself to death establishing the bar.

Mac had pledged to himself when he was still a teen that he would not be like his father and take life too seriously or let himself be tied down. As a result of his pledge, he'd resisted taking over the bar, instead studying architecture in college—much to Peg's disappointment. After college he started an architectural firm, and he made quite a name for himself and his company. When the steel industry collapsed, many Pittsburghers left for employment elsewhere and that combined with the scores of people who had moved to the suburbs, had left a number of city parish churches with empty pews. The Diocese of Pittsburgh had sold off several of these old churches, and Mac and his firm had been instrumental in turning them into nightclubs. Peg thought his work a sacrilege and had begged him to stop. Mac had refused. He was convinced that she had purposely taken a heart attack six years ago so that he'd have to dial back his business and do something he'd always avoided—running the family bar.

He hated to admit it but he enjoyed running it and was good at it. Sure, the hours were long and it was fraught with responsibility, but most of the time it felt like play. Where else could you make a great living serving drinks and flirting with women? Life was one endless happy hour. And he'd always assuaged his fears by telling himself that his running the bar was temporary.

Or it had been until Peg's last heart attack two weeks ago. Before she'd been wheeled into heart surgery, Peg had extracted a promise from him—that he'd run the bar and not sell it at least until she died.

He'd been so frightened at the time, he had agreed. Now Mac was even more frightened. He had made a pledge to keep Peg alive, but in doing so he had set himself up for an early death—just like his father. All he needed was a wife to seal his fate and early demise. And if Peg and her saints had their way, he'd be married and dead in no time. Just like his father.

"The hell I will." He pounded the desk. *I'll run this bar, but I will not settle down with any woman. I don't care how many strands of rosary beads my mother wears out or how many novenas she says. I'm not getting married. I'm taking my life back.*

That's why he'd hired Anne. He'd spent the past fourteen days dividing his time between work and the hospital. He'd thought things would be easier when Peg came home, but the amount of care she required was overwhelming. He needed help. He needed Anne.

Anne. He passed his hands over his face, running his fingers through his thick hair. Gently tugging his black locks as if to rip them out, he muttered, "What do I do about Anne?"

***

"Yoo-hoo." A white-haired woman who looked like Mrs. Santa Claus stuck her head around the doorframe.

"Come on in, Irma," Peg said.

Irma Schmitt teeter-tottered in, her lilac polyester pants making scuffing noises where her thighs rubbed together.

She walked to Peg's bed and plopped her ample backside on the mattress. She patted Peg's foot. "How you feelin' today, Kiddo?"

"Irma, this is my nurse, Anne Lyons."

Irma turned her head then chuckled. "Oh, I didn't see you there in the corner, Honey." She made an attempt to hoist herself up, but must have decided it required too much effort and settled back down on the bed. "Nice to meet you. Gerry told me you were starting today. I'm your relief."

Oh good. When I quit, I won't be abandoning Peg. "You're a nurse then?"

"Me, a nurse?" She put her hand on her chest, her large breasts quaking as she snorted. "Good heavens no."

"Irma's my friend," Peg explained. "She lives five doors down. Above the bakery. She's going to keep me company during the evening while Gerry's working down in the bar."

"So, Anne, how's my patient doing?" Irma eyed Peg with affection.

"Coming along nicely," Anne said. Peg smiled like a child receiving a gold star from her teacher. "It's simply a matter of her regaining her strength."

"Is there anything special I need to know or do for her?"

"No, only make sure that she gets her medication. I was just writing up a schedule when you came in. Here, let me show you."

Irma looked at the clock. "I can figure this all out. Why don't you leave now, Honey. We'll be fine. Beat the traffic. I'm sure a pretty young thing like you must have a date."

"She doesn't have a boyfriend," Peg said. "Can you believe it?"

Irma tsked. "Pity." Then she slapped her thigh. "Oops, I almost forgot. Gerry said for me to remind you to stop by his office on your way out."

All day Anne had dreaded facing him. She could kick herself for losing her temper again. Private duty nursing jobs were cushy and hard to come by these days and the pay was great. But she couldn't let some egotistical mama's boy tell her how to do her job. She'd quit before she'd let him dictate a patient's care.

Anne stood and Irma, laying her hands aside her plump cheeks, exclaimed, "Why, you're no bigger than a Kewpie Doll. I think I've finally found someone shorter than me, Peg. How tall are you, Honey?"

"Just under five feet."

"You could wear her on your watch fob," Peg interjected.

"I'm five-foot one. That's my height." Irma laughed. "I'd hate to tell you my width. I started out a little slip of a thing like you, but I married a baker." She spread her arms, showing off her ample figure. "As you can see, he was a good one. God rest his soul."

"God rest his soul," Peg intoned, her eyes closed reverently. Then she moaned. "Mmm, I can still taste Otto's cinnamon buns."

Anne picked up her bag. "Speaking of buns, I better get mine moving." She walked over, taking Peg's hand. Sadness tweaked her heart; Anne already had grown fond of her patient. "Listen, Peg," she squeezed the old woman's bony fingers, "take care of yourself."

"Thanks, Anne Dear. See you Monday."

Anne didn't want to mislead Peg, so she left without replying.

As she descended the stairs, her stomach flipped with anxiety. She fought the urge to sneak out the door and phone Gerry, "Mac," or whatever the hell his name was, later to tell him that she'd quit. But she knew that would be cowardly and unprofessional.

Inhaling deeply, she straightened her spine and walked into Mac's Place. The change in the atmosphere from the morning was amazing. People were crowded around the bar and the tables were nearly full. Music thumped in the background, and voices and laughter filled the place. The aroma of garlic and onions made her hungry. Anne scanned the bar area for Mac but didn't see him. She walked over, signaling the bartender.

"Excuse me. Do you know where Mr. McMaster is?"

"You must be Anne. He said you might be looking for him. He's in his office taking a call." He nodded to the phone hanging on the wall whose red busy light was flickering. "I'll let you know when he's off. Have a seat."

"No, I'll just stand."

"Come on, take a stool. He might be a while."

Anne looked at the phone. The light was still flashing. *He's probably talking to my replacement.* "Oh, OK." While she waited, she would formulate her resignation speech. She put her bags on the floor, climbing onto the vacant stool.

"I'm Dave . . . Dave Weber." The bartender extended his hand. When she shook it, it was cold. She imagined from handling so many chilled drinks. "Can I get you something while you wait?"

"No thanks." She didn't want a drink; she just wanted to get this over with and get out of there.

"Come on, it's on the house." He raised an eyebrow. "It's Friday . . . Relax a little."

Her mouth was dry from nervousness. "OK, I'll have a ginger ale."

He playfully arched an eyebrow. "Sure you can handle that?"

After blowing up and trying to punch Gerry, she wasn't sure she could handle anything anymore.

He grabbed a hose from below the counter, his thumb pushing the button. She watched him slide a coaster onto the bar's top and set a frosty Mason jar before her with a flourish.

She guessed him to be in his late forties as his mouse-brown hair was thinning, and he carried some extra weight around the middle. He looked like he should be selling insurance instead of tending bar. What an odd pair he and Mac must make—the Adonis and the Actuary.

"How is Mrs. Mac?" he asked.

"She's doing well." Anne ran her finger up the glass, tracing designs in the condensation. "A little weak, but that's normal."

"Good . . . good. She's a great lady, and it's nice to have her back upstairs."

What a lovely voice he had, deep and soothing. People must find it easy to converse with him after a long day at work. Anne sipped her drink. She felt more relaxed since beginning to chat with him.

"You'll love working for the McMasters. They're the best."

That may be true about Peg but not her son.

"I've been working for Mac for nearly three years. I'm a teacher. I moonlight here on the weekends when school's in session. In the summer, I pick up more hours."

Anne glanced around the bar. "It must be quite different from school."

"It's a nice change. I have a son in college. An art major at Carnegie Mellon. The tuition is just about sending me to the poor house and the extra money helps."

"Do you teach art?" Anne asked.

A wiry, blonde woman in a white shirt and black pants carrying a tray scooted behind the bar. "Dave, I need two Bud Lights; a Rolling Rock; a Margarita, no salt; and a mojito. I'll get the beers. You do the fancy stuff." The woman talked machine-gun rapid, flitting from tap to tap, pouring beers, reminding Anne of the hummingbirds that visited her parents' feeder. Dave grabbed a glass and began to fill it with ice.

"Vera," Dave said, "this is Anne. She's Mrs. Mac's nurse."

"How ya doin'," Vera said, keeping her eyes on the beer flowing into the mugs.

"I was just telling Anne how much she's going to like working here."

Vera grabbed coasters and briefly caught Anne's eyes. "Oh yeah, you'll love it. Mrs. Mac is a spitfire. What can you say about Mac?" She loaded the beers onto her tray. "He's Mac." Laughing and shaking her head, she zipped away into the crowd.

Anne glanced at her Timex. When would he get off the phone?

"So, Dave, what do you teach?"

"History. That's how I met Mac. I belong to the Historical Society. When his company began converting churches into nightclubs a few years ago, he came to the society to get some direction on how to preserve them properly since some of them were historical landmarks. We became friends. When my son, D.J., went to school, he offered me a job here."

"His company?"

"Yeah, he had an architectural firm and was big into preserving the history of the buildings, but he's sort of put the business into mothballs since his mom has gotten sick."

He's an architect and a history buff? He didn't seem the type.

Dave looked over at the phone. "He's free now. His office is down the hall, past the restrooms, opposite the stairs. You'll see the PRIVATE sign."

Standing before the wooden, six-panel door, Anne straightened her scrubs and knocked.

"Come in."

Mac was seated behind the desk, papers scattered on its top, his head cradled in his left hand. He looked up at her, his dark brows pinched together in a frown above his blue eyes.

The intensity in his gaze startled her. *If I could custom order the ideal man, he'd look exactly like him. Thank God I'm quitting.*

"Do you have any clout with medical supply companies?" He tossed a paper on his desk. "They lost the order for my mother's bath seat. I've been handed off to four different clerks."

"No, I'm afraid I don't." Anne stood in the doorway. *How can I be attracted to him and hate him at the same time?*

"Have a seat." He motioned to the vinyl chair in front of the desk. His cologne, clean and spicy, was hypnotic, tempting her to come closer into the room.

Anne held up a hand. "No, what I have to say will only take a minute—"

"Please sit, Anne." His jaw tightened as he adopted a serious look. "What I have to say will take longer."

She didn't move for fear that if she took one step toward him, she'd lose her resolve.

"Please, Anne."

How harmful could it be to sit and work this out like adults? After losing her temper, she wanted to salvage some dignity, leave this job with grace. Anne moved to the chair and sat, her bag perched on her lap. She cleared her throat. "I think it's best if you find someone else because—"

"I want to apologize."

Stunned, she leaned forward. "Pardon me?"

He rose and walked around the desk. Then he sat on its edge directly in front of her. He wore leather cordovan loafers with tassels. Her eyes traveled up to where his pants rode above his sock, at the dark hair on his shin. Then up his leg to his muscular thighs. Look at his face! But she was immediately captivated by his eyes. The irises were blue with a faint golden sunburst radiating out from the pupils. She clutched her bags to her chest like a shield. *Oh, I've got to get out of here.*

"I said I want to apologize."

"You do?" Her heart was beating wildly.

"Yes. I do." He looked at her sorrowfully like a puppy that had been chastised with a rolled up newspaper. "I've been thinking about you all afternoon."

Anne was glad she was sitting, because she felt her legs turn to pudding just thinking about him thinking about her. *Get hold of yourself, Anne. You know his type—he's trouble, another womanizing idiot. Oh, but a damn gorgeous one.*

"I'm sorry about this morning. You were here as a professional, and I treated you like one of my customers. It's my job to chat up the ladies who come in here, to make sure they have a good time. Sometimes I forget to turn off the charm."

"Do you really do that?"

"Do what?"

"Chat up the ladies—flatter woman to attract business?"

He looked pained. "I'm not that shallow. I like my customers, and the ladies don't seem to mind my teasing. They expect it from me. The flirting is all in good fun."

She could understand how he would draw the female clientele.

"And I'd like to apologize for second-guessing you upstairs. I'm on edge. I feel like I've brought a time bomb home from the hospital. I'm so afraid I'm going to forget a pill or do something that's going to hurt my mother. Dave even gave me his son's old nursery monitor." He waved a hand toward the receiver sitting on the file cabinet, "I'm so afraid I won't hear her if she needs me." He tilted his head looking mournful.

Anne didn't know what to say. Flustered, she played with the latch on her bag.

"I'll keep my nose out of my mother's care," he said, "and I promise I'll try to treat you as a professional."

"Professional?" Anne repeated, surprised that she felt disappointed.

"Strictly business."

What is happening to me? I was insulted when he hit on me. Now I'm annoyed that his interest in me was only an act. She shook her head. "Aw, I don't know."

"Look, Anne, I need you."

He needs me? Anne shifted in her seat. She felt her cheeks burning. *Get hold of yourself. So he's gorgeous. You've had gorgeous before. You know how that turned out. You want more than gorgeous. You want someone who's serious. And you want this job. Is there anything harmful in enjoying looking at him? Guys ogle women all the time. I can handle him. I'm strong enough now. I can enjoy the view and still be professional.*

She looked at him sheepishly. "Well, only if you'll forget that I tried to punch you."

"You tried to punch me?" He stood, scratching his head. "I don't recall . . . " Then he smiled broadly, and it was like the sun breaking through on a cloudy day. "So it's a deal then?" He held out his hand. "A professional relationship."

Anne cautiously fitted her small hand into his large one. At his touch, it was as if all her veins and arteries were converted to wire, and a charge tingled throughout her body.

"Professional," Anne said weakly, shaking on their arrangement.

Chapter 4

Anne sank back into the chair. *What have I gotten myself into?* Her mind told her that Gerry "Mac" McMaster was poison for any woman looking for a serious relationship. Her hormones, however, told her to gulp the toxin.

As she warred with herself, she watched Mac's broad shoulders rise and fall in a huge sigh. "Now that that's settled, Ms. Lyons—"

"I know we made a deal to keep this professional," she interrupted, clutching the handles of her bags to keep from reaching out and grasping the bulging muscles of his shoulders, "but please won't you call me Anne? Ms. Lyons sounds so formal."

"Whatever you want. You set the ground rules." He shifted so that he was facing her directly and leaned toward her, resting his elbows on his thighs. "So about her diet, Anne, what do I need to know?"

She was relieved to think of something else besides how physically appealing he was. "Not that much. Cut out saturated fats. Watch her sodium intake. Limit red meat. Eliminate junk."

Mac grimaced. "Oh great."

"It's not that difficult to follow."

He straightened up. "I'm sure it's not, but getting my mother to eat that way is going to be a nightmare. She's old school. Bacon and eggs for breakfast. Roast beef and potatoes for dinner. I assume you met Irma. Well, she and her late husband used to own the bakery down the street. She still bakes. A lot. My mother's a sugar addict and Irma's her supplier."

"I'm sure if you talk to them and explain how important it is for Peg to eat a healthy diet, they'll be reasonable."

Mac raised an eyebrow. "Reasonable? Those two?"

"Maybe if I talked to them."

"Nah, then I'd have to give you hazard pay. I'll do it."

"I can get you a copy of the Heart Association's recommendations and some recipes that are healthier versions of what she's used to eating, if you want."

"That'd be great, Anne. Then I can give them to Luis, my chef. I make Mum breakfast, but he makes our lunch and dinner. With his flair for food, maybe she won't notice the difference."

Sensing that he had many questions about his mother's health and that the conversation would be an extended one, Anne moved the bags she'd been holding protectively in front of her to the floor. "You really should relax, Mac—, Mr. McMaster. She's doing as well as can be expected."

He smiled, and she noticed a small dimple winking playfully under his left eye. She knew that dimples were nothing more than muscle imperfections, but even imperfections looked perfect on him.

"I wish you'd call me Mac."

"OK, Mac," she paused before saying his name for emphasis. "As I was saying. Relax. Your mother is doing just fine. She's weak that's all. You'll be amazed how fast she regains her strength."

"I certainly hope so." A vertical line of concern creased his forehead.

"There is one problem."

"What? What is it?"

The alarm in his question revealed how tightly he was wound. Anne touched his arm to reassure him. The light growth of black hair on it was soft to her fingertips in contrast to the thick, hard sinews and muscles of his forearm. "It's nothing serious, Mac. She's mildly depressed."

"Depressed?" He rose from the desk, her hand sliding off his arm. "Why would she be depressed? She's getting better and she's home now."

34

"It's common after major surgery. Her body has suffered a shock. Many people find it difficult to cope with being ill and having to rely on others for care."

"Well, my mother's always been independent. She'll be OK, won't she?"

"Give her some time. I can think of one thing that might perk her up though. She's worried about her hair."

He turned up his nose. "Her hair?"

"The roots. They need to be touched up. She needs a cut too. Do you think you could arrange to have someone come in to do it? That might lift her spirits a bit."

Mac went behind the desk, sat in the chair, and began taking notes. "Call, Dolly Sladik," he mumbled as he wrote. Then he looked up at Anne. "Is there anything else?"

"Nothing I can think of except my hours," Anne said. "Is nine to five OK with you? I'm flexible. I can start earlier or later."

"No, nine is great. Then I can squeeze a run in. Since she's gotten sick, I've slacked off on exercising. I can get a few miles in, be back, shower, shave, and get to work by eleven. Normally, I'm not in the bar as early as I was this morning, but I had to wait on that delivery. I hated to leave her alone upstairs, but she said she would be fine. It couldn't be avoided." He stretched his arms over his head. Anne noticed the powerful muscles braided along his bones and wondered what it would feel like to be wrapped in them. "Well," he said, sliding the chair out from the desk and rising. "I don't want to keep you any longer on a Friday night. You've probably got plans."

Anne picked up her bags and stood. *Why does everyone think I have plans?*

"Oh, I almost forgot," he said. "Please don't tell my mother I hired you. She thinks Medicare provided you. She'd have another heart attack if she knew I was paying out-of-pocket for a private-duty nurse."

"My lips are sealed." Anne noticed how he glanced at her lips for an instant as if to see if she should be taken literally. The predatory gaze that passed over his face made her heart beat irregularly. Flustered, she bent and picked up her bags.

Mac started for the door. "I'll walk you out. Where'd you park?"

"Down the street, in front of the pharmacy."

"You'll probably have a ticket waiting for you."

"Oh no, the meter! I forgot all about it."

"Don't worry. I'll pay it. You can park in the back from now on," Mac said.

"Oh, you don't have to do that."

"It'll be my way of making up for getting off to a bad start."

Anne let his offer stand, but she would never let him pay. It was hard enough resisting the attraction she felt for him without feeling indebted to him as well.

"I'll show you where." He guided her through the bustling kitchen. The aroma of the food made Anne's mouth water. In front of a burner, a slightly built, olive-skinned man in his early twenties was flamboyantly flipping a medley of chopped vegetables in a sizzling pan. There were two other young men in the kitchen. One was prepping salads; the other ladling soup out of a large stainless steel pot.

"Luis," Mac called, "got a minute?"

"Luis is my chef," Mac explained. "The other two over there are interns from the culinary institute. While we're here, Anne, you might as well tell him about my mother's diet." Mac lowered his voice. "He's a little high-strung but the best cook around."

Luis moved like a dancer, gliding between stove and the steam table. At Mac's summons, he handed off the skillet to one of the interns then sauntered over to Mac and Anne.

"Luis, this is my mother's nurse, Anne Lyons. She'd like to discuss my mother's diet with you. Anne this is Luis Ibarra."

The chef wore a small gold earring, and his eyes were the darkest Anne had ever seen. She couldn't discern pupil from iris. His curly black hair that he'd secured in a ponytail and a well-trimmed goatee made him look more like a poet than a chef.

Luis took her hand in both of his and said in his accented voice, "It is so lovely to meet you, Anne."

The way he pronounced her name with a soft "A" made her want to sigh. She was used to hearing her name pronounced the way Western Pennsylvanian's did, nasally like E-Anne.

"It's nice to meet you too."

Never releasing her hand, he said, "Come with me." He led her to a chair in the corner with such style she felt as if he were escorting her onto a dance floor for a Tango.

"Sit down, Senorita Anne. Tell Luis how I may help you take care of Senora Mac."

Anne tried to focus. Although he was too young for her, his exquisite manner had her rattled.

"Well," she said her voice sounding shaky, "I'll bring you some guidelines, but basically, we need to limit her fat intake and cholesterol."

"I see." He listened as intently as if she were professing her love for him.

"And she should have plenty of fruits and vegetables."

"Consider it done. Anything for a beautiful woman like you. Now I must get back before that imbecile," he nodded toward the intern, "destroys my kitchen." He took her hand again. "Come down here next week, and I will make you something special." Then he kissed her hand and dashed away.

Anne glanced up at Mac, who had a sour look on his face.

"Good God, he thinks he's Antonio Banderas or something," he said. "If you can get past all his b.s., he's not a bad guy."

Do I detect a note of jealousy in his voice? Perhaps there were two roosters working this hen house?

Anne rose and followed Mac. Before they reached the door, she heard someone beeping behind her. Startled, she turned and found that she was blocking the path of a short man holding a basin of dirty dishes.

"Oh my, I forgot to introduce you to the most important person in the bar," Mac said. "Anne, this is my good pal and champion dishwasher, Bernie Schmitt."

"Pleased to meet you," Anne said.

"Bernie is Irma's son—"

"And your best buddy," lisped the man with Down's syndrome as he set the dirty dishes near the stainless steel sink.

Anne shook his plump, food-soiled hand.

"Do you like kiss?" Bernie asked.

"Pardon me?" Anne asked, as she tried to locate a towel.

Mac grabbed one and handed it to her. "He doesn't want to kiss you. Although he might," Mac said nudging Bernie. "He's a big fan of the rock group, KISS."

"Oh, that kind of KISS," Anne said, wiping her hands.

"Yeah, Gerry and I are going to see them."

Mac laughed. "Lucky me." He took the towel from her when she was finished. "Years ago I promised to take him to their concert if they ever came to town. I never dreamed they'd have a reunion tour." Mac rolled his eyes. "He wants us to wear face paint and black leather when we go." He touched Bernie's shoulder. "Anne's got to leave now, Buddy. She'll be back on Monday to take care of Mum."

"See you, Anne." Bernie stood, his feet forming a near-perfect right angle, flipping his hand in a wave.

Mac showed Anne the lot out back where she could park. It was a square patch of concrete. "That's my car there," he said pointing to the silver BMW convertible. "You can park in the spot next to it." Anne looked up, noticing that the window in Peg's room overlooked the lot. She wondered what Peg and Irma were doing now. Probably eating forbidden foods.

Then Mac guided her back into the bar. As they threaded their way through the crowd, fifteen women must have said "Hi Mac."

Wow, he is the number one attraction here.

Mac opened the door and asked if she needed any help getting to her car. She assured him she could manage.

"Enjoy your weekend then," he said as he held the door for her. "And don't forget to give me that parking ticket on Monday."

She walked through the doorway, looked back at him, and said, "Hopefully, I won't have one, Gerard."

His face froze. "Gerard?"

"Yes, Gerard. I think I'll call you that instead of Mac."

"But every girl that comes in here calls me Mac."

She widened her eyes, looking up at him. "But I'm not every girl."

"Point well taken. But call me Gerry. I hate Gerard."

"Don't you think St. Gerard will be insulted?"

He covered his eyes with his hands, groaning. "Good God, did my mother tell you that story about how she prayed to him for me and how I'm the center of her universe?"

"She did." With a playful laugh, Anne walked outside. She looked over her shoulder. "Goodnight, Gerry."

Butler Street was now camouflaged with long shadows cast by the evening sun. She plucked the ticket off her windshield and got into her car. As she pulled away, she checked her rearview mirror. Gerry was leaning against the doorframe, his arms crossed, watching her.

She sighed dreamily. It would be so easy to make someone as handsome as Gerry McMaster the center of her universe. Then she reminded herself that the last time she'd made someone the center of her universe, her world had fallen apart.

Chapter 5

"Nothing." Anne shut the mailbox. She went through the security doors, put the key in the lock, and walked up the flight of stairs, entering her apartment. Passing by the kitchen, she headed down the short hall into the living/dining area, where she set her bags on top of the glass table. She noticed a stack of unopened mail there. Janetta must have been home. For a change.

Since high school, Anne and Janetta Orlando had always plotted to one day be roommates. In April, after Anne had been fired from her position at Latrobe hospital, Janetta, who owned a tanning salon in the area, persuaded her to move to Pittsburgh and room with her. Anne assumed they would pal around once she moved in, but since Memorial Day, Anne could count on one hand how many nights Janetta had spent with her in the apartment.

Anne sat and unlaced her running shoes. As she tugged off a sock and wiggled her toes, enjoying the freedom of bare feet, the bed in Janetta's room began squeaking.

Anne closed her eyes and curled her upper lip. Oh great, not only is she here, but she and Steve are at it again.

Moans and shrieks, sounds more native to a zoo, carried out to Anne. She whipped off her other sock, marched out into the kitchen, and flipped on the garbage disposal, letting it grind for a full minute. When she turned it off, there was silence. She smiled smugly. *In-sink-erator interruptus.* Anne grabbed a Lean Cuisine from the freezer and popped it into the microwave.

Janetta's bedroom was next to the kitchen and through the thin walls, she heard Steve's voice. His volume control was perpetually set on high. "Why don't you bring Anne in here too? I'm big enough for the both of you. Might loosen Miss Priss up a bit."

Anne stuck her finger down her throat. *What does Janetta see in him?* Gerry was a thousand times more handsome. Then again, their taste in men had never agreed.

They had met Steve Novak at a Memorial Day picnic thrown by their neighbor Jeff Dietz. Steve worked with Jeff, and was drunk when he had been introduced to them. Anne thought him a loud blowhard, but Janetta found him attractive. Maybe it was his size; she had a thing for large men. Steve had played college football and had a neck like a tree stump.

Anne had only been in his company on a few occasions since then, but each time her opinion of him had grown poorer. A few weeks ago for Anne's twenty-ninth birthday, Janetta and Steve had treated her to dinner. While driving to the restaurant, he had given the finger to so many drivers, Anne vowed she'd never ride with him again.

However, what disturbed Anne most about Steve was the way he behaved with Janetta. A computer programmer, he treated her friend as if she were a p.c., issuing commands like: "Get me a beer. Come here. Shut up." Never a please or a thank you. Whenever Anne had criticized him, Janetta defended him with excuses that sounded like they had come straight from his mouth. "He's tired," she'd say. "He's uncomfortable around you because he knows you don't like him." Anne tried to bite her tongue, but she was finding her mouth bloody too often.

She knew from experience it was useless to warn Janetta about him; she had a penchant for married men, alcoholics, and guys who couldn't hold a job.

The microwave bell dinged. Anne juggled her dinner onto a plate and blew on her fingers. Carefully pulling back the plastic film, she released a cloud of steam and walked to the table. While she ate the lasagna, she went through her mail.

When Anne was nearly finished with her dinner, Janetta and Steve emerged from the bedroom. He was flipping down the collar on his knit golf shirt, and she was carrying a duffle bag.

Janetta smiled innocently at Anne, exclaiming, "When did you come in? We didn't know you were here." She tossed back her long straight hair, an act she always did that when she lied. Her swan-like neck was red and scuffed. "Did we, Steve?"

He grunted.

Janetta's bronze skin, eyes as black as sin, and her stature, like a Grecian column, gave her an exotic air. Her features—long nose, generous mouth, chiseled cheekbones—when taken separately were not particularly attractive, but when viewed together resulted in striking beauty. Sometimes when Anne stood next to her, she felt like the proverbial red-headed stepchild.

"We just stopped by to pick up some things," Janetta said. "We're going camping."

Anne laughed. "You? Camping? For God's sake, you call me to kill spiders."

Janetta took Steve's arm, looking adoringly at him. "Steve said he'll protect me from all the creatures."

Anne almost choked on a lasagna noodle. It's the creature in the tent she should fear.

"I didn't see your car in the lot when I came home," Anne said.

"We were visiting Jeff. It's parked down by his place. Well, we better get going. What are you doing this weekend?" Janetta asked.

As Anne followed them to the door. She wished she had some wildly romantic weekend planned that she could brag about. "I'm going home tomorrow. I promised to help Patsy and Vince wallpaper their nursery."

Janetta looked at Steve. "Anne's sister and her husband are expecting twins."

He snickered. "There's a chick at work who's having twins. Man, she looks like an elephant."

What a moron.

43

"Is Patsy up to wallpapering?" Janetta asked.

"No, she's tech support."

Steve didn't even grin at Anne's attempt at a computer joke. She'd taken care of comatose patients with more personality.

"Sounds exciting," Janetta said. "Have a good time."

"You too," Anne said through clenched teeth as she closed the door after them. Wallpapering was dull but it was better than spending a weekend in the woods with Big Foot.

She went to the kitchen window, which overlooked the parking lot, watching through the slats of the mini-blinds as Janetta struggled with the bag. Steve strolled in front of her, his beefy hands stuffed into the pockets of his jeans.

Anne shook her head. What had become of that spunky girl she met in high school?

Sister Constance had seated her ninth grade class alphabetically, but a myopic Donna Markovich, who had been assigned the desk behind Anne, complained that she couldn't see the board, so sister moved her to the front row. Orlando was the next name in the roll book, and Janetta not only filled the seat behind Anne but the spot as her best friend.

As a teenager, Janetta spent so much time at the Lyons' home, Anne's father often joked that he'd declared her a dependent on his income tax return.

Janetta's parents, Fiore and Carmella Orlando, were Italian immigrants, who had eight children. Janetta was their finale. Her parents were Old World, but their youngest child was anything but. She was impulsive, daring, and nothing like Anne. That's why they meshed so well.

Anne watched their car pull out of the lot. The others Janetta had dated were bad, but there was something different about Steve. Something that frightened Anne. How can someone as feisty as Janetta fall for someone like him?

The same way you fell for Zach. But at least he was kind. Until he broke my heart and ruined my life.

44

A feeling of regret and longing overwhelmed Anne. She closed the blinds, retreating into the living room. They'd left dirty glasses on the wooden coffee table. Anne grumbled to herself as she picked them up. Water rings discolored the wood. She took the glasses to the kitchen and retrieved a towel. She was always cleaning up after Janetta.

At least, I had the sense to learn from my mistakes and avoid men like Zach. And Gerry. She felt proud of herself for standing up to Gerry's overtures.

As Anne blotted the milky-colored rings, she worried that one day she might not be able to clean up Janetta's mess.

Chapter 6

Golden ribbons of sunlight streamed through the slats of the blind, striping Anne's face with light. Lifting an eyelid, she looked at the clock—seven forty-five. She let the lid drop. *I'll just lie here for a few more minutes.*

The room was stuffy; the air conditioning petered out before it reached the vents in her room. She rolled over onto the other side of the queen-sized bed where the sheets were crisp and cool.

Janetta had already been living in the apartment for a year and had furnished it before Anne moved in. All Anne had needed was bedroom furniture. She fell in love with the honey oak sleigh bed suite the minute she spied it on the showroom floor.

She stretched out in the empty bed, feeling as if she were a cork bobbing on a lonely sea. Her thoughts drifted to Janetta, cozy in the tent with Steve, and wished she could be like her, able to let herself fall in love so easily. If she were like Janetta, she would have played along with Gerry McMaster and most likely he'd be lying next to her now. But wishing she were someone else was like trying to wear shoes that were too small. It just didn't fit.

She watched the sun warm and bring out the wood grain of the nightstand. Anne knew she should get up, but she dreaded going home. Now that she had turned twenty-nine, her sister and mother seemed particularly desperate to marry her off.

After ten more minutes of decadent lounging, she showered, dressing in khaki shorts and green T-shirt, gathered her things into an overnight bag, and headed out the door. On the way out of town, she hit the McDonald's drive-thru on McKnight Road, picking up an Egg McMuffin and coffee.

Traffic was light; she made it through the Squirrel Hill Tunnels without delay and headed for Latrobe, her hometown. The birthplace of Rolling Rock beer, Arnold Palmer, and Mr. Rogers, was only an hour's drive from Pittsburgh. Instead of going to her parents' home and dropping off her things, she drove straight to Patsy and Vince's house, arriving before eleven.

"You made good time." Patsy unlocked the aluminum screen door. Her sister's blond hair was pulled into a ponytail atop her head à la Pebbles Flintstone. The floral smock top hung like an awning over her enormous belly, providing shade for her navy maternity shorts and sandal-clad feet.

Anne walked in to the small ranch house and stepped back to look at Patsy. "You've gotten bigger in one week."

Patsy massaged her belly. "You're the nurse. Tell me, has medical history ever recorded a pregnant woman who exploded?"

"Not that I know of," Anne said.

"Well, I might be the first," Patsy said. "How am I going to last another ten weeks?"

"Poor Patsy." Anne laughed, patting her sister on the shoulder. The morning was still cool, yet she felt clammy.

"It's not funny. I think they're practicing punting with my bladder." She lowered her voice. "I almost wet my pants at Target yesterday."

"It's the pressure. Do Kegel exercises. They'll strengthen your pelvic floor muscles."

They walked into the cheerful kitchen accented with yellow sunflower border and curtains. Anne looked out the back door into the yard. "Where's Vince?"

"At his friend's house picking up the tools." Patsy sank into a chair. "Do you want something to drink? Some orange juice?" She dug her feet in, trying to push herself up, reminding Anne of a turtle on its back struggling to right itself.

Anne put her hand on her sister's shoulder. "Sit. I'll get it myself. Want some?"

Patsy stifled a burp and shuddered. "No, gives me heartburn."

Anne opened the refrigerator and poured herself a glass of orange juice. "You should put your feet up. They look swollen."

"Do they?" Patsy peered over her belly. Not only were her feet swollen but Anne thought everything on her appeared to be puffy. Her sister looked as if she were poked with a needle, she'd gush water.

"You don't think anything is wrong?"

"Want me to check your blood pressure? My cuff is in my bag in the trunk?" Anne could tell by the alarm that spiked in Patsy's eyes that her sister was not looking for medical advice but sisterly.

"I was just at the doctor's on Wednesday. It was fine then. The doctor said some swelling is to be expected."

"Don't mind me. Nurses tend to be overly cautious."

Patsy held up her sausage-like fingers. "I can't wear my wedding ring anymore. Mom loves that."

"I'll bet. She's probably afraid everyone will think you've been knocked up."

"She says she understands that I can't wear it, but do you know that she suggested I tie it to my wrist when we went shopping?"

Anne was not surprised. Appearances were everything with her mother. "Why don't we go sit on the patio. You can have the chaise longue."

"So how is life in the big city?" Patsy asked as she gingerly reclined on the chaise longue.

"Where are you two?" Vince called from inside the house. Then he appeared in the doorway, seeming to fill the whole frame. Vince Confortini was as big and warm as a bonfire. With reddish-blond curls and beard, he looked like a Norse god. "Hi, Anne. Ready to wallpaper?" He walked out onto the patio, planting a kiss on top of Patsy's head.

"Let Anne finish her juice," Patsy said. "I was just asking her how things were going in Pittsburgh."

Vince settled into a lawn chair, the metal frame creaked under his weight. "Honey, why don't you just ask her what you really want to know?" He faced Anne. "Have you met a husband yet?"

She loved Patsy dearly, but every conversation came back to this. Anne held up her left hand. "No engagement ring. I hate to disappoint you."

"It's none of my business," Patsy said with a frown. "It's just that you'd think with all the people in Pittsburgh, you'd find someone nice."

Anne was feeling mischievous. She knew Patsy had to be bored with all the restrictions she was under due to her pregnancy, so she thought she'd stir up some trouble. "Well, I did meet someone gorgeous yesterday."

Patsy tried to scoot upright in the chaise longue. "How gorgeous?"

"Road kill gorgeous."

"What? Road kill? I don't understand." Vince looked from Anne to Patsy.

"The kind of guy who's so good-looking no matter how hard you try to turn away from him, you can't keep from looking at him," Anne explained.

Patsy tried to lean forward over her enormous belly. "What's he look like?"

"He's tall and built with dark, wavy hair and beautiful blue eyes the color of the ageratums you have in the flower bed," Anne said.

Patsy was hanging on every word. "He sounds perfect."

"Sounds," Anne said. She set her glass on the table beside her. "But he's not."

"Why?"

"First, he's an egotistical player. Second, when he hit on me, I told him to get lost." Anne didn't dare reveal that she'd tried to punch Gerry; she didn't need to add to the lore of her notorious temper.

"You what?" Patty clutched the sides of her belly. "For God's sake why?"

"He was handing me this line of bull."

"But he was interested in you?" Patsy lifted her brows.

"He's interested in anything that secretes estrogen."

"Does he have a girlfriend?"

"I don't know. Probably. I never asked."

"Unless he's got a ring on his finger, he's fair game. Don't play hard-to-get, Anne. Flirt a little."

"Flirt? I can't stand all that cutesy crap. If he'd have been honest with me, I might have considered him."

"How do you mean honest?" Vince asked, looking deeply interested in the workings of his sister-in-law's mind and heart.

Anne pursed her lips and thought a moment. "Well, say if he had just been honest and said what he was really thinking like, 'Hey, you're cute. I'd like to get you in the sack.'"

"Nobody's that blunt," Patsy scoffed.

"I am," Vince said.

"Yeah, but you're one in a million, right, Vince?" Anne said.

Vince smiled his agreement with his sister-in-law's assessment of him.

"Admit it, Anne," Patsy said. "You'd be offended if a strange man walked up to you and said he'd like to sleep with you."

"True, but I guess what I really want is honesty . . . and maybe a little romance. I wouldn't be offended if a guy walked up to me and said he thought I was pretty, and he would like to get know me." She pointed to her chest. "Me. Instead of giving me the feeling that he's only interested in getting something from me. I want someone to want me not just sex with me. I don't think he's capable of that. Anyway, he's my boss, and a relationship would be inappropriate."

"But I was Patsy's boss," Vince said.

Patsy kicked him, laughing. "You see how that worked out. Look at me. Now I'm a whale. I knew I should have filed charges against you."

Vince laughed and grabbed her foot. "Hey, you're really swollen today. You better stay off your feet." He moved over, sitting at the foot of the chaise longue between Patsy's pink puffy feet. As he massaged her sister's swollen feet, he looked at Anne. "You're like every girl," Vince said. "You just want love."

Vince was right; she did want love. But he was wrong about one thing—her being like every girl. After what she'd done, what she'd been through, she knew she could never be like every other girl ever again.

Chapter 7

"Aw, you're not inviting Colleen." Anne groaned, tossing her pen onto the table.

"She's your cousin. Of course, we're inviting her," Grace Lyons, Anne's mother said. Her eyes, as she looked at her daughter, were as green and round as the tomato sitting on her kitchen windowsill. "Now that'll never ripen," her mother had said after Anne had accidentally knocked the green tomato off the vine while in the garden harvesting one to put on the chipped ham sandwiches they'd eaten for lunch. Anne insisted that they put the green tomato on the window sill, and if she could work miracles, she would have turned the tomato bright red to prove her mother wrong.

"How can you even think of excluding her from Patsy's baby shower? Eileen would never forgive me." Aunt Eileen was Grace's oldest sister.

It was Sunday and after wallpapering at Patsy's and spending the night there, she had attended Mass with her parents at her home parish, Holy Family. Instead of feeling uplifted from the service, she felt diminished, as if she were cast into a pit that she couldn't scale. Sometimes after Mass, she felt hopeful, as if she might be able to claw her way to the top, escape the blackness, climb out, but today, guilt and remorse uncurled her fingers, and she lost her grip and any hope of ever shaking the oppressive weight of regret that closed in on her life like the walls of shrinking room. It wasn't anything Father Bednarik had said. She knew it was all the talk about babies and showers that had stirred her emotions.

Kevin, Anne's youngest sibling at twenty-two, had wisely gone golfing rather than stay at home while their mother was planning

Patsy's shower. Anne would rather have had her legs shaved with a rusty razor than spend her afternoon discussing which color of crepe paper streamers to decorate with and whether to order a whole- or half-sheet cake.

Mrs. Lyons had been simultaneously dictating to Anne a guest list while running vinegar through the bowels of her Mr. Coffee to remove mineral deposits.

Anne had inherited her mother's green eyes and petite size, but that was about all they shared, other than a propensity to clash.

"Colleen is such a loser," Anne said, curling a nostril in disgust at the smell of vinegar permeating the air. "Always bragging about those big-eared brats of hers. I swear if they were to hang upside down, they'd look exactly like bats."

Her mother gasped. "Anne, my goodness, your tongue."

From behind the rustling sports page, Anne heard her father chuckle.

Her mother frowned. She walked over, pulled the paper down, glaring at her husband.

Anne had inherited her red hair from her father, only his was now dulled by the gray shot through it. He'd always had the light brows and smooth cheeks of a child. Sitting there at the table trying to look innocent, he appeared much younger than his fifty-two years.

"Don't encourage her, Bill." Mrs. Lyons wagged a finger at Anne. "That's her problem. You've always encouraged her."

Anne put a hand on her hip, feeling her temper beginning to boil over. "Problem? What do you mean? I don't have a problem." Anne turned to her father, fixing her eyes on him. "Do I have a problem, Daddy?"

"Your explosive temper," Her mother said, her voice sounding tight. "Since you were a baby, you've always taken temper tantrums. I thought you'd outgrow it, but you've gotten worse."

"Maybe it's that you've become more annoying," Anne shot back, feeling relief from giving into her rage.

The coffee maker slurped, gurgled, and spit like a patient with emphysema. Mr. Lyons rose, ceremoniously folded the paper, and tucked it under his arm. Picking up his plate, he said, "There's an infomercial on some new car wax that I've been dying to see. Fight nice, Girls."

Mrs. Lyons chewed her lip, watching her husband leave the kitchen. Then she must have sensed that the conversation was not accomplishing much because she sat back down and began rummaging through a plastic bag sitting on the table. "Now, back to the shower. I went to the craft store and assembled two sample favors." She placed them before Anne. "Which one do you like?"

Furious with her mother, Anne could barely see straight enough to make out the stork composed of bent pipe cleaners and the teddy bear made from glued together pompoms resting on the blue vinyl tablecloth.

She pushed herself away from the table, crossing her arms in front of her chest. "I don't care."

"Oh, pick one, Honey."

"I said I don't care."

"You have to care."

"No, I don't."

"Hmph," her mother sniffed with a jerk of her head. "Suit yourself then. With that attitude, let's see who will want to throw you a shower when you get married."

Anne's nostrils flared, her face flushing, drowning her freckles in a sea of red. She bolted out of the chair, nearly knocking it over. "Whoever said I want to get married?"

Mrs. Lyons laughed at her. "Oh, don't be ridiculous. Every girl wants to get married."

"Would everyone stop telling me about every girl. I am not every girl." She turned, storming out of the room.

Anne sat on the front step, fuming, her knees drawn to her chest. She heard the webbing of the aluminum lawn chair stretching behind her. She hoped it wasn't her mother.

"Got your quills up again, eh, Honey?" her father said.

Anne stared up the street, heat rose in waves from the asphalt. "She is impossible."

"No, she's not. She's your mother, and she loves you."

Anne blew out a gust of air between her lips, the only air moving on this sultry afternoon. "She'd love me more if I were married."

"No, Honey, you're wrong there. She just worries about you."

Anne looked over her shoulder at him. "Worry and love are not the same thing."

"To your mother they are."

With a sigh, Anne put her hands aside her hips, resting her palms on the porch floor, and leaned back. The gray cement was cool under hands. Stretching out her legs down the steps, she said, "You're the only person who understands me, Daddy."

Her father laughed and came to stand by her. He nudged her rust-colored curls hanging loosely down her back with his knee. "It's the hair. We red heads have to stick together."

He descended the three steps to the walkway and began pulling weeds from the cracks between the stepping stones. "You give me too much credit, Honey. I don't think anyone fully understands anyone else." He yanked out some moss. "I don't think most people even understand themselves."

***

On Monday morning, Anne pulled her car into the space next to Gerry's behind the bar. The sun was blazing, but no light found its way between the closely congregated buildings. Deep, cool shadows filled the lot.

Before she'd left for work, Anne called her mother and told her that she liked the teddy bear favor best, offering to make all of them. Pleased, her mother seemed willing to forget the confrontation of the day before, and Anne thought it easier to construct seventy-five pompom bears than it was to apologize or to live with the guilt of knowing that she'd behaved like a brat yesterday.

Anne rang the bell at the back door. It was humid. Her hair felt like a blanket on her neck. She reached back, pulled it together, and lifted it, fanning her moist nape. When the knob began to rattle, she dropped her hair. Gerry opened the door. His black hair was tousled, and he was unshaven. Dressed in running shorts and T-shirt, he looked rumpled and as comfortable and snuggly as a security blanket. And too sexy for Anne to deal with so early in the morning. This must be what he looks like in bed when he wakes up. *Professional, Anne. Keep it professional.*

Caught flat-footed, she plastered on a smile and said, "Hi. Me again."

"Morning, Slugger. Come on in."

"Slugger?"

He grinned. "Well, if you can call me Gerry, I figure I can call you Slugger."

"Fair enough," she said as she stepped inside. "How'd it go over the weekend?"

He moved aside, holding out a hand, letting her start up the stairs. "Pretty well. Although on Saturday I forgot to give her the baby aspirin. I called the doctor. He said not to worry about it. She'll be OK, won't she?"

"I'm sure she'll be fine. I've brought you something that should help with her meds." In the kitchen Anne set her bags on the table, retrieving a plastic container from one of them, she handed it to him.

"What's this?"

"A pill organizer. I'm going to make you a chart and sort Peg's medication for you. That should make it easier."

"Great." Gerry smiled. A shaft of sunlight beamed into the kitchen, touching the tips of his mussed hair with reddish gold highlights. "And I have something for you." He went to the kitchen counter, set the organizer down and slid an object into his palm. Then he held out a key to her. "For you. In case I'm in the shower when you come, you can let yourself in. The apartment that is." He winked. "Unless you'd like to scrub my back." He cringed and stepped back. "Hey, sorry. Old habits die hard."

She felt her face flush not from anger with him but from the images in her mind of them in the shower together, their bodies slick with soap and water.

"I promised you I'd behave. Let me redeem myself. Where's that parking ticket?"

"I took care of it."

"Now why'd you do that?"

"It was my fault, not yours."

"But I should have told you to move your car."

As they bickered, the nursery monitor sitting on the kitchen counter began to squawk. Alarmed, Gerry dashed toward Peg's room with Anne following.

When they entered her bedroom, they found Peg, her lips near the monitor on the nightstand next to the bed. "Irma," she whispered. "Sneak me some butter."

"What?" Gerry cried.

Peg jumped, looking surprised to see him standing in the doorway.

"Is Irma smuggling you butter, Mother?"

"Butter? Who said anything about butter? I heard people in the kitchen. I'd thought you'd gone for your run. Irma said she might stop in. I was just saying, 'Irma, is something the matter?'"

"How do you like that?" Gerry turned to Anne who had moved into the room. "Lying. Not less than an hour after Fr. Paul was here giving her Communion."

Peg blushed. "Well, I'm forced to." Peg appealed to Anne with her eyes. "He's a food tyrant. Hamsters eat better."

"I made you a good, healthy breakfast." He turned to Anne. "She had scrambled egg substitutes, soy sausages, and toast."

"Dry toast," Peg cried. "Can't I please have some butter, Anne?"

Anne dropped her things on the chair next to the bed. "So I see Gerry's been following some of my dietary suggestions. I've got the whole diet sheet in my bag."

"You told him to feed me this garbage?" Peg asked. She waved a hand at the half-eaten toast sitting on the plate. "I thought you were my friend." She crossed her arms in front of her chest. "If I can't have butter, then I should have died when I had my heart attack."

"Saturated fat isn't good for you," Anne said. "However, I'm sure diet margarine wouldn't hurt, and it tastes just as good."

"I don't have any," Gerry said. "I guess I'll add that to my list." He slapped his hands together. "Well, now that that's settled, Ladies. I'm going to go for a run before it gets too late. By the way, Anne," he said, setting the stopwatch on his wrist, "they delivered that bath seat for Mum on Saturday. I hooked up the hand-held shower hose yesterday."

Anne looked at Peg with expectation. "What do you think, Peg, are you up to a shower?"

"It certainly would feel better than these darn sponge baths. But I'm still shaky."

Anne patted her hand. "We'll take it slow. I think you can do it."

Gerry left. Anne took Peg's vitals, examined her, and then got everything ready for the shower. Anne helped her to inch the few feet to the bathroom on her walker. After entering the lime tile bathroom, Anne sat Peg on the toilet allowing her to catch her breath. Wisely, Gerry had placed a rubber safety mat in the bottom of the porcelain tub too. Anne helped Peg to stand, and while she clung to the walker, Anne stripped off her nightgown. Then she stepped into the tub, wrapping her arms around Peg's wrinkly naked body, helping the old woman to step over the tub's side.

"Oh boy," Peg laughed as Anne maneuvered her onto the bath seat. "I hope no one can see in the window. They'd wonder what in

God's name is going on in here. They'll think were a couple of thespians."

"Thespians?"

"You know," Peg said. "Girls who like girls."

"You mean lesbians."

"Thespians, lesbians." Peg shrugged.

Anne stepped out of the tub, turned on the water, and waited for it to warm up to the right temperature.

"I don't get them," Peg said.

"Get who?"

"Them lesbians, whatever you call them. They say they don't like men, but then they go for a girl that looks just like a fella. Why don't they just save themselves the aggravation and go after a man in the first place?"

Anne shook her head at the old naked woman sitting in the tub. She patted her shoulder. "You are too much, Peg."

"You like fellas, don't you, Anne?"

"Yes, of course."

"I was just checking. When you said you thought true love was old-fashioned, I thought maybe you were hinting around . . . trying to come out of the cupboard."

"I think you mean closet. But I can assure you that I like men. It's just that I've given up hope of finding the right one for me."

First, Anne washed Peg's two-toned hair, and then she helped her to lather her body. The exertion fatigued Peg so much so that Anne had to rinse her off and towel her dry the best she could. Then they reversed their dance. Anne helped Peg step out of the tub. While Peg held onto the walker, Anne dried her more thoroughly, rubbing her back with baby powder, and slipping a fresh, cotton nightgown over her head. Then she followed behind Peg as she slowly shuffled down the hall.

When Peg got into the room, she slumped into the chair, leaning against the arm, exhausted.

"You did fantastically," Anne said. "Why don't you sit there and catch your breath while I change your sheets."

Peg watched Anne as she moved about the bed tucking in the fresh linens. "So what's your type?"

"Type? What are you talking about?"

"Fellas. What kind do you like?"

"Oh, I don't know."

"Well, how are you going to find the right one when you don't even know what he should be like?"

Anne plumped the pillows. *If only love were as simple as Peg believed.*

"Do you think my Gerry is attractive?"

Anne shook her finger at Peg. "I know where you're going with this, and I'm not playing along. Now, back to bed with you, you little matchmaker."

Peg slid between the fresh linens and sighed. She smiled contentedly up at Anne.

"Ah, is there anything better than clean sheets?" Anne asked.

"Having someone handsome between them," Peg said, a devilishly look stealing over her face.

Anne laughed and tucked Peg in. Then she left her to straighten up the bathroom. When she returned to the bedroom, she gave Peg a comb and a mirror.

"Good God," she cried, viewing herself in the mirror, "I could haunt a house."

Gerry appeared in the doorway his face mottled with red blotches. His dark hair, glossy with sweat, curled around his forehead and neck. A smell of raw maleness filled the room, piquing Anne's senses.

"I got diet margarine. It's in the fridge," he said. Seeing Peg with the mirror, he grimaced. "Aw, I forgot to call for your haircut. I'll write myself a note."

"If you're busy," Anne said. "I can call for you."

Gerry ran his hand across his glistening forehead. His white T-shirt was soaked and clung to his broad shoulders and muscular pectorals.

"Could you?" he said, snapping Anne out of her lust fest. "That'd be great. When I get out of the shower, I'll get the number for you." He headed toward the bathroom.

When she turned her head from him, Anne noticed Peg staring at her with a crooked smile that made her feel uncomfortable.

"How about if we set your hair?" Anne quickly suggested. "That may perk you up a bit."

Peg directed Anne where to find her pink sponge hair rollers. The old woman's hair was as fine as cobwebs, and Anne did her best to roll it around the sponges that had become hard and brown around the edges with age.

As Anne tried to rig up the old bonnet hair dryer that Peg said she usually sat under, Gerry walked in wearing only light gray pants. She couldn't help but let her eyes sweep over his chest, the carved muscles of his abdomen.

"Here's that number, Anne."

She crawled out from behind the hospital bed, holding the bonnet of the dryer.

"Oh, is she making you use that old thing?" He raised an eyebrow at his mother. "Peg, how many times have I told you, no one uses them any more. I'll get my blow dryer."

He returned and handed the dryer to Anne. The scent of soap clung to his skin. She felt her nose leading her mind to take in the rest of him and wondered whether the dark hair on his chest would feel soft or coarse. *Professional, Anne.* She quickly turned to locate a plug and give her heart a chance to stop flipping. Thankfully, Gerry left the room.

Anne dried Peg's hair, doing her best to arrange the sickly, two-toned curls into an attractive style.

Gerry returned again, this time wearing a red and white pinstriped oxford shirt. "You look like a new woman, Peg," he said as he rolled up his cuffs. "So how did the shower go?"

"It felt great," Peg said. "Although I'm pooped out. But Anne and I did OK, didn't we?" She took Anne's hand and squeezed it.

"Great," Gerry said, stuffing his hands into his pockets. "I'll be downstairs if you ladies need me. Any special requests for lunch?"

"Something with butter," Peg said.

"Wait." Anne grabbed her bag. "Here's Peg's diet."

"Benedict Arnold," Peg grumbled as Anne handed the paper to Gerry.

When he took it, he focused his blue eyes on her. They made her feel as if they were a pair of heat lamps, warming her.

"I know she wants a pound of butter for lunch. What do you want?"

You on a platter. "Oh, I brought my lunch."

"Don't be silly," he said. "You may as well eat here. Remember, Luis will cook anything for you, Anne." He said her name like he was Luis, mocking his chef.

"A sandwich is fine."

"I'll bring you something good. See you later," he said then disappeared down the hall.

Anne called Dolly, Peg's hairdresser, to come to the house on Wednesday. Then Anne began to sort her medications, putting the proper dosages into the pill minder.

"So Annie Banannie," Peg said, speaking slowly from fatigue as she lay in the hospital bed. "What'd you do over the weekend?"

Anne told her about the episode with Janetta and Steve and how she worried about her roommate.

Anne's tale of how she spent her weekend seemed to have revitalized Peg. She scooted up a bit in the bed. "You know, I saw this Tyra," Peg said, referring to Tyra Banks, the talk show hostess like she was a close, personal friend, "and she had this psychologist on the show. You say Janetta is dark and slender and her boyfriend

63

is large and blond? Well, this doctor said that if a person picks someone that is totally opposite in looks, it means that person really doesn't like himself. Janetta must not like herself very much."

Anne had never considered that. Janetta had always appeared so self-assured.

"See," Peg continued, "you and my Gerry would be a good match. You're both Irish and fair skinned—"

"But I have auburn hair and Gerry's is black."

"In the sun, his hair has lots of red in it."

In the kitchen this morning, she had noticed his fiery highlights.

"You'd be perfect for each other." Peg screwed up her face. "More so than Claudia."

"Claudia?"   Anne's heart thudded in her chest.   "Who's Claudia?"

"His latest tootsie."

"Tootsie?"

"His little floozy."

Anne chuckled to cover her annoyance. "I take it you don't you like her."

"Let's not talk about her," Peg said. "She depresses me. What did you do on Saturday? Any dates?"

Anne felt sick but told herself she was being ridiculous. She had no reason to be jealous of Claudia. Nevertheless, Anne still wanted to know all about this "tootsie." Anne tried to refocus her mind. "I went home to Latrobe," she said. "I helped my sister and brother-in-law wallpaper their nursery."

"You're a regular Jack of all trades. When is their baby due?"

"Babies," Anne corrected. "They're having twins."

Peg clasped her hands together. "Oh God Bless them. Twins! Your family must be so excited."

"We are. She's due in ten weeks. Every time I go home she gets bigger and bigger. She's so uncomfortable. And scared. Carrying twins is high risk and well, she—" Anne stopped.

Peg picked up on Anne's distress. "What is it, Annie Banannie?"

"Nothing."

Peg peered skeptically above her glasses. "What's wrong?"

"Well," Anne said. "I'm just worried about her. I don't have to tell you how risky pregnancy can be."

"Honey, could you do me a favor?"

"Sure."

Peg directed her to a shoebox on the top shelf of her closet. Anne had to go on tiptoes and stretch to retrieve it. When she handed it to her, Peg rested it on her lap and removed the lid. She began sifting through the contents.

"What's that?" Anne asked.

"My war chest. My weapons for defending against the wickedness and evil of this world. It's full of things I've collected over the years. Some I've bought or gotten at church. Most I've received in the mail for making donations to charities." She held up holy cards, rosary beads, a 5" X 7" drawing of the Blessed Mother. "Here," she said holding out a medal.

"What's this?" Anne asked.

"It's St. Gerard. For Patsy."

Anne looked at the silver disc in her palm, the bas relief of a man holding a crucifix, a halo radiating about his head. She noticed something small depicted near the bottom of the medal but couldn't quite make it out. She held it closer to her eyes.

"They say in addition to his being the patron saint of expectant mothers that St. Gerard could also read the consciences of sinners," Peg said.

Anne moved toward the window where the light was brighter and squinted at the medal. Then her breath caught as she made out the article on the medal. It was a small skull. She felt her blood drain from her face as her peripheral vision narrowed and darkened to a tunnel of sight. Anne was going to faint. Closing her hand around the medal, she quickly backed away, sitting in the chair before she collapsed.

"Anne, dear, are you OK?"

Anne put her head between her knees. "I'm just a bit dizzy. I think I overdid it a bit this weekend." Her vision slowly returned and the fog lifted from her head.

"Are you sure? Maybe I should call Gerry."

She slowly raised her head. "No. No, I'm fine." She didn't want him to see her so rattled.

Peg stared at Anne for a moment, making Anne feel as if Peg could also read consciences. Then Peg sighed. "Well, as I was saying, St. Gerard is supposed to be able to reveal sins that sinners are too ashamed of to acknowledge."

As much as Anne wanted to toss the medal away, pretend she had never seen it, she opened her palm, gazing at it again. Then she curled her fingers around it, accepting it humbly as if she were Hester Prine taking her scarlet "A."

She turned to face Peg, a smile pasted on her face. "Thank you."

"Give it to your sister. It'll help her."

Then Anne went to her bag and dropped the medal into one of the side pockets.

Anne assured Peg that she would give it to Patsy, but she knew there was no way in hell she could give it away any more than Hester could tear off her scarlet letter.

Chapter 8

By the time Friday arrived, Anne and Peg had settled into a routine. Gerry, true to his word, had refrained from meddling in Peg's care, and since striking their professional agreement, he had dropped the Don Juan routine with Anne. She found that she liked him much better when he wasn't trying to charm her.

Medically, Peg was progressing steadily so Anne focused on gradually increasing the amount of time that Peg spent out of bed. The physical activity seemed to stimulate her circulation and improve her coloring. Her haircut had lopped off much of the red part of her hair. In a few weeks, it would all be grown out. She looked much healthier and stylish than the woman Anne had met a week ago.

Near four-thirty on Friday afternoon, Gerry unexpectedly walked into Peg's room. "Well, Girls," he said clapping his hands, "Irma just called. She's running late at the eye doctor's. I came up to tell you, Anne, not to wait for her. At five, I'll come up and sit with Mum until she gets here."

"It's Happy Hour. On Friday. You're too busy," Peg said. "I'll be fine by myself. I don't need a babysitter."

"I know you don't need a babysitter, Peg, but what if you have to go the bathroom? I don't want you getting up and falling."

"I can stay until Irma arrives," Anne said.

"Are you sure?" he said, relief relaxing the muscles of his face. "I don't want to take advantage of you."

"I'm sure."

"Really?" he said. "Things are crazy downstairs right now. Luis can't find the Sterno for the warming trays for the hors d'oeuvres. He thinks Bernie threw them away."

"Really, I don't mind," Anne said.

"Thanks, Slugger." He touched her shoulder. She felt herself go limp like those space creatures did on Star Trek when Mr. Spock grabbed their pressure point on their neck. "I owe you one. I'll see to it that you're compensated."

Anne regrouped her senses and said, "I don't want money. Peg's my friend." She patted the old woman's hand. "We'll consider this one girlfriend visiting another."

"You sure you don't mind?" Gerry asked. Anne nodded. "Well, at least let me send dinner up to you."

She agreed and he breezed out.

Peg grasped the bedrail, turning toward Anne. "I feel terrible cutting into your Friday night. I hope I'm not holding you back from something."

She knew Peg was fishing to find out if she had a date again. "I have nothing planned for this evening," Anne said, feeling the sting of admitting that her love life was a total zilch.

"I can't believe a beautiful girl like you doesn't have a date. You should start saying the St. Anne prayer."

"It's pretty sad when you have to pray for dates."

"You wouldn't be praying for dates, you'd be praying for the right husband. That's what you want, isn't it?"

"Well, yes," she reluctantly agreed, hating that her love life had become the focus of their conversation yet again.

"Would you get me my war chest, Annie Banannie?"

"What do you want it for?" Anne was beginning to hate her war chest.

"I gave you something for Patsy, now I want to give you something."

Reluctantly, Anne went into the closet, reached up, taking the box from the shelf. She handed it to Peg, who began riffling through the contents until she found a white envelope. "Here we are," Peg said, the envelope shaking in her hand as she reached into it with her twig-like fingers and removed its contents.

"Take this. It's St. Anne's holy card. If you want a husband, every day pray 'Dear Saint Anne, get me a man, as fast as you can.' I guarantee you it'll work. Why, I say it everyday myself."

"You do?" Anne said. She gazed at the pious woman on the card. Why do saints always have great complexions? "You told me no one could ever replace your husband."

"I'm not praying for me. I'm praying for Gerry."

"You want Gerry to get a man? Now, I am confused."

"No, no, no." Peg scooted up in the bed, her nightgown twisting. While Anne helped her straighten it, Peg explained. "I figure if St. Anne is out there finding matches for girls, then she needs fellas to pair them up with. I've been praying that she'll fix one of her girls up with my Gerry."

"I heard my name being taken in vain." Gerry stood in the doorway, his arms crossed, smiling. "Things have slowed some now in the bar, so I brought dinner up for all of us." He spied the box sitting on his mother's lap, rolled his eyes, then looked at Anne. "Is the Witch Doctor showing you her charms?"

"Witch Doctor?" Peg sneered, batting a hand toward him. "One day you'll learn, Wise Guy. This box is mightier than the nuclear bomb."

He laughed. "Maybe I should paint Enola Gay on its side."

Peg clutched her box reverently as if it were one of the gifts the Magi had brought the Christ child. "These artifacts are blessed and endowed with special graces," she said, "and you shouldn't laugh at them." She held the box out to Anne. "Will you put it back on the shelf, Dear, before he desecrates it any further."

Anne slipped the card into her bag and then took the shoebox, walked to the closet, stood on her toes, and struggled to push it back onto the shelf. Suddenly, Gerry was behind her, his arms reaching above her, encompassing her with his presence. "Here, let me get that, Slugger." He was so close she could feel his breath, warm on her neck as he spoke.

69

Anne looked up into his face. He smiled, and she noticed that no whiskers grew on the faint scar on his chin and his pulse beating in his neck kept time with her own thumping heart.

"Thank you," she said her voice ethereally soft. Her shoulders sagged as she melted with electric awareness that his body was as close as it could come to hers without actually touching.

He pushed the box back onto the shelf. "No problem."

Then he put a hand on her shoulder. She could feel its warmth on her skin through the thin cotton of her scrub top. He guided her to the side so he could shut the closet door.

"So, Peg," he said, seemingly unaware that Anne was paralyzed with desire for him, "are you up to eating with an infidel in the kitchen or should we eat in here?"

"I think I can make it to the table."

Anne unconsciously massaged the spot on her shoulder where Gerry had touched her as she walked behind Peg who slowly shuffled along on her walker. When they entered the kitchen, Anne was surprised to see that he had set the table.

"I hope you like shrimp, Anne," he said, pulling out a chair for his mother. "The old girl here won't eat meat on Fridays even though she's allowed to."

Peg looked over her shoulder at him. "I offer up my sacrifice for the salvation of your soul."

He patted her head playfully. "Don't do me any favors."

"You better hope someone's praying for it, Wise Guy. When's the last time you've been to Confession? Or Mass for that matter?"

"Aw, not this again," he said as he took his seat at the table. "You know Sunday is my only day off. I hate to get up early."

Peg glowered at him. "Well, I hope when you come knocking on the Pearly Gates, old St. Peter doesn't tell you to go to hell because he's too lazy to get out of bed and open them for you."

Anne took a seat across from Gerry; she kept her eyes on her plate so they couldn't see her smiling at their repartee. "This shrimp smells delicious," Anne said to change the subject.

Peg led them in a blessing. At the end of it, she tacked on a postscript. "And St. Monica, please remember my special intention."

Gerry rolled his eyes.

Peg made the sign of the cross, looking at Anne. "You've heard of St. Monica, haven't you?"

I'm going to have to borrow my dad's *Encyclopedia of Saints* when I go home again, Anne thought.

She opened her mouth to reply, but Gerry cut in speaking in a sing-song voice. "She's the mother of St. Augustine, and she prayed for seventeen years that her wicked, sinful son would mend his ways and return to God, blah, blah, blah."

"Well, it worked, Mr. Know-it-all," Peg said, making a face at him.

Before things deteriorated any further, Anne picked up her fork and said cheerily as she speared some of the shrimp scampi, "I never eat this well at home. I'm going to gain weight."

"Oh, hell," Peg said, "you're perfect. A girl needs a little meat on her bones. Something to hang on to." Peg had her hands up aping like she was weighing Anne's breasts. Anne blushed. "Don't you think she's built nice, Gerry?"

He lay down his utensils, tilting his head toward his mother. "Why are you out to get me tonight, Peg? If I say yes, Anne's going to think I'm out of line. If I say no, then she's going to get mad."

"All I'm saying," Peg said, looking disappointed at the dinner he had brought her—broiled scrod, tossed salad, and rice—"is that a girl should have some curves. Now take a girl like Claudia. So skinny. No meat. If I were a man, I'd be afraid to make love to her with all those bones of hers jutting out. Why, they could puncture your intestines or spleen or something."

Anne choked. She quickly gulped her iced tea to clear her throat.

"You always find a way to knock Claudia, don't you, Peg?" Gerry said setting his jaw. "I don't know why you hate her so much."

71

"I don't hate her. I don't hate anyone; that wouldn't be Christian. I'm just saying that she's too skinny. She probably won't be able to bear children. But if you like a girl you have to shake the sheets to find in bed, then that's your business."

"That's right, it is my business," he said. "She's coming home on Thursday. I wish you'd be a littler kinder to her."

Irma came up the back steps huffing and puffing wearing massive black plastic sunglasses. "Oh, I'm so sorry. I got held up." She paused behind Anne's chair to catch her breath.

"Who the hell are you supposed to be?" Peg asked. "Ray Charles?"

Irma took off the glasses. "No, they dilated my pupils." Then she patted Anne's arm and said, "Poor Girl, I've probably made you late for a date."

"She doesn't have a date. Again." Peg said.

Both women shook their heads in disgust.

Anne felt like she was a twelve-year-old.

Irma turned to Gerry. "I'm glad you're here. I forgot. Next Friday night is my turn to work the bingo at church. Ruth Sweeney offered to come and sit with Peg."

Peg slammed down her fork and eyed Gerry. "Oh, no! Not Ruth. She'll spend the whole night telling me about her diverticulitis, how the gas just rolls through her bowels. She came to the hospital and went on and on so long, I almost reached back and pulled the plug on myself to put me out of my misery. Get someone else."

"And who do you suggest, Mother?"

"Anne. She never has any dates."

"I didn't say I never have any dates." Anne stabbed a shrimp with her fork. "I just don't happen to have one tonight."

"Well," Peg said, "do you have one next Friday night?"

Anne sputtered, turning to look at the tea towel calendar hanging on the wall. "Well, what's the date? Hmm. August 9."

"Peg, that's unfair to Anne," Gerry said. "You're putting her on the spot." He turned to Anne. "Don't worry about it. I'll find someone or take off the evening and let Dave pick up the slack."

"No, don't do that," Anne said. "I don't have anything planned that night. I can do it."

"Are you sure?"

"Please let Anne do it," Peg begged.

"I'm sure," Anne said.

Peg clapped. "Thanks, Anne Banannie. I couldn't have faced a whole evening of discussing Ruth's farts."

Everyone laughed. Then Irma made herself a cup of tea and joined them at the table. After dinner, Anne began to clear the dishes.

"Don't clean up," Gerry said. "I'll get them. You've done enough for us already. Go on home."

After gathering her things, she stood next to Peg's chair. "I'll rent a movie for next Friday night," she said tucking a curl behind her ear. "What kind do you like, Peg?"

"Anything but one of those dirty ones," she said looking up at Anne. "Those Hollywood stars have no shame. I was reading an article about Britney Spears in an old *People Magazine* that Dolly Sladik brought me from her shop, and did you know Britney went out partying without wearing her panties. While she was getting into a car, she took everyone's picture. Can you imagine?" She looked at everyone as if waiting for their reaction. "What's she going to do for an encore? Show us her Pap smear? I mean there's nothing left to see."

Laughing, Anne kissed the top of Peg's head. "You are priceless. I'll think about it over the weekend and try to come up with something good." Anne wished everyone a good weekend and started for the stairs.

"Wait," Gerry said, "I'll walk you to your car.

"You don't have to."

"I know I don't have to but I want to. Joe, who owns the shoe repair shop, said there have been some shady looking characters hanging around the neighborhood lately. This area has always been pretty safe, but the lot's secluded. I'd feel better if I went with you."

They walked down the stairs together. Gerry opened the door for her, and she stepped outside. Shadows filled the lot and aromas from whatever Luis was whipping up in the kitchen laced the air. Muffled street sounds surrounded them. Anne opened the car door and bent to put her things on the passenger seat.

When she straightened, Gerry was standing in the sweep of the door, one hand on the doorframe, his other arm leaning on the roof of the car, trapping her. "Anne," he said, slowly moving the door back and forth, the hinges softly squeaking, "I just want you to know how much I appreciate everything you've done. You've been a lifesaver for me, and my mother loves you. I only hope you're not offended by the things she says."

His forearms were tanned and freckled but the underside was pale and looked soft, reminding Anne of the tender under belly of a puppy and she longed to stroke it. She caught herself and diverted her eyes to stare at her white tennis shoes. It was awkward standing so close to him in the shadows, and she wanted to leave.

"You're welcome," she said softly. "I like your mother. I think she's a riot."

"Well, she's right about one thing, Anne."

She tilted her head and gazed up at him. "What's that?"

"There's definitely something wrong with the world when a girl like you doesn't have a date on a Friday night."

His compliment rattled her composure. She had to get out of there before she said or did something stupid. Blushing, she quickly ducked inside the car, saying, "Have a nice weekend." She closed the door and wondered if he could hear her heart beating outside as she started the ignition and pulled away.

Chapter 9

Although Anne had blasted the air conditioner all the way home, when she pulled in front of her building, she was damp with perspiration. A trickle ran between her breasts, tickling like a tongue lightly licking her skin. Like Gerry's tongue. Professional, she reminded herself, yet she doubted that even Mother Theresa herself could remain professional around Gerry McMaster.

After retrieving her mail, she walked into the apartment, flung her things on the table and flopped onto the couch. When her heart finally resumed a natural rhythm, and she had cooled down, she kicked off her shoes and rose, and began to scan the mail.

It was nearly seven-thirty—too late for an early movie. She was bored. The pent-up energy Gerry had unleashed in her had made her restless. What should she do? Her paycheck had been deposited into her checking. She could go shopping. But by the time she would change out of her scrubs and drive to the mall, there wouldn't be enough time to do any real damage to her checking account before the stores closed.

She went to the answering machine, hoping that someone had called wanting her to go out, but there were only messages from Patsy and her mother.

She called her mother first. Nothing was new on the home front except that she had flipped her mattress today and had suggested that Anne might want to do the same. Kevin had had an interview in Greensburg, and the tomatoes in the garden were coming along nicely, except for the one on the windowsill that Anne had knocked off the vine. "For some reason," her mother said, "it still won't ripen."

The call to Patsy was equally as thrilling. She'd been to the doctors and was steadily growing bigger by the day and more uncomfortable. Someone Joe worked with had crocheted two baby blankets for them.

By the time she got off the phone, Anne decided the only sensible thing to do was to stay in. When she took off her scrubs, the St. Anne card fell out of her pocket. She placed it on the nightstand then took a shower. After slipping into an oversized T-shirt and fresh bikinis, she dried her hair. She read the paper, half-watching the Friday night sit-coms.

When she caught herself shouting out the answers to the questions on *Are You Smarter than a Fifth Grader?*, she stopped and immediately felt like crying. *My God, my life has reached a new low. I'm home alone on Friday night in my pajamas watching morons.* She went into the kitchen, opened a can of ready-to-spread frosting, and got herself a spoon. She dug into the tub of chocolate icing. *I am so pathetic I may as well take up knitting and start taking in stray cats.*

As she worked on polishing off the frosting and her blood sugar soared making her feel jumpy and even more restless, an advertisement for the *Oprah Winfrey* show blasted a teaser, "Next Oprah. Does life peak for women at 18? We'll discuss with the author of the new bestseller, *Is There Life After the Prom?*"

Obviously not.

Disgusted with her life and herself, Anne licked the back of her spoon, dropped it into the empty frosting tub, and then flicked off the TV. Her head humming from the sugar buzz, she walked into her room, turned down the covers, and crawled under the sheet. It had started to rain. She lay there alone in the dark listening to it drumming on the roof. She felt like a raindrop, solitary, falling aimlessly through the space without any control of her life.

She turned off the lamp, rolling onto her side. Then Anne did as she had done every night since she was a child, she said her prayers. After asking God to keep everyone she loved in His care, and requesting healthy outcomes for Patsy and the babies, she added another petition.

In desperation, Anne whispered in the dark, "I know I don't deserve it, but, Dear St. Anne, get me a man as fast as you can." Then grabbing the unoccupied pillow lying next to her tightly to her heart, she begged, "Please?"

Chapter 10

Anne looked down at her chest, gasping. On the front of her scrub top, was a scarlet letter "W."

Janetta spit on her. "Waster!"

"Waster? Of what?" Anne cried above the din.

"Of life," said her mother who was busily shining the brass rail in Mac's Place.

Steve grabbed her by the hair and shoved her through the crowd that had gathered. He forced her to crawl upon the bar where she stood before the angry patrons, who shouted, "Hot Head! Old Maid! Waster!"

Olives, cocktail onions, maraschino cherries pelted her. Ashamed, she hung her head. Then a voice rose above the din— Peg's. Anne looked down and saw the old woman unrolling a parchment.

"Anne Lyons, Waster," Peg shouted, "you are hereby charged with abstaining from life. Your punishment is—" Anne held her breath. "Making 623 shower favors or making love with Gerard McMaster, my son." Peg smiled wickedly while the crowd roared its approval.

Anne cried, "Please have mercy!"

"Choose," Janetta shouted.

"She needs a good roll in the hay," Steve said. He reached up, seized her wrist, hauling her down from atop the bar. The crowd parted as Bernie, dressed as an executioner and wearing a black KISS T-shirt and face paint, appeared. Steve handed her over to him, and Bernie dragged Anne down the hallway to Gerry's office. From his ring of keys, he extracted one and inserted it into the door. Anne felt faint.

Bernie shoved her inside, locking the door behind her. A thousand candles lighted the room. In the flickering glow, she spied Gerry. He was lying on the couch wearing nothing but black leather boots and a leer.

As he rose and strutted over to her, she trembled. He reached out, slowly running a finger up her throat, and whispered into her ear. "How do you want your punishment, Slugger?"

Her hair stood on end as she shuddered. Then defiantly, Anne set her jaw and flung her red curls back. "I'll take it like a woman."

Gerry smiled, pulled her to him, his body heat searing her flesh. He crushed her lips with a kiss. Then he backed away and looked her in the eye. Suddenly, he jerked the drawstring on her scrub pants. They fell to the floor in a puddle of cloth. Resigned to her fate, she ripped the "W" from her shirt, freeing herself from its sentence.

"Prepare for your punishment," Gerry growled as he pulled the top over her head, casting it aside. Then moving in to inflict her sentence, he lavished her mouth, her throat, her breasts with kisses.

Her nerves on edge and her flesh singing with desire, she wished for a life sentence of this. As his hands caressed every inch of her, out of the shadows, she saw St. Gerard emerge carrying a cross and a small skull.

A flash of light followed by a crack of thunder split the night. Anne bolted upright in bed, sweating. Another flash illuminated the room and the roar of thunder that followed rattled the windowpanes in an orgasmic shudder. Panting, she pulled out her T-shirt; there was no "W."

"Great," Anne muttered, falling back onto her pillow, her chest heaving, "even my dreams leave me unsatisfied." She ran a hand across her damp forehead and glanced at the clock. It was five-thirteen.

As more lightning flashed, Anne lay staring at the ceiling trying to burrow back into the mood of how it felt to have Gerry's lips on her mouth, his hands on her skin, but the moment was gone.

Rolling over, she watched the rain running in silver rivulets down the window. *I can't deny it. I am infatuated with Gerry. But am I wasting my life by not responding to my desire for him?* The imposing image of St. Gerard came to mind, quashing any lingering lust she felt from her dream. *Gerry's a player, and I just can't risk falling for someone like him again.* She snuggled with her pillow. *And what if I did want him? What good would it do me? Remember, professional, Anne.*

She drifted off, and when she woke again after seven, the rain had stopped. Slowly, Anne stretched and crawled out of bed. She went to the window. The storm had left behind a gray, damp morning. Raindrops, like glass beads, were strung along the window ledge. A strange mood settled over her as she watched the rain-beads, one-by-one, drop and fall. Her dream came to mind, intensifying the loneliness she'd felt the previous evening. She turned from the window, sighing. *I can't spend another Friday night like last night. Maybe my subconscious was not telling me to get involved with Gerry but to stop wasting time and make my life happen.* At that moment, she resolved to do something to improve her lot.

Anne decided that a run in nearby North Park would be the perfect start for taking charge of her life and burning off the extra calories she'd consumed the night before as well as the energy pinging through her from the dream. She washed her face, brushed her teeth, changed into her spandex running shorts and tank top and did her hair in a French braid.

As she drove into the park, she noticed that the puddles and downed limbs had not deterred the walkers, runners, and cyclists from their five-mile trek around the muddy, green lake. Anne preferred running the smaller, less-crowded course near the park's swimming pool.

The sun broke through the clouds as she pulled into the parking lot near Pie Traynor field. A few other cars were scattered throughout the gravel lot. A young couple coaxed a lazy mutt from the backseat of their car. She saw no other people there.

Anne parked, got out, and began to warm up. As she bent to touch her toes, the smell of wet earth filled her nose.

She crossed the road, heading out onto the hilly, one-way road that meandered through this part of the park. She started up the first hill, her lungs expanding and contracting mightily, the pounding of her blood beating in her ears.

She finished one lap and the fresh-washed morning spurred her to do another. Digging in, she attacked the hill again. As she ran alongside the soccer fields on her left, she glanced over, watching a small boy with blond mop-top hair kicking a ball. It rolled so slowly Anne laughed as it slid between the short legs of the bewildered goalie, who had been preoccupied with watching an airplane soaring overhead. Anne smiled and nodded as another runner passed her from the opposite direction.

"Anne?" she heard someone calling from behind her.

She slowed to a trot and turned around to find a tall man jogging back toward her.

"Anne, it is you?" the man huffed. "It's been so long—I wasn't sure."

Anne studied the face. Then she stopped running, her hands flying to her cheeks. "Oh, my God! Craig? Craig Love!"

He brushed back the fringe of blond hair that had fallen across his sweaty forehead. "I'd hug you if I wasn't such a mess."

"I'm a mess too," Anne said, looking down at herself. Then she glanced back up at him. "Who cares?" She hugged the friend she'd made in her freshman year at Penn State. A senior, he had tutored her in Biology. When he released her, she stepped back to take in the sight of him. Craig's blond hair was still thick though much shorter and the beard was gone, making him look more boyish. He had filled out considerably, not with excess flesh but muscle. Seeing him again, Anne felt as if she'd stuck her hand into a pocket and found a $1,000 bill. "What are you doing here?"

"Finishing up my residency. I'm over at Children's Hospital."
When he'd left for medical school, Anne had lost track of him.

"What are you doing in Pittsburgh?" he asked.

"I just moved here a few months ago. I'm a home health nurse.
In fact, now I'm taking care of a woman who lives in Lawrenceville.
Not far from Children's."

"Do you run here often?"

"I'd like to tell you everyday, but I'd be lying. When I get the
chance, I come on over. I don't live far from here." She touched her
forehead. "I can't believe you recognized me. It's been so long."

"Too long. And my fault. I'm afraid I've been rather negligent
in staying in touch with friends."

"You were in med school. You probably didn't have enough
time to sleep let alone to maintain a social life."

"Yes, but I must have been a fool to have lost touch with you.
God, you're as pretty as I remembered."

She laughed off his compliment though secretly she was pleased.
Running a hand over her hair, that curled in sweaty ringlets around
her face, she laughed. "Boy, what would you say if I were all cleaned
up?"

"Are you in a hurry?" he asked.

Anne told him no, and they walked over to a shelter and took a
seat at a picnic table. For the next half-hour, they brought each other
up-to-date on their lives. Craig had gone to med school at Johns
Hopkins and had served his internship in plastic surgery at The
University of Michigan. Only a few more days remained of his
residency at Children's, and he was considering a few practices that
were interested in taking him on as a new associate.

He got up and stretched. "So are you still with Zach?"

Anne chuckled derisively. "Zach? No."

"You two were pretty tight. I'd have asked you out back then if
it weren't for him and the fact that he could bench press me."

She'd always suspected that he'd had a bit of a crush on her, but at the time she was too blinded with devotion to Zach to encourage him.

"So what happened?"

She stood and casually touched her toes. "What usually happens to your first college romance. We outgrew each other. Or I should say he outgrew me."

"I watched draft day on ESPN and looked for you in the crowd when the Chargers picked him, but I didn't see you there."

"He'd moved on by then."

"Shame he blew his knee out in his first season."

"Don't feel too bad for him," Anne said. "He signed for a bundle. Last I heard he was out in Hollywood trying to parlay his fame into a movie career."

"Well, what'd they hype him as when he was up for the Heisman? 'The All American Boy.' I'm sure he can use that image to his advantage."

He uses everything to his advantage.

Craig glanced at his watch. "I'd love to stay and talk more, Anne, but I'm in a wedding today. I've got to go home to get ready."

"Your own?"

"No, I haven't taken the plunge yet. How about you?"

"Nope. Still kissing frogs," Anne said.

"Lucky frogs."

They headed back to the parking lot, and as he unlocked his car, he asked, "What's your number?"

Anne recited her number as he programmed it into his phone. "I'll give you a call on Monday. We'll make plans to get together."

"Great," Anne said.

"Too bad if I am sweaty. I want another hug." He laughed, wrapping her in his arms again.

She didn't mind at all.

Anne got into her car and waved goodbye. As she headed out of the park, she began to laugh. *Wow, St. Anne, I'm becoming a fan. If I had known that you worked this fast, I'd have prayed to you a lot sooner.*

***

Her spirits buoyed, Anne decided to indulge her addiction. She went home, showered, dressed, and went on a shopping spree. After buying take-out chicken for dinner, she spent the rest of Saturday trying on her purchases, coordinating jewelry and shoes for the three new ensembles she'd bought.

On Sunday, Anne attended ten thirty Mass then went for a swim at the apartment complex's pool. She left around two o'clock as she feared she was getting sunburned. Drowsy from the sun, she decided an afternoon nap was in order.

When she opened the door and stepped inside her apartment, the air conditioning chilled her, raising goose bumps. She was surprised to find Janetta in the kitchen unloading Tupperware containers from a bag. She was wearing shorts that had Ocean City written across her butt cheeks and a tight white T-shirt. The articles of clothing appeared to have come from the Daisy Duke collection.

"Hope you're hungry, Anne," she said. "I was home and mom sent spaghetti."

"That sounds delicious." Anne shivered in her wet suit. "Let me take a shower and change, then I'll help you." On her way to the bathroom, Anne peaked into Janetta's room expecting to see Steve in the bed. "Where's Steve?" she called.

"At a company golf outing."

After taking her shower and putting on a pair of navy shorts and pink tank top, Anne rustled up a salad while Janetta reheated the spaghetti. They dined at the tiny bistro table on the balcony that overlooked the woods behind their building.

Anne closed her eyes, moaning. "Your mother's spaghetti is still the best I've ever tasted."

"Tell that to Steve. He only eats Spaghetti-O's."

Figures, Anne thought. "I haven't seen you all week. How was camping?"

Janetta dipped another slice of bread into her sauce. "Horrible. We all drank too much around the campfire. Steve passed out in the tent, and I was afraid to get up by myself to pee because there were a lot of skunks wandering around. Must have been mating season or something."

Skunks mating—an apt description of a weekend in the woods with Steve.

"Anyway, I held it all night—I got a bladder infection."

Anne stopped chewing. "Sure it's a bladder infection?"

"What do you mean?"

"Did you see a doctor?"

"Of course, I saw a doctor on Wednesday."

"And he was sure it was a bladder infection?"

"What are you implying?" Janetta asked, her dark eyes growing blacker as she stared at Anne.

"Well, it could be something else."

"Like what?"

"Syphilis, gonorrhea, chlamydia."

"Chlamydia!" Janetta threw her garlic bread down.

"You don't know who he's been with."

"I don't have chlamydia."

"How can you be sure?"

Janetta rose, jerking her head, flinging back her black mane. "Look, St. Anne, I don't feel like one of your lectures."

"I'm not trying to act pious; I'm speaking as a health professional."

"Well, who do you think you are? The Surgeon General? After getting fired, you'd think you'd learn to keep your opinions to yourself."

Anne clutched the edge of the table. "I didn't deserve to be fired. Miller was being a bitch. All I did was let those little kids into the ICU to see their dad."

86

"That and telling her she had a lot of nerve citing health policy when her ass was as wide as a dumpster."

"But she was setting a bad example. I'm only looking out for you."

"Bullshit! You're just jealous because I have someone, and you're still sitting home alone keeping company with your virtue."

"That's not true!"

"You never like anyone I get involved with. It's easy to sit back and criticize when you're too afraid to take a chance on anyone."

Anne rose and faced Janetta. She hated the way Janetta towered over her. "I'm not afraid or jealous. I'd rather rot at home than settle for a Neanderthal like Steve."

"What's wrong with Steve?"

"What isn't wrong with him? He's loud, rude, and I hate the way he treats you. Always ordering you around. And you jumping through hoops for him like a trained poodle."

"Listen," Janetta said, pointing her finger in Anne's face, her eyes narrowing to slits. "If I jump through hoops, it's because I want to—only because I want to. No one makes me do anything." She yanked open the sliding door, storming into the apartment, her long black hair spinning like the skirt of a whirling dervish behind her.

Anne followed. "I just worry you're going to get hurt."

Janetta stomped through the apartment, gathering up her clothes, stuffing them into a bag.

"Don't go, Janetta."

Ignoring Anne's pleas, she slung her purse over her shoulder, and opened the door. Then she turned and her eyes burned into Anne. "You know, Anne, I hope this doesn't offend your saintly ears, but kiss my ass." Then she slammed the door.

Chapter 11

"Annie Banannie, we haven't lost it," Peg said. "It's in your hand."

Astonished, Anne looked at the puzzle piece lying in her palm. Peg had shaken out the blanket and looked down her nightgown searching for the last piece that would finish the reflecting pond in front of the Taj Mahal jigsaw puzzle they'd been steadily working on for the past few days.

"I forgot I had it. I must have taken a mental vacation," Anne said. She gave the piece to Peg, allowing her the honor of finishing the puzzle.

Peg inserted the piece and sat back with a look of satisfaction. "Oh, hell, at my age, I've taken so many mental vacations, I think I've been around the world three times." Her bespectacled blue eyes scrutinized Anne. "But your mind does seem to be elsewhere today. Is something bothering you? Is Patsy OK?"

"She's fine. Everything is fine."

Peg lifted her eyebrows as she murmured a skeptical, "Hmmm."

Anne moved the card table into the corner, and Peg settled back to say her daily rosary. Anne had to admit to herself that things weren't fine. It was Wednesday afternoon, and she was still replaying in her mind the argument she'd had with Janetta on Sunday. Why hadn't she kept her big mouth shut? *Janetta has never listened to me before. Why should she start now?* The only thing keeping Anne from despair was the other matter on her mind—Craig. True to his word, he'd called and asked her out. She hadn't been this excited about a date in years.

Anne watched Peg doze off in the chair. She turned off the television and thinking it a good time to catch up on paperwork, she went to her nursing bag, pulling out her binder. When she reached inside again to retrieve a pen, she felt the St. Gerard medal in the pocket of the bag. Slowly, she pulled it out. Although it weighed less than an ounce, it felt extraordinarily heavy in her palm. Anne sighed, slumping into the chair. She stared at the medal for a long time. Then as she ran her finger over the tiny skull, she felt tears welling in her eyes. *When would remembering get easier?* Peg stirred, and startled, Anne quickly wiped her tears away, rose, and deposited the medal back in the bag.

"Anne," Gerry whispered from the doorway.

Tucking a curl behind her ear, she turned toward him, hoping that she'd regained her composure enough so that he wouldn't notice she'd been crying.

"I don't want to wake her." He nodded toward his mother. "I've only got a minute, but if you're not busy after work on your way out, Luis has been working on a new menu. He's concocted a new dish, and he wants 'Senorita Anne' to taste it." He rolled his eyes.

"Sure," she whispered. "I'd be honored."

***

When Anne walked into Mac's Place, she was feeling a bit morose, but the energy of the happy hour crowd that was jammed into the bar invigorated her. Gerry and Dave were behind the bar serving up drinks. Businessmen with loosened ties were clustered around the bowling machine in the corner, and Vera was buzzing through the swarms of patrons. The air was heavy with aftershave and perfume.

"Hi, Dave. How are you today?" Anne asked, stepping up into a barstool. At first she had felt like an outsider in the place. Now after dropping by Gerry's office or the bar after work so many times to inform him of his mother's progress, or alert him that she needed

90

more baby aspirin, or to say that Peg didn't like the brand of laundry detergent he was using, Anne felt at home there.

"Fine," Dave said. He wiped up a water ring. "I hear Luis has created something special for you."

Anne looked at Gerry. "He made it especially for me?"

"Yeah," Gerry said.

He sounded annoyed. Anne's green eyes sparkled. "Wow, you didn't tell me that. I'm flattered."

"I'll see if Julio Iglesias has it ready yet. I told him you'd be down a little after five."

"You should be flattered," Dave said. "Luis takes his cooking seriously. Considers it an art, much like my D.J. regards his painting."

"How is D.J.?"

Dave leaned across the bar. "Get this, Anne. He wants to spell his name D-e-J-a-y." Then Dave shook his head. "Hmph, artists."

Luis in white chef's smock, checkered pants, and toque burst out of the kitchen door carrying a steaming platter. Gerry followed him with a set of silverware.

"Anne," Luis said, in his Spanish-infused English, as he placed the platter in front of her, "you are the inspiration for this dish."

Anne looked at the plate of raviolis smothered in a pinkish cream sauce and inhaled. It smelled heavenly, and she couldn't wait to taste it, but she knew she must first wait for Luis to give the go ahead.

"The pasta is stuffed with roasted red peppers and portabella mushrooms." He touched her curls. "The peppers remind me of your flaming hair, and the mushrooms the earthy goodness of your soul. The sun-dried tomato cream sauce is like the rosy blush of your cheeks, and I have added scallions because they remind me of your eyes. To finish the dish—garlic and cracked peppercorns, for you, Anne, are the spice that enlivens this place."

Anne blushed and glanced up at Gerry. His arms were crossed in front of his chest, and he was staring at the tin ceiling.

91

Luis took her hand, peering into her eyes. "You are the first to taste this creation, and if it meets with your approval, I will add it to the menu and call it 'Pasta Anne.'"

She giggled. "Thank you, Luis. I'm truly honored."

Luis kissed her hand. "Now, please eat. I will go back into my kitchen and await your appraisal."

As Luis walked away, Gerry mumbled and set the silverware down, "His kitchen? Ricky Ricardo, that's my kitchen."

Anne, feeling like a queen, bit into the plump ravioli. She closed her eyes, moaning with delight.

Gerry cleared his throat. "Sorry to interrupt your rapture, but would you like something to drink with that? Some wine?"

Anne opened her eyes. "Just water, please. I don't want anything to interfere with the flavor."

As she watched Gerry pour her a glass, she thought this is how life was meant to be—two gorgeous men attending to her. Maybe she could get them to peel her some grapes.

Gerry came around the bar and set the glass of water next to her plate. Then he took a seat beside her. Swiveling the stool to face her, he leaned an elbow on the bar. "Explain something for me, Slugger. That first day you came into the bar when I hit on you, you told me off. Luis slobbers all over you and you melt like butter in his skillet. I don't understand."

Anne swallowed, flashing her eyes playfully at him. "Are you jealous?"

He leaned back in the stool. "Jealous? Me? Are you kidding? I'm not jealous. What I want to know is: Why do you treat Luis so differently? Is it just me that you don't like?"

Anne set her fork down, looking him in the eye. He had long, dark lashes. It was so unfair. Anne had to stroke on mascara, and she still never achieved lashes like that.

"It wasn't you personally, Gerry. To be honest, it was your technique."

"Technique?"

"Yes, you know. The way you operate."

"But my technique has never failed me with every other girl."

"I told you I'm not every girl." She sipped her water. "That first day it was all about you." Anne's voice took on a deep male tone and swaggering in her seat, she draped an arm around his shoulders. "'Hey, Babe, I'd like to sample your bedside manner.' Big ego—big turn off." She withdrew her arm and sipped from her glass.

"Now, take Luis." She clasped her hands together at her chest, imitating Luis' accent, saying, "Oh, Senor Gerry," she panted, "your eyes are the most beautiful blue eyes I've ever seen. They are lovelier than the Aegean Sea where Aphrodite bathed."

Gerry sat quietly, apparently absorbing what Anne had said. Then he looked at her. "Do you really think my eyes are as blue as the Aegean?"

She shrugged. "I've never been to the Aegean." Perhaps she'd said too much. If she was going to maintain a professional relationship, it didn't seem wise to comment on the beauty of the boss's eyes. But by the serious look on his face, she realized he was seeking her approval. *My God, he's insecure. I'd completely misjudged him.* All that male huffing and puffing was a smoke screen. It was as if she'd been given a key to unlocking Gerry's mind. She almost felt sorry for him.

Anne slapped his wrist. "You missed the point, Gerry. Your come-on was all about yourself. Luis's focused not on himself but on me. That's why Latin men are such renowned lovers." She cut into ravioli. "Their first concern is their partner's pleasure. Not their own."

Gerry frowned. "Are you speaking from experience?"

Anne arched her eyebrows. "Would I tell you?" It was fun to turn the tables on him and toy with him as he had done with her that first day she'd come into the bar.

Gerry appeared to be thoughtful for a moment while Anne ate. "But either way you look at it," he said, "Luis and I are both after the same thing."

"And neither of you are going to get it." Anne laughed. Although she'd always found flirting to be silly before, tonight with him, she was having fun. "Besides I know Luis is engaged. With him, it's a game. It's harmless. With you I felt like the last loaf of bread at the Giant Eagle when they predict a heavy snowfall."

"That's not true."

"Oh, yes it is. Admit it, Gerry. You weren't really interested in me." She thumped her chest with her hand, "Me. Anne. The person. You just wanted to get something from me."

Gerry turned his head sharply like he'd taken a blow to the head. "Man, I've never had it put to me that way before. You're right." He touched her arm, his fingers cool on her skin. He kept them there. "I never realized . . . I'm so sorry, Anne."

Anne patted his hand. The fine, dark hair on the top of his hand felt like strands of the softest angora wool. "Don't be too hard on yourself. Women put up with it all the time. I'm used to it." He still looked remorseful. "Aw, Gerry, don't feel bad. I do like you. In fact, I consider you a good friend. When I said your blue eyes were the most beautiful I'd ever seen, I wasn't teasing. They really are."

His face brightened. She was amazed at how she easily her words could influence his mood.

"Let me see if I've got this right, Slugger. If on that first day when you came in here, had I used Luis' technique, I might have had a chance with you?"

As much as she wanted to admit to him that she'd never been so attracted to a man in her life, she couldn't. No matter how handsome Gerry McMaster was, Anne was well aware that a man like him was toxic to her. It would do her nothing but harm if she allowed him to know that she found him irresistible. However, it didn't hurt to have a little fun—make him sweat.

"We'll never know now, will we?" Anne said, feeling quite puffed up by their conversation. "I'd better finish this before it gets cold." She picked up her fork.

Gerry stood, started to walk away, and then stopped. He walked back to her, bending so that they were at eye level. "Tell me, Anne," he said softly, "whose eyes are nicer do you think—mine or Patrick Dempsey's?" He opened his lids widely so Anne could get a good look at them.

She wanted to laugh, but restrained herself. "Oh, yours. Definitely, Gerry."

"Hmm," he mused, then smiled and walked away.

As she ate, she watched him and Dave talking down at the far end of the bar. Gerry was very animated; no doubt he was relating their discussion to Dave.

When Anne was finished with her meal, she headed back to the kitchen with her dirty dishes. She gave them to Bernie then found Luis near the walk-in cooler. "Luis, that was absolutely magnificent. I'd be honored to have it named after me. You are a wonder."

"With you as my muse, it is easy to create masterpieces," he said, then kissed her hand.

Anne giggled, feeling like the woman who inspired the *Mona Lisa*.

Before she left, she went over to the bar and said goodnight to Dave. Gerry was bent over, talking to some women seated at a table near the door. She walked toward him and gently placed a hand on his back. In a heavily accented voice she whispered into his ear, "Adios, Senor Gerard."

Gerry stood. Then Anne pointed at him. "I'll see you and those baby blues tomorrow."

The corners of his mouth curled into a self-satisfied smirk. He usually offered to walk her to her car, but Anne guessed that he was so stunned that he forgot. He just stood there as she passed through the door into the vestibule.

On the way home, Anne stopped for an ice cream cone to top off her wonderful meal and evening. She had a date with Craig, a dish named after her, and Gerry begging for her approval. What more could a girl want?

Chapter 12

That night when Anne entered her apartment, the answering machine's red light was blinking incessantly. Holding her breath, she hit the button, hoping that Craig hadn't called to cancel their date.

"Anne." It was Janetta's voice. She sighed with relief that it wasn't him, yet she braced herself for a tongue-lashing.

"I didn't want to call your cell because I knew you were at work, but I'm sorry for storming out." She hesitated then stumbled over some words, finally saying, "I don't agree with anything you said, but we've been friends for too long to let something like this come between us. Call me. I'm at Steve's."

Anne dialed Steve's apartment. "Hello, Steve," Anne said dryly. "I'm returning Janetta's call." He responded to her as if she were a telephone solicitor.

After a few moments, Janetta came on the line. "Oh, I'm so glad you called. I'm sorry for blowing up at you."

Anne could hear the remorse in her voice. "I'm sorry too." Anne felt she better not embellish her apology or they'd end up fighting again. She vowed to herself that she'd refrain from meddling in Janetta's love life.

Back on good terms, Anne then filled her in on her upcoming date with Craig and how Patsy's pregnancy was progressing. Near the end of their conversation and much to Anne's chagrin, Janetta invited her and Craig to Steve's house for a party on August 17. Although the thought of being in Steve's company made Anne's skin crawl, she couldn't refuse now that they had made up.

She hung up the phone and poured herself a glass of wine. Oh well, my life is becoming so interesting maybe I won't even have the time to worry about Janetta.

***

The next day after Anne and Peg placed their bets for the *Price Is Right's* Showcase Showdown, Anne settled in the chair in the corner to do her charting. Peg, who Anne insisted get out of bed for awhile, was seated in the chair next to the hospital bed. She was, once again, alternating between watching television and saying the rosary during the commercials.

The beads jangled between her gnarled fingers then stopped at the sound of voices in the hall. Anne looked up.

"Damn it," Peg whispered. "That's Claudia. I forgot. It's Thursday. She's back."

A willowy woman appeared in the doorway with Gerry. "Mrs. McMaster," she gushed, holding out her arms as if to sweep Peg up into an embrace, "it's so good to see you well. I brought you a little—"

"Shhh," Peg hissed, holding her finger to her lips as Drew Carey reappeared on the screen. "It's the Showcase Showdown."

Claudia swallowed her sentence. Standing next to Gerry, she let out a sigh and examined her manicure while she waited for Peg's permission to speak.

Claudia had society page written all over her, Anne thought. Delicate bone structure—high cheekbones and pointed chin—lent her an air of nobility, but her puffy, no doubt injection-enhanced lips were not in sync with her blue eyes. Even as she smiled at Peg, her almond-shaped eyes remained icy. Anne noticed that she was dressed in an expensive, understated pale yellow suit that was the same shade as her straight blond hair. She reminded Anne of a banana Popsicle.

Peg slapped her leg. "I knew that dunce overbid." Placing her rosary beads on the nightstand beside her, she then turned her attention from the television to Claudia. "Did you lose weight while you were away, Dear? You look so frail."

"No, I haven't lost weight," Claudia said, clipping her words. "You ask me that every time I see you."

Peg smiled sweetly. "I worry about you, Dear. That's all."

Anne knew Peg well enough to tell that she was being insincere. Anne also knew that Claudia knew it too.

Claudia took a shopping bag from Gerry. "As I was saying, Mrs. McMaster, I brought you a little something." She placed the bag on the hospital bed.

"You haven't met our Anne," Peg said, sweeping her hand toward the corner of the room.

Claudia turned her head, and a look of surprise registered on her face when her eyes landed on Anne sitting in the corner. "Oh, I'm sorry. I didn't see you there. You must be Mrs. McMaster's niece." Claudia smelled of expensive perfume and money.

Anne stood, put her paperwork on the chair, took a few steps forward, and extended her hand. "No. Actually, I'm her nurse."

"Oh," Claudia said. The icy smile melted on her face. "The scrubs . . . I should have realized. Mac said a nurse was taking care of his mother. I pictured someone . . . I didn't think . . . It's nice to meet you."

After shaking hands, Anne saw Claudia surreptitiously wipe her palms on the side of her skirt.

Anne's blood pressure rose along with a growing dislike for Claudia. She picked up her file and sat down, keeping her eyes fixed on the paperwork on her lap so as not to shoot visual daggers at the Ice Princess's back.

"I don't know what we'd have done without Anne," Peg said. Anne looked up and saw Peg's blue eyes as she smiled genuinely at her. "She's been such a help. Never impatient. Always kind. She's been a godsend. Hasn't she been, Gerry?"

He winked at Anne. "Oh, she's like no other girl." He was obviously alluding to their conversation of the night before. Anne crossed her eyes at him.

Claudia had been rummaging in her shopping bag and missed their exchange.

"It's nice to meet you too, Claudia. I've heard so much about you," Anne said to be polite. *I may not have been a debutante, but at least I have manners.*

"All good," Peg said. She tried to look so innocent but everyone knew she was fibbing.

Claudia pulled out a gift wrapped elaborately in gold and purple striped metallic paper and gold net bow.

"Peg," Gerry said, "Claudia brought you a present from California."

Claudia handed the box to Peg with an anxious look on her face, like someone making an offering to appease a harsh god.

Peg examined the box. "Honey," she said, scowling at Claudia, "you shouldn't waste your money on expensive wrapping paper. If you ever marry Gerry, you'll have to learn to cut corners. He's not an architect anymore, and even though he still likes to put on the dog, barkeepers aren't millionaires you know."

Claudia pulled her lips into a sour smile. "You were worth the extra expense."

Peg unwrapped the present, lifting the box's lid, wading through purple tissue paper. She fished out the gift, held it up, looking strangely at it.

"It's a crystal," Claudia said brightly.

"A what?" Peg turned it over and over in her hand.

"A crystal . . . you know . . . "

Peg brought it up in front of her glasses, staring quizzically at it. "It's a sparkly rock. Is it a paperweight?"

"No, no." Claudia chuckled. "I found the most charming New Age boutique out in San Francisco. The clerk there advised me that this particular crystal is good for healing."

Peg let the crystal fall into her lap, its heaviness making a trough in her cotton housecoat. "I don't know about healing, but it's so heavy you could kill someone with it."

Claudia looked like a child waiting to be praised for a drawing she'd made. She was so intimidated by Peg, Anne almost felt sorry for her.

"Thank you, Dear. It's . . . ah . . . lovely." Peg scuttled the crystal to the nightstand.

Claudia's face fell. Gerry must have sensed her distress because he quickly touched Claudia's elbow and said, "Well, Mum, Claudia needs to get to her office."

"Sorry, I can't stay longer, Mrs. McMaster," she said, jumping on his suggestion. "Now that I'm back and you're home, we'll have to schedule a little chat."

"I'll be waiting" Peg said dryly.

"It was nice meeting you," Anne called to Claudia as Gerry hustled her out. Anne could hear Claudia whispering furiously as they walked down the hall.

After they had gone, Peg waved her hand toward the crystal. "How do you like that? I damn near die, and all she brings me is a rock. She could have at least stopped up Wardzinsky's Drug Store and gotten me a box of Russell Stover candies. That would be better than this stupid thing."

"She seems very nice," Anne said, playing devil's advocate.

Peg turned up her nose. "Seems is right."

Anne chuckled. "Don't hesitate to reveal your true feelings, Peg."

"Oh, you probably think I'm mean," she said, looking remorseful. "God forgive me, it's nothing personal against the girl. It's just that she's not right for my Gerry."

"He seems to like her."

"What man doesn't like a shameless tart?"

"She hardly looks like a tart."

"Do you know how he met her?" She put a hand on her hip. "She bought him."

"Bought him?"

"Bid on him like he was a stud up for auction."

"What?"

"He was nominated one of Pittsburgh's most eligible bachelors, and she outbid everyone at some charity bachelor auction to get a date with my son." She crossed her arms with deliberation. "In my estimation, that makes her a tart."

"From what I've heard from Dave and Vera, Gerry seems to be serious about her."

"Oh, phooey. He's never been serious about a girl in his life. He says he never is going to get married."

"I don't know. Dave told me that Gerry's asked him if he can work some extra hours because he needs to spend more time with her."

Peg looked up at Anne with panic in her eyes, grasping the chair's arms. "You don't think he's changed his mind? You don't think he'd actually marry her, do you?"

"You'd better ask him that question."

"If he does, he may as well just stab me in the heart."

Suddenly, Peg moved her hand to her chest. A troubled look crossed her face, and Anne could she that she was holding her breath.

"Something wrong, Peg?"

"No, no," she said, waving a hand at Anne. "Just a burp that was stuck."

Anne stood. "You sure?"

"Of course."

Anne came to Peg, feeling for the old woman's pulse. Peg wriggled out of her grasp. "Don't get your knickers in a twist. I'm fine. It was just a burp."

"I don't like your clutching your chest while talking about dying."

Peg raised her eyebrows, and spoke snottily as if she were a teenager confronting an overprotective parent. "I am fine. Geez, if you get this upset over a burp, I'd hate too see you if I fart."

***

Gerry closed his office door. Claudia turned, practically lunging for him, wrapping her arms around his neck and kissing him. Off guard and balance, Gerry's back slammed into the door. He heard a click as she reached behind him, locking it. She continued to maul him with her lips, and he suspected it was more an act of defiance aimed toward his mother than a sudden wave of passion for him.

She pulled back, sliding her hands down his chest, her slender fingers playing with the buttons on his shirt. "Why does your mother hate me?"

The inside of his lips hurt from her mouth forcing his flesh against his teeth. "She doesn't hate you."

"You saw what happened upstairs. I can't do anything right by her."

He ran his tongue around the inside of his mouth, feeling a groove imbedded into the soft tissue. "She's just old and cantankerous, Claudia, that's all. It's not you. She thinks no one is good enough for me."

Claudia undid a button and kissed the skin she had exposed. She looked up at him with her cool blue eyes. "I've missed you so much, Mac. With your mother's illness and my trip to the coast, I feel like I've hardly seen you." She undid another button and began kissing his neck and chest.

He moved away. "I can't now, Claudia. I'm needed in the bar."

Her lower lip curled into a pout. "But it's been so long." She moved closer and began to yank his shirt out of his pants. "I want you so much, Mac. I can't wait any longer."

He pulled away, knifing a hand inside his pants, tucking his shirt back in. "I feel the same way. We'll get together, but not right now."

"When?"

"Soon."

103

"But I want you now."

"God, Claudia. I have work to do and someone could come in."

She crossed her arms, glaring at him.

"I promise."

Claudia walked to him and took his hands, placed them on her small breasts. Her nipples—buried under linen—registered as minor blips on his palms.

"I'm tired of your promises, Mac. I feel as if we're spinning our wheels. When are you going to make time for me?"

He broke free of her grasp, walked toward the desk, and began rearranging the papers scattered on top of it. "It's not as easy as it used to be to get away, Claudia. It takes planning now."

She came from behind him, playing with the hair at the nape of his neck. "I hate the idea of your living here with your mother. You promised me when you bought the townhouse that we'd be together more. You promised you'd make more time for me."

She was whining now and Gerry hated when she did that. He whirled around and fluffed out the hair she'd been playing with. "Can I help it that my mother got sick before I could move in? You don't expect me to leave her now, do you?"

"No, but she's better. And she has that nurse—Hanna."

"Anne. Her name is Anne."

"I don't care what her name is. What I care about is you. When are you going to move in, Mac?"

"I have to wait until she can manage on her own. It shouldn't be much longer. She's made a lot of progress since Anne's been here."

She slapped his chest. "Why didn't you tell me she was beautiful?"

"Who? My mother?

She tilted her head, looking out the corner of her eyes. "Stop being coy. You know who I mean. Anne."

"Anne's beautiful? I hadn't noticed."

"Liar. If you weren't interested in her, you would have told me about her. You're attracted to Anne, aren't you?"

"She's an employee."

"Like that's ever stopped you before." She grabbed his rear-end, pulled him closer, grounding her hips into him. "What are you paying her to do?"

It had been a while since they had made love, and Gerry missed the physical release of sex with her. "Anne and I are just good friends." He kissed Claudia, long and hard to reassure her, and against his will, felt himself stirring with desire. He broke away from her before he lost control. He walked behind his desk. "Listen, I have an idea. Tomorrow she's going to sit with Mum in the evening because Irma's can't be here. I'll have Dave cover for me for an hour, and I'll sneak over to my place. Why don't you meet me there at seven? Then I can welcome you home properly."

"I don't think I can wait until then." She slinked over to him and licked his earlobe. "Couldn't you just welcome me home in here. Right now?" She moved a thigh between his legs, rubbing it against the length of him. He felt himself rising and succumbing at the same time.

He ran a hand up her bare thigh and backed her onto the desk. Stepping between her legs, he forced them wide open. Then he kissed her, and as he moved his lips down her neck to her throat, he saw the picture of his mother and father staring up at him. His desire wilted.

He pulled his hand out from under her skirt. "I can't. Not here. Not now." He backed away leaving Claudia sitting on the desk, her mouth open, her legs apart, looking like a startled equestrian, who'd just been bucked from her horse.

Chapter 13

Anne stepped out of the bathroom after changing into her khaki shorts and green cotton sleeveless sweater and walked into Peg's room.

"Woo, Kiddo," Peg said, eyeing Anne. "You got great gams."

Anne stuck out a leg, appraising them. "You think so?"

"They're nicely shaped and in proportion to the rest of you. Take it from someone who knows a nice set of pins when she sees them."

"Well, thanks," Anne said. She rubbed her hands together. "Since work is officially over, it's now time to play."

Anne felt that she and Peg had fallen into a rut, spending the majority of their day tending to Peg's convalescence and their free time building jigsaw puzzles, doing word searches, and solving crosswords. Peg resisted any exercise; Anne had to coax her just to walk into the kitchen for meals. When she suggested that they try an excursion and visit down in the bar, Peg balked as if Anne had suggested she go hiking in the Himalayas.

What worried her was that Peg still showed signs of being depressed. She cried occasionally and seemed to be content to sleep when Anne wasn't engaging her in activities. Anne thought that if she shook things up a bit, maybe Peg's spirit might lift.

It was Friday night, and after Gerry had delivered dinner and they'd eaten, Anne deliberately made a big deal out of changing into casual clothes in hopes that it would delineate the evening from their daily routine.

"Oh boy," Peg said, giggling and looking up at Anne from the hospital bed. "What are we going to do?"

"Well, I've got a few tricks up my sleeve." Anne rooted through a bag she had retrieved from her car.

"You didn't hire those Chippendip dancers, did you?"

Anne knew she meant Chippendale but didn't have the heart to correct the old woman since the promise of an evening of fun seemed to have cheered her. "No, they were booked," Anne said, keeping her eyes focused on the inside of the bag. Then she looked up, holding two DVD boxes. "I brought two of my favorite movies. You can pick. We have *True Lies* and *Pride and Prejudice*."

"I don't know anything about either of them. You decide, Anne."

"Well, are you in the mood for action or romance?"

"I don't think my heart needs any action." Peg smiled girlishly, "I'm overdue in the romance department though."

"Romance it is then." Anne popped *Pride and Prejudice* into the DVD player. "You're going to love this movie, Peg. I watched it and had to go out and buy it. I swear this is the most romantic movie I've ever seen. Mr. Darcy has these smoldering eyes that . . . Oh, I don't know . . ." Anne felt a chill rush through her.

Peg chuckled. "Sounds to me like you're a little over due in the romance department too."

If you only knew, Anne thought.

***

"Well," Anne said, as the credits scrolled by on the TV screen, "did you like that?"

"It was swell, and you were right. The fella who played Mr. Darcy . . . Mmm, was he a looker! But that Lady Catherine. What a pain in the ass! And that Mr. Collins." One nostril curled in disgust. "He gave me the creeps. Reminded me of Junior Joswiak. I sat next to Junior in second and third grade, and he was always playing with his saliva, making spit bridges between his fingers, watching how the sun lit up his drool drawbridges."

Anne shuddered and reached into her bag. "I brought some snacks. Hungry?"

"Oh, goodie. Treats."

From her bag, Anne produced a sleeve of rice cakes and bottles of Perrier water.

Peg bit into a rice cake and exclaimed, "Quick, I need a drink." Anne opened one of the bottles and handed it to her. Peg gulped it down. A few grains of the puffed rice stuck to the moisture on her lips. "Thfppt," Peg sputtered, sticking her tongue out and blowing air through her mouth trying to dislodge the rice morsels. Finally, she brushed them away. "What the hell are you feeding me? An old mattress?"

"They're rice cakes."

"If you call that a snack," Peg snorted and shrugged, "you need more than romance, Annie Banannie."

Anne ejected the DVD. As she put it back in its case, Peg screwed up her face. "You know, I've been wracking my brains trying to figure out who that Mr. Darcy puts me in mind of, and now I know. Guess?"

"I don't know," Anne said, snapping the plastic case shut. "Who?"

"My Gerry."

Anne blushed, feeling suddenly exposed. She'd never made the connection, but Gerry with his dark good looks, did resemble the leading man. When she was around Gerry, Anne had to admit that she felt the same electric excitement that thrilled her whenever she watched this movie. "I guess there's some resemblance."

Maybe I'm not really attracted to Gerry at all. Subconsciously, I must have transferred the feelings that the Mr. Darcy character stirred in me to Gerry because they looked similar. Relieved that she'd finally figured out why she was attracted to such a shallow man, she dropped the DVD into her bag, sat down in the chair, and pulled out a rice cake.

Suddenly, Gerry appeared in the doorway, his face seemed flushed. Anne caught his cologne as it wafted into the room. It made the lining of her nose prickle like a dog that had smelled roasting meat. She felt her blood surge through her heart. "I've got to run out for a minute." He sounded a bit breathless. "You ladies, OK up here?"

"We're fine," Peg said.

"Fine," Anne echoed softly.

"Good then. Be back in an hour or so." He disappeared.

Anne's heart thundered in her chest. *You're not really attracted to him. It's just transferred feelings.* She sunk her teeth into the rice cake, biting off a chunk with a loud crunch. *Yeah, right, Sigmund Freud. Believe that and believe that nonsense about penis envy too.*

***

Gerry opened the door and flicked on the light. The newness of the townhouse screamed to him. Pristine white walls and shiny oak planked flooring looked operating-room bright. The smell of fresh paint and new upholstery reminded him of how little time he'd spent here since closing on it two months ago. The place seemed sterile; it had not taken on the fragrances of living—cooked meals, soap, his favorite cologne.

Gerry walked up the flight of stairs to the first level and strode to the massive bay window that looked over a back channel of the Allegheny River. The evening sun, like some large orange tablet, was dissolving into the placid water. A mallard with three ducklings cruised near the shore tracing patterns on the flat river like a skater doing school figures. *This is why I bought this place. For the serenity.*

Washington's Landing, a development situated on miniscule Herr's Island in the middle of the river, seemed like a world away from the bustling bar and the noisy, crowded streets of Lawrenceville, but it was merely minutes away across the Fortieth Street Bridge. The complex of raised wooden townhomes with large porches looked like a seaside village found in North Carolina instead of Pittsburgh.

Gerry walked into the kitchen, his footsteps echoing off the ceramic tile floor, and retrieved two wineglasses and a corkscrew. He opened the bottle of Chardonnay he'd brought with him from the bar. As he poured it into the crystal goblets, he thought how much the wine suited Claudia. It was light in color to match her delicate complexion and hair, and it had a sting to it that matched her personality.

From the kitchen window, he watched a black Mercedes pull into the driveway. Claudia stepped out, touching the sides of her hair, which had been pulled back into a chignon. Gerry hated her hair that way. It reminded him of the old women who toddled up and down Butler Street. The dress she wore, however, was anything but an old woman's attire. Skimpy and black, this brief slip of fabric made it clear what her intent was in meeting him here.

Gerry set the glasses on the teak credenza in the living room, made his way down the stairs, arriving at the foyer as the doorbell chimed. He squared his shoulders and opened the door.

"Hello, Mac." She greeted him as if he were a business associate. When she stepped inside and Gerry closed the door, it was like someone had thrown some sort of switch. She was all over him tongue, lips, and hands.

He was pressed for time and was grateful she wanted to dispense with preliminaries. "I poured us some wine," he said making a stab at trying to appear interested in the woman in the dress not just what was under it.

"Forget the wine." Claudia mumbled her lips pressed against his. She pulled his shirt out of his pants and ran her cool, slender fingers up his chest. Goosebumps sprinted up his spine.

"Good," he said, pulling the shirt over his head and tossing it aside. "I told Dave I'd only be gone an hour. Anne's sitting with my—"

Claudia bit his lip. "Don't mention her." Her eyes looked sharp. "Don't mention anything. Just take off your pants."

He needed no coaxing; in seconds he was naked. The air pouring from the vent felt chilly on his bare skin. Reaching behind Claudia, his fingers searched for the dress's zipper.

She pushed him away. "Stop. I have a surprise." Taking him by the hand, she led him upstairs to the master bedroom, the new tan

111

carpet was thick and spongy under his feet. Perhaps he should take her on the rug.

Now, get on the bed," she commanded, nixing that idea. A compliant participant, he stretched out on the bed, leaning against the wrought-iron headboard. The metal was cold on his back so he grabbed another pillow and plumped it behind him.

She pulled the pin securing the chignon, unleashing her blond mane. As she shook her hair out, she turned her back to Gerry, and then she reached up behind, unzipping her dress. Slowly, seductively, she eased it off her shoulders, revealing a black, lacy bra.

Gerry folded his arms behind his head, his pupils dilating from the visual stimulation. "Go to it, baby."

She let the top of the dress fall to her waist. Looking over her shoulder at him, she ran her tongue across her lips, then shimmied her hips. The dress landed in a heap at her feet, revealing a black lace thong, garter belt, and black hosiery.

Gerry wolf-whistled.

"Surprise," she said. "I got this on my trip."

"Come on over here," he said. "I've got a surprise for you too."

Claudia laughed and stepped out of the dress. Then she turned around, and Gerry was astonished to see that the bra was cupless. Her breasts looked like two bullseyes pasted to her chest. He had never noticed how small they were before. Seeing them in the black lace contraption accentuated their meagerness. Suddenly, he felt his desire ebbing.

She gyrated and shook them in front of him, but they barely moved. There wasn't enough flesh to raise a good jiggle.

What is wrong with me? Breasts are breasts no matter what size. I've got a live, half-naked woman in front of me who wants sex.

He smiled, trying to look lustfully at her, but he couldn't help noticing the way her ribs protruded, how sharply her hip bones stuck out under the garter belt.

Anne would do that lingerie justice. He imagined her standing before him, her flaming hair cascading down her creamy shoulders, curling over her full breasts, her nipples like red jujubes. His mouth began to water.

Claudia crawled cat-like up the bed toward him, her eyes in a predatory gaze, her manicured nails honed like claws. As she drew closer, the bare-breasted fantasy of Anne dissolved from his mind. Claudia, on all fours, hovered over his exposed body, ready to pounce, and he felt his blood surging. As she nuzzled his neck, his mother's voice intruded in his head. *She's so skinny.*

He noticed how angular her shoulders were, how ridge-like her clavicle, and his passion wilted. *Think of Anne's breasts. Think of Anne's breasts.*

Then as Claudia lowered herself onto him and began grinding her bony hips against his pelvis, his muscles knotted involuntarily in an act of self-preservation, and he heard Peg's voice warning again. *I'd be afraid she'd puncture your spleen.*

Damn my mother! He closed his eyes, tensing as he awaited imminent organ damage.

Chapter 14

Craig arrived Saturday night promptly at six, dressed in black slacks and a gray sport shirt, the dark clothing accentuating his blond hair.

"You look lovely," he said, as he gave Anne a peck on the cheek. She grabbed her knock-off Chanel navy purse hanging from the closet doorknob and slung it over her shoulder. She'd indulged her shopping mania, buying white pants, a red and white striped tank top, and in case the breeze coming off the rivers at the stadium made it chilly, a navy linen blazer.

"You don't think it's too nautical?" she asked. "I don't want to look like the captain of *The Good Ship Lollipop*." *The Good Ship Lollipop* was the children's riverboat cruise that plied Pittsburgh's three rivers.

Craig touched her shoulder, laughing. "I'd forgotten how good natured you always were, what a great sense of humor you always had, Anne."

Shocked that someone had found her good-natured, she almost missed the note of heaviness in his voice.

"Is everything OK? You seem down."

"Nothing an evening with you won't fix." He escorted her out the door. "I'm just facing a decision, and I'm not sure what to do."

"Oh," Anne said. She hoped he wasn't trying to decide whether to come out of the closet or join a monastery.

"I'll tell you about it on the way to the game."

Craig's car, a late-model blue Honda Civic, was clean and fresh inside, no gum wrappers in the ashtrays, no fast food wrappers on the floor in the back. *He probably has his tires rotated regularly and his oil changed every 3,000 miles too. My mother would love him.*

He shut off the radio when he started the car. Anne took that as a compliment. She didn't like having to compete with music. She'd been on a date with a drummer once who blared Phil Collins while he drove and beat time on the steering wheel.

"So what's the dilemma?" she asked.

"It's not really a dilemma. Everyone should be so lucky; I have too many choices. As I told you, I'm nearing the end of my training, and I've been offered several great positions. I don't know which one to take."

"Well, are you leaning toward any of them?"

"Two. The first is in town with the city's premiere cosmetic surgery practice. The money is unbelievable, Anne. I've also been offered a position in Las Vegas. I've always loved the West."

Anne silently hoped he wouldn't take the Las Vegas position. She didn't want to lose him after finding him again.

They were so involved in discussing Craig's career plans, before they knew it they'd arrived at PNC Park.

The smoky aroma of grilling kielbasa and hot dogs from tailgaters filled the parking lot. As they walked to the park, the wind whipped the banners attached to the lamp posts and tousled Craig's blond fringe that fell over his forehead.

He took her hand, and they threaded their way through the crowd. Anne wondered what he expected from the evening. Were they just old friends reuniting to reminisce about the past? Or were they beginning a new phase? A relationship? If his interest in her was romantic, how would she fit into his career plans?

They barely paid attention to the baseball game they were so busy bringing each other up-to-date on their lives. He told her about a trip he'd recently taken, with some other doctors to the Dominican Republic, where the physicians donated their surgical talents to aid the poor.

Craig was the first man Anne had been out with in a long time that she didn't feel she needed to be on guard with. He had no hidden motives, played no games, and she knew his compliments were not said to get her into bed. With his powerful build, boyish good looks, intelligence and strength of character, in another era, King Arthur would have pressed him into service at his Round Table. But was he her knight in shining armor?

When they stood for the seventh inning stretch, all doubts about his intentions vanished. Craig put his arm around her waist and whispered in her ear. "I'm so glad you're no longer with Zach."

She relaxed into his embrace, feeling safe and secure.

After the game, he suggested that they get a bite to eat. Anne was reluctant to see the evening end and agreed.

"You've told me so much about Mac's Place, why don't we go there?"

Anne opened her mouth to recommend another place then stopped. *Why shouldn't we go to the bar?* She was proud to be seen with Craig, and perhaps if she appeared with him, everyone would stop commenting that she never had dates.

***

When they arrived there, it was crowded. This time Anne took Craig's hand and led him through the throng. Dave was busy with customers and didn't notice her as they made their way. She scanned the place for Gerry but didn't see him. Oddly, she felt disappointed, but she blamed it on the fact that she wouldn't get to see his reaction when she showed up with a date.

Anne, familiar with the layout, guided Craig to a small table in the corner which people always seemed to overlook. Vera, in a rush carrying a tray of drinks, breezed past, calling over her shoulder, "Be with you in a sec." She did a double take and quickly came back to the table. "Anne, when did you come in?"

"Just got here."

"Let me serve these, and I'll come right back."

Vera returned, the large brown tray resting on her hip. "What are you doing here? Can't get enough of us, huh?" While she spoke, she was sizing up Craig.

"We were at the baseball game. This is my friend Craig Love," Anne said. "Craig, this is Vera Kowalski, the best waitress in the universe."

"Pleased to meet you," Vera said, her eyes lingering over Craig. Anne had never seen her still for so long.

"We'd like to order dinner." Anne glanced at her gold wristwatch. "If it's not too late."

"For you, Luis would reopen the kitchen. How about some drinks first?"

"I'll have a mojito," Anne said.

"How about you, Craig?" Vera asked. Anne noticed that she was enjoying the opportunity to stare into his face while she waited for his reply.

"I'm on call tomorrow. I better lay off the hard stuff. A Pepsi is fine."

Vera brought them their drinks and menus. "You'll notice," she said, pointing to a slip of paper attached to the inside of the menu, "that tonight's special is Pasta Anne." She turned to Craig. "It's named for none other than your friend here."

Craig winked across the table at Anne. "I've always thought she was some dish."

"Vera, I'll be the only one ordering dinner." Anne laughed as she pretended to hit him with her menu. "He's already full of baloney."

When Vera returned to take their order, Anne selected the chicken Caesar salad and Craig, of course, ordered the Pasta Anne. As he closed his menu, Vera, standing slightly behind him out of his vision, pointed her thumb toward him, making goo-goo eyes.

Anne raised her eyebrows, signaling to her that she was well aware of how hot her date was.

Vera stopped at the bar. Anne saw her say something to Gerry, who was now there mixing drinks. She motioned with her head towards Anne and Craig's table. Before Gerry could catch Anne staring at him, she turned back to Craig, but she sensed his eyes on her. This was a mistake coming here, she thought. He'll probably come over to the table now, tease her, and tell Craig about what happened her first day here, about her horrible temper, about how she tried to slug him.

When they'd finished their dinners and Gerry had not dropped by their table, Anne felt relieved. Perhaps since tonight she was a customer and not an employee, he felt it out of bounds to intrude on her date. Yet, it wasn't as if she were just anyone who had come into his bar. She took care of his mother for, goodness sake. You'd think he could spare a minute to say hello. Annoyed, Anne decided she'd ignore him if he did stop by their table.

Vera removed their dishes and asked if they'd like some dessert. Anne had a craving for one of Luis' Napoleon's, but she didn't want to appear to be a glutton before Craig so she declined.

"Nothing for me either," Craig said.

"If I can't tempt you," Vera said, "then I'll bring the check." She walked away.

"You know, Anne," Craig said, his velvety brown eyes soft and disarming, "I've had a wonderful time." He reached across the table and took her hand. "I have a feeling that we were meant to run into each other again. Like fate had—"

"And you thought I'd let you get out of here without ordering dessert!" Gerry plunked an enormous Napoleon in front of Anne. "Anne here is a fiend for these. You must be her brother, Kevin. She talks a lot about you. If you'd like something too, I can get it for you."

"This isn't Kevin," Anne said sharply. "This is my date."

"Date? Oh, my mistake." Gerry offered Craig his hand. Craig, ever polite, stood to shake it. Gerry's head rose as he gazed up at Craig, who was a good two inches taller and about twenty pounds heavier with muscle.

"Gerry, I mean Mac," Anne said, not sure if she should call him by her pet name when others were present, "this is Craig Love."

"Nice to meet you," Gerry said, wearing one of his best smiles, but Anne knew him well enough now to know that it was his false charm at work. "So how do you know our Annie?"

What's this "our Annie," crap? I'm not his anything.

"Oh, we go way back to college," Craig said. He looked around the bar. "You've got a great place here. I work up at Children's. I've run by here but have never had time to stop in. I know this place is a favorite of the O.R. staff."

"Yeah, we get a lot of you nurses in here," Gerry said.

Anne sensed derision when he said the word "nurse." If Craig noticed how condescending Gerry was treating him, he didn't let on. *He's too refined to acknowledge Gerry's rudeness.* But she wasn't.

"Gerry," Anne said.

He looked down at her sitting at the table. "Yes?"

"Craig's a doctor."

"Doctor?" Gerry repeated raising his dark brows. "Like a proctologist? Or something?"

"Surgeon," Anne said dryly. "Plastic surgeon."

"Hmm," Gerry mused. The muscle twitching ever so slightly near his mouth told Anne he'd been put back into his place. Gerry looked askance at Craig. "You say you run?"

"Yes."

Gerry puffed out his chest. "So do I. Eight minute miles. What's your p.r.?" He looked at Anne. "A p.r. is a personal record."

"I know what a p.r. is, Gerry," she said.

Gerry, trying to one-up Craig, reminded Anne of the rams on nature programs who butt heads in order to establish their superiority. *Gerry can't stand not to be the lead male.* He was the same way whenever Luis was around.

"I haven't timed myself lately," Craig said, "but last year I qualified for Boston."

"The marathon?" Gerry asked.

"No, the Tea Party," Anne said.

"Oh," Gerry said, and Anne listened to see if she could hear the air hissing out of him as his ego deflated before their eyes. He could not depose Craig as the alpha male.

Before he could challenge Craig to an arm wrestling match, Anne interrupted. "Gerry, thanks anyway for the Napoleon, but I'm too full to eat it now. Perhaps I could have a box?"

Gerry caught Vera as she scooted by. "Please have Bernie bring out a box for Anne."

"Sure thing, Mac," she said before dashing away.

While she waited, Anne asked how Peg was doing. A few minutes later, Bernie, wearing his apron, came out of the kitchen carrying a Styrofoam container. His eyes lit up when he saw her. "Hi, Anne," he said, raising his hand.

"Hi, Bernie. How are you tonight?"

"Busy. Always busy."

Anne stood and touched Craig's arm. "This is my friend Bernie Schmitt. He's Gerry's chief dishwasher."

"And best buddy," Bernie added. He was as tall as Anne, and she placed a hand on his shoulder, looking him in his eyes.

"Bernie, you've got something on your glasses. Let me clean these for you," she said. Anne removed them and picked up a clean napkin from the table. After wiping off the spots, she handed them back, and he put them on the almost non-existent bridge of his nose. "Bernie, this is my friend Dr. Love." Anne used Craig's title to annoy Gerry.

Bernie began bouncing on his feet. "Dr. Love!" His head started bopping as he drummed on the table and sang, "They call me Dr. Love . . . Calling Dr. Love . . . I'm the doctor of love."

"Not that Dr. Love," Gerry sneered.

"I'd forgotten about that KISS song," Anne said. She turned to Craig, "Bernie is a big KISS fan."

"So am I. I saw them at Madison Square Garden a long time ago," Craig said, seeming pleased to find someone who shared this interest. "You know they're touring again. If I'm in town, we should go."

Gerry's face turned red. "Ah, doc. I've got that covered."

Gerry was doing his best to provoke Craig. She wanted to get out of there before his behavior deteriorated further. "Bernie, why don't you take Craig over and show him your KISS poster?"

"Wanna see it?" Bernie asked.

"Sure do," Craig said as he placed a hand on Bernie's shoulder. "So, what's your favorite album, Bernie? Mine's *KISS Alive II*."

While Craig followed Bernie to over to the wall where Gerry had allowed him to hang his autographed KISS poster, Gerry helped Anne put the Napoleon into the container.

"Dr. Love," he groused. "You sure he's a plastic surgeon? Sounds more like a porn star."

"What it sounds like is that you're jealous of Craig." Anne said to tease him. "Can't take the competition?"

To her surprise, Gerry did not laugh. He stiffened, his jaw tight, his eyes sharp. Thrusting the container at her, he snapped, "Me, jealous of him? Why would I be jealous of Craig? So he's a doctor. Big deal! I've got one of the most successful businesses in the city. Women love me. What's he got that I haven't got?"

Anne didn't want to argue with him. "Can I have our check please?"

He touched her arm. "Answer me."

She moved away from him. "Gerry, give me the check."

His face turned the color of red wine. "No charge."

"Gerry, don't be ridiculous—"

"I said no charge," he barked, stalking away, leaving Anne standing there dumbfounded, holding the Styrofoam container.

What does Craig have that you don't have, Gerry? Manners!

Every time she began to think that Gerry was a nice guy and his playboy image was just an act, she was reminded of what a jerk he really was. He deserved a woman like Claudia.

She walked to Craig and Bernie, where she explained about the check and wished Bernie good night.

"That so generous of him. I'd like to thank Mac," Craig said.

Good. And I hope when Craig thanks him, Gerry feels very small.

As soon as Craig moved toward the bar where Gerry was standing, Anne saw Gerry turn and make a beeline for his office.

"I'll thank him for you on Monday," she said. He has the emotional maturity of a 16-year-old boy, she thought. He was right. He really had no reason to be jealous of Craig. He was as equally handsome and successful in his own right. There was nothing that Craig had that Gerry didn't.

"OK," Craig said, putting an arm around Anne.

She looked over her shoulder as she left the bar and glimpsed Gerry standing in the back, his arms crossed, glowering at them.

Then it dawned on Anne what exactly it was that Gerry didn't have. *Me. Gerry doesn't have me.*

Chapter 15

On Monday morning Anne knocked at the McMaster's door. Her scrubs clung to her skin. Already the day was blast-furnace hot, but she wasn't sure if it was the heat or the prospect of confronting Gerry that had her perspiring.

Usually he came quickly to answer, but when no one responded, she was relieved. She hated to ring the bell for fear Peg was sleeping, so she let herself in with the key. The coolness inside the entry embraced and revived her. The only sound was the faint hum of the air conditioner. She opened the door that led into the bar and peeked inside but saw no one. Perhaps Gerry was out running.

She made her way up the avocado-carpeted stairs. After his childish behavior on Saturday night, she hoped he'd stay away all day.

Anne entered the kitchen. A dish with toast crumbs was in the sink along with a pan that had dried egg-lace sticking to it. The butter was still out on the counter. She tucked it into the refrigerator. Usually Gerry was very meticulous about the kitchen. He's losing it. He certainly seemed to have left in a hurry. Was he avoiding her? Why? Was he embarrassed by how silly he'd acted around Craig? He should be. His jealousy had puzzled her. *Maybe it is because he doesn't have me.* Some men just can't stand the fact that a woman isn't interested in him. Zach had been like that too. She stopped before the Sacred Heart statue and whispered to it. "Well, he can just get over it. I'm not one of his bar bimbos who can't stop fawning over him."

She looked into Peg's room. She lay sleeping peacefully in the hospital bed. Her gray roots were growing out. They'd soon have to make a decision about her hair, whether to dye it or have the red tips cut off. For now she'd have to be content with looking like a geriatric punk rocker.

"Peg?" Anne whispered from the doorway, not wanting to startle her.

Peg's eyes flew open, and she looked so alert, Anne knew she had been pretending to be asleep. She let out a long sigh. "Thank goodness it's you."

Anne dropped her purse and medical bag. "You were expecting somebody else?"

"No, I thought it was Gerry. I was hoping he'd think I was sleeping."

"Why?"

"He's crabbier than a bear with a sunburned ass. He's in his office already. I hope he stays there."

That makes two of us.

"Have you two been fighting again, Peg?"

Peg waved a hand, sneering. "I don't know what his problem is. He was fine on Saturday. Then yesterday, every time I opened my mouth, he bit my head off."

"Maybe he's tired," Anne said.

"Tired of me probably."

Anne stood over Peg. "Don't be ridiculous. He's devoted to you."

"I've thrown a monkey wrench into his little romance with Claudia." The way Peg turned up her nose when she said Claudia's name, you'd have thought she was sniffing ammonia. "I heard him on the phone last night with her. They were arguing."

Anne knew Gerry's love life was none of her business, yet she couldn't stop herself from prying.

"About what?"

Peg made her voice whiny and babyish. "Evidently, she thinks he's not paying enough attention to her. That's why he's downstairs so early. He's interviewing another bartender so he can have more free time."

126

Anne raised the bed. "Well, he probably could use the help."

Peg clutched her arm. "Get this. He's talking about hiring a housekeeper too. Me—with a maid? I'll be the laughing stock of Lawrenceville. Mae Corcoran up the hill had a maid, and she was the laziest damn woman I've ever known and the talk of Butler Street. I'd rather die first than have someone keeping my own house for me."

"It's probably just until you're well enough to take care of it on your own."

"Or until he puts me in a home."

"Oh, Peg." Anne took her hand. "He'd never do that. He's probably just overwhelmed."

Peg snorted. "He doesn't know what overwhelmed is. Try being a widow with a young son and a business to run, that's overwhelming. But you know what I really think has him in a snit?"

"What?"

Peg's eyes twinkled behind her thick lenses. "Something a little birdy told me about you."

"What birdie was that?" Anne asked suspiciously.

"Bernie."

Anne presumed the bird would have been the big dodo, Gerry.

"I heard you came into the bar Saturday night. With a beau." Peg widened her eyes. "I think Gerry's jealous."

Anne tried to appear shocked. "Jealous? Of what?"

Peg pointed to her glasses. "I know these are thick, Annie Banannie, but that doesn't mean I'm blind. I see the way he looks at you. How he's always finding an excuse to eat with us. He's jealous of your date. "

"Oh, phew," Anne said. "No offense, Peg, but I've seen your son in action. He's a big flirt. He's not interested in me. And besides he has Claudia."

"What about you?" Peg said. "I see the way you look at him."

Anne blushed. "Oh, Peg, I'll grant you that Gerry is handsome, but we are not suited for each other. We don't want the same things from life. We're just friends."

"Whatever you say."

"Besides, I'm dating someone."

"Speaking of which, why didn't you bring him up and let me meet him."

"It was late. I thought you might be sleeping."

Peg frowned. "So what's he like? I asked Gerry, but he said he was too busy to notice." She raised her eyes at Anne, giving her an I-told-you-so look.

Liar, Anne thought. If Gerry could have fingerprinted Craig and run a make on him, she knew he would have.

"Oh, he's an old friend from college," Anne said. "I ran into him recently."

Peg spent the greater part of the morning pumping Anne for information about her date. As Anne extolled Craig's virtues, Peg spirits seemed to sink deeper and deeper until she seemed as touchy as Gerry had been on Saturday night.

Finally, Anne felt she had to say something. Moving to the bed, she took the old woman's hand. "Look, I know what's going on here, but it's never going to happen, Peg. I'm very flattered that you think enough of me to believe I'd be good for your son, but I wouldn't."

For the rest of the morning, Peg was quiet. Gerry remained scarce, letting Bernie deliver their lunches.

At three o'clock as she often did, Irma arrived early and sidled silently into Peg's room, taking her seat. This was the sacred hour—*General Hospital* time—and everyone had their assigned seat—Peg in the chair by the bed, Irma near the door, and Anne in the corner—all facing the television. No one ever talked while the soap opera was on, and Anne was glad of that. With Peg sulking, she found it hard to make conversation with her. So when Peg spoke, Anne jumped.

"Irma," Peg called, "our Anne had a date."

"She did? Who'd you go out with, Honey?"

"A doctor," Peg said.

Irma pursed her lips, looking worried. "Hmm, a doctor."

"And he's handsome. Big blond fella."

"What kind of doctor?" Irma asked, turning away from the television.

"Plastic surgeon."

Her brows knit together for a moment as she appeared to be mulling that over. "I'd don't think I'd like that," Irma said, shaking her head. "I'd be afraid he'd want to operate on me—redo me. Why I'd be afraid to fall asleep around him. You could wake up to find you have a new nose, or something."

Peg batted the loose skin under her chin. "That might be a problem for you, but not me. I wouldn't mind waking up with a new face. Or breast implants."

"Breast implants?" Irma cried. "I'd want them like I'd want a hole in my head." She crossed her arms over her ample bosom. "Just what I would need. I have a hard enough time corralling the ones I've got."

"I'm not necessarily talking bigger, but perkier." Peg looked down at her chest. "Sometimes I'm grateful my Martin died when I was still in my prime. He used to tell me my breasts were delicious like two cupcakes with cherries on top. I'd hate for him to see them now." She cupped her saggy breasts. "They look like two day-old coffee cakes topped with raisins."

The trio erupted in laughter. Irma blushed and Peg held her side snorting, while tears formed in Anne's eyes.

"What's going on in here?" Gerry stood in the doorway, his eyes scanning the laughing women.

"Just girl talk," Peg said, her face flushed.

"During your story? That's a sacrilege."

Anne crossed the room to get a tissue. As she began to blot her eyes, Peg said, "We were just talking about Anne's date."

"Is that why she's crying?" Gerry said.

"I'm not crying," Anne said indignantly.

"She's not crying," Peg said.

"She's laughing," Irma said.

"Laughing? He wasn't that bad, was he?" Gerry frowned. "OK, so the poor sap wasn't Prince Charming, but it's really cruel of you ladies to make fun of the guy behind his back."

"Poor sap!" Anne cried.

Peg looked at Anne. "I thought you said he was tall and handsome."

Gerry crossed his arms in front of his chest, leaning against the doorframe. "Hmph, to Anne, everyone's tall."

"He is tall," Anne said, planting her hands on her hips. She looked at Peg and Irma. "And handsome. And a doctor." Then she turned to Gerry, and angry now, she stared him down. "He's charming and kind . . . and . . . and . . . and he kisses exquisitely. And I'm going to marry him!"

Their mouths all dropped open at once as they looked at her.

Her mouth almost dropped open too because she couldn't believe she'd said that. "Well, we haven't made any plans, but we're very serious," she said, trying to mitigate her declaration.

"But you've only been out on one date," Peg cried.

"Oh, but I've actually known him for years. It's like we've never been apart."

Gerry, looking like he'd taken a blow to the gut, shook his head. "I thought I was a fast operator."

Anne glanced at her watch. "I forgot to tell you, I have a dental appointment. I need to leave early today." She quickly gathered her bags. "See you tomorrow." Her face flushing a deep crimson, she rushed out of the room.

Gerry stood dumbfounded as Anne rushed past him. Puzzled, he turned toward Peg and Irma who greeted him with scowls.

"What?" he said innocently.

The two old women put their hands on their hips.

"Now you've done it," Peg said.

"Done what?"

"Obviously, her date was a real stinker," Peg said. "Probably, one of those bald, tubby doctors with cold hands. And she was too embarrassed to admit it."

"Where'd you get that idea?" Gerry said. "He was tall and good looking."

"I thought you didn't notice them."

Gerry stuttered, "Well, I mean . . . "

Peg pointed to the door. "Go apologize to that girl."

"For what?"

"For embarrassing her so badly about her date that she had to lie and say she's going to marry this fella. She told me all about her date this afternoon, and never once did she mention that they were thinking about marriage."

Peg and Irma glared at him. Rather than facing their icy stares, he turned and dashed after Anne. He wanted to talk to her anyway, but he damn sure was not going to apologize for anything.

"Wait, Anne," he called, catching her as she was about to go out the door.

Anne stopped and whirled around. "What? Did you remember another of Craig's flaws?"

"Hey, I was only teasing. You're so defensive."

"I'm not defensive," she said her voice shrill. "Craig is handsome, intelligent—"

Gerry touched her arm. "OK, Slugger. OK. He's the second-coming. Whatever you say, but that's not why I stopped you." He tried to avoid the subject of marriage, if she'd only blurted it out to save face.

She sighed impatiently. "Well, then what do you want?"

"I want to discuss my mother's—"

"Gerry, I told you, she's progressing as—

"Birthday."

"Her birthday?"

131

"Yes, she'll be eighty on the eighteenth. That's Sunday. I'm planning a small party for her that afternoon. Here at the apartment." His face relaxed into a smile. "And I'd . . . we'd like you to come."

Anne felt her anger evaporating. "Oh, sure I'll come. Is there anything I can bring or help you with?"

"No, Luis is taking care of the food. But thanks for offering."

Anne put her hand on the door knob. "Peg will love a party. It should be fun." They stood there in awkward silence for a moment. "Well," Anne said, "then, I'll be going. See you tomorrow."

"Let me walk you out," he said.

She looked up at him. "It's daylight, Gerry. You don't have to."

"No, I'm coming. Someone robbed Wardzinsky's last night. They think they were looking for drugs."

"Anybody hurt?"

"No, old Pap Wardzinsky got a little banged up, but he managed to fend the robber off with a barbecue fork that he was marking for discount."

As she stepped outside, the stifling heat caught her off guard and seemed to press on her.

"I just called Kathy up at the card store to see if she had any eightieth birthday decorations she could put away for me, and she told me one of her customers had her purse snatched yesterday. In daylight. She told me to warn everyone to be careful."

"I will," Anne said, walking to her car. The exhaust fan from the kitchen blew hot air and ruffled her hair.

"I'm thinking of getting a security system," Gerry said, strolling behind her, his hands in his pockets. "My mother refused to even consider installing one before. She thought it was putting on airs. But I don't care what she says. I'm getting one. Eventually, I'll be moving into my own place, and I'd feel better leaving my mother if she had one."

Peg will have a fit, Anne thought, but she could see Gerry's point. Leaving Peg alone living above the bar would worry her too. "If it gives you peace of mind," Anne said. She opened her car door.

He took his hands out of his pocket and held the door. "You can bring him with you."

"Bring who?"

"Dr. Love. Your friend. Craig. You can bring him to the party too if you want."

"Thanks. I'll ask him and let you know."

She started into the car.

"Wait, there's one more thing."

"Yes?" She stepped back out, facing him.

"This Craig—all kidding aside, Slugger—he's a good guy? He treats you right?"

"Yeah, he treats me right." She was touched that he was concerned.

"I mean doctors are known to have egos as big as their wallets."

Maybe I've been wrong about Gerry. Perhaps he wasn't jealous of Craig. Perhaps he had given him the once over because he was protective of me, like my father had been around any dates I'd brought home, like I am with Janetta.

"You've known him for a while?"

"Since I was eighteen," she said.

He touched her lightly on the shoulder. "Well, good then. Good. Because you're a great girl, Anne." Slowly he withdrew his hand, and as he walked away, she heard him whisper, "The kind who should be kissed exquisitely."

Chapter 16

Anne stood in front of the mirror on Saturday evening, combing brown mascara over her lashes, wishing she could put on a new attitude toward Steve as easily as she put on makeup. She dreaded his party but knew Janetta would be upset if she didn't come. If she valued their friendship, she had to make at least a brief appearance.

As she applied lip gloss, she leaned toward the mirror. Then she suddenly stopped, the wand poised in mid-air as Gerry's face appeared again in her mind. His eyes as they gazed at her were filled with longing, and she heard his voice again. *The kind who should be kissed exquisitely.* She sighed. "Oh, Gerry. Just when I think you're the biggest idiot, you go and mess with my head." *Or maybe it's my heart.* Whatever it was he was messing with, Anne knew it had to stop.

She finished applying her makeup, then appraised herself front and back. The lilac wrap-dress fit well; the way it tied on her hip whittled her waist, and the coolness of its color toned down some of the brightness of her coppery hair. The macramé sandals that she'd purchased in the exact same shade as the dress were a true find. It was a shame she had to waste this outfit on a party for Steve.

Her only consolation was that Craig would get to see her in it, and that she'd be spending the whole evening with him. Anne was as shocked as Gerry, Peg, and Irma had been when she blurted that she was going to marry Craig, but on reflection, she decided her outburst was merely her subconscious expressing her true desire. *Dear, St. Anne, is Craig my man?*

Why shouldn't she want to marry Craig? He was the perfect man—handsome, intelligent, kind, and with a promising future.

A little after six, Craig called to say that he'd been detained. Anne was glad they'd get to the party late; she'd have to spend less time in Steve's company.

While she waited, she balanced her checking account. Mistake. She'd certainly put a dent into her finances with her recent shopping spree, and by the time Craig rang the bell at eight thirty, she was flirting with a tension headache.

Anne pressed the button to let Craig in. When she opened the door and saw him, she felt that same rush she did as kid when playing the *Mystery Date* board game and was lucky enough to open the little plastic door to the handsome date wearing the tuxedo.

"Sorry I'm late," he said, stepping into the apartment.

"No problem."

"Of course, it is. That means less time with you." He kissed her on the cheek, and then sighed, his broad chest rising and falling. "I had a hard time extracting myself from the hospital. I took a quick shower there and just threw on these clothes."

Anne wished she could throw on clothes and look so spectacular. His khaki pants and tan shirt seemed as if they'd been tailored for him.

"Well, there's no rush," she said. "The party will be going on all night. Sit down and unwind a bit. Would you like a beer?"

He took a seat on the flowered sofa. "I'll pass on the beer, but water would be nice. I'm working again tomorrow, and I'm sorry I won't be able to go to that birthday party with you."

Anne was disappointed but was well aware of how few free hours residents had. She was also relieved because after dropping the bomb that they were going to marry, she wasn't eager to bring Craig to the McMaster's, where they could question him and embarrass her. "Oh, I understand. It's just a small get-together."

She went to the kitchen to get his water and while there, popped some Tylenol to quell the headache. When she returned, she sat next to him on the sofa. He took a drink and said, "Janetta, your roommate? I've met her before, haven't I? Tall, thin, dark hair?"

"You have a good memory. She did visit me at school once before you graduated. We all went to that game against Iowa. Remember, when it hailed and snowed?" She rubbed her arms. "I still don't think I've thawed from that one."

He sipped his water. "Well, it would be hard to forget someone like her."

"Why's that?"

He grimaced. "She's your friend. Forget I ever said anything."

Anne shifted to face him. "No, tell me. She's my friend, but nothing she does shocks me."

He gulped his drink, then set the glass on the end table. "Well, like you said. It was bitterly cold that day, and you brought some blanket that we spread across the three of our laps."

"It was an afghan, my mother had crocheted."

"With one minute left in the fourth quarter, we were down by six points, and by then she was smashed on the rum she'd smuggled in to spike her Cokes. The game was a real nail-biter, and I was so into it, I almost fell out of the bleachers when I felt her fingers on my zipper."

"Oh, my God," Anne said, her hands flying to cover her mouth. "She didn't."

"Yeah, she'd slid her hand under the blanket and tried to unzip my jeans."

Anne closed her eyes, shaking her head. "I can't believe it." *Then again, I can.*

"Thank God, they threw a Hail Mary and we scored. I stood to celebrate and never sat back down."

Anne felt embarrassed for her friend. "I wonder if she remembers that?"

"Why, do you think she'll be embarrassed to see me? I don't have to go. I wouldn't want to cause any problems."

"Oh, knowing Janetta she'll probably think it's funny." Anne was afraid to ask the question, but she had to know, she had to know if Janetta had succeeded later in the weekend in seducing him. "It's none of my business," she said, wearing a pained smile, "but did she ever come on to you again?"

"I avoided her the rest of the weekend."

Relieved, Anne said, "Wow. That's unbelievable."

"What is?"

"That you didn't take advantage of her." She patted Craig's hand. "Every other guy has. I guess that's one of the things I've always liked about you, Craig. You're always a gentleman." *I bet Gerry would have been all over her.*

He took Anne's hand and kissed her knuckles. "Maybe I'm not all that much a gentleman. Maybe I just prefer to make the first move."

Then he leaned over, kissing her tenderly on the lips.

Anne felt safe with him, she knew he'd only go as far as she permitted him, and not pressure her for more. So she let herself enjoy his lips without holding back.

She touched his cheek, his skin was soft from being freshly shaved and smelled of menthol shaving cream. When they broke the kiss, she said softly, "I'm glad Janetta didn't snag you."

"Me too."

"In all honesty," Anne said, snuggling into his arms, I'm not really looking forward to this party."

He smoothed her hair. "Why's that?"

"Steve—her boyfriend—I detest him. But if I don't go, she'll be furious."

He kissed her forehead. She couldn't remember feeling so peaceful in anyone's arms before. He gazed at her with his warm brown eyes. "Let's go. I'll protect you from Steve if you'll protect me from Janetta?"

"Deal," Anne said.

They sealed their pact with another kiss.

***

It was nearly nine o'clock when Anne and Craig drove down Martindale Street. Cars lined the curb on both sides of it. Anne was surprised that this many people would want to spend an evening with Steve.

They found a parking space four doors away from Steve's tiny two-story brick home. When they stepped out of the car, the noise from the party carried to them on the cool night air. Light from the street lamps filtered down through the leafy canopy of trees. Anne carried a plate of brownies she'd baked earlier in the day.

"Man, Anne, they look good," Craig said, eyeing the plate longingly as they walked.

Anne stopped, reached under the plastic wrap, and gave him one. "Here, it'll fortify you for the battle."

Craig looked at the brownie. "I never knew they gave you strength."

"Oh, anything chocolate does," Anne said. "It's a little known fact that David had a hit off a Hershey bar just before he slew Goliath."

They walked up the short asphalt driveway that ran along the side of the house to the backyard. About sixty people were buzzing about the small square patch of grass. A boom box balanced on the kitchen windowsill pumped out Metallica's *Nothing Else Matters*. The song was punctuated by the occasional sizzle of the bug zapper hanging from the patio awning. The aroma of grilling hot dogs and hamburgers filled the air. In the far corner of the lawn sat the center of attention, the beer keg. Men in shorts and T-shirts were huddled around it holding red plastic beer cups. Most of the women were seated at the picnic table and on the various lawn chairs scattered about the concrete patio.

Anne scanned the crowd for Janetta, but couldn't locate her. Then the screen door opened, and she emerged carrying a roasting pan heaped with Buffalo wings.

"There's Janetta," Anne said to Craig.

She was wearing white shorts that accentuated her long, tan legs and a skimpy little top. She set the roasting pan on the picnic table. They crossed the yard, and Anne placed a hand on her friend's

139

shoulder. "Hello, where should I put these?" Anne asked, holding out the tray of brownies.

Janetta turned around and hugged her. "Oh, you finally got here. I was afraid you weren't going to come."

Craig stepped forward and thrust out his hand. "It's my fault we're late. Craig Love. I believe we met along time ago."

Janetta sized him up, and by the smile she gave him as she took his hand, it was obvious that she'd forgiven him for detaining her friend. "We've met before?" She frowned coyly at him.

Anne couldn't tell if she had truly forgotten meeting Craig or was pretending to. Anne handed the brownies to her. "You met him that weekend you visited me when we went to the Iowa game where it snowed and hailed."

Janetta laughed, her unfettered breasts bouncing under her top. "No wonder I don't remember. I was blitzed all weekend." She turned to Craig. "Forgive me for being blunt, but I didn't sleep with you, did I?"

Craig flushed a little. "Well, no, you didn't."

"Didn't think so." She touched his forearm. "You're so handsome, even bombed out of my mind, I think I would have remembered being with you." Sighing, she shrugged. "It's just as well, isn't it? I mean it would be a little awkward if I had now that you're seeing Anne."

"Yes, I guess it would be a little bit uncomfortable," he said.

"Where's Steve?" Anne asked, hoping to take Janetta's mind off the thought of sex with Craig.

Janetta reached behind her, setting the brownies on the picnic table. "He and a bunch of his buddies went down to the basement to play pool. They'll be up soon. Let me introduce you around and get you something to eat."

Janetta introduced them to a few people and then showed them where the beer keg was and the makeshift bar, fashioned from some boards supported by two saw horses. Anne and Craig helped themselves to drinks and food, scoped out two lawn chairs under a maple tree, and sat to enjoy their food under the moonlight.

"I've got to have another of your brownies," Craig said. "They were delicious. Want one?"

"Sure."

The chocolate along with the aspirin seemed to have helped her headache. When only a bite remained of her brownie, Anne saw Janetta leading Steve across the patio toward them. By the way he was staggering, it was obvious that he'd had too much to drink already. She popped the last morsel into her mouth.

"Craig," Janetta said, "I'd like you to meet Steve."

Craig rose, transferred his glass of ginger ale to his left hand, and extended his right.

"Steve, this is Anne's date, Craig Love."

Steve looked at Anne sitting in the lawn chair then to Craig. "Hey, how ya doin'" he slurred. "Glad to see Anne with a guy. I been startin' to think she was a dyke or something."

Anne rose, ready to tell him off, then checked her temper and said with restraint, "No, I just have very discriminating taste when it comes to men."

Steve was too drunk to catch Anne's sly jab.

Janetta, looking alarmed at the tone the conversation was taking, took Steve's arm and changed the subject. "Steve, Craig is a plastic surgeon."

Steve grinned. "No shit?" Alcohol fumes blasted from his mouth when he spoke. "You do nose jobs and face lifts?"

"Sometimes."

"Ever do anybody famous?"

"Ah . . . no, I don't think so."

"You do boobs?"

"Pardon me?"

"Boob jobs, you know. Implants?"

"I have on occasion. Mainly reconstructive surgery after—"

Steve clapped. "Oh man, I'm in the wrong field. Nothing I'd like more than to be paid to play with breasts all day. You know, you guys should get the Nobel Prize."

"Excuse me?" Craig said.

"Hell, yeah. For your service to humanity." Steve slapped Craig on the back. "For bringing boob jobs to mankind." He leered at Anne's chest. "Anne's got a nice set of jugs. I've always wondered if they were real. You two meet doing her tits?"

"Steve!" Janetta cried.

If Anne were a cartoon character, she knew steam would have been streaming out of her ears. "You disgusting—"

As she was about to slap him, she felt Craig's hand on her shoulder. She didn't want her ugly temper to reveal itself to him so she caught herself.

"Listen, Steve," Craig said. "You're being rude."

Steve leaned his head in towards Craig and spoke conspiratorially. "Man to man, Doc. Do they feel natural? I mean Janetta's are puny. I think she could use a new rack."

"Steve, shut up," Janetta said.

"You shut up," he snapped.

"Hey, Anne," Steve said, reaching toward her, "mind if I feel yours? Just for research purposes."

"Steve!" Janetta cried.

Out of the corner of her eye, Anne could see conversations come to a halt as all eyes turned to them.

Craig stepped between Anne and Steve, intercepting his hand before he could grope her. Craig bent Steve's hand back, twisting his wrist into an unnatural position. He whispered very calmly, "If you ever try that again, you're going to need the services of a friend of mine. He's an orthopedic surgeon." Craig flung Steve's hand away.

People crowded around to see what was going on. Anne felt her cheeks burning with embarrassment.

Steve shoved Craig. "Don't you threaten me, you Ivy League fairy."

"How dare you!" Anne cried.

Janetta grabbed Steve's shoulders, trying to push him away. "Go in the house!" She looked pleadingly at Anne and Craig. "He's had too much to drink. He doesn't know what he's saying."

"Get the hell off me," Steve roared, flicking Janetta off him. She turned her ankle, stumbled into the lawn chairs, hitting the ground.

Craig and Anne scrambled to her, pulling off the overturned chairs, while Steve swayed.

"Are you OK?" Craig asked, kneeling beside her and examining her ankle.

She nodded that she was fine, but to Anne, she seemed stunned.

Anne stood. She could no longer control her anger. "You animal! You hurt her—"

Steve leaned in toward Anne, his breath repulsing her. "Get off my property," he slurred.

"What?"

"I said, get off my property!"

Craig rose. "Let's go, Anne."

"That's right, Anne, listen to your sissy doctor and get the hell out of here before I kick both of your asses."

She went to Janetta and helped her to her feet. "Come home with me."

Janetta began to cry. "I'm fine. I just lost my balance that's all."

"No, you didn't. He pushed you," Anne cried. "Dump him. Please before he really hurts you."

"No," Steve yelled, storming over to Anne. "You leave before I hurt you. And don't you tell her what to do." He pulled Janetta to his side. "She's staying here."

"Go," Janetta sniffled. "I can take care of myself."

"You call letting him abuse you taking care of yourself?"

Caught between Anne and Steve, Janetta cracked and exploded. "Just go, Anne. Go! Butt out of my life!" She turned her back, limping away.

"Come on." Craig took Anne's hand and led her away.

Anne felt like crying, but she didn't want to give Steve the satisfaction. She bit her lip, and they hurried down the driveway. Before she reached the sidewalk, Anne glanced over her shoulder. Janetta was standing there crying, watching Anne walking away, while Steve stumbled over to a group of guys and took another swig of his beer.

Chapter 17

Anne didn't feel much like going to another party when she awoke Sunday morning. Her headache had intensified after the scene at Steve's, and she'd slept poorly. After leaving the party, Craig had driven to Station Square where he'd bought her a drink at the Gandy Dancer. He sat silently, patiently while Anne fretted about Janetta and ranted about Steve's behavior.

By the end of the evening, his calm, methodical demeanor and rational reasoning had convinced Anne of what she already knew: She couldn't help Janetta. Only Janetta could help herself.

But that realization hadn't eased Anne's mind. She'd tossed all night with bad dreams. Even attending Mass, which usually had a calming effect on her, gave her no peace.

After church, Anne came home and wrapped the gift she'd purchased for Peg. It was only when she changed into her coral-colored dress, the third of the new outfits she'd splurged on during her last shopping excursion, that her mood began to lift. Sleeveless with straps that crossed in the back, the dress looked absolutely perfect on her. Its color picked up the peach undertones in her skin, complementing her red hair.

Her hair. She had fussed with it so much, trying to decide whether to wear it up or down that, she was twenty minutes late when she arrived at the McMaster's with her curls hanging loosely about her shoulders.

Although she had the key to the apartment with her, today, she was there as Peg's friend, not her nurse. She rang the bell, waiting to be let in as all the other guests had.

It was Dave who answered the door. "Woo-wee, Anne, you look delicious, like a dish of orange sherbet."

"Thanks. Sorry I'm late."

"Oh, just fashionably so," he said closing the door. "And looking that fantastic, you deserve to make an entrance."

"No wonder you're such a good bartender," Anne said as she started up the stairs to the apartment. "You know exactly what to say to put a person at ease."

When she walked into the kitchen, it was humming with activity. Luis, garnishing a silver platter of raspberry tartlets with mint leaves, was so intent on his work he didn't see her. A petite, young woman with wavy, brown hair pulled back into an unruly ponytail stood at the sink brandishing a small knife, fluting tomatoes. From the wonderful aromas in the kitchen, Anne knew Luis had knocked himself out preparing the food for Peg's party.

"Luis," Anne said, closing her eyes and inhaling deeply, "what have you made now? It smells absolutely delicious."

He looked up, holding his arms out to her like she was a long-lost friend. "Anne, you're here! Now it is a party."

Dave reached for a tart, and Luis slapped his hand.

"You've outdone yourself." She glanced around at the trays of delicacies spread across the table and counters.

He smiled. "I've had help. Teresa, my love." He held his hand out to the girl. "A moment please."

The girl at the sink turned around and came toward him. Her skin was the color of weak tea and her large black eyes were only dwarfed in size by her huge smile when she took Luis' hand.

"Anne, this is Teresa, my fiancée."

"It's nice to meet you," Anne said. "You and Luis certainly know how to cater a party."

"I've asked them to adopt me when they get married," Dave said. "Could you imagine dinner every night at their house?"

Teresa giggled. "You are most kind."

Why did accents sound so charming? Anne wondered.

"Come on, Anne." Dave touched her elbow. "Let's join the party." On his way out, he snatched a chocolate covered strawberry and popped it into his mouth.

Anne walked into the living room. It was festooned with crepe paper and balloons. When Peg, who was sitting in the recliner wearing a paper crown, saw her, she exclaimed, "Annie Banannie, you've come too!"

Peg looked healthier than Anne had ever seen her. Her hair had been dyed a becoming silver and curled, and she was wearing large faux-pearl earrings and broach, and a powder blue dress that accentuated her eyes.

Anne went to the old woman, kissing her on the cheek. "Happy Birthday, Peg. Your hair looks fantastic."

Peg touched her white curls. "Dolly did it yesterday."

Anne handed her a gift. Peg sat the box on her lap and took Anne's hand. "You didn't have to bring me a present." She looked Anne up and down. "You don't look so bad, yourself. What a fashion plate you are." Peg scanned the room. "Gerry, look. Anne's here. And doesn't she look beautiful?"

Gerry disengaged himself from a conversation and came to Peg. Following him, wearing a white linen sheath and a ton of gold jewelry, was Claudia.

"Hello, Slugger," Gerry said. "I was beginning to worry you weren't going to come."

Peg, sitting in the chair, slapped Gerry's thigh. "Doesn't she look beautiful?" Peg gazed at Anne. "You always look pretty, but we're used to seeing you in your nurse's clothes."

"You look very nice," Gerry said evenly. But the way his eyes lingered over her, Anne knew he thought she looked more than nice.

Peg slapped his thigh again. "Look at her legs, Gerry. Don't she got great gams?" Peg lifted her own legs, admiring them. "Why they're as nice as mine were when I was young."

Anne couldn't tell which was colder, the ice melting in Claudia's empty glass or her eyes as she stared at Anne.

Gerry, looking like he'd been trapped, stepped back and bent his head eyeing both Claudia's and Anne's legs. "Why Peg, I certainly am a lucky man. I'm surrounded by beautiful women with lovely legs. There's you . . ." Peg smiled as she admired her ankles. "Anne . . ." Peg bumped Anne with her knee, tittering. He put his arm around Claudia. "And Claudia."

Peg's smile dimmed. Taking a long look at Claudia's legs, she paused then gazed at Gerry. "That reminds me," she said. "Do we have any more of those chicken legs? They were delicious."

Claudia smiled sweetly, but the grip she had on her tumbler made Anne afraid she'd crush the glass.

Quickly changing the subject, Gerry said, "Anne, do you know everyone here?"

He led Anne around the room, introducing her to some of his fellow proprietors on Butler Street and to Dave's wife, Nancy. All the time Claudia shadowed them.

After the introductions, Gerry excused himself to ask Luis if everything was going well in the kitchen. He left Anne with Claudia, Dave, and Nancy. Claudia thrust her glass at Anne. "Now that you've familiarized yourself, you can start refilling drinks. I'll have a gin and tonic. No lime."

"Pardon me?" Anne said.

Claudia took Dave's drink from his hand and shoved it toward Anne. "Dave needs another too. What were you drinking?"

Apparently stunned too, all Dave could do was mumble, "Scotch and soda."

Anne felt angry and hurt all at once. Maybe she had misunderstood Gerry's invitation. She thought she was an invited guest. Afraid she was going to punch Claudia, she took the glasses and turned. She felt as if hot sauce were coursing through her arteries and veins instead of blood. But she couldn't lash out and ruin Peg's party.

Before she could get away, Claudia touched her wrist. "And Anne, when you're done freshening drinks, you might want to tidy a little. Remove some of these dirty plates."

In the dining room, Anne stood in front of the buffet arrayed with liquor bottles trying to compose herself, mumbling invectives.

"Anne," Dave said, rushing toward her, grabbing his glass. "Don't you dare make me a drink."

"It's OK," she said, her voice quivering.

Dave turned her around, his baritone voice more deep and somber. "You are a guest. You don't have to serve that . . . that she-devil."

She had to smile at him. "It's OK. Maybe I misunderstood. Maybe Gerry invited me to help at the party."

"I would have been asked to help out if he'd needed someone. I'm a bartender. He knows you are a nurse and not a waitress."

Nancy walked into the room and put her arm around Anne. "I saw what happened out there, and you are not to touch a thing. I took orders. Peg and Irma are the only others who need refills. I'll get the drinks. That witch treating you like Cinderella. We'll fix her. Dave, go into the kitchen, get another tray of canapés from Luis and offer them around."

Dave patted Anne's shoulder. "Good idea, Nance. We'll show up the wicked stepsister by being so gracious and servile, it'll make her look bad." Dave, with an evil grin on his face, strolled from the room.

Nancy slammed ice into glasses. "I understand she's jealous of you, but her behavior is inexcusable."

Anne was so consumed with controlling her rage, Nancy's words didn't initially register. "What did you say? She's jealous of me?"

"Are you blind? When you walked into the room her face pickled like she was drinking brine."

"Well, it's not my fault Peg likes me better."

Nancy looked over the tops of her bifocals. "Everyone likes you better, but it's not Peg's affection Claudia is vying for."

"Whose then?"

Nancy stopped pouring drinks and touched Anne's arm. "Sweetheart, wake up. Mac is gone on you."

"Oh," she waved her hand, "he just acts that way with me because I'm off-limits to him."

"Who made you off limits?"

Flustered, Anne began chopping limes. "We both did."

Nancy popped an olive into her mouth. "Well, rules are made to be broken. I'd fight for him—if only just to piss off Claudia."

Of course, he likes me now that that I've found Craig. Gerry is handsome and nice enough for a friend, but why would I dump Craig, who is solid and dependable, for a man who is so insecure he has to charm every woman he meets? But maybe I should flirt a little just to annoy Claudia.

"Now what was Claudia drinking?" Nancy asked.

"Gin and tonic," Anne said in her snippiest voice. "No lime."

Nancy poured gin into the glass and then looked all over the bar, searching for something.

"Here's the tonic," Anne said, handing her the bottle.

"I was looking for arsenic."

Anne and Nancy laughed conspiratorially and then loaded the drinks onto a tray.

As they were about to rejoin the party, Gerry flew into the room, his face scarlet with Dave following behind. "Give me that," he said, taking the tray from Anne. "I am so sorry, Anne. I apologize for Claudia. No matter what she may have assumed, you are a guest at this party, and I will not have you acting as a waitress."

"You don't have to apologize for her," Anne said, feeling somewhat vindicated.

Gerry set the tray of drinks on the dining room table. "You're absolutely right. I'll speak to her. She owes you an apology."

"Oh, Gerry, please don't. I don't want to ruin Peg's party by making a big deal out of this."

"Nonsense. Claudia's reasonable. When I explain the misunderstanding to her, she'll want to apologize to you. Now, go back into the room and have a good time."

Anne put her hands on her hips. *He's not ordering me around.*

"Please?"

Those blue eyes should be registered as a lethal weapon; she couldn't resist. "Fine." She let her hands fall to her side. "But I wish you'd just let it drop."

Dave took the tray and followed Nancy and Anne into the hallway. Nancy whispered to Anne, "I'd like to see him tell her anything and get away with it!"

Anne walked into the room and took a seat between Irma and Bernie on the couch, while Nancy passed out drinks and Dave offered everyone water chestnuts wrapped in bacon. Bernie immediately began to beat Anne's ear about the upcoming KISS concert. She could feel Claudia's eyes on her as she tried to focus on what Bernie was saying.

A few moments later, Gerry appeared in the archway. "Claudia, could you come here? I need a little help."

Out of the corner of her eye, Anne watched her saunter out of the room, her nose in the air. Gerry took Claudia by the elbow, guiding her into his bedroom.

As Bernie produced a well-worn map of the Consol Energy Center and showed Anne exactly where his and Gerry's seats were for the concert, Anne heard Claudia from all the way in the bedroom shout. "I will not." Gerry's muffled voice followed her outburst. "I refuse to apologize to her," Claudia said even louder now. "I don't give a damn who hears me. Why do you defend her all the time, when she sits there beside your mother acting like little St. Anne ridiculing me?"

Anne looked up, blushing. Everyone in the room was pretending not to hear the argument. Only Peg sat with her hand over her mouth giggling.

Gerry mumbled something again.

"I am not paranoid," Claudia shrieked. "Why did you invite her anyway? You say she's just an employee. Oh, I know, you invited her so she could change water into wine for you?"

Peg slapped her knee, laughing silently.

The argument continued for a while then there was silence. Everyone sat staring, their ears straining to hear more. A few minutes later, the two of them walked back into the room. Gerry looked frazzled. "Dinner is ready," he announced. "Luis has set up a buffet in the dining room. Help yourself."

"Anne," Peg called, "would you be an angel and help me into the dining room?"

Anne rose and helped Peg up. Peg latched onto her arm and grabbed the cane leaning against her chair.

"You've graduated to a cane?" Anne asked, proud of Peg's accomplishment. "Yesterday you refused to try it."

"Canes are classier than walkers."

"I'm impressed," Anne said.

"Well, I couldn't have done it without you, Annie Banannie," she said loud enough so that Claudia could hear.

They walked toward the archway where Claudia stood glaring at Anne.

"I know you're skinny, Honey," Peg said to Claudia, "but you're going to have to move out of the doorway. Anne and I can't get through.

"Oh," Claudia said sarcastically. She put her hand on her chest. "Excuse me . . ."

As they walked past, Anne swore she heard Claudia snarl under her breath, "Blessed Mother and St. Anne."

Chapter 18

It was raining heavily the next morning when Anne let herself into the McMaster's apartment. There were so many things weighing on her mind that it was only after depositing her dripping umbrella into the porcelain kitchen sink that she noticed Gerry was not there to greet her. She was relieved; she was not up to rehashing the previous evening's embarrassing episode between her and Claudia with him.

Janetta was still worrying her. Since Steve's disastrous party on Saturday night, she'd heard nothing from her friend. When Anne had returned from Peg's party, Anne's mother called concerned about Patsy, whose glucose tolerance test had come back indicating she was on the border line for having gestational diabetes. Anne reassured her mother that Patsy would be fine, but even though she could calm her mother's fears, she was concerned. Anne would be going home on Sunday for Patsy's shower. Then she could see her sister for herself, and she hoped put her fears to rest.

When her mother asked how the favors for the shower were coming, Anne felt sick. She'd completely forgotten about offering to make them. Where was she going to find the time to make seventy-five teddy bears? Maybe she could get Peg to help her.

What weighed most heavily on Anne's mind, however, was Craig. He'd phoned her last night when he'd gotten off work to make a date for the following Saturday night. Instead of going out for dinner, he asked to bring over Chinese food. He wanted to discuss something with her and didn't want to do it in a crowded restaurant. She'd tried to pry out of him what he wanted to talk about, but the seriousness of his voice when he said he'd rather wait until Saturday, made her heart race.

He'd certainly made it clear that he had feelings for her. She knew it was rather soon, but maybe her dreams were going to come true. Perhaps St. Anne had taken pity on her. Perhaps Craig was going to ask her to get married. She put the thought out of her mind. It was too exciting to think about.

In the hallway on her way back to Peg's room, she stopped in front of the mirror and fluffed out her damp hair. The Sacred Heart Statue, offering his ensnared heart caught her eye. "I think it might be time to unchain my heart," she whispered to it.

Anne found Peg sitting in the chair by the bed, her eyes dancing with delight. She waved Anne inside. "Come, come. I've got something to tell you."

Her curiosity piqued, Anne quickly set her things down. "What is it?"

"Gerry and Claudia had a doozie of a fight last night."

Anne looked behind her. She didn't want Gerry to hear her gossiping with his mother about his love life.

"Don't worry. He's down in the bar already," Peg said picking up on Anne's apprehension, "interviewing another bartender."

"Oh, I feel terrible," Anne said. "I apologize for ruining your party last night."

Peg looked incredulous. "You didn't ruin it. You gave me the greatest gift. To see Claudia fuming was priceless."

"But my being here caused problems for Gerry."

"It's his own damn fault. What does he see in her? Speaking of gifts. Anne, would you hand me that one sitting on my bureau." Peg took the box from her and lifted off the lid. "Get a load of what Claudia got me." She held up a lavender bed jacket embellished with ecru lace and satin rosettes. Peg screwed up her face. "Who the hell does she think I am? Loretta Young?"

Anne felt the jacket's fabric. It had to be pure silk. "It's beautiful though."

Peg tossed it to her. "You have it. Put it in your hope chest. Save it for your honeymoon with Craig, Dear. That is if you get to take one. You know those doctors are never home, and I understand they have a very high divorce rate. That's something you should consider before you marry him."

Great, Anne thought, folding the expensive piece of lingerie and putting it back in the box. Another thing to worry about.

***

At noon, Gerry arrived with lunch. He nodded and said hello to Anne, and she could tell from his subdued manner that he was embarrassed about the previous evening. Under his arm, he had tucked the mail. After setting down their sandwiches, he leafed through the stack and then handed a thick white envelope to Peg.

"What's this?" she asked, looking as excited as Cinderella receiving an invitation to the Prince's ball. "Mrs. Martin McMaster and Son," she said, reading the address. Then her face fell as she read the return one. "The Honorable and Mrs. Francis X. McMaster. Oh no, what's Fran up to now?"

"Son? I'm not a kid anymore. You think he could used my name. They're probably inviting us to another of his campaign fundraisers," Gerry said.

"Fran is my brother-in-law," Peg explained. "He was my Martin's younger brother."

"He's a judge," Gerry said.

"I've heard of him," Anne said. "I never made the connection."

Peg tore into the envelope, pulling out another one upon which was written in calligraphy: Aunt Peg, Gerry and Guest. "Hmph," Peg said, "Gerry gets to bring a guest, and I don't. Guess Fran thinks I'm too old. What if I was one of those bobcats, like we saw on *Good Morning America* this morning?"

Gerry rolled his eyes. "I think the term is cougar, Peg. And you can forget about it. Chasing younger men is bad for the heart."

"My heart's fine. Right, Anne?"

"Leave me out of this," Anne said.

155

"I'm talking about my heart," Gerry said. "Just thinking about you with a guy my age gives me palpitations."

Peg slipped the invitation out of the envelope and a tissue and reply card fell into her lap. Peg read the finely engraved script, then clutched the invitation to her chest. Astonished, she looked up at Gerry. "It's not an invitation to a fundraiser. God bless her, Maeve's getting married."

"Who's Maeve?" Anne wanted to know why they had to bless the prospective bride.

"My cousin," Gerry said.

Peg picked up the reply card. "Who's as ugly as a mud fence."

"That's cruel, Peg," Gerry said.

"It's the truth. I could draw a better face in the sand with a stick."

"How old is she?" Gerry asked.

"Oh, God Lord, let me see," Peg said scrunching up her eyes. "She's pushing fifty."

Curious, Anne asked, "This is her first marriage?"

"Yes," Gerry said.

"I hope to hell she doesn't wear white," Peg said.

"Because she's not a virgin?" Gerry asked.

"No, because of the size of her ass. She'll look like an iceberg coming down the aisle."

Gerry shook his head. "When is the wedding?"

"September twenty-eighth."

"That's the night before the Great Race," Gerry said.

"At St. Paul Cathedral." Peg read on. "And the reception's at the Pittsburgh Field Club." Peg raised her eyebrows. "Woo, fancy. I imagine there will be a lot of dignitaries invited."

"I'm sure the mayor will be there," Gerry said.

Peg traced her knobby fingers over the invitation's lettering. "I hope I'm up to going." She looked at Anne. "Do you think I'll be strong enough by then?"

156

"That's what, about six weeks away?" Anne said. "If we work hard, I don't see why not. That will be our goal: To get you well enough to attend."

Peg's face lit up. "You could be Gerry's guest."

Gerry, caught off guard, began to stutter.

"Oh, no," Anne said. "I couldn't. I'm sure Claudia—"

"If I need assistance in the bathroom, do you think Claudia will help me?"

Gerry and Anne said nothing because they both knew Claudia would not.

"When does the reply card have to be in?" he asked.

"September sixth."

"Well," he said, taking the invitation from Peg, "let's not commit to anything today."

Peg agreed to wait, but the faraway look in her eyes told Anne that the wheels in Peg's brain were already moving, scheming for a way to scare off Claudia and replace her with Anne.

***

To appease Claudia's demands that he make more time for her, Gerry hired a new bartender, Bob Butterbaugh, who taught at the same school as Dave.

On Wednesday, Dave and Gerry interrupted Bob's training to bring him upstairs to meet Peg and Anne. A burly man, in plaid button down shirt and elastic waist pants, he was bookish-looking. When Gerry introduced Peg, who had been lying in the bed, Bob's eyes misted over. "Nice to meet you, Ma'am," he said. Then he whipped off his silver aviator glasses and dabbed at his eyes. "Sorry," he sniffled. "The hospital bed and all. I recently lost my mother."

Peg pulled out a tissue and handed it to him. "Ah, Poor Dear, have a seat. Your mother was sick?"

"Not long. Pancreatic cancer. By the time I got over the shock that she had cancer, she was already gone. Sixty-three days from diagnosis until the end." He shook his head.

"Bob took care of her," Dave explained.

"I have a sister in Toledo I don't see too much," Bob sniffled. "Mom was my family. I really miss her."

Peg looked at Gerry smugly. "I'm sure you do." She patted Bob's pudgy, hairless hand. "I'm always telling my Gerry, that's Mac's baptismal name, to appreciate me. I'm not long for this world."

Bob blew his nose and looked up at Gerry, who was standing with his arms crossed in front of his chest. "Treasure your mother, Mac. I have no one now."

Gerry rolled his eyes.

"You don't have a wife or children?" Peg asked.

"I'm sorry to say, no."

"Hear that," Peg said seizing onto his words. "He wishes he'd gotten married and had a family." Bob lowered his head to replace his glasses. Peg pointed her finger at Gerry, nodding knowingly. He avoided her admonishment, casting his eyes toward the ceiling.

Then Anne heard Gerry whisper to Dave, "You sure he'll be OK? Bartenders are supposed to listen to sob stories not tell them."

"I've never seen him like this," Dave whispered. "Peg must have gotten to him."

Gerry talked out the side of his mouth. "She gets to me too."

"Well, Bobby," Peg said, patting his forearm, "you're not alone anymore. You're working for us now, and we're one big happy family." Peg glanced around the room at Anne, Gerry, and Dave. "Aren't we?"

Anne thought she sounded like Lindsey Lohan in the *Parent Trap*.

All three of them smirked at Peg's childlike bonhomie, nodded and voiced their agreement.

"Take Anne there," Peg said. "She's all alone, too."

Anne straightened up. "I'm not alone."

"She has family," Peg said, ignoring Anne's protests, "but they don't live around here, and she has a boyfriend, but I'm not convinced he's right for her. So basically we're all she's got. We've taken her under our wing."

Flabbergasted, Anne started to speak but couldn't think of anything to say that wouldn't make her life seem even more pathetic.

Gerry shot Anne a knowing look that said *see what I'm up against.*

"Speaking of family," Dave said, his hands in his pockets jingling his change. "D.J. is coming home tomorrow. He's going to stop in the bar on Friday."

"Good, I'd like to meet him," Anne said. "What time is he coming?"

"Six."

"I'll stick around for a while after work then."

"Make sure you bring him up to see me," Peg said. "I want to ask him what in the God's name those artsy-fartsy people see in some of that junk they call art. I read about this one fella who sculpted the Blessed Mother out of animal dung. I'd like to be there on his judgment day. See how he explains to Our Lord why he was picking on his mother."

Gerry closed his eyes, shaking his head.

Dave and Bob chuckled. Peg, offended that they found her remarks funny, turned to Anne. "You're a nurse. I'm sure you've had to change your share of diapers and empty bed pans. You ever seen any art in them?"

Anne couldn't believe the conversation. "Well, no and actually, I'm partial to Elvis on velvet."

"Well, you art mavens," Gerry said, "it's back downstairs for us. Bob, I want to show you our inventory procedures."

Bob rose.

"Wait," Peg called. "Gerry, get me my war chest."

Gerry growled, but did as instructed. Peg opened the lid, sorting through it. "Here," she said, pulling out a picture. "This is St. Rita. The patroness of the lonely. Pray to her."

"But I'm Lutheran."

She shoved the card into Bob's hand. "She'll overlook that."

***

Friday was Bob's first night at work. Anne left Peg at five-fifteen and went downstairs to await D.J.'s arrival. Bob, looking stiff and nervous, stood behind the bar. Anne slid into a stool, and Bob jumped to attention. "Would you like something to drink, Anne?"

"How about a Czechoslovakian Daiquiri?"

He froze, his eyes wide. "A Czechoslovakian Daiquiri? Don't think I've ever heard of that. Let me get the mixology guide—" He bent beneath the bar and began rummaging around. "It was right here. Maybe Vera knows—"

Anne rapped on the bar. "I'm only teasing. I made that up."

He straightened up, looking relieved.

"I'm sorry. I'll just have a glass of white wine."

"That I can handle."

As Anne sat at the bar sipping her drink, Dave came from the direction of Gerry's office carrying a carton of coasters. Behind him, Gerry followed wearing a tuxedo.

Bond, James Bond, Anne thought, her eyes dazzled by the sight of Gerry looking knock-out handsome and debonair in his formal wear. Suddenly, she felt hot; she wished she'd ordered water instead so she could gulp it down.

"Hi Anne," Dave said as he came and stood near her stool. He handed the carton to Bob, who stowed them under the bar.

"Can you do me a favor, Anne?" Gerry said. "Can you help me with these cuff links?"

"Sure, but I didn't know meeting D.J. was a formal affair."

As he handed her the cuff links and she began threading them through the holes, he said, "Aw, Claudia is on the board of some charity, and she's dragging me to some fundraising dinner. She should be here soon, but I'm going to try to stall a bit so I can see D.J."

He was a man born to wear a tuxedo, Anne thought. The jacket set off his jet black hair, and the cut of it emphasized his broad shoulders. His cologne was seductively sexy.

"Oh, Ger-ree," Claudia called as she strutted across the floor in a white dress that skimmed her bony hips. Her hair was pinned up.

She looks like a Q-Tip, thought Anne.

When she saw Anne, she pasted on a fake beauty queen smile. "Nice to see you again." Then she insinuated herself between Gerry and Anne. "Is something wrong with your tux?"

"Anne's just helping me with the cufflinks."

"Here, let me." Claudia practically elbowed Anne out of the way. When she was finished, she patted his chest and kissed his cheek. "There you are, darling."

Gerry stepped back and adjusted his sleeves.

Claudia grabbed his arm; diamonds sparkled at her neck and earlobes. "Ready?"

"I want to wait a few minutes. Dave's son, D.J., is coming in. I'd like to see him. He's been in Florence studying all summer."

She looked at the diamond-encrusted watch on her slender wrist, sighing. "Oh, I guess so."

"Have a seat next to Anne."

"I can't sit," she snapped. "I'll wrinkle."

Bernie, carrying a basin filled with dirty glasses, toddled over. He set it on the bar and waved. "Hi Claudia."

"Hello," Claudia said, looking down her nose at him.

"Hi, Anne."

Anne reached out and touched his shoulder. "How are you doing, Bernie?"

"How am I doing what?"

"Work," Gerry said. "She wants to know how work's going, Bernie."

"Busy," the little man said. "Always busy."

"You headed back to the kitchen with these dishes?" Anne asked.

He nodded.

"Well," she said. "Do you want to take this glass?" As Anne handed it to him, it slipped out of her hand, bouncing off the edge of the bar. Instinctively, Gerry reached out and caught it, the glass shattering in his hand.

"Damn!" he cried, dropping the shards and wincing. "I'm cut."

"Badly?" Claudia took his hand. When he opened his palm, blood dripped onto her white dress, leaving a red splatter like a ruby broach above her left breast. She dropped his hand, shrieking, "My dress! My new dress!"

But Gerry was not concerned with her dress. His face turned pale as his blue eyes dulled, rolled up into his head, and he began to sway.

Anne leaped from the stool. "Dave, help me. He's going to faint."

Anne and Dave each grabbed one of Gerry's arms. "Claudia, get a chair," Dave commanded.

She didn't hear him. She was holding the fabric of her dress out, swearing.

"Do you want me to dial 9-1-1?" Bob asked.

"No," Anne said, "he's not that serious."

He was very heavy, and she and Dave struggled with the crumpling Gerry. "Just tend the bar," Dave said.

As Gerry's knees buckled and blood ran down his wrist soiling his pristine white cuffs, Anne stretched and dragged a chair over. She and Dave guided him into it. Then she shoved his head between his knees and elevated his arm.

"Bernie, get a clean towel," she called.

He quickly scurried away, his arms flapping at his side.

"Dave, support him," Anne said. "I think I've got smelling salts in my bag." She dashed to her bags by the barstool, found them, ran over, and knelt in front of Gerry, sticking the smelling salts under his nose. He jerked his head and sat up, pushing the foul-smelling capsule away.

Bernie hurried toward them with a clean bar towel, but as he passed, Claudia snatched it from his hand.

"Hey," Bernie said, taking it back.

"Give me that, you retard," Claudia demanded, grabbing a corner, beginning a tug-of-war with Bernie.

Gerry's hand was gushing blood. Anne rose. "Claudia, Gerry needs this," she said, wrenching the towel away.

Claudia stomped her foot. "But what about my dress?"

"Screw your damn dress," Dave mumbled.

Claudia looked at Bernie. "Don't just stand there, Forrest Gump, get me another towel."

He crossed his arms in front of his chest. "No."

"I said get me a damn towel!"

"No. You have to say please."

Disgusted, Dave stood. "I'll get you one."

While Anne applied pressure to the wound, Gerry watched the white towel turn red and became woozy once more.

"Don't look at the blood, Gerry," Anne ordered. She kept the pressure on the cut, holding his hand up in the air. "Or you'll pass out again."

"How bad is it?" He stared at the ceiling, tapping his feet nervously.

Dave returned with two towels. He handed one to Anne who wrapped up Gerry's hand. "You need stitches," she said.

"Bernie," Dave said, "have Bob put some club soda on this."

When Bernie returned with the other towel, he handed it to Dave who gingerly began to dab at the spot on Claudia's dress. The stain spread.

"You idiot!" she screamed batting Dave's hand away. All eyes in the bar fixed on her. "This is imported French taffeta! You've ruined it."

Dave backed away trying to look remorseful, but Anne could see the ghost of a smile on his face. "Sorry."

"Sorry? You're sorry? I paid $1,400 for this dress."

Gerry, his arm raised like the Statue of Liberty, called, "Hey, Claudia, take it easy."

"Take it easy?" She looked at Dave and Bernie. "Tweedle Dum and Tweedle Dee here have ruined my dress."

"Gerry," Anne said gently, "you need to go the hospital. Can you stand?"

"I think so." He rose on unsteady feet. "After we go to the hospital, Claudia, we can stop by your place and you can change."

"I can't go to the hospital. I'm expected at the gala. I'm an honoree. I'll be lucky if I can change and get there on time."

Gerry's face turned red, the first color he'd had in it since he'd been cut. "I'll take myself then."

"I'll take you," Dave said.

"You can't take me. D.J.'s coming and Bob's new. He and Vera can't handle the bar by alone. I'll take myself."

"You could pass out," Anne said. "I'll take you."

Claudia looked at her watch. "For god's sake, someone take him."

Gerry looked at Anne. "You don't mind?"

"It's no problem," Anne said.

"Don't anyone tell my mother. You hear me?" Gerry said, holding on to Anne's shoulder to steady himself. "It'll only upset her, and I don't want to tax her heart."

"I've got to leave," Claudia said. "Meet me when you're done." She started to walk away, then stopped. "Be sure to change your shirt first."

As she walked out, Bernie put his hands on his tubby hips and stuck out his tongue at her.

Chapter 19

They arrived at the Emergency Room near six o'clock. Anne signed Gerry in with the receptionist who directed them to a cubicle, where they found an attractive black woman sitting behind the counter at a computer. Her hair was a fountain of black, glossy loops, a style so elaborate, it reminded Anne of the coiffures found on characters in Dr. Seuss books. Her nameplate said Letitia Pinkney, and she was sucking on a lollipop. Removing the sucker with a great smack, she put it in an ashtray. "Gave up cigs," she explained. "Blood pressure was sky-high. Trying to fool myself by substituting these."

"Is it working?" Anne asked as she took a chair across the counter from her.

"Nope. It's like taking Chris Rock to bed and telling yourself it's Denzel Washington." She looked at Gerry who had also sat down. "So what'd you do, Handsome, slash your wrist to keep from getting hitched to this pretty lady? She eyed Anne. "Don't even tell me you're walking down the aisle in that sorry get up."

"No, a glass broke in my hand," Gerry said.

Anne looked down at her scrubs, laughing. "We're not getting married." She fumbled for some words that explained their relationship then finally said, "We're just friends."

"Friends?" the clerk mumbled, her eyes on the computer, her thumbs tapping the space bar. "Second biggest lie next to The check's in the mail."

Letitia took Gerry's name and address. When she asked for his insurance card, he stood, holding the towel to his hand, and tried to reach into his pants pocket to extract his wallet but couldn't.

165

"Anne, could you get into my pants?"

Anne's eyes grew wide. "Pardon me?"

"Hell," Letitia mumbled. "Now that is what I'd call one of those offers you can't refuse."

"I can't grab my wallet," he said, motioning to his injured hand.

Anne slowly rose. Wearing a huge smile, Gerry held up both of his hands. Hesitantly, Anne moved beside him, and she reached out.

"Woo, Honey," Letitia whooped, "you need any help there? I'd like a piece of that action."

Anne blushed as she slid her hand inside Gerry's tuxedo pants pocket.

Gerry flinched and giggled. "I said grab the wallet."

"You go for it, Girlfriend," Letitia said.

Anne looked up at him. "Will you behave yourself?"

As she fished around for it, she felt the hard muscles of his thigh and embarrassed as she was, she fought the urge to explore whatever else was concealed in those trousers.

"Me, behave myself?" he said, obviously enjoying the attention by the way the dimple in his cheek winked at them. "You're the one who's groping a gravely injured man!"

Letitia put a hand on her hip and cocked her head. "Hmph. Gravely injured? Looks pretty healthy to me."

Anne pulled the wallet out. Gerry closed his eyes and sighing heavily said, "Was it as good for you as it was for me?"

Anne had to laugh as she opened the wallet. "Keep it up and I'll have them stitch your lips together."

"It's in the second slot there," he said.

Anne passed the card to Letitia. After typing all the information in, she printed out a form that she placed before Gerry. Anne had to hold it steady for him to sign. Letitia separated the copies, handing the yellow one back to Anne. "Have a seat in the waiting room. You shouldn't have to wait too long. You take care, now, Handsome. Something tells me a man who looks like you does his best work with his hands."

Gerry stood and winked at Letitia, and as Anne rolled her eyes and pushed him out of the cubicle, she heard Letitia mutter, "Just friends, my ass."

The waiting room was not particularly crowded. A mother holding a toddler, who kept pulling his ear, whining, "It hurts," was walking the floor. A young man in a softball uniform was sitting in a wheel chair, his right leg propped up, an ice pack on his knee. He was accompanied by a teammate, who was swigging from a bottle of Gatorade. A TV blared the evening news.

Gerry and Anne took a seat. She noticed that he was once again tapping his feet. "Is it hurting?" she asked.

"More like throbbing." He watched the woman walking her sick son, his eyes following her, shifting like a metronome. "How bad is it?" he asked.

"Your cut?"

He turned to Anne. "No, getting stitches. I've never gotten them before." She could see the fear in his eyes; James Bond was a wuss.

"What about that scar on your chin? You must have gotten stitches to close that."

"I did, but I was only two. I don't remember. Can they put me to sleep?"

Anne snickered. "For stitches? No."

He looked pale.

"You'll be fine, Gerry."

He tapped his foot nervously. "I don't know about that. When I get my teeth cleaned, they sedate me."

She touched his shoulder. "Try to relax."

"I am," he said nearly shouting. The little boy resting on his mother's shoulder raised his head and looked at them. He lowered his voice. "Come in with me."

"Huh?"

"Come in with me, Anne. You know all this medical stuff. You can make sure they don't hurt me. Please."

"Gerry, you're a grown man. You don't need me—"

"Please. Your beauty will distract me from the pain."

His plaintive blues eyes left her no choice.

"Well, if you think it'll help; I'm sure they won't mind."

She saw him let out a deep breath. "Thanks. I owe you, Slugger." He eyed the clock. "You didn't have any plans with Dr. Love tonight?"

"Tomorrow," Anne said. "He's on call tonight. What time does your dinner start?"

"Cocktails are at six; dinner's at seven."

"Maybe they'll have you patched up in time for dinner." As Anne said those words, the faint wails of sirens caught her ear and steadily grew louder until the piercing sound seemed to envelop them. Suddenly, it was quiet for a moment. Then the double door opened and all hell broke loose. A gurney wheeled in by two paramedics crashed through the doors. Another quickly followed. The person lying on this one was so bathed in blood, Anne couldn't tell if the patient was a man or woman.

She turned to Gerry. "Must have been a terrible accident." He didn't seem to hear her. His eyes were fixed on the door, where another victim had just been brought in. This time the EMT was sitting on a middle-aged man doing chest compressions. Gerry's eyes looked like they were about to roll back. Anne didn't want him to pass out. She touched his arm. "We're probably going to be here awhile." She pulled her wallet out of her purse. "Come on, I'll treat you to some cheese crackers."

He seemed relieved at her suggestion yet kept looking over his shoulder as she held on to his arm. They walked to the vending machine alcove just down the hall. Anne had enough change for two Cokes and a pack of Lance crackers that they shared.

When they were finished with their snack, they walked back the short hallway to the waiting room. Joining the others now was a girl who looked to be about nine, holding an ice pack on her forearm. Her mother and a younger brother, who kept rolling on the floor, accompanied her. The mother was admonishing her son to get off the floor. "Hospitals have germs," she said. "Get up now."

Anne and Gerry fidgeted in the uncomfortable vinyl chairs. The clock now said six-forty. "Looks like you're going to miss dinner," Anne said.

"Looks like it."

"I forgot my phone back at the bar," Anne said. "Did you bring yours?"

"No."

"Maybe you should call Claudia. Wonder if there is even a pay phone here anymore? "

"Why? So she can bring me a doggy bag?"

"No, she might be wondering how your hand is." Anne felt she had to say that so as not to hurt his feelings, but from Claudia's tantrum, Anne knew that Claudia's prime focus was Claudia.

Gerry adjusted the bar towel wrapped around his injured hand. "Let her wonder."

Anger was plainly in his voice. Anne didn't know what to say, so she picked up a magazine and began leafing through it. She sat silently, her eyes scanning Heloise's column on how to remove stubborn orange grease stains from Tupperware.

Gerry sighed. "God, I hope they take me soon. I hate this waiting. And those cheese crackers just didn't cut it. I'm getting hungry." He looked at Anne. "I bet you're hungry too."

"A little."

"How about after I get stitched up, we go get something to eat? My treat."

"Oh, you don't have to—"

"Come on, Anne."

"But what about Claudia?"

His jaw tensed. "What about her? I know a great Italian place in Bloomfield. Ever been to Gino's?"

"No, I only moved here a few months ago. I'm not even sure where Bloomfield is."

"You did? I didn't know that. You've got guts."

"Because I moved sixty miles from my home?" she said. "I'd hardly say that's bold."

"I've never lived anywhere but above the bar. I even commuted to college. I've always felt responsible for my mother." He shook his head. "God, I lead a narrow life."

"You're your mother's only support. She relies on you. You couldn't just up and leave her."

He half smiled. "It was Claudia who encouraged me to buy the place on Washington's Landing. She's never really understood what it's like to be the only son of a widowed mother. I'm glad you understand."

"Do you mind Peg being so dependent on you? Or living and working in the same place you were born?"

Gerry looked thoughtful for a moment, and then he straightened up in the chair. "No, I don't. I love the continuity of it. For years I resisted running the bar, but when my mom couldn't do it anymore, she pleaded with me to take it over. So I relented and put my architectural career on hold. I've been surprised at how much I enjoy running it. I love knowing that the bar is the place where my father grew up. I love our customers. I love walking up Butler Street and knowing everyone. And Peg can be a pain," he said, his eyes getting misty, "but when I almost lost her . . . " He stopped because his voice was choked with emotion. "I've promised her I won't sell it while she is still alive."

Moved by his love for Peg, Anne felt herself getting weepy too. She patted his shoulder. "Well, Scarlet, if you love Tara that much, why leave the plantation?"

"I guess I've been paying too much attention to what others want and not what I want."

Was he alluding to Claudia? She wanted to tell him what she really thought of Claudia but it wasn't her place.

"There's nothing wrong with taking care of your elderly mother," he said.

"I'd say it's downright noble," she declared. "Why, that's the fifth commandment."

"And many people live in their ancestral home," Gerry said.

"Prince Charles didn't move out of Buckingham Palace," Anne observed.

"And being a barkeeper is a respectable position," he said puffing out his chest a bit.

"You provide a safe, comfortable environment where people can enjoy themselves."

"Damn right, I do. You know," he said turning to her, his jaw set with determination, "I'm through with listening to everyone else's opinions. I'm going to do what I want. I'm not going to deny my feelings."

"You do that," Anne said.

A nurse in scrubs came through the doors that led back into the E.R.'s exam rooms. She read a sheet of paper, and called, "Gerard McMaster."

He turned to Anne and grabbed her wrist. "Since I'm no longer going to deny my feelings," he said, melting before her eyes like the wicked witch in the *Wizard of Oz*, "I have to tell you that what I'm feeling now is faint."

Chapter 20

With his good hand, Gerry poured them wine and then raised his glass. "Here's to the best nurse ever."

Anne smiled, clinking her goblet to his. "Here's to smelling salts."

When Gerry began to black out in the waiting room, Anne, quick on the draw, whipped out her smelling salts again and called for the E.R. nurse. She held them under his nose, and he quickly came to. Despite his protests, she and the nurse insisted that he ride back to the exam room in a wheel chair.

While the attending physician gave Gerry five internal stitches and nine external ones, Anne kept his mind off the needle mending his flesh by engaging him in conversation. He held her hand tightly and kept his blue eyes fixed on her, wincing every so often. As he lay on the table looking up at her, Anne could see the specter of the boy Gerry had been.

Now as he sat across the table from her in the dimly lit restaurant, she no longer saw the frightened child, but the handsome, confident man, comfortable with charming women.

Anne twirled pasta around her fork and watched him as he undid the top stud on his tuxedo shirt. To the other customers, they must look so odd, she thought, with him dressed in formal wear and her in scrubs. "So you met Dave at the historical society?"

"When I was restoring the bar." He struggled to butter a roll.

"Let me help you," Anne said, taking it from him. "You restored it?" She returned the buttered hard roll to him.

"Over the years, my grandfather, father, and mother had made changes to the place. Some not so good. Like the windows out front. In the early fifties they leaked, so my father had glass block installed. When I took over, business was not brisk to say the least. Mostly locals. To survive, we needed to attract a larger clientele, and to do that, the place needed to be remodeled. I'm a history minor and felt restoring the place to its original state would be the key to its success. I went to the historical society for guidance. That's how I met him."

"I never figured you for a history buff?"

"Don't be so shocked." He pointed to his head. "I'll have you know there are brains behind this gorgeous face."

He is gorgeous. And now that he'd taken off the bow tie and opened his shirt, he was even more so. He looked sexy like a groom loosening his clothing in preparation for a night of lovemaking with his bride. What am I doing thinking about Gerry and making love? Keep your mind on history, Anne. "But history is so cerebral and solitary," she said, "and you're so gregarious."

"Well, when a chunk of your past is missing, you value the links to it."

"Part of your past is missing?"

He swallowed and then said softly, "My father."

"Oh," Anne whispered, not sure what to say. Peg had often talked about her late husband, how she missed him so, but Anne couldn't recall Gerry mentioning his father before.

He stared at the candle flickering in the glass globe on the table. "Sometimes, it's so strange, Anne, but I'll be standing at the bar pouring a beer or sitting at his desk in my office, and I get this feeling—it's not a creepy feeling, but a good one—that he's there with me." He looked at her, sadness dimming the sparkle in his eyes. "I don't know how I know it's him. I barely remember my father. But I know he's there. I never wanted to work in the bar, but since I've been forced to do it, I'm finding that I'm loving it. To know that I'm sitting where he sat, standing where he drew beers, doing the same things he did. Do you understand what I mean? Have you ever been haunted by a memory?"

Anne touched his hand. "Yes, I understand what it's like to be haunted."

"I'm sorry. I didn't bring you here to depress you. I'm as bad as the old lushes who used to hang out in the bar when I was growing up. They were always calling me over to tell me that I 'Looked just like my old man. What a good egg he was.' Then they'd buy me a Slim Jim. I know they were trying to make me feel better, but it made me feel worse to know they knew my father and I didn't."

When he stopped speaking, she realized she was still touching his hand. She felt awkward, and she quickly withdrew it and reached for her wine, taking a long sip.

Gerry picked up a knife to cut his Veal Oscar, but couldn't with his wound. "Let me," Anne said. She took his plate and cut his meat. As she handed it back to him, she said, "How are you ever going to be able to work?"

"I'll manage. Good thing I hired Bob to take up some slack. I was planning to cut back my time in the bar anyway."

"Why's that?"

"Oh, I don't know." He sipped his wine then stared pointedly at her. "So how's Dr. Love?"

"Fine."

"Come on," Gerry said. "Are you two really getting that serious?"

Anne smiled and looked at her dinner. She couldn't admit to him that she'd exaggerated about their relationship the other day. "All I know is he called and said he wants to talk to me about something important tomorrow night."

"You said you thought he's going to propose."

"We get along so well, and all the signs are there, but who knows?" she said with a shrug. "You're a man. You know how men think. You tell me."

"I'm not him, but I know what I'd do."

"And what's that?"

His face colored pink. "I'd marry you."

"You'd marry me?" Flustered, she quickly said, "You mean you think Craig would marry me?"

"Why wouldn't he? You're beautiful, intelligent, kind, and you pack a mean punch."

Flattered, she laughed. "Ah, the attributes of the perfect wife."

Through the rest of their dinner, no matter what the topic of conversation—Peg's progress, how Anne liked living in Pittsburgh, the upcoming KISS concert Gerry had promised to take Bernie to—all Anne could think of was how handsome Gerry was and how she'd misread him. He was much deeper than the image he projected.

When the waiter brought the check, Gerry's customary devilish smile crept back over his face.

"What is it?" Anne asked.

"I need my wallet again."

She held up her hand. "No way. I'll pay."

"No, I insist on paying." He rose and stood next to the booth. "Just reach in and pull it out."

Anne crossed her arms, staring dubiously at him.

"Look, I'll behave myself."

"You? Behave yourself?"

"We'll be discreet. No one will see."

She wasn't convinced but remembered that she didn't have much cash. She huffed. "Oh, OK." Rising, she sidled up next to him and slid her hand into his pocket.

"Goodness, woman," he shouted, attracting the attention of all the other patrons in the dining room, "have some decorum. Can't you wait until we get to the hotel?"

Anne's face turned the color of the marinara sauce remaining on her plate. She clenched her teeth and muttered, "I'm going to kill you."

He turned to an elderly man who was taking the whole scene in. "She can't keep her hands off me."

She pulled out the wallet and tossed it on the table." She sat back down in the booth, covering her face with her hands. While they waited for the server to return to take his money, she kept mumbling, "You're dead, Gerard."

When she uncovered her face, she saw him sitting across from her grinning.

"If you're smart, you'll hide your knife," she said, "or you'll be needing more stitches."

After the check was settled, they stood to leave. As Anne made her way out of the restaurant, she felt someone touch her arm. She looked back. It was the elderly man. "I have arthritis," he said softly. "Could you take out my wallet for me?"

Anne ignored him and stomped out of the restaurant.

When they stepped outside, Gerry was roaring with laughter.

Anne wanted to be mad at him, but his laugh was so infectious, she felt her anger fading and she started to laugh too.

"You are incorrigible, Gerry McMaster," she said, giving him a shove.

"Sorry," he said. "Next time I'll try to be more 'corrigible.'"

When they got to his car, Anne began to root inside her purse. "Where'd I put your keys?" She looked up and Gerry was wearing a huge smile, his arms outstretched.

"No," she groaned. "Don't tell me."

The dimple in his cheek became deeper as he grinned at her. "Oh, yes. Don't you remember? You gave them back to me."

She closed her eyes. "Let me guess. They're in your pocket."

He laughed wickedly.

She moved toward him, stuck her hand in his pocket, and slid her hand along his powerful quadricep. He moaned and writhed as if in ecstasy. "Oh, be gentle," he cried. "I've lost a lot of blood."

Looking up into his playful blue eyes, she said, "You're enjoying this, aren't you?"

He kept his eyes locked on hers. "Yes. Aren't you?"

She was, but she couldn't admit that to him, so instead of answering, she grabbed a hunk of thigh and pinched him.

"Ouch!"

She took the keys from his pocket. "Get in the car, Merv the Perv."

As she drove him back to the bar, he insisted on putting the convertible's top down. It was a warm, clear night. The breeze as they drove along Butler Street, was like a thousand fingers caressing her skin, and the stars seemed to twinkle more brightly. People throughout Lawrenceville recognized his car and waved at them as they drove by. Anne felt as if they were in a parade. When they stopped for a light, one teenager walking up the street called to them, "Mac, you dog, I gotta get me a chauffeur that looks like that." Anne had to laugh as she watched Gerry smiling smugly and waving as she drove him home. She pulled his car into the space next to hers and handed him his keys.

"Want to put them in my pocket for me?"

"No," she said, stepping out of the car.

When they walked into the bar, Dave, Bob, Vera, and Bernie crowded around, asking Gerry how he was. Satisfied that he was fine, Dave gave Gerry a slip of paper. "Claudia called. Said you could reach her at this number. She's at some after-party, and she wants you to join her there."

"Thanks," he said, crumbling the paper and tossing it into the trash. They exchanged glances behind Gerry's back.

Shocked that he'd thrown away her number, Anne cleared her throat. "Well, I suppose we missed D.J."

"He promised to stop by again," Dave said.

"Good," Anne said. "Then I guess I'll be leaving."

Dave reached below the bar. "I put your stuff back here for safekeeping."

"Thanks, Dave." She took her belongings and waved at everyone. "I'll see you all on Monday."

"I'll walk you out," Gerry said.

"Why? Is there something you need in your pocket? I can take care of myself. Go call Claudia."

"No, I'll walk you out. It's pretty dark out there."

"Remember, I pack a mean punch."

"And a mean pinch," he said rubbing his thigh. "Besides I also want to put the car's top up."

As they walked down the short hall, past his office to the door that led out to the back, Anne again went over the instructions for taking care of his stitches. Stepping out into the soft night air she said, "If you have any problem with them, give me a call."

"If you haven't eloped."

With all his shenanigans, she'd forgotten about Craig. Thank goodness, he never acted as silly as Gerry. "Craig's not the eloping type."

Gerry leaned against his car, folding his arms in front of him. In the tux next to the convertible, he looked like a model posing for an advertisement for luxury cars.

"What type is he?"

Anne had to think for a moment. "He's the gentle, reliable type."

"Sounds like a laxative."

Anne laughed and smacked his arm.

"Hey, don't hit the infirmed." Gerry straightened up.

"No, I'm serious," she said, trying to put her finger on exactly what it was about Craig that she found so appealing. Then she finally hit upon it. "He's honorable and trustworthy."

"So are priests."

Insulted that he thought Craig stodgy, Anne replied "Believe me, he's no priest."

"Yeah, yeah," Gerry mumbled as he examined the bandage on his hand. "So you like that sort of guy, do you? You know, a Boy Scout?"

"He's not a Boy Scout. But what's not to like about gentle and reliable?"

He slowly strode toward her until he was so close that she was pinned against her car. He smelled of cologne, antiseptic, and maleness. Lifting her head to see his face as he towered over her, she noticed something in his eyes that she'd never seen before—fierce determination, and she knew she didn't stand a chance against his raw sensuousness. Anne heard her heart thud as it fell to the pit of her stomach.

"He doesn't sound like much fun," he said, his voice husky. Anne braced her hands behind her on the car and bent away from him. He moved in closer, his powerful thighs pressing against hers. "Don't you find it boring, Slugger?" He whispered as he twirled one of her curls around his finger, then tucked it behind her ear. "Don't you crave a little excitement?"

All she could do was gulp before he moved his hand to the back of her neck, drew her to him, and kissed her, kissed her wildly, kissed her so passionately and with such heat that she thought the rubber soles of her shoes would melt.

After allowing herself to indulge in his lips for several moments, panic flared in her, and she quickly got hold of herself and broke free. Breathless, she stared him in the eye. Then without saying a word, she slipped into her car, started the ignition and pulled away. And although the sky on this warm summer night was studded with stars, to Anne, they were nothing but dull pinpoints compared to the ones dancing in her eyes.

Chapter 21

Gerry's kiss haunted Anne's dreams that night and occupied her thoughts all the next day, quickening her pulse every time she recalled how soft yet demanding his lips felt on hers. What did his kiss mean? Was he truly interested in her, or was she merely another woman to conquer? It didn't matter anyway, she told herself, because Craig was the man for her.

What did Craig want to talk to her about tonight? Did he plan to propose? Did she love him? If love was admiring and wanting to be with someone, then Anne guessed that she did love Craig.

The possibility that he might pop the question that evening at dinner made her jittery. With nervous energy to spare, she made some of the shower favors, but grew bored with the repetition and decided to clean the apartment and catch up on laundry.

Late Saturday afternoon when everything was spic and span, she took a leisurely bath in gardenia-scented bubbles and gave herself a manicure and pedicure. She then slathered on body lotion in the same scent, laughing that she'd prepped her body like an Egyptian waiting to be mummified.

She chose a cream-colored skirt and a shell the color of a honeydew melon from her closet. Before sliding into some strappy sandals, she hiked up her skirt and studied her legs. Too many darn freckles. *Why don't I have Janetta's skin?* Anne could tan any time she wanted free of charge at Janetta's salon, but she knew it was no use. The end result was always the same—burns, blisters, and peeling skin.

As she rifled through her drawers for the perfect shade of pantyhose, she worried about her roommate. She still had not heard from her. Anne wanted to call, but sensed that Steve viewed her as a threat and took out the wrath he had for her on Janetta. Afraid to make the situation worse, she figured it would be best to let Janetta call her whenever she was ready.

She wiggled into a pair of nude-colored hose and fussed with her hair.

With her apartment and her body groomed to perfection and nothing left to do, she sat on the couch and clicked on the television, flipping through the channels. Finally, she settled on a golf match because she thought the hushed voices and rolling green hills on the screen would calm her.

When the buzzer sounded, she shot off the couch like someone had hit an ejector button. She pressed the intercom, heard Craig's voice, and released the lock to admit him inside. While she waited for him, she stood at the door, her hand over her heart, taking deep breaths. He knocked softly. Before answering it, she checked herself in the mirror and then put an eye to the peephole. She saw a distorted image of him standing in the hall. He was wearing a navy sport jacket and his arms were full with brown bags, a bottle of wine, and a bouquet.

"Oooh, flowers," she whispered and shuddered with delight. "He means business." She whipped open the door with a placid expression hiding the excitement weakening her limbs.

"Here, let me help you," she said, reaching for the bag.

"Take these," Craig said shaking the flowers, signaling that she should relieve him of the bouquet. "They're for you. Hope you like roses."

Anne shut the door behind him. "Who doesn't?" She peered into the green tissue paper cone and saw that they were peach-colored blossoms, not her favorite—red—but she didn't want to tell him that. Sticking her nose into the bunch and closing her eyes, she basked in their fragrance. She didn't know which smelled better, the flowers or his cologne.

"Their color reminded me of you," he said. "Your hair in the sun."

He was waxing poetic and had brought flowers. *I wonder if he brought a ring too?* Her heart was tripping like a machine gun.

As she followed him into the dining area, she studied his pants pockets to see if she could make out the outline of a ring box inside his khakis. Her thoughts flashed back to last night and the episode with Gerry's pockets and she had to smile.

She had set the table with her mother's old ironstone dishes. Craig unloaded the containers of shrimp fried rice, General Tsao's chicken, Mongolian beef, and egg rolls. He held the bottle of Chablis out for Anne's approval. "I didn't know what, if anything, goes with Chinese. Hope its OK."

Anne touched the bottle. "You could have told me all fine Chinese restaurants serve this for all I know about wines." She opened a container and stuck a serving spoon inside. "It seems so tacky serving out of cardboard. Maybe I should get some bowls."

She stepped toward the kitchen, but Craig grabbed her before she could get away. "Sit," he said. "Just being with you makes everything seem elegant." He kissed her until Anne felt as if someone had reached into her chest and polished her heart until it was glowing.

She was so excited she could barely eat. Her mind raced with thoughts of wedding dresses, cakes, and flowers. *It will be such a relief to no longer have to wonder if I'll ever find a suitable husband. Craig knew her, knew Zach; he'd understand about her past.*

Anne suspected that he wouldn't propose until after dinner. So she tried to eat slowly and concentrate on what he was saying even though all she could think about was what china pattern she should register for to replace these sorry plates.

When they had finished, she quickly cleared the table while Craig stored the leftovers. After everything was tidy, he refilled their drinks, and they headed into the living room.

They sat on the couch in silence. Anne could hear him breathing. Craig took a sip, gulped, and then set the glass on the table. He looked at Anne and smiled.

He's nervous too, she thought. Charmed by his shyness, she smiled back.

He chuckled, a faint pinkness washing over his chiseled cheekbones. "I don't know where to begin."

Anne giggled. "Just jump right in."

Taking a deep breath, he picked up her hand and held it in both of his. "Anne, I have something to ask you."

This is it. She straightened her spine, pivoting to face him. His warm, dark eyes settled on her. "What is it?" Her voice sounded shrill, her vocal chords taut with anticipation.

"Anne, will you . . . "

She leaned in closer.

He shifted in his seat. "Oh man, I'm so nervous."

Anne was trembling. "Will you . . ." She stared into his eyes. *God, please just spit it out!* "What?"

"Will you . . ." He paused then blurted, " . . . go to Guatemala with me?"

Anne blinked a few times, not sure what he had said. "What?"

"Guatemala. I want you to come with me."

She felt the breath she'd been holding slowly escape her chest. Then she pulled her hand away. "For vacation?"

"No. To live. Work."

She felt tears stinging her eyes, but choked them back. "I don't understand."

"My career." He took her hand once again, but this time Anne let it lie lifelessly in his palm. "You know how I've been struggling to make a decision. Well, I've searched my heart, and I've decided to go to Guatemala."

"To practice medicine? You're going to some third-world country?"

"Yes. And I'd like you to come."

"To visit?"

"To be my nurse."

"Nurse?" She pulled her hand away again and waved it around the room. "You bring all this—wine, flowers—to coax me into coming to Guatemala for a job?" Her anger was spilling over into her voice. What's next? she wondered. Him trying to sell me some Amway?

"That and more."

She crossed her arms in front of her. "What? As your office manager too?"

"No, no." He grasped her knee and she stiffened. "Let me explain. Anne, ever since Steve made those comments the other night, they've been weighing on my mind. I've struggled with this decision so much. Finally, I asked myself why I became a plastic surgeon? Was it to amass a fortune? To enhance the breasts of vain women?" He touched her cheek. "No, Anne, the reason I became a plastic surgeon is because I wanted to help people. Before I met you, I was leaning toward leaving the country to practice somewhere where I can really make a difference."

He stroked her cheek. "Then you came back into my life, and I didn't want to lose you."

She felt her anger subsiding.

"So I ignored my desires and decided to narrow my choices to practices here. But, Anne, I know I'll never be happy doing nose jobs and facelifts. You should see the kids out there with cleft palates—deformities you can't even imagine."

She uncrossed her arms.

"But I also won't be happy in Guatemala without you. I know we haven't been seeing each other very long, so I think it's premature to ask you to get married, but would you please consider coming to Guatemala with me?"

Anne sighed. "Craig." She stood and walked to the balcony doors. Looking out at the horizon, she saw the sun fading fast, shadows lengthening in its dying rays. "I don't know." She did enjoy helping others; that's why she had become a nurse. *Maybe this is God's way of allowing me to atone for what I've done.*

He came to her and grasped her shoulders, turning her to face him. "We'd make a great team. Doctor and nurse helping the unfortunate. I know what kind of person you are. Your compassion and skill could make a world of difference for so many people."

"Oh, I don't . . ."

His eyes pleaded with her. "There'd be no expectations. If our relationship develops, then fine. If not, you're free. At least give us a chance."

"But—"

Before she could refuse, he pressed his lips to hers. While he kissed her, a thousand thoughts crossed her mind. *Guatemala? I'm not even sure where that is. What about my family? Patsy's babies? Could I live a life of deprivation? Where would I shop?* His lips were soft and warm on hers. They tasted like ginger and wine, and she felt safe and secure in his arms.

Safe and secure.

The way Gerry looked at her before he kissed her flashed in her mind. When she felt vibrations on her thighs, she'd thought she'd aroused Craig, but when he pulled away and thrust his hands into his pocket, she realized it was his pager going off.

"Damn," he said. "I've got to go in, Anne. But please. Please promise me you'll think about it."

As he dashed out the door, she wondered how she could possibly think of anything else?

Chapter 22

It was nearly midnight when Gerry went upstairs to change out of his tuxedo and soak his bloody shirt. Usually by this time, Peg would be sleeping in her hospital bed, and Irma would be dozing in the chair. She stayed with Peg until the bar closed then she and Bernie would get a ride home from either Vera or Dave.

Gerry didn't want to disturb them so he tiptoed down the hall. He stopped when he heard a strange sound like the tinkling of glass and whispering coming from Peg's room. Puzzled, he peeked inside the darkened bedroom and found both old women working their rosary beads, the lights from the television reflecting silver-blue on their faces.

He didn't want to have to explain about the cut, so he tucked his bandaged hand behind him and whispered, "You two doing penance for thinking impure thoughts?"

Irma jumped, clasping the beads to her chest. "Oh, God help us. He's come to say goodbye before departing for his final judgment."

Peg made the sign of the cross.

Gerry flicked on the overhead light. Both women clamped their eyes shut, recoiling from the harsh glare. "What the hell are you talking about?"

Irma, her eyelids pinched tightly together, her face as white as her hair, turned toward Peg and whispered, "Sometimes spirits don't know they've died. Tell him it's OK, Peg. Tell him to go toward the light."

Gerry strode over and touched Irma's shoulder. She screamed, cowering from him.

"It's OK. "I'm alive."

Both women squinted at him, trembling.

"You weren't killed?" Irma said, her voice quivering.

"Where did you get that idea?"

"It's really you?" Peg held her hands out to him, tears streaming down her cheeks..

"What? Do you want to probe the nail marks in my hands, Doubting Thomas?"

"But Claudia said—" Peg began to sob.

"And Bernie said—" Irma choked back tears.

Gerry's face turned the color of the blood stains on his shirt. "Claudia called here? After I specifically told her not to?" His lips became tight as he shook his head.

"About half an hour ago," Peg said. "All upset, wondering where you were. You left here in your tuxedo at five thirty. We didn't know what to think."

"So I called Bernie down in the kitchen," Irma said tag-teaming on Peg's explanation. "He was so upset. He said you'd had an accident, and they'd taken you to the hospital, and he wasn't allowed to say anymore."

"You could tell by Claudia's voice that she was furious with you," Peg said, wiping tears from her wrinkled cheeks. "We assumed you'd never gotten to pick her up because you'd had an accident on the way."

"And that Dave and Vera had gone to the hospital and weren't telling us the bad news," Irma added. "I called the hospital, but they won't tell you anything unless they have permission."

Gerry held out his bandaged hand. "I cut myself on a glass. Anne took me to the hospital for stitches."

Peg sighed heavily. "Is that all? We've been going out of our minds with worry."

"We must have said five rosaries," Irma chimed in.

He plucked a tissue from the box on her dresser and handed it to his mother. He smirked and kissed her on the forehead. "I'm touched by your grief, Peg."

"You're going to be more than touched, Wise Guy. If I was stronger, I'd get out of this bed and kick your ass for scaring us so badly."

He set his jaw. "Oh, there's going to be an ass kicking all right. But it won't be mine." He glanced at his watch. "I'll leave you ladies to your beads; I have a phone call to make." He patted his mother on the head. "You can say them in thanksgiving for the safe return of your precious son."

Peg slapped his hand away, and as he left the room, she muttered, "Wisenheimer."

***

While Gerry removed his jacket, he went over the evening in his mind, recalling each of Claudia's selfish and rude acts—from her shouting at Dave and Bernie to phoning his mother and worrying her unnecessarily—until his anger was packed together in a tightly wadded ball sitting in the pit of his stomach. He remembered her behavior at Peg's party, how condescending she had been to Anne and her lack of understanding when it came to how much time he had to devote to Peg.

Having the use of only one hand, he struggled with the cufflinks until he became so thoroughly frustrated that he ripped them out, followed by the studs up the front of the shirt.

His bloody shirt in tatters, he threw it aside and picked up the phone. With his uninjured hand, he punched in the numbers.

"Claudia," he said sternly when she answered.

"It's about time you called. I texted you. Where have you been? My big night and you go and screw it up."

"Where was I? Try the hospital, Claudia. The place you were too busy to take me."

"Oh, don't be a baby, Gerry. It was only a cut. And I couldn't take you. You bled on my new dress. And then those idiots that you employ—"

"I will not allow you to call my friends names," he shouted. He knew Peg and Irma had probably heard him. He reached over with his foot and kicked the door closed.

"Fine, your friends and their grubby paws destroyed my brand new dress. Then I waited for you all night. How long does it take to get stitches?"

"If you'd have taken me to the hospital, you'd know."

"What? You didn't expect me to miss the dinner? They were honoring me!"

"That's it," he shouted into the phone, "I've learned to expect too little from you."

"Well, maybe if I didn't have to compete with St. Anne for all your time, things would be different."

"Leave Anne out of this."

"Oh, that's right, protect poor little Annie. You treat her better than me. I swear you're in love with her."

"I am not in love with Anne!"

"You can't fool me," Claudia shouted. "I can see the way you two behave around each other. Exchanging little jokes and glances, and you calling her Slugger. And the way she looks at your ass. Oh, please. Do I have to spell it out for you?"

"You're crazy," Gerry cried into the phone. "Anne's in love with someone else. In fact, she's probably getting engaged this weekend."

"Bullshit," Claudia cried. "She salivates like a St. Bernard when you come near."

"She does not. You are so self-absorbed, Claudia, that you don't recognize common courtesy."

"Me, self-absorbed? You are the most egotistical, immature—"

"Shrew. That's what you are, Claudia. A shrew."

"How dare you talk to me like that."

190

"And you know what else?" he said, feeling the ball of rage in his stomach unraveling as he let loose all that he'd been holding in. "You're too skinny and you have no breasts." Then he slammed down the phone.

***

Irma stood in the doorway, covering her mouth to stifle her laughter. "He told her she has no breasts."

Peg slapped her thighs, laughing.

Irma jumped. "Oh, my gosh, he hung up on her." The hinges on his door squeaked. "Here he comes." She scurried to her chair, her thighs rubbing together like a cricket.

Feigning sleep, they tilted their heads back and closed their eyes.

The floor creaked as Gerry walked down the hall. He stopped at Peg's doorway. "You two better say an extra decade as penance for eavesdropping," he snarled.

When they heard him walk into the kitchen, Peg and Irma opened their eyes and looked at each other. Then they giggled like school girls.

Chapter 23

Their date cut short, Anne tried to watch television after Craig left, but she couldn't concentrate on the program because her thoughts kept intruding. Should she go to Guatemala with Craig? Why had Gerry kissed her? What did she want? Who did she want? Sleeping was useless; she knew she'd never be able to calm her mind enough to nod off. So she changed into her pajamas and set out to finish the rest of the shower favors. As the night wore on and she glued pompom after pompom together and wiggly eyes onto the little bear's faces, she began to get weary.

When her fingers became so tacky from the glue that the pompoms were sticking to them, she broke down, giving into self-pity. *Only I get asked to go Guatemala instead of being asked to get married.* Tears streamed down her cheeks. She tried to wipe them away, but her hands were so sticky and fuzzy, she ended up getting lint in her eyes.

Sobbing, she shoved the favors aside, shut out the lights, and flung herself onto her bed. *Now, what do I do, St. Anne?* She let the tears fall freely until she drifted off to sleep.

When she awoke on Sunday morning, she shuffled into to the bathroom, and caught a glimpse of herself in the mirror. A pompom was stuck to her cheek. "What the . . . ?" she said as she plucked it off. It hurt like pulling off a bandage and left a huge red blotch. When she remembered the unfinished favors, she stood ramrod straight. "Damn," she muttered, quickly splashing water on her face and then hurrying into the living room. The glue and pompoms had dried to the newspaper covering the dining room table.

Panicked, she looked at the clock. It was nearly seven-thirty. The shower was at two. Why hadn't she drafted Peg into helping her with these? She had to finish the favors, shower and dress, go to Mass and drive to Latrobe by noon to help set up. How was she ever going to make it? Caffeine power that's how.

She grabbed a 16-ounce Pepsi from the fridge and began gulping it down while she counted out the favors she'd already made. Thirty-three were done; she needed forty-two more. Setting herself a deadline of eight thirty to get them all finished, she worked like an automaton, gluing and gluing.

At eight twenty-five, she did a final count. Sixty-two were done. She hastily made a few more before she had to stop. Exhausted, she wasn't sure if she'd put bow ties on the last few bears. Too bad. Perhaps she could finish the rest at the shower while everyone played Baby Bingo. She gathered the favors and leftover supplies into a shirt box and set them with her purse so she wouldn't forget them when she left.

She took a quick shower, dressed in a new butter-yellow suit and bone-colored heels she'd bought for the occasion, and made it to church just as the priest was processing down the aisle. Even though it was cold in the church from the blasting air conditioner, it took her a good twenty minutes to cool off from all the rushing around she'd done. Anne felt guilty, but she left right after Communion so she could get to Latrobe at a reasonable time.

When she pulled into her parents' driveway at twelve twenty-three, Kevin, dressed in shorts and T-shirt, stepped out onto the porch and called, "They left already. You're supposed to go to the hall." She tried her mother's cell phone, but she never remembered to turn it on.

With the needle of her speedometer perilously in the range of a traffic violation, she zoomed to the Croatian Hall, a square, flat-roofed building with glass block windows.

When she pulled into the gravel lot behind the building, her father was taking boxes out of the trunk of his Regal.

"What can I do?" she asked as soon as she stepped out of the car. She hoped to jump right into the preparations before anyone could fault her for being late.

As her father was handing her a glass punch bowl to carry in, her mother appeared at the door. She had the same suit on as Anne. *Oh, great.*

"There you are, Anne." Her mother squinted into the sunlight. "Are you wearing my suit? Did you get that at Macy's?"

"Yes," Anne growled.

Her mother smiled. "Oh, it's just like when you were little, and we got those mother-daughter outfits from the Alden's catalog. Isn't that something!"

"It certainly is," Anne snarled, making plans to burn the suit as soon as she got home. "Where do you want me to take this?" she asked, twisting her ankle on the gravel.

"Into the kitchen. You're late. I thought you'd never get here."

"Father's sermon ran long," she said.

"You should have gone last night."

As she limped into the hall, she thought that maybe Guatemala wasn't such a bad idea. She wouldn't have to put up with her mother's nagging.

When Anne saw Patsy sitting at a table trying to assemble a tissue paper stork, she said, "What are you doing here already? You're the guest of honor."

Patsy whispered out the side of her mouth, "She panicked when you were late. Wanted help with the decorations." She scrunched up her nose. "Is that the same suit as—"

"Yes, and if you don't want me to crash this punch bowl over your head, you'll not mention it again."

Patsy snickered.

Anne set the punch bowl down. "I hope you don't think you're going to be decorating."

Mrs. Lyons walked in carrying a crockpot filled with baked beans. "Did you remember the favors?"

"Yes, they're in the car," Anne said sarcastically.

By the time two o'clock arrived and the shower began, Anne was ready for a nap. Besides having to acknowledge numerous times that she and her mother were dressed like twins, she had to help her mother greet guests, lug presents to the gift table, make punch, and help put out the luncheon.

After everyone had eaten and played Baby Bingo, Anne cleared away the dirty plastic plates and utensils. Then Patsy began to open the mountain of gifts. Anne plopped into a folding chair. Her new shoes were killing her and her ankle seemed to be puffy. She was glad to let two pre-teen girls act as ladies-in-waiting by handing the gifts to Patsy, and her mother was recording who gave what gift.

It was the first time that Anne had a chance to study her sister. Was it possible to get any bigger? She looked like she'd swallowed a brick of yeast and risen too much. Anne's eyes took in Patsy's ankles. They were puffy, but not unusually so. Patsy was wearing a brown dress, and although she would never tell her, Anne thought it made her sister look as big as a grizzly bear.

Bear? "Damn it!" she muttered. She'd forgotten about the unfinished favors. Her shoes pinching and her ankle aching, she hobbled to the car as Patsy was opening up her third diaper bag.

Taking the box of favors into the kitchen, she stood at the stainless steel counter hastily assembling some more. She stopped when she heard her mother calling for her. Quickly, she threw the rest in the box and prayed that some of the guests hadn't showed up so she wouldn't need all seventy-five bears.

When the gift opening was completed, her mother asked her to serve the shower cake. After everyone had consumed enough sugar, and drank an urn of coffee, the guests began to get restless and moved to leave.

"Wait," her mother cried. "You're forgetting your favors. Anne, pass them out."

Gladly, Anne thought, as she went into the kitchen and grabbed the box. She never wanted to see them again. Stationing herself near the door, she handed them out as the guests departed. She breathed a sigh of relief when all the guests were gone, and she still had two favors left over.

As Anne and her mother turned to begin removing the paper tablecloths, they heard a "Hello," from the doorway.

It was her cousin Colleen. Anne gritted her teeth and groaned.

"Oh, Aunt Grace," Colleen ignored Anne and addressed her mother. "I was wondering whether I could have two more favors? I'd like to take them home for the kiddies."

"We don't have any more," Anne said. Colleen's face fell. "Oh, I can't give one to Courtney and not Dabney and Whitney. You don't have children, Anne. You wouldn't know how hard it is to see your children be disappointed."

There it was. Colleen's first shot across the bow. She always gave her a dig about not being married and having kids.

Mrs. Lyons turned toward Anne. "There should be a few left. Not everyone showed up." She looked at Colleen. "You heard Mrs. Norton fell last night and broke her hip. Beth is with her at the hospital so that should be two extra favors."

Anne couldn't tell her mother she hadn't finished all the favors, so she whispered a prayer that the last two looked something like bears. While Mrs. Lyons ducked into the kitchen to get the leftover favors, Anne started rolling up the dirty tablecloths, ignoring Colleen.

"So how is Pittsburgh?" Colleen asked, following behind her.

Anne didn't want to answer because she knew how Colleen operated. Anne would reply and she'd use the opportunity to brag about herself.

"It's fine," she said, without looking up.

"We were just in Pittsburgh in May. Actually, the airport. We all flew down to the Cayman Islands. Byron had a conference. It's just a spectacular place. Ever been there, Anne?"

"No," Anne said, stuffing the soiled tablecloth into the trash.

"You really should go. The color of the sea—"

"Here you go, Honey," Anne's mother said as she walked back into the hall and handed Colleen two bears.

"Thanks, Aunt Grace. I was just telling Anne about our latest trip." She glanced down at the favors in her hand. "Oh my, this bear is missing an eye and a bow around his neck."

"They must have fallen off in the car," Anne said.

"Did you make them?" Colleen asked.

"Yes." Anne's tone of voice dared Colleen to make a catty remark.

Colleen chuckled as she looked at the bear in her hand. "It's a good thing you're not making babies."

"Any kids I'd make would be a helluva sight better than ones you and your geek-freak husband produced."

"Anne!" her mother cried.

"Well, at least I have a husband."

"Big deal," Anne snapped, ignoring her mother's warning. "I could have a husband too if I lowered my standards and settled for someone like Byron." Anne said his name in a sing-song voice.

"Girls!" Mrs. Lyons shouted.

Colleen narrowed her eyes. "You're just jealous because he's a well-respected physician, and I have a beautiful house and kids."

"Who are all as ugly as he is."

Colleen's face turned scarlet. She fired the bears at Anne. "You know where you can shove your damn bears. That dried up old place where no man would ever want to go." She spun around and started out the door.

"That's what you think," Anne said as she followed after her. "I'll have you know I've got plenty of men wanting to go there," she shouted out the door.

As Colleen sped away in her Mercedes, Anne hurled the shirt box at her.

Her heart beating in her ears, she turned and saw her mother standing there, her mouth agape.

Anne brushed past her mother who closed her eyes and shook her head, mumbling, "Now you've done it."

Yes, I have. And I feel fantastic.

Chapter 24

Anne felt like hell.

As she drove home into the setting sun, she fought the urge to bypass her exit and drive until she caught the horizon. *Why did I let Colleen get to me like that?* Her father had arrived just as Colleen was storming out. He stood in the doorway, the afternoon sun lighting the thinning red strands atop his head, pointing at his niece. "What's with—?"

Anne shot him a withering look that warned him not to ask. Her mother, her lips firmly set so that it looked as if she were wearing white lipstick, stalked off into the kitchen. Anne headed to the utility closet leaving her father alone in the deserted hall.

When Anne returned, her father looked at her and held his hands open. "What did I miss?"

"You don't want to know," Anne said, handing him a broom. In truth, she didn't want to tell him because she was ashamed of herself. *I must be such a disappointment to him.* She watched her father as he swept the floor. He was such a gentle man. He rarely raised his voice. *He doesn't deserve a daughter like me.* She wished she could leave, but she couldn't abandon them to clean up alone. Anne took down the decorations, rolled up the rest of the soiled paper tablecloths, and stuffed them in the trash.

She dumped the box with the mutant pompom bears in the garbage and wrapped up some cake to take home. As she was about to tell her father to say goodbye to her mother for her, Mrs. Lyons appeared.

"Dan, do you have any steel wool? I was going to scour the stove. Whoever rented this place before us did a lousy job cleaning the burner pans."

Her father felt his pockets. "Oops, sorry must have left my steel wool in my other pants."

Her mother's nostrils flared as she exhaled. "Just what I need. Another person making my life difficult."

Anne took that comment as her cue to leave. She kissed her father on the cheek and waved at her mother and left.

As she drove, she did a mental inventory of all the people who were angry with her—Janetta, Colleen, Claudia, and now her mother, and if she refused Craig's offer, he'd no doubt be angry with her too. Soon there would be no one left to alienate.

Her cell phone rang several times while she drove, but she ignored it. She rationalized that it was unsafe to talk while behind the wheel, but she just didn't want to talk to anyone. When she arrived home, there were three messages on her answering machine. Probably Colleen, her Mother, and Aunt Eileen calling to ream her out, she guessed. Bracing herself, she pressed the button.

"Oh, my God, Anne," Patsy laughed on the tape, "did you really call Byron 'a geek-freak?' That's the best shower gift of all. Finally, someone shut up blowhard Colleen. I wish I had your nerve. I keep calling your cell, but you're not answering. Give me a call when you get home."

One down, Anne thought.

Beep. "Anne, look, this is silly. Steve just had too much to drink the other night. He's been an angel ever since, and you should see the ring he bought me. A ruby. It's gorgeous. You and Craig seemed to be hitting it off. Miss you. Please call me."

Steve an angel? The angel of darkness.

Beep. "Anne, Honey, I'm worried about you." It was her mother. Anne rolled her eyes and mimicked her mother as she removed her suit jacket. "I didn't want to call while you were driving, but Aunt Eileen phoned all upset about how you treated Colleen. I smoothed things over. But I wanted to let you know that I sent Colleen a flower arrangement with an apology and signed your name to it."

"What?" A Venus Flytrap large enough to swallow Colleen and her whole family, Anne hoped.

"Maybe you should reduce your sugar intake, Honey," her mother said. "I heard too much can make you cranky."

Anne kicked off her killer shoes. "Cranky?" she talked back to the machine. "My obnoxious cousin insults my genetic compositions, my best friend is dating Cro-Magnon Man, and to top it off," she said as she bent and looked at her heels, "I have blisters the size of bubble wrap. I have a right to be cranky!"

Anne reached up under her skirt and peeled off her panty hose, tossing them on the back of the chair. She thanked God she didn't have a job that required her to wear hose and heels everyday.

After changing into shorts and a T-shirt, she headed to the kitchen where she got a fork and the shower cake she'd brought home, along with a glass of chocolate milk. Then she took her snack and cordless phone out onto the balcony.

You think sugar is my problem, Mother? Watch this.

While Anne massaged the ankle she'd twisted, she dialed Patsy. She needn't fill her in on the gory details of the argument; her mother had already done so.

"I am so sorry I missed it," Patsy said. "Bet Colleen turned purple."

"Actually," Anne said, digging into the cake, "she was red. Like she'd spent a week under one of Janetta's sunlamps."

"I owe you one. Thanks to your wicked temper, maybe Mom won't insist I invite her to the babies' baptism. She won't want to risk World War III."

My wicked temper hasn't done me a lot of good though, Anne thought.

"Oh, I'm tired," Patsy yawned into the phone. "Opening shower presents is hard work."

"I wouldn't know," Anne said, the words bitter on her tongue.

She'd expected Patsy to say something encouraging like your wedding shower will be the next one, but she only replied, "I'm going to lie down, Anne," and hung up.

Her spirits plumbing new depths of despair, Anne decided there was no better time to call Janetta. She stuffed some more cake into her mouth and punched in the numbers, praying that Steve wouldn't answer. After four rings, she closed her eyes and gently sighed with relief when she reached their machine. She left a brief message. Then shrugging, she pushed the off button and set the phone on the plastic table beside her. There was nothing more she could do. She'd met Janetta half way.

Anne finished her cake and milk and then, exhausted, went back inside and turned in early. The overdose of sugar hadn't left her cranky but jittery. She felt like she had a swarm of bees buzzing in her bloodstream. As she lay staring up at the ceiling, she whispered in the dark, "Dear, St. Anne, I've blown it again. Help. Please."

***

As soon as she limped into the kitchen on Monday morning, she heard Peg calling, "Annie Banannie, is that you?"

The urgency in Peg's voice alarmed her. "Yes?" Anne quickly hobbled to her. "Is something wrong?"

Anne entered and scanned the room and Peg for a problem.

Peg waved her inside. "Why the hell didn't you tell me?"

"Tell you what?" Anne came to the side of the bed.

Peg frowned, shaking her head. "It's not a good sign to be ashamed."

Anne grabbed the bed's metal rail. "Ashamed? What are you talking about?"

Peg picked up Anne's left hand from the rail, looked at it then peered at Anne. "Your ring. Where is it?"

Anne pulled her hand away, letting it hang against her side. "I don't have a ring."

"He's going to let you pick it out?"

Weary, Anne plopped into the chair by the bed. "There's no ring."

Peg crossed her arms over her saggy breasts and focused on Anne. "I don't like to butt my nose in, Dear, but I'd think long and hard before I'd marry a fella who's too darn cheap to pop for a diamond. Especially one who's a doctor."

"He's not too cheap. And I'm not sure I'm going to marry him."

The corners of Peg's mouth twitched, as if wanting to smile. "What? But I thought . . . You told us—" Her voice bubbled over with joy.

Anne covered her face with her hands and groaned.

Peg softened her tone. "What happened?"

Anne gripped the arms of the chair and sprang out of it, then winced as she put weight on her foot. "Look, Peg, what happened is none of your business. I'm your nurse. My personal life is private."

Peg blew out a puff of air. "Pardon me, for taking an interest." Then glancing up at the crucifix hanging on the wall, she addressed Jesus, mumbling, "Another one with a bee up their ass."

Go ahead, Anne, lose your temper with Peg. Ruin another relationship. She touched the old woman's arm, "I'm sorry. I didn't mean to bite your head off. I had a rotten weekend."

Peg tilted her head puppy-like and gazed at Anne sympathetically. "What happened, Dear?"

Sighing, Anne sat down again in the chair and began telling Peg about everything—twisting her ankle, her argument with Colleen, and her offer from Craig.

"Well," Peg said, glancing conspiratorially toward the door, "I don't want Gerry to hear me, but I've got great news."

"I sure could use some."

Peg's eyes twinkled. "Gerry dumped Claudia."

Anne's mouth dropped open. "You're not serious."

"Oh, yes I am. They had a big fight on the phone. He told her she was selfish." Peg's shoulders shook as she chuckled. "And get this, Anne. He told Claudia her boozles were small."

"Boozles?"

"Her breasts."

"He didn't."

"Oh, he most certainly did."

"Oooh, that had to sting," Anne said, trying to contain her glee.

Peg tapped Anne's hand. "Guess what else? She accused Gerry of being in love with you."

Anne tried to speak. Her mouth moved but no words came out. When she managed to form sounds, all that escaped was a humpf and then, "Oh, that's ridiculous."

"Is it?" Peg arched her brows, her eyes boring into Anne.

Anne wanted to ask how Gerry had replied to Claudia's accusation, but she didn't want to encourage Peg. To avoid her stare, Anne began riffling through her bag for her blood pressure cuff.

"You have to admit, Honey, that you and Gerry get along swell. She had reason to be jealous of you."

"Right. She's only beautiful and worth millions. She has every reason to be jealous of me."

"Honey, a woman could be the Queen of Sheba and if she doesn't have what she wants and another woman does, it doesn't matter. She'll be jealous."

That may be, Anne thought, but like Claudia she didn't have Gerry either. She believed that no woman would ever possess him. That observation saddened Anne, but then she thought about the rich, beautiful Claudia being jealous of her, and her spirits lifted.

Gerry didn't show his face upstairs all day. Peg said it was just as well because ever since his phone call on Friday night with Claudia, he'd been surly. Anne thought it was just as well too. She was embarrassed to tell him that Craig hadn't asked her to get married. And even though she felt Claudia had gotten what she deserved, Anne also felt bad that she had come between them.

At five when it was time for her to leave, Irma arrived and then entertained Anne with another blow-by-blow replay of Gerry's phone conversation with Claudia. Then she told her how she and Peg had thought Gerry was a ghost when he'd come home from the hospital.

Anne laughed all the way down the stairs picturing Irma and Peg's faces when they saw what they thought was Gerry's ghost. She imagined the two old women, their eyes bugging out, telling Gerry to go into the light. She was still chuckling as she dug around in her purse for her car keys and walked right into a solid wall of flesh.

"Oops, you OK?" Gerry said as he grabbed her to prevent her from falling. His fingers were strong and firm on her shoulders.

"Oh sorry, Gerry." She tucked a curl behind her ear. "I didn't see you."

"Delirious with love, no doubt."

"I couldn't find my keys."

"I thought maybe you were blinded by the sparkle of your engagement ring." He took her purse.

"Watch, your cut."

"I've got a bandage on it. It'll be OK." He grabbed her left hand. "Let's have a look."

She cast her eyes toward the tin ceiling and tapped her toe impatiently. "Hard to be dazzled by something that's not there," she said sarcastically.

"He asks you to get married and doesn't buy you a ring? Oh what a romantic! Have him call me. I'll give this rookie some pointers on how to woo a woman."

"No need to. I'm not engaged, Gerry." She tried to pull her hand away, but Gerry, looking stunned, held it tightly.

"He didn't ask you to get married?"

"He did and he didn't."

"What does that mean?"

"He asked me to go to Guatemala."

"Guatemala?"

She pulled her hand away. "He wants me to help staff his practice helping disfigured children. He wants me to accompany him as his nurse." She tried to sound unaffected but heard her voice quiver. "And then he said if things work out, we could marry."

"What did you say?"

The tenderness in his eyes unnerved her, sending a large lump to her throat and tears to her eyes.

"Let's go to my office."

"No, I'll be fine." Her lower lip began to quiver. She wanted to leave before she fell apart.

"Liar. Get into my office." He placed a hand on her back, guiding her down the hallway.

"You're limping," Gerry said.

"I twisted my ankle yesterday."

"And I thought my weekend sucked."

She struggled to compose herself. It was bad enough what had happened with Craig, now Gerry was going to make her go into detail. She just wanted to go home. He opened the door and directed her to the couch where he took a seat next to her.

"Now start from the beginning."

She started out rationally, telling Gerry what had happened, then despite all her control, she felt herself crumbling. "I thought he was going to ask me to marry him, Gerry, not join some service project with an option to marry the director if things work out." Hot tears spilled from her eyes. Embarrassed, she hung her head, covering her face with her hands. When she felt Gerry touch her shoulder, she lifted her head.

"What did you tell him, Slugger?"

His gesture touched her and unlocked all the emotions she'd been bottling up. They came out in a flood of tears. "Oh, Gerry, I'm so confused." She sobbed into her hands. Anne flinched when she felt his arms encircle her, but she was weary of being prickly and maintaining her defenses. It felt good to be comforted, and she cuddled into his chest. He was so solid and strong, and he smelled like herbal shampoo, laundry starch and beer. She pulled back and looked at him through her tears. "What am I going to do?"

He pulled her close again and stroked her curls. "What do you want to do?"

"I want to marry a man who's madly in love with me and who doesn't want to live in a mud hut," she sniffled into his chest.

"Did you give him an answer?"

"No. I told him I have to think about it. But if I have to think about it, Gerry, don't you think that means my heart is not in it?"

"You're asking the wrong person, Slugger. I'm no expert on love." He paused. "I broke up with Claudia."

Anne moved away from him and brushed away her tears. "I heard."

"Let me guess, from my mother?"

Anne nodded and straightened up. "I shouldn't be blubbering on you when you've got troubles of your own."

"Aw, I'm OK. I never intended to marry her, but even just being with her was a chore. We never really fit together. We had to force ourselves to be people we weren't to make it work. I'm surprised we lasted this long. What bugs me though is my mother was right." He paused then asked. "I suppose she told you what Claudia said about you."

Anne's blush affirmed that his mother had told her that Claudia had accused him of being in love with Anne.

"I hope I didn't do anything. I mean, we're just good friends," Anne said.

He reached out and brushed a tear from her cheek. "I told her that." As he lightly dragged his finger along her jaw, he whispered, "I told her we were just good friends."

Anne gulped.

He gazed into her eyes and then crushed his lips to hers.

As a nurse, she'd touched all types and textures of skin, from the satiny smooth skin of infants to the thin, crepey flesh of the elderly. But never had she felt skin so warm and exciting as that of Gerry's lips. Startled by the reaction they were causing in her body, Anne's breath caught and she froze a moment. Then something primal asserted itself in her soul, and like a river with a swift current, she let herself be swept along with the passion she felt.

She slid her hands along his face. The stubble of his beard and the smoothness of his cheeks, were a tactile feast. A wanting rose up inside her. Whether it was a need to be comforted or to satisfy the long-burning lust she'd felt for him, she didn't know. What she did know was that she must keep his lips on hers. She kissed him back fiercely, trying to satisfy all those urges.

Gerry plunged his hands into Anne's curls, drawing her even closer, storming her mouth with his tongue. When she finally pulled away, she was panting and her cheeks matched her flaming hair. She stared at him, looking like someone who'd been surprised when a fire flared after dousing it with kerosene.

Chapter 25

After two sleepless nights spent pondering what she should do, Anne knew she had to give Craig her answer. He came to her apartment Wednesday evening bearing a pizza and dressed in his scrubs. God, he is gorgeous, Anne thought, as he entered the apartment. He'll look like a Titan walking amongst the smaller Guatemalans. While they ate, she could sense his nervousness, and her mouth was so dry, she could barely swallow the pizza. They talked of many things but not the subject that was occupying both of their minds—her answer. Anne poured them refills. "Want to go out on the balcony?" she asked.

They stood at the railing looking over the woods behind the apartment complex. Birds chirped their goodnights in a cacophonous racket. Craig slid his arm around her waist. She stared up at him. The setting sun had bathed him in fiery light. He looked handsome like a bronze statue of a god. And that was precisely the problem. He was handsome, perfect, unreal. And non-threatening. He was the path of least resistance. He was no more a man to her than Peg's statue of the Sacred Heart.

"Craig," she said softly, "I can't. As much as I want to want to, I just can't." She knew she had to be insane to refuse a man like him, but she also knew herself and even though men like Zach and Gerry frightened her to the quick, they also made her feel fully alive.

"Please don't be angry with me. I feel like someone who's tossing away a winning lottery ticket, but I can't go to Guatemala with you."

He grasped her shoulders. "I know moving there would be difficult, but I've only committed to five years."

Anne couldn't tell him that Guatemala had been the easy part of the decision. What was really holding her back was him. She placed her hand on top of his. Those long fingers held the skill and magic to transform the lives of disfigured children. But they couldn't transform her twisted heart; she was doomed to fall for bad boys. "I don't want to say no, Craig, but I have to. I'd never be happy living there. I'd miss my family. I want to watch Patsy's babies grow up." She lowered her eyes. "And I'm ashamed to admit it, but I'm too shallow. I'm not cut out for missionary life."

"You're not shallow. You're compassionate and caring. You'd be great there after you get used to the place."

I'm shallow in that I want excitement and passion. "You give me more credit than I deserve."

"You could come home for visits."

She clasped his hand to her heart, wanting to be gentle but firm. "Craig, Guatemala is your dream, not mine."

His shoulders slumped. "Then where does that leave us?"

"I guess as we've always been," Anne said. "Friends." She gave him a peck on the cheek.

He seemed subdued but resigned and only stayed long enough to outline his plans. He'd already sub-let his apartment and planned on leaving as soon as he could tie things up and finalize the arrangements in Guatemala. He estimated he'd been gone in less than two weeks. "It's going to be so crazy, but I want to see you again before I leave."

The fear of being alone once again overwhelmed her, and it so shook her that she almost reached for him and the safety and security he offered. Then she got hold of herself and said softly, "Maybe it's best that we don't."

When Anne walked him to the door, she told Craig to be sure to call her before he left. He hugged her, whispering in her ear, "Why does that line from that poem 'What might have been' keep echoing in my mind?" He put his hand on the doorknob, but before turning it, he swept her up into his arms, kissing her once more. Anne felt him throw everything—his heart and soul—into his kiss, as if to change her mind.

As she pulled away from him and closed the door, she knew she was making the right decision. Safety and security wasn't what she really longed for.

Hugging her waist, she closed her eyes and leaned against the door. *What do I really want?*

Suddenly, her eyes flew open as the truth burst from her heart like a supernova exploding in space.

I want Gerry.

So what? I want world peace and to be 10 pounds thinner, but wanting doesn't mean having. And even though she wanted him, she still wasn't sure that he wouldn't be poison to her. She sighed. *Dear, St. Anne, now what's the plan?*

***

Anne arrived earlier the next morning and found Gerry sitting at the kitchen table, wearing running shorts and a T-shirt, his hands wrapped around a coffee mug.

"Wow, you getting your passport photo taken?" Gerry asked.

"What are you talking about?"

"You. You look great. You have that glow of love."

Anne blushed. "You really don't know much about love, do you?" She paused as he looked quizzically at her. "I told him no."

He set the mug down with a clank and rose. "No kidding?" A smile appeared on his lips. "Well, that's good news. I knew you were confused, but I thought for sure in the end, the handsome doctor would win out. Peg will be so happy."

"What about you, Gerry?"

"What do you mean?"

She stepped toward him, looking into his eyes. "Are you happy?"

He leaned in as if to kiss her then stopped. "Ah, we've got to talk. Can you come down to my office when you're done today?"

***

Anne knocked on Gerry's office door and poked her head inside. When he saw her, he moved his paperwork aside. He looked very serious. "Hey, come on in. Have a seat."

Anne sat in the chair across from the desk. Since Gerry had cut his hand, it had become Anne's routine to stop into the bar to check on his injury before leaving for the day. Wanting to ease the tension, she asked, "How's your hand?"

Gerry extended it across the desk. Anne leaned across the desk and gently lifted the bandage. She slowly brushed her finger over the flesh of his palm. It was pink and healthy and healing nicely. She looked up at Gerry who stared at her with a look of intensity on his face she'd never seen before. With his free arm, he quickly slid his hand under Anne's hair, clasping her neck and pulling her to him, kissing her fiercely across the desk. Then just as swiftly, he drew back, breaking the embrace, leaving Anne slumped over the desk top. "Oh, man, we've got a big problem here," Gerry said, standing and backing away from the desk as if Anne were a bomb ready to detonate.

Anne sat back in the chair. "What's wrong?"

He paced, running his fingers through his thick black hair. "You."

"Me?" Anne asked a bit annoyed.

Gerry looked at her. "And me. Everything."

Anne folded her arms.

He raised his hands as if beseeching God. "I want you, but I don't want to want you."

Anne came up behind him and wrapped her arms around his chest. As she laid her head on his back, she laughed. "Oh, my God, Gerry, I don't want to want you either."

He spun around in her arms. "Great. Now what do we do?"

She fiddled with the buttons on his shirt. "Start a relationship, but promise to hate every minute of it?"

Gerry took both of her hands and held them. "I'm serious. Anne, I've been attracted to you since you walked into the bar, but I know you play this game for keeps. I don't."

She reached up and held his face. "I know that. I know your type. You're a male Molotov cocktail. But after you kissed me in the parking lot, I realized that I can't be happy with nice, safe guys. Unfortunately, I'm defective; I'm attracted to you too."

"So that brings us back to my question: What do we do?"

"Well, I can either quit," Anne said, "or we can start seeing each other." She held her breath, afraid that he'd accept her offer to quit.

"I need you here so I guess we're going to have to suck it up and go with it."

"I guess we have no other choice."

"So our professional arrangement is over? You won't deck me if I touch you?"

"No, you'll be safe."

"Good, but because this could blow up in our faces, I think it would be a good idea to keep our relationship a secret."

"You mean keep it from your mother?"

"And Irma. I don't want them to get their hopes up in case we want to call it all off."

"OK, now that that's settled," Anne said. "I think you should kiss me."

"Yeah, I guess I better," Gerry said, with the enthusiasm of patient waiting to have a tooth drilled.

When their lips met, their desire rekindled. Anne felt as if all the tethers that had been binding her broke, freeing her to enjoy Gerry.

She was breathing heavily when their lips parted. Anne looked up into Gerry's indigo eyes and said, "Wow! I'd hate to see what would happen if we really wanted to want each other."

***

"They seem to be hitting it off," Irma said on Wednesday night. "Annie flits around Gerry like a moth around a flame. And he can't take his eyes off her."

"But they haven't even gone out together," Peg said frowning. "We need to speed things up a bit. Throw them together. But how?"

"What about that wedding you've got coming up? Why doesn't Gerry take Anne?"

"I've already suggested that," Peg said, the wheels turning in her mind, "and he nixed the idea. But Claudia was in the picture then. I could bring it up again. I can say I need Anne's assistance. Only problem is they still won't be alone, because I'll be there too."

"Maybe when the day arrives you can say you don't feel up to going."

"Oh, but I really want to go."

"Couldn't you go and leave early?"

Peg smiled. "You are so good at secret operations, you should work for the CIA. I'll give Marty's cousin, Mary Gallagher, a call and fill her in on my plan. Maybe she could drive me home early, and then Gerry can have some time alone with Anne and take her home by himself."

"Maybe they'll do the nasty." Irma blushed, covering her mouth as she tittered.

Peg frowned. "The what?"

"The nasty. Sex," Irma whispered. "That's what they call it on MTV."

"I certainly hope they don't do that," Peg said, rolling her eyes. "He's done the 'nasty' with enough women. I hope he does the honorable thing. I know he'll try something, but I hope Anne's smart enough not to let him get anywhere. That'll make her more desirable."

"The old why buy an appetizer when the hors d'oeuvres are free?" Irma smiled shyly. "Heard that on MTV too."

"Why in the hell are you watching that trash?"

"Oh, Bernie's been watching it for news on the KISS concert."

Peg made her lips tight. "I don't think I'd let him watch that, Irma. All those girls gyrating, it might give him ideas."

The next day when Gerry brought in Peg's breakfast, she slid the wedding invitation toward him. "It's the twenty-ninth. You know we have to reply by September 6. Are you going to take anyone?"

"No, I could ask someone, but I really don't know a girl worthy of my charms." He winked at Peg.

"In that case," Peg said, "I'd like to take a guest."

"You would?" He looked suspiciously at his mother and smiled. "Have you been calling up that singles network they advertise on TV?"

"No, Smartass," Peg said, sipping her decaf. "I want to ask Anne to be my guest. She could help me get around and take me to the ladies room. When she gets here, I'm going to ask her."

"Why don't you let me do it?" He tapped the invitation against his lips, narrowing his eyes. "She has a hard time refusing you, and I don't want to impose on her if she has other plans that day."

"OK," Peg said, containing a smile so that he wouldn't realize that he'd swallowed her bait whole. "Maybe it would be better if you asked her."

***

Gerry had gotten so busy on Friday he'd had no opportunity to ask Anne to the wedding. Perturbed, Peg kept on him all Saturday morning. He called Anne in the afternoon, but couldn't reach her on her cell or home phone. He didn't leave a message, because he wanted to invite her in person.

Sunday, his only day off, dawned bright and clear. While Irma came over to visit with Peg after church, Gerry took his convertible out for a drive. After checking on his place at Washington's Landing, he punched Anne's address into his GPS and set out for her apartment.

He parked in front of her building, and after appraising himself in the rearview mirror, he strode to the entrance and went inside, where he pressed the buzzer to her apartment

"Yes?" Anne's voice came squawking out of the speaker.

"It's Gerry."

"Gerry? Gerry! What are—"

"I was out driving around," he talked into the speaker, "and I found myself in the area. Thought I'd stop by. But if this is a bad time—"

"No! No. It's a good time. Come on up."

Gerry heard the security door unlatch, and he headed for the stairs.

***

Inside the apartment, Anne turned into a tornado of activity. When the buzzer had sounded, she had just kicked off her black sandals and was going to changing out of her church clothes. *What is he doing here?* Since deciding to pursue a relationship, they'd only had a few moments to steal into his office to be alone. He'd seemed fine when she'd left on Friday after using the pretense of meeting him in his office to check up on his hand. And when he took a few moments last night from the frenzy in the bar to call her, he'd been in a great mood. Maybe he met someone else?

She quickly tidied the Sunday paper and stuffed her breakfast dishes in the dishwasher while she wiggled out of her black Capri pants. Dashing into her room, she threw off her white cotton sleeveless blouse, grabbed a teal printed cotton dress and slithered into it. Balling up her church clothes, she threw them in the bottom of her closet.

Gerry knocked on her door. She slid her feet into a pair of white open-toed mules.

She exhaled deeply and opened the door. Gerry stood there leaning on the doorframe. He was dressed in an electric blue sport shirt that intensified the color of his eyes and a pair of jeans that were worn in places that accentuated all the right areas on him. "Sorry, Anne, I should have called first."

"Is Peg OK?"

"She's fine. Irma's with her."

"Good," Anne said. "Well, come on in."

218

He stepped inside. "Hope I'm not interrupting anything."

Anne swept her hand toward the dining room table. "I was just reading the paper."

"You always look this good when you read the paper?"

She smiled. "Only the Sunday paper." She waved her hand toward the couch. "Have a seat."

He touched her arm. "Look, I've got the top down on my car and it's a gorgeous day. Want to go for a ride?"

Still not certain what he wanted, she hesitated then said, "Yeah, sure. Why not?"

As they walked to the car, Gerry put on his sunglasses. While he started the car, Anne found a ponytail holder in her purse and tied back her curls. Then she put on her sunglasses too. The sun was intense but the air rushing over her skin as they drove kept her cool. She enjoyed how the other motorists stared at them. He was made for convertibles, and sitting beside him, she felt as glamorous as Grace Kelly cruising The Riviera.

The traffic was too noisy to hold much of a conversation. Gerry called over the din, "How about an ice cream cone?"

"Sure," she said.

He pulled into a stand on the outskirts of North Park. Anne joined him at the window, where he ordered them both large vanilla cones.

"Want to sit by the lake?" he asked.

The day was rapidly getting warmer. "It's probably cooler there."

Anne held Gerry's ice cream cone while he drove the short distance to the lake, periodically handing it back to him to lick up the drips. They found a vacant grove near the shore, walked through the sun-browned grass, and sat on a bench. It was shady and a light breeze blew from the lake. The scent of smoke from of a barbecue grill wafted their way. The lake was still, reflecting the sky and billowy clouds on its glassy surface.

She watched Gerry licking his ice cream cone. Anne found herself fantasizing about his tongue and the pleasure it could induce.

"When I was a kid," he said between licks, "I thought North Park was in the country."

Anne laughed. "If I'd have come here as kid, I would have thought it was the city. I guess it's a matter of perspective."

Gerry was silent for a while; the mystery of what he wanted was killing her. He took one more swipe at the ice cream then finished the cone while he looked out over the lake. "That's kind of what I wanted to talk to you about."

Anne finished her ice cream. "I don't follow."

"Perspective. How two people can see the same thing differently."

He turned to her, gently placing a hand on her shoulder. "Could you have gotten sunburned already?"

Anne glanced down at her skin where Gerry's hand lingered. She shivered. "Probably. I burn so easily."

He moved his hand toward her neck, stroking the side of her throat with his thumb. "That's what I find so attractive about you, Anne," he said, his blue eyes searing her heart. "Under that ferocious temper, I sense that you're fragile and easily burned."

Anne lowered her eyes, embarrassed that he could read her so well.

He brushed back her hair and kissed her neck, his lips chilly from the ice cream on her warm skin. Goosebumps rose along her spine, giving her a chill even though it was eighty-six degrees.

He took her hand. "I don't know about you, Anne, but I think things have been going great. Between us, I mean. How do you see it?"

"I agree." She smiled impishly. "I haven't wanted to hit you once."

"Good," he said. His eyes warmed her like a tropical sea.

He kissed her temple. She closed her eyes and moaned involuntarily. Then he whispered into her ear, "Now that that's settled. I want to ask you something."

"Yes," Anne heard herself croak.

"Would you go to my cousin's wedding with me? We haven't had a chance to go anywhere because with my schedule, it takes a damn near act of God to get a Saturday night off, so at least we'll have a real date to look forward to."

She opened her eyes and did something she'd longed to do. She played with the curls at the nape of his neck. "I'd love to."

"But the only thing is. . . "

Anne held her breath waiting for the caveat.

"See, my mother wanted me to ask you to go as her nurse." Anne felt her spirits plunging. It must have reflected on her face. He took her hand. "I want you to go as my date, but I hate how she meddles in my life. So as a favor to me, Anne, could you please keep up our charade, pretending that you're going as her nurse? Only you and I will know you're really my date."

"Sure," she said.

He touched her chin, bringing her lips to his, kissing her gently. His lips cool tasted of vanilla.

"Ahh," she sighed.

She'd don grease paint and leather pants and pretend to be Gene Simmons if he wanted.

Chapter 26

Anne looked over her shoulder at the back of her dress. *It certainly is skimpy.* That observation sent her rushing back to her closet to search for something else to wear. Although Gerry had been nothing but sweet to her, she still was a bit wary of him. She wasn't sure if this sexy dress was leaving her vulnerable.

The weeks leading up to Maeve McMaster's wedding had been some of the happiest of Anne's life. Even when Craig called to say goodbye, it didn't depress her. Why shouldn't she be happy? She was in love. Unlike with Craig, where she had mistaken affection and safety for passion, she was sure that what she felt for Gerry was genuine. She hadn't yet professed to him how deeply she felt for him, but tonight if the evening went as she dreamed, that would all change. She planned to tell him that she loved him.

Gerry also hadn't declared how he felt about her either, but from the way he spent every free moment with her and how ardent his kisses were, she sensed that he was in love with her too.

After finding nothing in her closet, she gazed at herself once again in the mirror. The dress, a plum crepe sheath that skimmed and accentuated her curvaceous figure, plunged into a deep V terminating at the small of her back. It was daring, but that's exactly what she had in mind when she purchased it. It was time to start taking chances. It was time to take a chance on love.

Along with the dress, she'd also splurged on shoes with skyscraper heels and a matching bag. Her afternoon had been spent at the salon where she had a manicure and pedicure and had the stylist arrange her hair into an upsweep of red curls. The amethyst earrings and bracelet that she already owned added just enough glitter to enliven the darkly hued dress.

Even though she wanted to be a head-turner in the nearly backless dress, she felt it was a bit too bare for church. She had made another purchase in the accessories department—a plum satin wrap that would cover her back in church. The wrap was her security blanket in case she lost her nerve. Anne was walking a tightrope. She wanted to dazzle Gerry but not look cheap.

The buzzer sounded. Too late to change now. Anne trembled with anticipation as she walked to the intercom and pressed the button. "Hello?"

"It's me." Gerry's voice sounded deep and sexy. Tingles traveled her spine.

Anne released the lock. "Come on up." She dashed to the mirror for one last look, then stood by the door, her hand resting on her chest, trying to calm herself as she waited for his knock. When she finally opened it to greet him, she felt that same rush she'd experienced the night she'd first seen him in his tuxedo. The navy suit he'd recently purchased for the occasion gave him an air of sexy sophistication.

"You look fantastic," she said, thinking that didn't nearly come close. "It's a wonder the women in the bar ever let you out."

He smiled, the dimple in his cheek twinkling, as he patted his breast pocket. "I have a stun gun. They get too close. Zap."

Anne felt as if he'd already used one on her. She laughed nervously. "I'll keep that in mind."

"For you, I'll turn it off."

She smiled. "I'm ready—just let me get my things."

Before she could move, he took her hand, pulling her closer, kissing her neck. "Speaking of stunning, you look fabulous."

Anne blossomed under his approval. "Thank you."

She broke free turning toward the table to pick up her bag and wrap.

"Wow, Slugger, I think you forgot the back of your dress."

She gasped and straightened up. "I knew it was too much. I'll find something else to wear. It'll only take me a minute." She turned, heading for her room.

He grabbed her arm, stopping her short. "Don't change." He picked up her bag and wrap and handed them to her. "You look beautiful. No man in his right mind would ever tell you to change out of that dress."

"What do you think Peg will say?"

"Don't worry." He glided his hand along side her neck and fiddled with her earring. "I think you look great. So will she."

She arranged the swath of purple fabric over her shoulders. Anne walked out the door with Gerry following behind. As she locked her apartment door, he whispered in her ear. "Lose the shawl." Then he gave the fabric a tug, pulling it off.

***

Autumn sunlight gave the world a golden glow as they drove back to Mac's Place to pick up Peg. When they arrived there, Anne was surprised to see that a crowd was waiting for them. Peg sat at a table with Irma. Dave, Bernie, and Luis stood at the bar. As she walked into the room, Dave wolf-whistled, making her blush.

Luis strode over and kissed her hand. "I am undone by your beauty."

Anne giggled. "Oh, Luis."

Bernie did his flipper wave. "Hi, Anne. You look pretty."

Touched by his sincerity, she got a bit choked up, but managed to say, "Thank you, Bernie."

"Oh, Kiddo," Peg said, as Anne came over to her, "aren't you the fashion plate!"

"You don't look so bad yourself." It pleased Anne to see Peg looking so well. She was wearing a silver blue dress embellished at the neck and sleeves with crystal beading. She was glad Dolly had talked Peg into letting her hair go natural. It was a soft shade of white and now that it had been set and teased, it looked like white cotton candy.

"Hell, anything would look better than my housecoat."

Irma patted Anne's arm, smiling. Then she looked around. "Where's Vera? She wanted to see you."

"She went in the back to get some cherries," Dave said. "Bob went to help her."

"Bernie," Gerry said, "would you please go and get them?"

Bernie toddled off while Irma took pictures of Anne, Gerry, and Peg.

"Jeez, I feel like I'm going to the prom," Peg exclaimed.

Bernie came back and stood next to the wedding-goers, obviously wanting to have his picture taken too.

"Are they coming?" Gerry asked as he posed with Bernie.

The camera flashed then Bernie announced. "Yeah, they were busy sucking face again."

"What?" Gerry cried.

Dave's and Anne's mouths dropped open.

"Sucking face?" Peg asked. "What's that mean?"

"Kissing," Irma said.

"How do you know that?" Peg said.

Irma grinned. "Heard it on MTV."

"Vera and Bob? Are you sure?" Gerry asked Bernie.

"I'm not sure. I'm Bernie."

"What I mean is," Gerry said "were Bob and Vera kissing?"

"Yeah, they do it all the time. They like each other."

"That explains why Bob is always so eager to get supplies." Dave smiled. "That old dog."

Vera and Bob walked into the bar each carrying a large jar of maraschino cherries. Her cheeks were flushed and his thin hair was disheveled. Everyone smiled politely at the pair.

"Don't you all look lovely," Vera said. Bob nodded in agreement.

Peg slapped her hand on the table. "So what's with the hanky-panky in the stock room?"

Everyone chuckled. Then Vera began to laugh as Bob turned the color of the cherries.

"Mother!" Gerry cried.

"It's OK," Vera said. "You found us out."

Bob cleared his throat and stepped forward. "If there's a problem, I'll resign."

"For making out in the stockroom?" Gerry said. "Why, I've already—" His eyes traveled to Anne, who blushed and stared at her shoes.

The only places Anne and Gerry could carve out some privacy had been in his office and the stock room. Often he would catch her while she was walking past the stock room door and pull her inside for a kiss.

"No," Bob said, straightening his posture and wrapping an arm around Vera, "for being married."

"Married?" Peg cried. "Who's married?"

Vera looked starry-eyed at Bob. "We are."

"I hope there's no rule about married couples working together here," Bob said.

"If there was," Gerry laughed, "my father would have had to fire my mother."

Everyone swarmed around Bob and Vera congratulating them and hugging them.

"When did you get married?" Anne asked.

"Last weekend," Vera said, holding Bob's hand.

"You don't waste any time, do you, Bob?" Dave said

Bob smoothed down his hair. "Well, when it's right, you just know it."

Vera beamed at her new husband.

"Why didn't you tell us?" Gerry asked.

"We didn't want to make a fuss. And Bob was nervous about standing in front of a crowd."

"Well, you could have at least told us afterwards. I would have given you some time off for a honeymoon."

"Hmph," Peg snorted, "instead of taking it in the stockroom."

Gerry shook his head at his mother's comment.

"We really can't afford to take the time off," Vera said.

Gerry put his arm around her. "How about as my wedding gift to you, next weekend you two take off at my expense and you can you use my place on Washington's Landing? The back deck overlooks the river."

"Oh, Mac, you're the best," Vera exclaimed and hugged him. Bob shook his hand.

Peg rose on her shaky legs, gripping her cane. "Well, I hate to break up the party, but we have another wedding. I don't want to be late."

She shuffled out to the parking lot with Gerry and Anne aiding her. Irma followed like a lady-in-waiting carrying her pocketbook.

While Gerry unlocked the doors, Peg looked all around. "I haven't been out of the apartment since I came home from the hospital. Lazarus has arisen from the dead."

After Gerry opened the passenger side door, Peg started for the front seat, then said, "I'll sit in the back."

Anne protested, but Peg wouldn't hear of it. They settled her in the back seat with her cane.

"Have a good time," Irma called while waving. Peg winked and gave her friend a thumbs-up as they pulled out.

***

"Oh, it feels so good to get out." Peg turned toward the window, taking in the sights of Butler Street.

She put her hand on Anne's seat and leaned forward. "Doesn't my Gerry look handsome tonight, too?"

Anne turned to look at Peg. "He does clean up rather nicely." Gerry smiled and slid his hand over and patted Anne's knee.

His gesture didn't escape Peg's notice. Everything was progressing according to plan. Satisfied, Peg sat back and enjoyed the ride, thinking how what she was wearing would make a lovely mother-of-the groom dress.

It was a short ride to St. Paul Cathedral in nearby Oakland. Anne noticed that the leaves bore the first blushes of crimson and rust, and high wispy clouds floated in the blue Indian summer sky past the tall spire of the church. Gerry pulled in front of the massive stone cathedral, put on his flashers, and dashed around the back of the car to help his mother. Taking his arm, Peg slowly ascended the stone stairs. Anne scurried ahead of them to open the huge door. As they reached the last step, Anne pulled on the handle, her shawl sliding off her shoulder. She fumbled with it and the door. When Peg caught sight of her bare back, she let out a whistle that would make a construction worker proud.

Embarrassed, Anne struggled to cover herself and keep the huge door from closing on Peg and Gerry.

As they entered the hushed vestibule filled with people waiting to be escorted to their seats, Gerry transferred Peg to Anne's arm. "I'm going to move the car before it gets towed," he said. When he opened the door to leave, his mother, in a voice loud enough to reverberate throughout the vestibule, proclaimed, "I guess you're not wearing a bra under there, Annie Banannie."

Anne felt all eyes scanning her. Her cheeks burned scarlet with embarrassment. Gerry rolled his eyes at Anne and quickly left the cathedral.

An usher, whom Peg explained was a nephew, escorted them to a seat near the front with the family. Anne wished she were sitting in the back so that all those behind her could not sit in their pews speculating whether or not she was wearing underwear. A few minutes later, Gerry slid into the pew next to Anne just seconds before the parents of the groom and the bride's mother, his Aunt June, were seated.

Anne sat through the nuptial Mass enraptured by the beauty of the ceremony. Tears welled in her eyes when the couple exchanged vows, promising to love each other in good times and bad, in sickness and health, for richer or poorer. When I marry, those are the kind of vows I want to take, she thought. Not those lame ones they recite at Hollywood weddings, where the starlet says something vague like I promise to help you grow to be the best you can be. And the leading man says something as equally non-committal.

When she got married, she wanted it all spelled out. She wanted to know where she stood, what was being put on the line. In short, she wanted promises. She wondered as the priest introduced the new Mr. and Mrs. Norris, whether she would ever have that.

She smiled at Gerry. "Wasn't that beautiful?"

"Now that we've gotten that out of the way, let's go have some fun," he said.

The reception was held at the Pittsburgh Field Club. The huge ballroom was filled with flowers. The scent of lavender and roses perfumed the air. There was a champagne fountain and ice carvings and an orchestra playing, "Misty."

After navigating the receiving line and fielding kisses and compliments from his Uncle Fran, Aunt June, and Cousin Maeve and her new spouse, Gerry led them to their assigned table. People were already seated around it. They were more relatives—his father's cousin, Mary Gallagher, and some of her grown children.

Mary, who was in her late-sixties, rose and gave Peg a big hug and kiss. Peg introduced Anne to the family. "Mary, this is Anne, my nurse and good friend." She turned to Anne. "Mary and I have been friends since the day Martin introduced us," Peg said. "She was a junior bridesmaid in our wedding."

"Both Fran and I were in it." The gray-haired woman made a gesture with her hand to the father of the bride, who was busy greeting guests, martini in hand.

"This wedding was nothing like mine," Peg said. "We held it at the bar, and my mother and her lady friends made all the food."

"We've certainly come a long way." Mary laughed as she surveyed the opulent ballroom.

"Oh, Fran would like us all to forget that he's nothing but pig-shit Irish, wouldn't he?" Peg said.

Everyone laughed while Gerry covered his face with his hand. "I need a drink," he whispered. He and Anne went to fetch a round.

After everyone had been served, Gerry and Anne began to mingle. Mike, his paunchy, middle-aged cousin, poked Gerry in the ribs and winked at him when introduced to Anne.

Dinner was an elaborate five-course meal. Afterward, the orchestra picked up the tempo and began to play dance music. The crystal chandeliers were dimmed. Cousin Mike, who had taken great advantage of the open bar, walked over to their table and asked Anne to dance. She sputtered, trying to make an excuse. Gerry stood, holding out his hand to her. "Sorry, Mike, she's promised them all to me."

"Peg," Gerry said. "I hope you don't mind if I steal a dance with your nurse."

Peg smiled. "I'm fine. Go have some fun."

Gerry took Anne's hand, leading her toward the dance floor. As they threaded their way through the crowd, he laughed, "I think Mike's taken with you."

"I think he's taken with St. Pauli Girl," Anne replied, referring to the bottle of beer in his beefy hand.

The dance floor was packed; they made their way to an open spot. Gerry slid his arm around her, placing a hand on her bare back.

Anne kept a respectable distance between their bodies. Gerry's hand, like a branding iron on her bare skin, held her gently. She wondered if it would leave an imprint on her flesh.

The rhythm of the orchestra and the hypnotic swaying of their bodies calmed her, coaxing the nervous tension from her. Little by little, she melted into Gerry's body until there was no longer any distance between them. The stiletto heels made her taller, elevating her head so that it came to his chest. She rested it next to his heart, closed her eyes, and inhaled his intoxicating cologne. She could feel the strength of his muscles beneath the gabardine suit as he held her tightly. The heat from his body penetrated her and fused them together. She would be content to spend eternity like this.

Lost in his arms, she was no longer conscious of their movement or of anything else. Their bodies were like a slow moving centrifuge that spun away reality leaving only Anne and Gerry forged together in the center with a thousand sensations. Anne began to feel a little dizzy. *This is what it means to swoon.* She'd always wondered when she read old novels what that felt like. Now she knew.

She stepped back from Gerry for a little air. His smile and the dreamy look in his eyes told Anne that he was also languishing in the same pleasurable sensations.

Gently pulling her back into him, he softly kissed the top of her head and his fingers inched under the dress until they nearly skimmed the side of her breast. A shiver surged through her body.

They stayed enmeshed on the dance floor until the orchestra finished its set. Slowly, he released her from his arms. She led them through the labyrinth of tables back to their place.

Anne observed the wistful smiles on the two old women's faces as she and Gerry sat down at the table. She knew they had been aware of the magic taking place on the dance floor. Anne took a sip of her drink. There was an awkward silence. Mary fanned herself and said, "My, it's close in here." Everyone nodded in agreement.

Peg, never at a loss for words, said, "Speaking of close. Could you two have gotten any nearer? The nuns used to make us leave room for the Holy Ghost to come between us when I was girl and going to dances." She shrugged. "Oh well, you looked nice together out there. Reminds me of my Martin. He was quite the stepper." Peg looked thoughtful for a moment. "I've never told you this, Gerry, but you were conceived after we came home from a wedding. I think the dancing got your Dad in the mood." She rolled her eyes devilishly as she struck a dance pose and sashayed in her seat.

Anne giggled.

"Thanks for sharing that, Mother," Gerry said dryly.

Peg had started to go into the miraculous details of his conception and birth when it was announced that the bridal party would now have their turn on the floor. Gerry looked at Anne. "Let's cool off outside."

They walked through the French doors onto the terrace that overlooked the rolling hills of the golf course. Muffled music and clapping as the bridal party was announced filtered outside. Anne stood looking off in the distance. It was twilight now. The sun had melted below the horizon in a puddle of peach light, backlighting the shadowy trees. The evening's first stars twinkled to a chorus of cicadas.

"Oh, how beautiful" she murmured, closing her eyes and slowly taking in the cool September air. It was laced with the sweet smell of ripe apples and turning leaves.

"Yes," Gerry said. Anne opened her eyes and found he was not looking out on the grounds but at her.

Gerry kissed her.

Could this night be any more perfect? she wondered. Slowly they pulled away from each other. Anne rested her head on his chest, savoring the splendor of the moment.

He wrapped his arms around her. "Are you cold?"

Anne shook her head and lay there listening to his beating heart, wondering if it was bursting with joy like hers. *God, I love him. I think he loves me too.*

Someone near the door called that they were cutting the wedding cake. They agreed that they probably should go back in. A crowd had gathered around the bride and groom as they cut the multi-tiered confection. A photographer with high-powered lights captured every moment. Calls of "smash it" came as the newlyweds fed each other bits of cake.

When they went back to their table, Peg yawned loudly. "Gerry," she said, "Mary's going to take me home. I'm pooped."

"Are you sure you don't mind, Aunt Mary? If my mother's tired, we can leave now," Gerry said.

"Don't be silly. Stay and enjoy yourself. We'll have a nice visit."

"I won't be too late," Gerry said. "I have to get up early. I'm running in the Great Race tomorrow morning."

Gerry and Anne helped Peg and Aunt Mary to the entrance and waited for the valet to retrieve the car. On her way out, Peg had grabbed a piece of wedding cake. "Don't forget," she warned Anne, "to get some too. They say if you sleep with it under your pillow, you'll be the next to get married."

Anne assured her she wouldn't forget. Between the magic of this night, wedding cake, and prayers to St. Anne, how could she not be the next one to get married?

Chapter 27

After a respectable amount of time, Gerry and Anne said their goodbyes to the bride and groom. As they passed by the bar, Cousin Mike, who was draped over the top like a rag on a nail, picked his head up, looked at Anne with bleary eyes, and slurred, "I never got my dance."

"Maybe next time," she said.

Gerry thanked his uncle for a lovely evening, and Judge McMaster shook his hand. "You are the spitting image of your old man. Your father would be very proud of you, Gerard. You turned the bar into a grand success. Now all you need is a wife and son to pass it on to." He winked at Anne with tears glistening in the old man's eyes. "Take care of your mother." He slapped Gerry's back and strode away.

On the way out the door, Anne heeded Peg's reminder and grabbed a piece of wedding cake wrapped in a monogrammed bridal napkin. As they waited for the valet, Anne held the cake. It smelled so delicious, she believed it might possess magical properties. *Dear St. Anne, I'll take whatever help I can.*

***

It was early, only ten o'clock, when they got back to her apartment, and Anne asked if Gerry would like to come inside. While she poured herself some wine and Gerry a beer, she battled with her conscience. She'd promised God she wouldn't have sex again until she had gotten married, but that promise had been easy to make then. The man she had fallen in love with hadn't been sitting on her couch when she'd taken her vow. *What am I going to do? I'm sure he's expecting me to make love to him.* She took a large gulp of wine and headed into the living room.

She set the drinks on the coffee table and Gerry closed his cell phone. "Called Peg. She's fine. Sounds like a party there. Irma came over for a blow-by-blow description of the wedding and to sample the cookies my mother stashed in her purse."

"What?"

"Didn't you see her? She was slipping them into her purse all evening. She must have two dozen in there."

"That little sneak. They're not on her diet."

"I know. She's like a teenager with cigarettes. I can't police her all the time. Anyway, Irma's going to stay with her until I get home."

Anne kicked off her heels while Gerry took off his tie, stuffed it into his jacket pocket, and draped the jacket over the back of the dining room chair. Then he sat next to Anne on the couch.

"I think she enjoyed herself," Anne said. "She's progressed so well. You know, she probably could do without me now."

"That may be." Gerry gazed deeply at her, his blues eyes washing over. "But I couldn't."

"You always know exactly what to say." Anne snuggled closer.

Gerry noticed her bare feet. "Do you mind if I kick off my shoes too?"

"No, go ahead. That's your beer."

He slipped out of his tasseled wingtips and unbuttoned his collar. Then he leaned forward and picked up his Yuengling. "What shall we drink to?"

"I don't know."

"How about we toast . . . " Gerry thought for a second. "Me."

She laughed. "You?"

"Yes, me. I kept Mike away from you all evening, didn't I?"

"True." She took her drink in hand and ceremoniously hoisted it. "Here's to Gerard McMaster, a true knight in shining armor. A friend to maidens everywhere."

They clinked their glasses then both took a sip. Anne reached forward to put her glass on the table, and when she leaned back on the couch, she noticed Gerry's arm was now around her. There were a few moments of awkward silence, weighted with anticipation. He put his beer on the end table to the side of the couch and smiled at her, a smile that held a million promises. "You'd think I'd let him steal you away?"

Nobody could do that. I'm all yours, Gerry, if you want me.

He took her hand and brought it to his lips, kissing each fingertip.

Blood surged in her. If this was her reaction to his kissing her fingertips, she was afraid she'd perish when his lips moved elsewhere. He slowly slid his hand up her bare arm to her cheek and gently turned her face toward him. His eyes locked on hers and he kissed her.

She moved her hands up his broad chest, around his neck, returning the fever of his lips. Then a force took over in Anne. Love, like a tidal wave, swept her up, and she began to consume him with kisses. Slowly, deliberately she kissed the curve where his shoulders met his neck, his eyelids, the tip of his nose. She ran her hands through his thick curly hair.

She heard Gerry moan with every brush of her lips and stroke of her hand, giving her confidence in her skill. She'd only been with one man so she was a bit afraid she wouldn't be as exciting as all the other women he'd been with.

He eased her back on the couch, shifting his weight so that he was on top of her. Her heart started to pound wildly, from arousal. From fear. Somehow he'd taken the lead, and she could feel herself losing control, feel the power of his passion. She flashed back to when she had been with Zach. *Do I want this? Am I ready for this?* He kissed her, as he ran his hand up her thigh. *Do I want Gerry?*

The early warning system that had kept Anne safe for years triggered. Sirens and buzzers sounded in her brain. Gerry was breaching her security. With his head buried in her neck nuzzling her flesh, she fought with herself. She wanted him, and yet she knew this went against all the promises she'd made to herself and to God. *How can I refuse him when every other woman he's had a relationship with has been giving him free samples?*

He slid his hand back down her thigh and then moved it to her shoulder.

God forgive me. Please don't be angry with me. I know what I did with Zach was terrible, but this time it's different. Don't I deserve another chance? I love Gerry. And I'm sure he loves me too. It's not like this is some random hook-up.

Gerry began to slide her dress off her shoulder. "Oh, my Anne. You're even more beautiful than I had fantasized."

Her breathing became more rapid and shallow as he kissed the hollow at the base of her neck.

It had been so long since she'd felt this way, and it surprised her that her ability to be passionate still remained in her. She'd thought it, along with so many other things, had died when her relationship with Zach ended. It felt so glorious to be held, to be wanted, to be loved again.

Clinging tightly to Gerry, she was overcome with emotion and desire for him, and it terrified her to allow herself to become so vulnerable. But she promised herself she'd no longer hold back. She astonished even herself when she heard herself whispering in his ear, "I love you, Gerry."

He sat up and quickly began to unbutton his shirt. Anne, too, sat up and touched his cheek. Looking deeply into his eyes, the ones that had devastated her the first time she gazed into them, she said more emphatically, "I love you, Gerry." And she kissed him hard on the mouth.

They were both panting when their lips parted, and she waited for his response. He seemed even more consumed with desire for her and began to work more furiously to get his clothes off.

"Did you hear me, Gerry? I said I love you."

"Uh, huh."

Anne ran her hands over the taut muscles of his chest. His flesh was feverish. "Gerry, I said I love you. You love me, don't you?"

"Oh, you know I do." He was struggling with the buttons of his cuffs.

Anne grabbed his hands. "Stop, Gerry. Look at me." When she held his gaze she asked: "Do you love me?"

He broke free and practically ripped the buttons at his wrist off. Then he took her face in his hands. "I love your lips," he said as he kissed her ravishingly. He slid his hands down her spine so that back arched and brought her flesh to his lips. "I love your creamy skin," he said nibbling on her neck. "And this blue vein," he said, blazing a trail of kisses, "that goes all the way to your lovely breasts."

"I know you love all of that, but do you love me?"

"Oh, yeah. Sure." He eased her back onto the couch. His fingers moved to his belt.

She scooted upright. "No, Gerry. I don't want a 'yeah, sure.' I want to hear you say you love me."

"I love you," he said quickly while tugging on his belt.

She crossed her arms. "You didn't say that with conviction."

He leaned in and tried to kiss her, but she turned her head.

"Oh, come on, Anne. Work with me here."

She batted his hand away. "Oh, come on yourself."

"Anne, what the hell's the problem?"

"Do you love me? Answer me right now!"

"What's this? Your version of 'Paradise by the Dashboard Light'?"

She pushed him off her.

He sat back, letting out a heavy sigh. "Geez, Anne. OK. OK. I love you." He tried to kiss her, but she turned her head.

She felt tears coming, but she choked them back. "No, you don't. You're just saying it."

"If you mean do I like you and want to be with you, then yeah I love you. Isn't that what love is? Isn't that enough?"

"No." She could feel her anger starting to bubble up. "You can like and want to be with a dog."

She began to pull up the straps of her dress.

"Aw, come on, Anne. Don't get all Oprah on me. What is love anyway?" He tried to nibble on her neck.

He takes me for some kind of fool. "What is love? What is love, Gerry?" Her voice was becoming shrill.

He stared at her like he hadn't a clue what was going on, which made her furious.

"I'll tell you what love is," she roared. "It's your mother being so connected to your father that even decades after his death, she still misses him. It's my pregnant sister being big as a house and my brother-in-law, seeing her as some beauty queen. And it's me, Gerry," as she moved to get off the couch, "being foolish enough to ignore my head because my heart was telling it that I loved you."

He grabbed her arm and pulled her back down beside him. "Oh come on, can't we figure all this stuff out afterward?" He nuzzled her neck and she jerked away.

"So I can be another notch on your bedpost?" She shoved him. "No way."

"You invite me in here, get all cozy and then spring this soap opera crap on me. What is wrong with you?"

She rocketed off the couch. "What's wrong with me? You're nearly forty years old, and you don't even know what love is. You think you're Don Juan, screwing every girl you lay your baby blues on, but you're really a coward who can't sustain a relationship."

He stood, his face turning red. "Listen, sweetheart, every girl I've ever been with has gone away happy."

"Yeah, they were happy with you for the moments that their orgasm lasted, but I don't see any of them hanging around for the long haul with you. Gerry McMaster sex machine. Emphasis on machine. You're no better than some sex toy."

The scar on his chin turned white as his lips hardened into a taught line. "Ok, maybe I don't have a handle on this love stuff, but

I sure as hell know one thing. I know I wouldn't fall in love with a hot-head like you."

Infuriated, she screamed, "Maybe I am a hot-head, but at least I'm real!"

He turned to walk away. She grabbed his arm and caught him. "I thought there was a Gerry McMaster in there." She stabbed a finger into his bare chest. "But I was wrong. There is no such person. You're just Mac, a shallow poor-excuse-for-a-man."

"I'm leaving." He stuffed one foot into a shoe.

"Leave. Go ahead. You're such a zero of a person, I won't even notice you're gone. And know this, Gerry McMaster. I hate you, and you'll never have me. I'll never make love to you. The next man I make love to is going to be a real man!"

He held the edge of the table to steady himself while he bent and hurried to put on the other shoe.

"If you really want something to sleep with tonight," Anne said, her rage spiraling, "try this." She grabbed the wrapped up wedding cake from the table, bent over and smashed the cake into his face. Startled, he stood as she ground the icing, cake, and napkin into his eyes.

As he sputtered and swiped at his eyes, she pushed him out the door. "My shoe!" he cried. "I need my other shoe."

She slammed the door behind him. Then she went inside and spied his shoe. She didn't want any part of him defiling her life. Enraged, she opened the door again and fired the shoe at him, hitting him square in the back as he was limping down the stairs.

"Ow!" he exclaimed. Surprised, he turned around, his face smeared with icing.

Anne slammed the door. She leaned against it breathing deeply, her blood pumping wildly. Then she slumped to the floor, dissolving into a puddle of tears.

Chapter 28

Anne sat on the floor, her purple dress rucked up around her thighs, the top hanging off her shoulder, crying. She felt like the time her Aunt Eileen had given her a chocolate rabbit for Easter. Assuming it was solid, she sunk her teeth into it expecting to bite off a chunk, but received a mouthful of air. Gerry was the hollow rabbit. There was nothing beneath his delicious façade. *How could I have been so stupid? I promised myself and God that I wouldn't let myself be suckered by another man. Why don't I ever learn?*

She looked at the cake crumbs littering the carpet. Damn him! Now she didn't even have cake to drown her sorrows.

Dear, St. Anne, how could I have ever thought I loved that man?

She sobbed until her eyes began to ache. With a sigh, she rose and started to pull out the pins securing her upsweep. The roots of her hair hurt when she let it down. Tossing the pins onto the table, she then unzipped the dress, letting it fall to the floor next to the couch. She wiggled out of her hose, tossing them over the arm of the couch. Worn out, she crawled into bed wearing just her new purple lace panties.

After switching pillows because her tears had dampened the first one, she eventually drifted off into a restless sleep. She dreamed of ants in her bed carrying off wedding cake stashed under her pillow and scenes of Gerry's cousin Mike kissing her.

Then she dreamed she heard someone calling her name. When she realized she wasn't dreaming, she woke with a start. It was a little after two. Anne threw on her robe. Maybe Gerry had returned to apologize and profess his love. Her heart pounded as she stumbled into the dark living room, tripped over the dress and walked through the crumbs on the carpet. They had hardened and felt like grains of rice beneath her feet.

"Anne, it's Janetta," a voice whispered. The door was open a crack, the security chain restraining it. The hall lights silhouetted her frame. "Let me in."

Anne cinched the robe's belt. "Wait, let me turn on a light."

"No, don't do that."

"Why?"

"I'll tell you when I get inside."

She sounded peculiar, and Anne quickly closed the door, fumbling in the dark to undo the chain. When she opened it, Janetta walked in, her head cast down.

"Why can't I turn on the light? What are you doing here?"

"Steve and I had a fight." A sob escaped her and then there was a long pause before she said, "He hit me, Anne."

"What? Oh, my God! Are you hurt?" Anne ran and turned on a lamp. The sudden brilliance pained her eyes. Squinting and clutching her robe, she moved to Janetta. "Where'd that bastard hit you?"

"Don't get upset. I'm fine."

Janetta lifted her head, and Anne, her sight now adjusted, gasped. Janetta's right eye was swollen shut, her cheeks bruised, her nose looked a couple of degrees off kilter and the nostril was crusted with dried blood. Her lower lip was a pink inner tube.

"Fine? He didn't just hit you; he beat the hell out of you. Jesus, Mary, and Joseph! You look like Mike Tyson got hold of you." Anne touched her chin. "Let me see you." Janetta flinched. Anne frowned, eyeing her friend's face. "Your nose might be broken. Did he hit you anywhere else?"

"No, but he threw me into the wall."

"Does your back hurt?"

"My side hurts a little." She was having trouble talking, her lip was so swollen.

"Let me put on some clothes. We're going to the hospital."

She started for her room, but Janetta grabbed her arm. "No, I don't want to go."

"You have to."

"I don't want anyone to see me like this!"

"But you could have broken bones, internal injuries, or bleeding."

Janetta looked at Anne, her features rearranged like a Picasso portrait, and crossed her arms defiantly in front of her chest. "I'm not going. I refuse."

"Well, at least let me get you something to put on your face to stop the swelling while we discuss this." Anne ran into the kitchen and wrapped some ice in a tea towel. "Here," she said.

Janetta gingerly sat down on the dining room chair, and applied the compress to her nose and eye, wincing at the contact.

"Why won't you let me take you to the hospital?"

"I can't. It was hard enough to face you like this. I don't want strangers staring at me and asking me questions."

Anne sat at the table across from her. "What do you mean?"

"Oh come on," she said, turning her head so that Anne couldn't see her face. "You're loving this. Why do you think I haven't been calling you? I didn't want to hear you say I told you so."

Anne sighed and rested her head on the table. The glass was cold on her forehead. "So you're going to turn this on me? Make this my fault." Slowly, she raised her head. "Look, Janetta, I'll help you any way I can, but tonight is not the night to get into it with me."

Janetta, subdued by Anne's curtness, turned her head, and then her mouth fell open, her pendulous lip a shelf of flesh over her chin. She looked around the room at Anne's hosiery on the arm of the couch, her dress on the floor, the suit jacket draped over the back of the chair. "Oh my God, you've got someone here. I assumed you'd be alone. I didn't realize." She stood. "I can go somewhere else."

"Sit down, Janetta," Anne said dryly.

"But I don't want to interrupt."

"You're not. There's no one here."

She swept her hand around indicating the clothing. "But your dress and panty hose? And whose jacket is this?"

"Oh no," Anne groaned, raking her fingers through her hair. The roots still hurt.

"Whose is it, Anne?"

"Gerry's. He left it when I threw him out."

"Threw him out? You threw him out? What happened?"

Anne sat up straight in the chair. "Nothing."

"Well, it certainly looks like something happened."

"Nothing happened," Anne said, feeling tears starting again.

Janetta tilted her head and stared dubiously at Anne with her one good eye.

"Really," Anne said, tears skipping down her cheeks.

Janetta reached across the table and took her hand. "Did he hurt you?"

Anne pulled her hand away. Then swiped at her eyes. She shook her head no.

"Then why are you crying?"

Anne let out a loud sob. "Because I love him, and he doesn't love me."

"How do you know that?"

Anne rose and went for a tissue. "Because when we started to make love, I told him I loved him, and he couldn't say he loved me." Anne wailed.

Janetta slapped the back of the chair. "That callous son of a bitch. He couldn't tell you he loved you?"

"He did."

"I thought you said--"

"But I wanted him to say it, and I wanted him to mean it."

Janetta's bony shoulders rose and fell in a great sigh. "Anne, none of them ever mean it."

Chapter 29

Gerry stomped up the back steps, through the kitchen, past Peg's room.

"Is that you, Gerry?" Peg called.

'No, it's the Pope," he snarled as he went into the bathroom and grabbed a cloth to wash the rest of the cake off his face. He'd had to use an old map he found in his glove compartment to scrape off the big globs so he could see to drive home.

Peg raised her eyebrows and looked at Irma. "What are you doing in the bathroom?" she called.

"Getting ready to say Midnight Mass."

"I didn't think he'd get home this soon," she whispered to Irma. "Bet he got fresh with Anne, and she put him in his place. I wouldn't have called you over after Mary left if I'd have known he was going to be home this early."

"Oh, I don't mind. I want to be where the action is."

Peg crossed her arms. "Good for Anne." They heard the bathroom door open. "Listen to this. I'll rub it in a little." Peg cupped her hands around her mouth, shouting, "Gerry, did Anne have a good time?"

"If you're so interested, why don't you call and ask her?"

The two old women tittered. "She might be asleep," Peg shouted. "What did you do at her apartment?" They covered their mouths, laughing silently.

Gerry suddenly appeared in the doorway. Caught, Irma and Peg quickly straightened up and looked serious.

"You want to know what happened at her apartment, do you?" His face reddened and his jaw tightened. "Well, I'll tell you. Your

247

sweet little nurse threw a shoe at me and assaulted me with wedding cake."

He stepped away, leaving the old women speechless. Then after a moment, Peg raised her eyes to heaven, and exclaimed, "Thank you, St. Anne." She looked at Irma and grabbed her hand. "Oh, Irma, they're in love."

**

Anne and Janetta talked until it was nearly dawn. Janetta told her that she and Steve had gone to a club with a bunch of other couples, and she'd danced with one of his friends. Drunk when they had arrived home, Steve accused her of cheating on him. He called her filthy names, beat her, and then passed out. She told Anne she considered doing a quick castration but decided she'd better make a run for it instead. She promised Anne that she'd call her physician in the morning and a lawyer on Monday to inquire about filing protection from abuse papers.

Anne gave Janetta some pain killers and another ice pack. Exhausted and emotionally drained, both women shuffled off to bed, but Anne couldn't sleep. She lay there going over the night's events. Near six she looked in on Janetta. Predawn light seeped into the room. Even in the dusky grayness her friend's face was a Technicolor mess. It would take weeks for the pain and bruises to go away.

As she padded off back to her bed, Anne didn't think her pain would ever go away. She didn't know how she'd ever get over Gerry. Anger, embarrassment, hurt, tormented her. *I almost allowed myself to be used again, and now I'm paying.*

What was even worse was that no matter how hurt and humiliated she felt, she still loved Gerry. And knowing that she would never have him hurt most of all.

By the time the birds' first songs heralded the arrival of morning, Anne had resolved that she could never see Gerry again. But what about that damn jacket of his? Part of her felt like taking scissors to it, but after he had called her a hothead, she wouldn't give him the

248

satisfaction of proving his estimation of her temperament right. Then she remembered that he would be running in the Great Race this morning. She'd drop the coat off while he was out. That way she could say goodbye to Peg too. She was nearly back on her feet so she could get by without a nurse now. Anne was going to miss her new friend terribly, but she couldn't face seeing Gerry every day.

Anne lay in bed until six-thirty. Then she rose, showered, and pulled on a pair of shorts and T-shirt. She left Janetta a note telling her where'd she'd gone and that she'd bring doughnuts home for them.

Fat and sugar was exactly what the situation called for, Anne thought, as she picked up Gerry's jacket. The smell of his cologne lingering on the fabric stopped her. She held the jacket to her chest. The memory of how it felt to dance with him, how right they fit together, how filled with promise the previous evening had been came flooding back. But he was as empty as this jacket. She wanted to cry, but she bit her lip, inhaled deeply, and headed out the door.

***

Anne pulled into the parking lot and was relieved to find, that as she had expected, that Gerry's car was gone. Using the key he'd given her, she let herself in. She knew Peg would be up because she usually watched the Mass for shut-ins on television early Sunday morning.

When Anne entered the kitchen, Peg called, "Irma, is that you?"

"It's me. Anne."

She walked into her room, and Peg, seated in the chair, turned off the television.

"I thought you were Irma on her way to church. What a nice surprise. What are you doing here?"

Anne glanced around. "Gerry's gone, isn't he?"

"He left a while ago for the race. Wasn't that a lovely wedding?" Peg's eyes widened expectantly.

Anne put Gerry's jacket on the bed. "I wanted to return this. He left it at my place."

"You didn't have to make a special trip. You could have brought it tomorrow."

Anne dragged the chair from the corner over next to Peg's and sat. "Peg, I need to talk with you."

"I know what you're going to say, and you did the right thing, Dear. Irma and I have been working hard to get you two together, and I'm proud of you. You have to leave a man begging for more. I don't understand girls today. Their biggest bargaining chip is their chastity, and they give it away as soon as a fella winks at them. Oh, he might be but a little put out, but you've set the hook, Annie Banannie. Now all you've got to do is reel him in."

"Listen, Peg, I have to tell you something." Anne paused. This was going to be more difficult than she thought; she hadn't realized the depth of emotion she felt for Peg until now. She sighed. "I can't be your nurse anymore. I'm not coming here anymore."

"What?" Peg cried. "Why? You can't leave me. I need you."

Anne took the old woman's bony hand. "You've made remarkable progress. You can get by on your own now."

"No, I can't." She gripped Anne's hand tightly. "I'll die without you."

Peg looked so frightened Anne's heart ached. "Don't be silly." She patted the top of her spotted hand. "You've got Irma and Gerry."

"But I want you, Anne." Tears shone in Peg's blue eyes. "I know I'm a pain in the ass. I'll try to behave. I'll eat your awful diet and do your exercises."

Anne broke free of her grasp. "You're not a pain in the ass, and I'm not leaving because of you."

Peg was crying now. "Then why? Why won't you stay?"

"I can't."

Peg took off her glasses and wiped her eyes. "Is it because of Gerry? He's been in a snit ever since he came home last night."

Anne didn't answer.

"Why would you leave when you love him?"

Anne lost her composure, tears rolled down her face. She stood and walked to the dresser, catching a glimpse of herself in the mirror. Her eyes were bloodshot and her skin paler than ever. "Because he doesn't love me, Peg."

"He loves you. I know he does."

She turned around. "No, as much as you and I wanted him to, he doesn't." Anne was sobbing now. "And as much as I'm going to miss you, I can't come here anymore. It's too hard." She covered her face with her hands.

Anne was surprised to feel Peg's hand on her shoulder. She uncovered her face and looked up. Peg was standing in front of her, resting against her cane. The old woman's eyes were tear-filled and brimming with sympathy.

"Is it because of your baby?"

Anne recoiled, feeling as if she'd just been slapped. "Baby? What are you talking about?"

Peg wrapped an arm around her. "I know, Honey. You don't have to pretend. You thought I was sleeping all those times, but I've seen you crying while you were holding that St. Gerard medal. And when I told you about all my miscarriages, your hand went to your belly. When did you lose yours? Recently? Or was it when you were younger?"

Anne broke out of Peg's embrace. She felt as if she were being pursued and had come to a dead end. Anger and shame gripped her, and she wanted to lash out at Peg for cornering her. She moved around the side of the bed. "I don't know what you are talking about. Maybe Gerry was right that you're too old to be alone. I think you're losing it."

Peg held out a hand to Anne. "Sweetheart, don't be afraid. Your secret will be safe with me. Tell me about it. You can't keep all that sadness and pain bottled up."

In the core of her being, Anne felt something rend. She thought it was her soul, and she felt demons and furies escaping, taunting her with guilt and recriminations. She feared the better part of her nature would sink and be swallowed by the gaping hole of her sin.

"Oh, Peg," she wailed.

Peg shuffled over to her and drew her close, and Anne collapsed into her arms, sobbing. She wrapped her arms around Peg and rested her head on the old woman's shoulder, crying uncontrollably.

"There, there, Annie Banannie," Anne heard Peg saying as the old woman's hand smoothed her curls. Anne felt foolish but she couldn't control herself; the grief swept her up, washing away all of her dignity. Although Peg was weaker physically, Anne felt the old woman's goodness and strength of character emanating from her feeble frame.

"Losing a baby is not easy, especially when you're not married, Sweetheart. But with time it will get better."

Anne bristled and raised her head. Peg was looking so lovingly at her, it made Anne sick to her stomach. She didn't deserve Peg's sympathy.

"Peg," she sniffled, "you're wrong. It's never going to get better."

She felt Peg's bony fingers stroking her cheek. "It may seem that way, Sweetheart, but with time—"

"No, Peg, time won't help. Nothing will help. It won't because I didn't lose the baby." Anne could almost hear squealing in her mind as everything inside her fought to apply the brakes to her tongue to keep her from admitting the unspeakable. But she had to get it out or she would lose her mind. "Peg," she whispered, "I got rid of it."

Anne could see the shock register for a moment on Peg's face, but she quickly recovered and tried to appear unfazed, but the cloud that had come over her bright blue eyes revealed that old woman remained stunned.

She saw Peg swallow. "You mean adoption?"

Anne lowered her head. "I wish. I wasn't brave enough." She paused and said softly, "I had an abortion."

If words were made out of glass, these would have caught the light and fallen to the floor and shattered at Anne's feet. How many times had she thought those words? *I had an abortion.* In the hours and days afterward, she repeated them incessantly, partly to make sense of what had happened, but mostly to punish herself. And now for the first time she had actually voiced those four little words that had for so many years been locked inside her mind, never passing over her lips.

She knew Peg would be horrified and probably even hate her. How could someone of her religious convictions and deep faith ever tolerate someone such as her? Perhaps that's why she'd told Peg. Maybe it would make leaving easier. Even as Anne looked at the sorrow etched on the old woman's face, she knew that it had been cruel of her to drop this bombshell into Peg's life. But all endings were cruel, weren't they? Abortion was an ending and it was cruel. The breakup with Zach was another ending and it had also been cruel. Life was just a string of cruel endings.

She's certainly not proud of me now. Anne couldn't bear seeing the disappointment on Peg's face. And yet she couldn't take her eyes off her. She wanted to see Peg's recriminations. She wanted to be condemned before she left. Anne went for a tissue to wipe away her tears. Peg shuffled over and sank into the chair. Tilting her head back, she closed her eyes. At first, Anne was afraid that her disclosure had killed her. But then she saw that she was breathing. As she watched the old woman, Anne she realized that Peg's lips were gently moving. *She's praying. Probably for my eternally damned soul.*

Anne reached into her pocket and placed the key on the table beside the chair. As she turned to leave, she heard Peg exclaim, "Oh, my poor, poor girl." Anne turned to see a tear roll down her lined cheek as she held her hands out to her. "My heart aches for you."

Anne had expected condemnation not empathy, and she was overwhelmed with emotion. Tears welled in her eyes.

"Tell me what happened," Peg said.

"Oh, Peg," Anne said, her lip quivering, as she stood near the door. "I don't think I can. No one, not even my parents know about this. I'm so ashamed."

Peg reached out. "Come. They won't ever have to know. It'll be just between you, me, and Our Lord."

Anne felt herself being drawn into the room by Peg's warmth. She reached out and clasped Peg's hand as if it were a life line.

"Sweetheart, I can see how tormented you are. You need to get this off your chest. When did this happen?"

Anne pulled away. "I can't talk about it. I'm too afraid."

"Don't be afraid. I love you."

Then Anne sunk to her knees in front of Peg. Laying her head in the old woman's lap, she began to sob. *Where do I begin? How do I make her understand how I could have done such a thing when I can't even understand it myself sometimes?*

When she could cry no more, Anne sat back on her heels. Peg offered a tissue and waited patiently while she blew her nose. "When I was a freshman in college, I fell madly in love with someone—a senior, named Zach." Her heart was pounding, and she could hear that her voice was reedy. "He was a star linebacker, and I thought he loved me. At least, he told me he did. A lot of the things I thought about him turned out to be wrong. He had this all-American boy image that the media just ate up. He was going to be drafted high in the NFL draft and stood to make a lot of money through endorsements. Everything was great. I was the girlfriend of a future NFL star. Then I got pregnant." Anne sniffled. She looked pleadingly at Peg. "I didn't do it on purpose. It just happened. I wasn't happy that I got pregnant, Peg, but I did want the baby. Our baby. *My baby.* He'd soon be making a lot of money so I figured we could get married, I'd quit school to take care of our baby.

"When I told Zach I was pregnant, he freaked. He said it would ruin everything. His squeaky-clean image would be shot to hell, and he'd lose his endorsements. He pleaded with me to get rid of the baby. At first I refused. He said we could have others. He told me to consider my parents. What would they think? He told me my mother would be horrified. She would never be able to deal with it. I was so confused; I didn't know what to do. Then he told me he'd deny it was his and break up with me if I didn't."

Tears spilled from Anne's eyes. "Oh Peg, it was horrible. My teeth were chattering. I've never been so cold as when I lay on that table while they suctioned my baby out of my body." Anne had to stop for moment because she was crying again.

"Oh, my poor Annie," Peg's lip quivered as she spoke and rubbed Anne's arm reassuringly. Anne pulled two tissues from the box; keeping one for herself and handing one to Peg, who was now weeping as well.

Anne sighed heavily. "Afterward, I went to Zach's apartment to tell him that I'd taken care of it, that everything would be fine. But, of course, it wasn't. Within a few weeks, he was already sleeping with someone else." A wail rose from Anne that shocked her. "How stupid could I have been? I chose him over my own child. I killed my own baby for him!"

Peg patted her reassuringly. "You were young and frightened and under pressure."

Anne rose. "Yes, but I knew it was wrong. I knew it was wrong when I was on that table. And I knew it was wrong afterward. There's not a day that goes bye that I don't regret what I've done, that I'm not haunted by this."

"Have you been to Confession, Dear? Our Lord is big enough to forgive even this."

Anne stared at Peg. "I have and I know I've been forgiven, but I don't feel forgiven. It still hurts like hell. Maybe it's best that I don't forget—that the pain never goes away. It keeps me from doing something stupid again, like getting involved with Gerry."

"Anne, I know him better than you. He's in love with you. He just doesn't know it."

Anne took the old woman's gnarled hands. "I don't want to hurt you, but Gerry's just like Zach. Handsome, charming, but shallow. For some reason, I fall for that type. That's why I can't come back. It's self-preservation. And he's better off without me. I can't cope with what I've done."

"You've got to forgive yourself. Give yourself a second chance. Give Gerry a second chance. God has forgiven you."

Anne released Peg's hand. "He's God that's why he can forgive me. I'm not. I don't think I'll ever get over what I've done." She sighed. "I've got to go."

"You can't leave me, Anne." Peg began to tremble. "I can help you. I won't—"

Anne's cell phone rang. She hoped it wasn't Gerry or Janetta. She wasn't up for any more drama. Wiping her eyes, she answered the call.

"What? Oh my God!" She straightened her back. "I'm glad you caught me." Anne ended the call. She quickly walked to Peg and kissed her on the forehead. "I've got to go."

Peg grabbed her arm. "Don't leave me, Anne."

"I have to. Patsy's in labor."

Chapter 30

"God love her," Peg said. "Please," she grabbed onto Anne's arm with both hands, investing her strength like someone clinging to a life preserver and pleaded. "You have to call me. At least, to tell me what she had. And because I'm worried about you. Please."

"I will." She slid out of the old woman's grasp.

Anne dashed through the apartment, a jumble of tears and excitement. She flew down the stairs, opened the door, and ran right into Gerry, so startling her that she lost her balance.

He grasped her arm to keep her from falling.

"Anne!"

"G-Gerry? But-but I thought you were at the race."

"I went to vacuum my car—there were cake crumbs everywhere in it. And I didn't feel much like running today. You come here to firebomb the place?" He laughed.

He's making jokes? She couldn't meet his eyes, let him know how wounded and vulnerable she was. She looked at her sandals, her manicured toes peeking out. "No," she said firmly, jerking her arm away from his grasp, "I came to return your key and suit jacket."

"The key? What the hell for?"

She peered up at him. His dark brows were laced together in puzzlement. "I'm not coming back."

He grabbed her by the shoulders. "Aw, I'm sorry if I came on too strong. We can take it a little slower."

She wrenched herself out of his grip.

"Hey, can't you cut me some slack? I'm not mad at you for smashing cake in my face."

She turned her head away, feeling the tears stinging her eyes.

257

He jerked her to his chest. "Look at me, Anne."

She closed her eyes, feeling a wash of tears run down her cheeks. "Why the hell are you crying?"

She opened her eyes, and when she saw how confused he was, she almost pitied him. "You are so thick," she said, and squirming out of his arms, she turned and rushed to her car.

He followed after her, beating her to it, and blocking the door. "Then enlighten me. What don't I understand?"

"You didn't hear a word I said last night, did you?" Her voice rose, scaring pigeons from the telephone lines.

He screwed up his face. "You mean that love stuff? You were serious?"

Furious now, she put her hands on his chest and shoved him away. She moved to put her key in the lock.

He touched her arm. "Weren't we getting along just fine?" She jerked it free. Not deterred, he asked, "Why'd you have to drag that into it?"

She wanted to rake her nails, the nails she'd paid $45 to have manicured for their big night, down his handsome face, but she didn't want to give him the satisfaction of losing control.

The door unlocked, she extracted the key and reached to open it.

And like the first day when she'd come into the bar, he held the door. *He doesn't love me, but he's perfectly willing to torment me.* Something snapped in Anne. She didn't care if he thought she was the most irrational woman he'd ever met. In a blind rage, she went at him with her fists, beating his chest, cursing him. When he captured her wrists and held them, she kicked him in the shin.

"You little witch!" he grunted, reaching for his shin. Free, Anne opened the door, but before she could enter the car, Gerry grabbed her, whirled her around, and kissed her, crushing her against the frame. She fought him for a bit, then weakened to enjoy his warm, sweet lips, their passion nearly erasing her pain. Then she recovered her senses, got hold of herself and tried to wrench herself out of his embrace. When he tightened his hold and continued to kiss her, she bit his lip. He jerked backward, releasing his hold on her. He clutched his mouth staring at her with anger blazing in his eyes.

Defiantly, she looked up at him, panting, her green eyes brimming with anger. "You think kissing me will make everything right? Well, you're wrong, Gerry. I'm not that stupid. I've learned my lesson. The hard way. Maybe you can live on winks, and smiles, and kisses, but I want more. I want something deeper. I want love." The fury began to subside and the tears started again. "But you're not man enough to love me."

"Man enough?" His eyes were cold like steel. "I'll show you who is man enough."

He swept her into his arms, crushing his lips to hers once again. She tasted blood and rage on them, but there was nothing she could do; his size and strength overpowered her. She lay limply in his arms while his lips worked to prove that he was truly a man.

He abruptly released her, and the smug smile that crept across his face told her that he was sure that his kiss had convinced her of his manhood.

Anne's anger changed into pity. He truly had no idea what she needed. She reached up, gently touching his cheek. Then shaking her head, she let her hand slide from his face. "That's not enough, Gerry." She got into the car and drove away.

Chapter 31

When Gerry went inside, Peg was leaning on her cane, waiting for him at the top of the stairs. "Anne was here," she said.

"I know. I saw her in the lot." He wiped his lip and looked at his fingers.

"What did you do to that girl? She says she's not coming back."

"Me, do to her?" He brushed past his mother. "She has a problem."

Peg followed him, her cane clomping on the kitchen's linoleum floor. "I'll say she does. You."

He wheeled around. "So this is all my fault?"

She reached for his arm. "Gerry, you're my son, and I love you, but you're the biggest horse's ass. Anne loves you, and you're driving her away."

He pulled back. "I don't need you butting into in my life."

"Somebody has to. You've messed it up so royally."

"Stop," he held up a hand, his jaw set firmly, "I'm not in the mood for one of your lectures. I've taken enough grief."

She gripped her cane, her hand white on the handle making the liver spots more vivid. "Well, too bad, Buddy Boy. You're going to take some more. You're wasting your life, Gerry. Have you taken a look at yourself? You're not a kid anymore. For God's sake you're nearly forty, and what have you got to show for it?"

He waved his hand wildly about the place. "You call my architectural career a waste? You call turning this rundown bar into one of the city's finest a waste?"

"I know you're successful professionally. I'm talking about your personal life. I've put everything I had into raising you. For what?

261

So you can act like a tomcat, hopping from one woman's bed to another? You think that's what a real man does?"

Gerry's face became lava red. "I'm sick of everyone telling me I'm not a real man. Times have changed, Peg. It's not 1945 anymore."

The blood pounded in Peg's temples. She felt dizzy, but she didn't care if it killed her. She was going to straighten him out. "Listen, Mr. Know-it-all, get my Bible. You show me the expiration date on the Ten Commandments. Your life's a joke. You sleep around, never go to church, and when someone comes along who really loves you, you toss her aside." Peg began to tremble, her voice breaking as tears swam in her eyes. "If only your father hadn't died. I tried to raise you the best I could, but a mother's not a father. He was a real man, not some . . . some playboy like you."

"Stop it," Gerry shouted. "I am not my father. I will never be my father. All my life that's all I've heard, 'your father was a saint, my Martin was a dear.'" Gerry made his voice singsong, mocking his mother. "Don't you understand? I can't measure up to your idealized memories."

"Idealized? He was all those things. He was an honorable and responsible man. A man who knew how to love."

"If he loved you so much, why did he leave you with nothing but a rundown bar and mountains of debt?"

Peg stomped her feet. "Gerard Martin McMaster!" Her heart was pounding so loudly she could barely hear herself. "Don't you dare talk about your father that way. You don't know how hard things were. He tried his best."

Gerry looked his mother in the eye and calmly said, "Can't you see that I'm trying my best?"

She waved her hand in the air, tears of hurt and anger streaking her lined cheeks. "Oh, baloney, you're not trying, you're hiding. You love Anne, why won't you admit it?"

"Will you leave me alone!" He turned and stormed down the stairs.

She tottered after him shouting, "What are you so afraid of, Gerry? What?"

Tightness seized Peg's chest. Her mouth went dry. She leaned against the wall for support, willing the pain to subside. Sweat beaded on her forehead as she staggered to the kitchen chair and slumped into it, fearing more for what would become of her son than her own health.

***

Because Patsy's pregnancy was deemed a high risk one, she and Vince had decided to deliver at Magee Hospital in Pittsburgh's Oakland section instead of one closer to their home. Magee had a well-respected neonatal intensive care unit in case one of the babies needed special attention.

Anne wished that Patsy were delivering her baby in Latrobe instead of Pittsburgh because she needed the extra time in the car to cry and get her pain out of her system before facing her family.

She pulled her car into the hospital's lot, shut off the engine, and checked the rearview mirror. Her eyes looked like someone had drawn on the whites with a red felt tip pen and her nose glowed. "Argh, I look like I could guide Santa's sleigh."

Rummaging through her purse, she found a tissue and wiped her nose. Then pressing the heels of her hands into her eye sockets, she tried to staunch the tears.

She found the room where her mother, father, and Kevin were waiting. Her father's thin red hair was gently waving like flimsy tentacles as the air conditioning vent blew freezing air above his head. He clutched a coffee cup, with a white-knuckle death grip as he stared out the window at the Cathedral of Learning. Kevin, dressed in jeans and T-shirt, was half reclining in the loveseat, his head propped up by his elbow. Her mother was leafing through a magazine. Anne knew she must be nervous because the magazine was *Field and Stream*; her mother was no outdoors enthusiast.

"Any word?" Anne asked as she walked into the room.

"Oh, you're here," her mother said then heaved a sigh. "Vince came out a little while ago. Her water broke, and she's in labor, but they're doing a C-section. One of the babies was trans—trans something. It was blocking the entrance to the birth canal.

"Transverse," Anne said. "It isn't an emergency section, is it?"

Mrs. Lyons looked alarmed. "He didn't mention anything about an emergency, did he, Bill?"

Her father came and kissed Anne on the cheek. "Nope."

"Why, do you think something is wrong?" her mother asked.

I hope the babies aren't in any distress, Anne thought, but she didn't express her fears because she didn't want to worry her mother. "No, I was just trying to guess how long before we have the babies. C-sections are quick. It should be over soon."

Her mother folded her hands tightly. "I just hate to think of her lying on that table, cut open."

Anne had no patience for her mother's histrionics this morning. "Then don't think of it."

"You don't have to be so short with me. Wait until your daughter is in labor. We'll see how calm you are."

There's no chance of that ever happening, Anne thought. I'm never getting married, I'll never have children, and I'll never have grandchildren. She felt tears threatening again.

Mr. Lyons came over and patted her on the shoulder. "Want me to get you some coffee?"

"You can't leave the room," Mrs. Lyons said. "You might miss the birth."

Mr. Lyons shrugged and whispered to Anne. "We're being held hostage."

Feeling the lack of sleep and the stress of the emotional upheaval, Anne sighed, pushing Kevin over so she could sit on the loveseat too.

"Jeez, you look whipped," Kevin said. "You out all night?"

That got her mother's attention. "You do look terrible. What were you doing last night?"

"I was out trying to score some heroin." Anne picked up a *Woman's Day*.

"Do you always have to be so smart?"

Anne closed the magazine. "Do you always have to be so annoying?"

"Girls! Girls!" Mr. Lyons shouted over their voices. "Who wants a candy bar? I saw Almond Joys in the vending machine out in the hall. I haven't had one of those in ages. Anne, Honey," he said, acting like a court jester trying to get a rise out of a miserable monarch. "Want one? You know how you love almonds."

Anne looked at the clock. "Not right now."

Her mother said softly, "You should eat some chocolate. Maybe it'll sweeten you up. You know, you catch more flies with honey."

Anne turned toward her mother. "And what's that supposed to mean?"

"Well, maybe if you sweetened your disposition, someday we'd be here waiting for your husband to tell us news of your baby."

Anne shot out of the seat. "Why should I change? To accommodate the assholes in the world? You never changed your annoying ways, and you still got married."

Mr. Lyons put an arm around Anne. "You're fine the way you are, Honey. If I were a young man today, I'd go for a girl like you."

"Sure," Mrs. Lyons said. "That's because you have no spine. You let her walk all over you."

Flustered, Mr. Lyons cheeks puffed in and out as he exclaimed, "I do too have a spine."

"Daddy, you don't," Anne said. "She ripped it out of you."

"Don't talk about your mother that way!" Mr. Lyons said sharply.

"I think Anne's jealous of Patsy," Kevin mumbled, his eyes closed.

Mrs. Lyons crossed her arms in front of her chest and bent her head as if about to cry. "I never thought that sweet little baby I gave birth to would grow up and turn on me."

"Would you all just leave me alone!" Anne shouted.

Vince appeared in the doorway looking awe-struck and wearing a wide smile. "It's a boy and a girl!" he boomed.

They all rushed to him.

"How's Patsy?" her mother asked.

"Are the babies OK?" Mr. Lyons said.

"What were their weights?" Kevin said. "I want to play the lottery with those numbers."

Anne felt as if champagne had been poured into her veins, she bubbled with excitement. "Who do they look like?" Anne asked, ashamed that she'd allowed her emotional upheaval of the morning to spill over onto such a joyous occasion.

"You can judge for yourself in a few minutes. The nurse is going to come get us when we can see them."

Forgetting their argument, they peppered Vince with questions about the delivery until a nurse summoned them. They followed her to a room, chattering excitedly.

Patsy was still in recovery when Vince and the nurse brought the babies to them. A chorus of "ohs" and "ahs" greeted them. One bundle was crying like a banshee. Vince presented his baby to Mrs. Lyons. "Grandma," he said, "this is Aaron." Mrs. Lyons burst into tears when she peeked inside the blanket at her sleeping grandson.

Vince took the wailing baby from the nurse. "And this, Aunt Anne, is your namesake."

Stunned, Anne stared at him open-mouthed. "My namesake? I didn't know you were considering my name."

She was flattered that they had named her niece after her until Vince handed her the squirming baby and joked, "From her wicked temper, I think we chose wisely."

Everyone chuckled, but Anne began to cry. She unwrapped the squirming baby and looked at her. The infant's gaping, shrieking mouth eclipsed all its other features. Bunching her tiny fists, she thrashed wildly. One of Anne's tears plopped onto the baby's cheek

266

and instantly it rooted for the source of liquid. Anne brushed the tear away wondering, "Is this how I really appear?"

Chapter 32

Anne sat in the leather recliner, resting her head against its back. The soft hum of the ventilation fan lulled her. She watched the babies as they snoozed in their incubators, marveling that those two little beings had a few hours ago been inside her sister. Is there anything more peaceful than sleeping babies?

She glanced over at Patsy, who was also dozing. Although she looked exhausted, the corners of her mouth were turned up in a smile as she slept.

After being discharged from Recovery, Patsy had been brought to this room. All afternoon, she'd been awake, chatting with the family and admiring her babies. As the late September sun sank and shadows grew longer in the room, Patsy had begun to tire.

Anne offered to sit with her and the babies while her parents and Kevin treated Vince to a celebratory dinner. They wanted Anne to join them, but she had no appetite. And she certainly didn't feel sociable.

Little Anne lifted her arms over her head and stretched, arching her back and drawing up her legs. She snorted and snuffled. Anne didn't want her to wake Patsy so she went to her tiny niece and, gently sliding her hands under her head and diapered bottom, she picked her up. Wide, gray-blue eyes stared up at Anne. She smelled fresh and new, a mixture of baby wipes and milk. Little Anne stared intently at her aunt like she was trying to place her face, and Anne had the sense that she'd known this tiny soul in a former life.

"Hello, Sweetheart, I'm your Aunt Anne," she softly crooned to her.

"Is she behaving herself?" Patsy asked, her voice groggy.

Anne stroked the baby's cheek. "Yes, she's been a very good girl.

"How are you feeling?" Anne asked, gently swaying on her feet to soothe her niece.

"Exhausted and happy."

"Do you want to hold her?"

"No, you two get to know each other."

Anne walked over to the chair by the bed and sat, cradling the baby in her arms. "She's so alert." She smiled down at the tiny face. "Aren't you, Anne?" She turned toward Patsy. "Sounds odd to be calling someone else Anne."

"You don't mind, do you?"

"Mind?" Anne said, raw emotions bubbling up in her. "I'm honored. Overwhelmed." Her voice was reduced to a whisper as tears filled her eyes. "I never expected you to do that." She put her index finger near the baby's hand, and she quickly wrapped her tiny fingers around it. And it occurred to Anne that this child in her arms maybe the closest she would ever get to motherhood.

Aaron burped loudly. Anne and Patsy both laughed. As though he were insulted by their laughter at his digestive distress, he let out an ear-piercing shriek. "I'll get the little piggy," Anne said as she placed her namesake in her mother's arms and went to the little boy thrashing and twisting his blanket.

Anne put him over her shoulder and patted his back, coaxing out another belch. As she kissed his cheek, she was thankful that these two were born when they were. She could throw herself into helping Patsy to get on her feet. They would be a lovely diversion, and she wouldn't have to think about Gerry and her baby that might have been.

***

She sat and reached for the amber prescription bottle on the coffee table. Anne was so tired her eyes could barely focus on the label's fine print. It was late on Sunday night. It had been an exhausting and emotionally charged day—breaking up with Gerry,

Peg guessing her secret and the euphoria of the twins' arrival. "What did they give you for pain?" She narrowed her eyes. "Ah, Percocet." Yawning, she looked at Janetta, who was sitting stiffly on the chair. Her cracked ribs had been taped at the hospital giving her the perfect posture of a Southern Belle wearing a corset. Swollen, purple bruises had bloomed all over her face. "Is it helping?"

Janetta yawned too and winced. "Yeah, I'm glad I went to the hospital. I hardly slept last night, I'm so sore."

"At least we know your nose isn't broken."

Janetta stuffed a pillow behind her back. "Speaking of broken," she said gently, "how's your heart?"

Anne sighed and stretched out on the couch, on which she and Gerry not more than twenty-four hours ago had nearly made love. How was her heart? In the same shape as Janetta's ribs. The breakup with Gerry had devastated her, and her mother's comments and Vince's joke about her temper ripped her wounded heart open even further. She had never felt so drained and humiliated.

"Oh, I'm OK. The twins were a happy distraction. It was hard telling Peg that I couldn't come back though."

"She called while you were out. I guess your phone was off while you were in the hospital. Hope you don't mind, but I told her what Patsy had."

"Good, I'm not up to talking to her yet, and I certainly don't want to get *him* on the phone."

Closing her eyes and leaning her head back, Janetta murmured, "I don't think men are worth the aggravation, do you?"

After a long silence, Anne rolled onto her side, propped her head up, and faced Janetta. "Can I ask you something? And please be honest."

Janetta looked pointedly at her.

"Is there something wrong with me?"

"Wrong?"

"I know this is going to sound crazy because you're all banged up, but in some way I'm envious of what you and Steve had."

"What?" Janetta exclaimed then caught herself, grabbing her ribs.

"Not of how he abused you, but I'm envious of how you can abandon yourself in love."

"What Steve and I had wasn't love, Anne."

"But at the time you believed it was."

"For a while."

Anne sat up. "See, that's it. I love Gerry." Her voice caught. She covered her face with her hand. "Why couldn't I just go with it, and let myself believe he loved me?"

"Because you can't be anything but true to yourself, Anne."

Maybe I have learned something from the past, Anne thought. I wasn't true to myself when I allowed Zach to bully me into the abortion. She felt tears begging to be released. She was tired of crying, so she sucked in some breath and held them back. Then she uncovered her eyes and said, "But at least I would have felt loved for a little while."

Janetta hobbled over and sat next to her. She put her arm around her. "Look, Anne, you don't ever want to be like me."

Anne gazed at her with eyes bleary from crying and lack of sleep.

"See," Janetta said, "I've been doing a lot of thinking, and I realized something today. I wasn't fooling myself into believing that I was in love, I was fooling myself about something entirely different."

"Like what?"

"You know my family. How angry I've always been at my mother for letting my father treat her like dirt? All my life I've rebelled, wanting to be nothing like her. I was going to be the independent, sexually uninhibited modern woman." She rolled her eyes. "Look where I've ended up." Gently dabbing at tears rolling down her bruised cheeks, she shook her head. "A doormat. Just like my mother."

Anne gently pulled Janetta close and held her, careful not to squeeze her ribs.

"Only I'm worse, Anne. Only one man abused her. I've allowed myself to be abused by dozens."

Anne could do nothing but rub her friend's back as she sobbed.

After a few moments, Janetta composed herself. Raising her head she said, "I've decided to take some time off. Lilah, the manager of my shop, has a timeshare in Hilton Head. She's given it to me for a week. I'm going to go down there and let myself heal." She paused, her dark eyes looking soberly at Anne. "When I come back, I'm going into therapy. A super-nice social worker talked with me at the hospital today."

Anne squeezed her; Janetta yelped, backing away. "Sorry," Anne said. "I'm just so excited. I think that would be good. I've worried for so long about you." She patted her hand. "Well, you've figured out your problem. What's mine?"

"I don't think you have a problem. Gerry does."

Anne thought for a moment then said softly, "But what about my temper?" Anne had told her about her mother and Vince's comments.

Janetta laughed. "Your temper's what makes you special. It comes from that sense of being true to yourself. As someone who's been a victim of that temper, let me tell you sometimes it's not easy to take, but you've never said anything that wasn't true or wasn't what I needed to hear. I think Gerry needed to be set straight too. Promise me, you'll never lose your backbone and become a doormat like me, Anne."

"Why don't we both make a pact," Anne said. "No more doormats."

Janetta held out her hand. "You got it. No more doormats."

They shook on the deal.

***

On Monday morning, Anne called her office and arranged for a new position. She didn't want to tell her supervisor that she'd made a mess of her job by becoming romantically involved her patient's son. Instead, she stretched the truth, telling her that she felt Peg had progressed enough that she didn't need full-time care, that she was afraid that Peg was becoming too attached to her. The only assignment available would begin on Thursday. It was caring for a man named Herbert Dunmire, who was one of the agency's intermittent cases. Mr. Dunmire was an elderly, lecherous, bachelor alcoholic suffering from end-stage cirrhosis. He was in and out of the hospital. No one wanted to take care of him. Anne had been forewarned to be on guard when taking his blood pressure as he had a nasty habit of fondling a breast then.

For the next few days, Anne's ears were attuned to the phone, longing for Gerry to call to tell her that he did love her. By Tuesday, Anne faced reality: their relationship was over. That morning Janetta deemed herself recovered enough from her injuries to drive. After hugging Anne goodbye, she left for the beach, leaving Anne alone in the apartment with an aching heart and a silent phone.

The one McMaster who did call was Peg. She rang daily, but it pained Anne to hear her voice, so she made their conversations brief. As much as Anne wanted to, she reused to inquire after Gerry.

Without the camaraderie of her friends at Mac's Place and without Janetta in the apartment, Anne was lonely. So lonely, that when her mother called Tuesday evening, Anne was happy to hear her voice. What her mother had to say, however, did not make her happy.

"Anne," Grace Lyons said, her voice threaded with anxiety, "can you come home?"

"What is it? Is Daddy OK?"

"He's fine. It's Patsy. Vince is taking her to the Emergency."

Anne felt like the air had been knocked out of her lungs. "Why? What's wrong?"

"I don't know. She's very sick. She's burning with fever."

Infection, Anne thought, a wave of panic washing over her.

"Vince is so upset and she's so weak, she nearly passed out. I'm going to help him get her to the hospital. Your father and Kevin are with the twins, but they're clueless. I'd feel better if you were here with them."

Anne, cell phone in hand, was already pulling her suitcase out from under her bed and stuffing clothes into it.

"Don't worry," she said, "I'm on my way."

***

Anne arrived at Vince and Patsy's house near ten o'clock. When she walked inside, her mouth dropped open. Empty bottles, soiled baby clothes, dirty diapers, and dishes littered the place. A smell of sour milk permeated the air. Her father walked out of the nursery, his hair mussed, his shirt stained with baby barf, carrying Little Anne. "Thank God, you're here," he said. "Can you take her a minute? I've had to go to the bathroom for the last hour, but every time I put her down she screams."

Anne took the baby and noticed that her father had put the child's sleeper on backward, the snaps running up the baby's spine. Anne wrinkled her nose. The baby had spit up so much, she smelled like a glass of spoiled milk. As he headed toward the bathroom, Anne called, "Where's Aaron?"

"On the dryer." He closed the door.

"What?" Alarmed, Anne, carrying the baby, hurried down to the basement where she found Kevin in the same state of dishevelment as her father. He was bent over the dryer, holding onto an infant seat, into which a snoozing Aaron had been strapped. The dryer was humming on the perma-press cycle.

"Why are you doing laundry?"

Kevin raised his head. "I'm not. My arms got tired from holding him. I read in Patsy's baby book that infants like this. Every time I take him off, he wakes up screaming. I hope she comes home soon. He doesn't like the bottle; he wants to nurse." Kevin massaged his neck. "He latched onto my neck before like a sucker fish."

Anne could see a red mark below her brother's ear.

Kevin smiled at the sleeping boy. "They should have named this little guy Count Dracula."

"Why don't you take her," Anne said, holding out her namesake, "and I'll see if I can do anything with him."

"Won't work," Kevin said. "Dad and I tried that. She hates me." Kevin's stomach growled loudly. He looked at Anne. "You think you can stay here with him a minute? I haven't eaten anything in a while."

"Sure." Anne assumed his post at the dryer, and after he disappeared upstairs, she held up Little Anne and kissed her cheek. In just a few days, she'd put on weight. Her skin had lost that redness that made newborns look as if they'd been scalded. Now she was a delicate pink like a blush wine. Looking into the baby's slate-colored eyes, she whispered, "I suppose you noticed, Sweetheart, that men are lame. What can be so hard about taking care of twins? Why, when I did my rotation in maternity in nursing school, I took care of four babies at once."

Little Anne's only reply was violent turbulence in her diaper.

"Ah-oh, what are you doing?" Anne said, chuckling as the baby grunted and her face froze in concentration. Her laughter ceased when she felt a warm wetness soaking her shirt. Holding the baby away, she eyed her poopy shirt. "Dad? Kevin? Somebody? Help!"

Chapter 33

Kevin came, taking Aaron up to the kitchen and sat his infant seat on the table so he could watch him while he finished eating. Anne ran into the bedroom and changed into a clean T-shirt. Her father held Little Anne out in the hallway at arm's length like she was radioactive. Anne, in a fresh shirt, quickly bathed Little Anne, who had managed to poop all the way up her back. Aaron serenaded the bath with incessant screams from the kitchen.

Anne swabbed the stump of the umbilical cord then nuzzled the baby's neck, noticing her satiny soft cheeks. Anne's mind flashed to Gerry's cheeks, his scratchy beard. Her knees buckled with longing for him. She had been so preoccupied she'd forgotten about both Gerry and Patsy.

Forgetting about him was good, she told herself, but now that she remembered her sister, she was worried. When would her mother call with some news from the hospital?

The baby clean, she handed her off once again to her father and went into the bathroom to take a shower.

When she came into the kitchen freshly showered wearing her flannel pajamas, it was approaching eleven-thirty. Kevin, seated at the kitchen table, was trying to coax Aaron into taking the bottle. The child was crying, thrashing, and turning his head away from the rubber nipple. Little Anne was asleep in her grandfather's arms. Anne noticed her father's eyelids sagging and his head beginning to bob. "Daddy!" Anne cried. "You can't fall asleep. You'll drop her."

Startled, Mr. Lyons sat up straighter in the chair. "Sorry. Maybe you better take her. I don't trust myself."

"Go to bed, Daddy. You have to get up for work. Kevin and I will wait up for them to call."

"They already did. While you were in the shower," Kevin said trying to get the nipple into the baby's mouth.

"What did they say?"

Disgusted, Kevin set the bottle on the table. Aaron screamed louder. "You try him. Maybe you can get him to eat."

Anne handed Little Anne off to her brother. She immediately scrunched up her face and began to bawl.

Kevin, looking flustered, stood and shouted over the din. "They're keeping Patsy. They ran some tests. The results aren't back yet, but they suspect an infection."

Anne hoped it was a "garden variety" infection and not something more serious like staph or MRSA.

"Mom and Vince are going to stay with her until they get her settled into a room."

"When is that going to be?" Anne asked.

"They didn't have any idea, but Vince is going to stay the night. Mom will need a ride home. Told her I'd come to get her."

"That could be awhile. In that case," Anne yelled over the racket, "I guess we should try to get these two to sleep."

As Anne bounced Aaron, she went to the cupboard and began rummaging through them. "I think the problem is these nipples. If they were more naturally shaped, he might suck." She closed the doors and looked at Kevin. "They don't have any. Maybe you could go to the grocery store and get some."

Kevin screwed up his face. "I can't go buy nipples. They'll think I'm a pervert or something."

Mr. Lyons yawned and pushed himself away from the table. "I'll go."

"You'll fall asleep at the wheel," Anne said sharply. "Go to bed, Daddy."

Mr. Lyons stood. "OK. I guess I'll go and crawl into Patsy and Vince's bed."

After her father left, Anne looked at Kevin. "You have a choice. Either you go get nipples, or I go and you stay here with these banshees."

"Some choice," he said, digging the car keys out of the pocket of his Levi's. "Now, what do I need?"

Anne handed him Aaron while she drew on a sheet of paper the shape of the nipple he was supposed to buy. He handed both of the babies back to her and picked up the paper. He curled his upper lip. "If I'm branded the town freak, it'll be your fault."

Of course, as soon as his car pulled out of the driveway, Anne's nose started to itch. With both hands filled with shrieking babies, she couldn't scratch it. She tried rubbing her nose on her shoulder, but that didn't satisfy it.

With her nose tingling, she quickly went into the living room, sat on the couch, propped her feet on the coffee table, and lay Little Anne on her thighs. Aaron, she put over her shoulder. Both babies screamed as she scratched her nose. To soothe them, she rocked her legs back and forth, lulling Little Anne into dreamland while at the same time patting the inconsolable Aaron's back.

When Kevin returned and held out the nipples, she snapped at him. "What took you so long? You were gone for forty minutes."

"I didn't want anyone around here to see me buying these so I rode over to the supermarket in Greensburg."

Anne rolled her eyes. "Take her off my legs and put her in that cradle. I'm stiff."

Anne rose, her joints cracking, and handed the squirming, starving Aaron to Kevin. "Think you can manage him while I go wash these, or are you afraid someone might see you?"

"Ha-ha," Kevin said, making a face at her and taking the baby.

A few minutes later, Anne returned with a bottle and took Aaron. Sitting on the couch once again, she attempted to stick the new natural-shaped nipple into Aaron's mouth. He smacked his lips at the formula that had leaked out onto his lips, hungrily searching for the source. He reminded Anne of Gerry when he was ravishing her breasts with kisses. How hungry he seemed to be for her. She couldn't deny, she had been equally starved for him. Her heart beat hollowly in her chest, aching to be, once again, in his arms, feel his lips on her flesh. Thinking about him was too painful. She couldn't deal with Gerry and Patsy's illness too, so she closed her eyes and banished him from her mind.

As soon as Aaron got his mouth around the rubber nipple, he began to suck vigorously. Anne heard the milk splashing as it hit his empty stomach. She kissed his downy head. "Poor Boy, you just didn't know how to get the milk out."

After gulping down the whole bottle and burping like a grown man, Aaron fell asleep in her arms.

Anne looked at Kevin who was half-dozing in the recliner. "Guess we should go to bed too. Who knows when Mom will call for her ride. I don't want to risk waking Anne to move her into her crib; I'll sleep out here on the couch with her. I'll put him in the nursery, and you can have the spare bedroom."

After the babies were all settled in, Anne found a quilt, curled up on the couch, quickly falling asleep.

It seemed like only a few minutes had passed, but when she heard Kevin whispering her name as he stood over her, she looked past him to the clock and realized she'd been asleep for nearly two hours.

"What?" Anne whispered, trying to get her bearings. "You have to go get Mom now? I didn't hear the phone."

"No. Aaron pooped. He needs his diaper changed."

Anne growled, threw back the quilt, and stomped off to the nursery, muttering. "Men are so stupid. They can build a rocket ship and send it to the moon, but they can't change a damn diaper."

She found Aaron thrashing in his crib, the place reeking. Scrunching up her nose at the smell, she picked him up and carried him to the changing table. After opening his kimono and removing the dirty diaper, she wiped the folds and crevices of his groin and small bum. Covering his tiny penis with her hand so she wouldn't get peed on, she tried to put on his new diaper, but he squirmed like the Hydra. Finally, she was able to swathe his bottom, and as she fastened the tabs, she crooned to him in a singsong voice. "All men are stupid, and I hate to tell you, Sweetheart, that you're a boy, and you're going to grow up and be stupid too. It's not your fault. Uncle Kevin is stupid. Zach is stupid. Craig's stupid. And Gerry McMaster is the King of Stupid."

"I never said I wouldn't change it, Anne."

Startled, she looked over her shoulder and was surprised to see Kevin watching her from the doorway. She'd assumed he'd gone back to bed. "Then why did you wake me up?" She quickly pulled the kimono down over Aaron's legs.

"Because I didn't know how, and I wanted you to show me."

She was glad there was only a nightlight on in the room, because she knew her face was red from embarrassment.

"You know we're not the enemy."

Anne picked up the baby and kissed his cheek.

"What are you talking about?"

"I heard what you said."

She ignored him and walked to the crib.

"Is that what you really think of men?"

She turned and stared at him. His blond hair was mussed, and he needed a shave as he stood in his boxers and T-shirt eyeing her. Even though he was her little brother, she had to admit that he'd grown into a handsome young man. "Who are you? Dr. Phil?"

"Get nasty, if you want, but your temper doesn't scare me. I know you unleash it whenever you feel threatened."

Aaron was squirming in her arms, and under Kevin's penetrating gaze she felt as uncomfortable as the baby. She moved to the rocking chair and sat.

"How do you know so much?" she said sarcastically. "I thought you majored in accounting not psychology."

"I know so much because I've watched you all my life. You used to be different. I don't know what happened, but you're miserable."

"Of course I'm miserable. I've been awakened from a sound sleep and my sister is sick."

"I'm talking about your personal life."

She began to rock furiously, feeling cornered. "My personal life is none of your business."

"See that's just what you do. Anytime someone threatens you or makes you feel vulnerable, you get scared and unleash that temper."

"I do not."

"Yes, you do. It's like you've mined your heart. Whenever someone breaches your security—Bang! You get defensive and detonate on them."

Kevin was getting too close, but she knew erupting on him would not help. She closed her eyes and exhaled. "Look, I'm tired. Can't you let this psychoanalysis wait until morning?"

He yawned and stretched. "OK, Anne, but I'm telling you, men aren't your enemy. You're enemy is you."

***

After she fed Aaron again and put him back to sleep, the phone rang, waking Little Anne. Anne dashed to the baby and rocked the cradle to settle her while Kevin staggered out of the spare bedroom and answered it. It was their mother asking to be picked up. He pulled on his jeans and shirt, stuck his feet into his Nikes without tying them and headed out, laces flapping.

Anne didn't even attempt to go back to sleep because she knew as soon as she dozed off, they would arrive and wake her. The light from the street lamps shone through the window and cast an amber glow on the baby. Anne lay on the couch watching her sleeping niece. The baby's eyes shifted rapidly under her lids and the rosebud lips pouted, as the baby seemed to be shuffling through a series of emotions while dreaming. Anne knew she had started out a blank slate just like her namesake but wondered how she had ended up the way she was. Alone and miserable.

By the time Kevin returned with their mother, Anne was having trouble staying awake. She and her mother exchanged information like sentries relieving one another's post. Anne brought her mother up-to-date on the status of the twins, and Mrs. Lyons shared what little information she had on Patsy. The tests had not come back yet, but they had started IV antibiotics and Patsy was settled in a room. They'd find out more in the morning.

Anne yawned and staggered off to the couch. Tucking the quilt under her chin, she willed herself to fall asleep quickly, knowing that one of the babies would probably be waking up soon.

Her slumber was tortured by fractured dreams. A particularly vivid one so disturbed her that it roused her to consciousness. As she lay on the couch in the silent darkness, she wondered if she had some psychosexual problem. In the dream she was holding Gerry to her naked breast trying to make him suck, but he kept turning away from her nipple, saying, "I don't know how. I don't know how!"

She stared at the ceiling, her heart pounding at how real the dream had seemed. *Oh, why couldn't he have just loved me?* A tear rolled down her cheek. Then as she wiped her eyes on a corner of the quilt, something occurred to her. Gerry had never said that he didn't love her exactly. In fact, he had said that he loved her, although with no emotion. Perhaps when he had asked, "What is love anyway?" he was being honest. Perhaps he really didn't know. Perhaps, like Aaron with the bottle, Gerry didn't know how to love.

I didn't matter, Anne told herself as she turned onto her side. Their relationship was over, and she wasn't going to humiliate herself trying to teach him how to love.

***

The next morning, Vince called to say that the doctor had just come in and that she had pyelonephritis. Anne explained that that was a severe kidney infection. Patsy's physician said that the IV antibiotics were working as Patsy's fever had diminished and she felt much improved. Her doctor estimated that they'd be keeping her at least for another day or two. Vince had gotten in touch with his parents in Chicago, and they were due to arrive at the Latrobe airport later that day to help take care of the twins.

Anne was relieved to hear that Patsy was doing better and that reinforcements were on the way. She would stay until the Confortinis arrived, then drive home so she could begin her new assignment on Thursday. She offered to come back on the weekend.

Wednesday passed in a whirlwind of baths, diapers, bottles, and when Anne kissed the twins goodbye after dinner, handing them over to their grandparents, she felt a mixture of longing and relief. In the short time she'd spent caring for them, she'd fallen in love with them and knew she'd miss them, yet she had never been so exhausted.

When she arrived home, she checked the mail—only solicitations for charge accounts—and the answering machine. No messages.

Dropping her suitcase in the corner of her bedroom, she washed her face, brushed her teeth and fell into bed.

On Thursday she drove to Mr. Dunmire's apartment and found him in such bad shape that he didn't have the energy to make a pass at her when she took his blood pressure. His condition was so much worse than Peg's; he required more care, keeping Anne busy all day, which was good because it gave her little time to think about how much she missed Peg and Gerry.

While eating her dinner that night, she called to see how Patsy was doing and learned from Kevin that she would be released from the hospital the next day. Anne was elated and relieved. "Well, good. Is there anything you want me to bring when I come?" she asked. "Diapers? Wipes? Food?"

"To be honest, Anne," Kevin said, "do yourself a favor and stay home. Mom and Mrs. Confortini are battling it out for alpha-grandmother and things are little tense."

"You sure they don't need my help?"

"Look, when Patsy comes home tomorrow, there's going to be two babies and six adults here fussing over them."

"I get the picture. Be sure to tell mom I called, and tell her that if they need help, I'll gladly come."

Now what was she going to do with herself all weekend? She vowed she would not mope about the place, mooning over Gerry.

"I will as soon as she and Mrs. Confortini decide whether the babies look more like Joe or Patsy."

Anne spent the weekend catching up on sleep and laundry. When she came home from church on Sunday morning, Anne was surprised and relieved to find that Janetta was there waiting for her.

"I didn't expect you home until tomorrow," Anne said, giving her a hug.

"Oh, Lilah called yesterday. Her niece was going to the beach and wanted to use the time-share. She said I could still stay, but I thought it best to just come back early."

Anne noticed that Janetta's bruises had faded to a mottled blue-green under her tan and that she looked refreshed.

Anne was glad to have her back. For the next week they stayed in the apartment licking their wounds, filling their free time by shopping, eating quarts of ice cream, devouring pounds of chocolates, watching every man-hater movie they could lay their hands on.

It was nearing mid-October now. The days were growing shorter and frost often silvered the small patch of grass outside their building. One chilly, rainy night after Anne and Janetta had polished off a bag of Hershey's kisses and drank two bottles of Yoo-hoo each, Anne stood and walked over to the DVD player. She picked up two movies. "What's it going to be tonight? *The Burning Bed* or *Thelma and Louise?*"

"Did you take back that Betty Broderick movie?" Janetta covered her face with her hand. "Oh, I'm having a sugar rush. I feel sick."

"Want me to get the Doritos? The salt will cut the sweetness."

Janetta opened her eyes, clutching her stomach. Her bruises were gone. "Look at us, Anne. It's eight o'clock on a Saturday night, and we're already in our pajamas. This has got to stop."

Anne dropped into the chair. "I know. My clothes are getting tight."

"I'm not just talking about the pigging out. We've got to get a life."

"You're right."

"I was thinking. Why don't we go to that Halloween Party they have on the *Gateway Clipper*?

"I don't know," Anne said, frowning. "I'm not sure if I'm ready."

"Come on. It'll be fun dressing up. We'll go for laughs."

"I'm not in the mood."

"Please. We'll design costumes. Get your sewing machine out. It'll take your mind off Gerry."

She couldn't pine for him forever; she might as well start getting over him. After a moment, Anne said, "OK, but what will we dress as?"

Janetta thought for a moment. Then her black eyes sparkled like onyxes. "I got it. How about doormats?"

Chapter 34

Gerry sat at his desk, his head resting in his hands. Pain flared in his back. Things had been so strained with Peg that for the past four weeks, he'd been sleeping on the couch in his office to avoid her. He still delivered her meals and oversaw her care, but they barely spoke.

He couldn't wait until the security system was installed. Then he could move into his townhouse at Washington's Landing and sleep in the king-sized bed.

There'd been another break-in on Butler Street, two doors down at the dry-cleaners, making him a little anxious about leaving Peg alone. The representative who sold him the system for the bar and apartment suggested a personal alarm for Peg as well. She could wear a device on a chain around her neck and call for help in an emergency.

Peg had informed Gerry that she would never wear the alarm. She would not be a "cow with a bell hung around her neck."

The agency had sent another nurse, a heavy-set, middle-aged woman named Nelda, to replace Anne. Thanks to Nelda, Peg had made tremendous progress. Peg claimed Nelda trained under the Third Reich. Unless Peg did her conditioning exercises, Nelda would not allow her to watch her soap operas. Peg hated Nelda and worked doubly hard at regaining her strength "so she could get that tyrant out of my house."

Nelda was definitely not Anne. Everyone who worked at the bar made sure that Gerry knew that. Anne's sudden departure, for which they all held him responsible, made him enemy number one. Irma responded to him with curtness. Dave, Vera, and Bob never gave him any grief because he was their boss, but he sensed tension and a distance between them. Luis doled him out smaller portions. Even Bernie took back his coveted KISS poster.

When Anne had failed to show up the Monday after the wedding, Bernie asked where she was. Gerry told him they had an argument, and she was not coming back. Bernie put his hands on his hips, and said to Gerry, "I want Anne. You stink." Then he gave him the raspberries.

Gerry hated to admit it, but he wanted her too. Though in what sense he couldn't say. The place seemed dreary without her, as if all the color had been drained from his life. He missed the way she sashayed around the place, her red curls swinging as she walked. He missed their verbal repartee, and, of course, he missed her physically. He tried not to think of their last night together on the couch, how beautiful she had been, her succulent breasts as she lay beneath him. It only produced an unquenchable longing for her.

Why couldn't I have just told her sincerely that I loved her? In the heat of passion with other women, he'd certainly never had trouble saying those words like he meant them to get his way. What was holding him back? Maybe because he sensed that if he said them with meaning to Anne, she'd believe them. All he knew was that in the weeks that had followed their breakup, he'd not had one happy day.

This one promised to be no better. It was Halloween, the thirty-fifth anniversary of his father's death. He picked up the picture sitting on the corner of his desk. "What is wrong with me, Dad?" he asked the smiling figure in the photo.

He studied the pose; an act he'd done thousands of times. His father had an arm around Peg's waist and a large hand resting on his Gerry's shoulder. How did his father's touch feel? As much as he strained his memory, he couldn't remember how his father felt when he was alive.

Unfortunately, I can never forget how he felt when dead.

In the photograph, his father looked healthy. Who would have believed that he would suffer a fatal heart attack two weeks later?

That Halloween day was forever etched in Gerry's memory. Early that morning Peg had gone up the street to the store to get candy to hand out to the trick or treaters and to buy a bandana at the five and ten. Gerry was dressing up as a cowboy and needed one for his neckerchief. After that, she had an appointment with Dolly, to have her hair dyed and set. She'd left Gerry home with his father.

Gerry remembered that his father had been reading the morning paper while he'd been hiding behind his father's chair, playing with his cap gun, pretending he was in a shoot-out with a desperado. He fired his gun. Pop! Pop! Pop! The sulfur smell of gunpowder fouled the air. Then he heard a strange noise coming from his father. "Gotcha, you varmint," Gerry said, thinking his father was pretending to be shot.

Laughing, Gerry peeked around the chair expecting to see his father slumped over, his eyes crossed, his tongue hanging out as he faked death. Instead, clutching his chest, his father rose, and staggered across the floor.

Gerry giggled, delighted that his father was going to play along. He fired again. "Prepare to meet your maker."

When his father vomited, Gerry knew he was no longer pretending.

"Yuck," Gerry said, running out of the room.

If we'd had 911 back then, Gerry wondered, would I have been one of those bright children they feature on the news who has the presence of mind to call for help?

Gerry remembered how wooden and heavy his father felt as he tried to shake him alive. It was a feeling he never wanted to experience again.

When Peg returned, her hair coiffed and dyed her customary Maureen-O'Hara-red, she found her husband dead and her small son sitting rigidly in the chair, his eyes frozen in fright. He'd sat vigil with his father's body for nearly two hours.

Now rendered thoroughly morose, Gerry leaned back in the chair, covering his face with his hands. He sat there for a moment wondering if life offered anything other than pain, heartache, and death. Then his hands fell away from his face as he thought of Anne. When she was here, it seemed possible that there might be something more.

But Anne, like his father, was part of the past, and he had no time to waste thinking about the past. Tonight was the bar's Halloween party. The place would be packed, and he had a lot of work to do. With a sigh, he rose and left the office.

***

The *Gateway Clipper* was jammed with people. The boat seemed to be bouncing on the river from the throng dancing on the deck below to the blaring music.

Anne took off the round sunglasses whose lenses she had painted white to be Little Orphan Annie and checked her watch. "Ten more minutes and we'll be off this thing," she said to Janetta, who was shivering in her skimpy Cher costume. The approaching dock looked like the Promised Land. Anne nervously glanced over her shoulder. "You don't see him, do you?"

"No."

They'd retreated to the open upper deck because a man dressed as a dog, had followed Anne all over the boat, claiming he was her dog, Sandy, and begging for her to pet him.

"I think we lost him when he visited the fire hydrant," Janetta said.

After avoiding the canine Casanova and departing the boat, they drove back to the apartment, arriving there a little after one. Janetta walked in, kicked off her leopard printed heels, and sat in the chair massaging her feet.

Anne whipped off the red Afro wig, and as she set it on the dining table, she noticed the answering machine's light blinking. "Hope nothing is wrong," she said to Janetta. "We've got five messages."

"If something was wrong with Patsy, they would have called your cell phone. It better not be Steve," Janetta said. Since being served with protection from abuse papers, she'd heard nothing from him.

Curious and concerned, Anne pressed the button.

Beep. "Anne."

She stopped breathing. It was Gerry.

"Look, we should talk. Give me a call. I'll be in the bar all night."

Janetta walked over to Anne, who stood staring at the machine as if she'd never seen one before.

Beep. "Ah, hi. Me again. I just have a minute. If you're there, please pick up." He paused. "I guess you're not home. Please give me a call."

Janetta grabbed Anne's arm. "He said 'please.' Twice!"

Anne shushed her. The sound of his voice alone turned her knees to mush.

Beep. "Anne. Look, I need to talk to you."

"Need? He said 'need.'" Janetta giggled. "He sounds whipped."

Anne folded her hands and pressed them to her lips, listening intently.

Beep. "Aw, Anne." There was silence, then he softly said, "I miss you."

Janetta clapped her hands. "You hear that? He's a broken man." She snapped her fingers and did a little bump of her hips. "You've brought him to his knees."

Anne smiled. He misses me.

Beep. The last message was just a desperate, "Please."

Anne fished her cell phone out of her purse. It said there were two missed messages. They were both from Gerry. "He called my cell too. It must have been too noisy on the boat to hear it."

Janetta gave Anne a bear hug. "Oh, man. He's miserable. You can hear it in his voice."

Anne frowned, playing with the white cuffs of her Orphan Annie Dress. "Do you think so? Do you think he wants me back?"

"I've never heard anyone so pitiful."

They replayed the messages two more times, analyzing every word and inflection of his voice.

"Do you think he's drunk? Should I call him?" Anne asked. If he was just calling because he hoped to reconcile because he needed someone to have sex with, then she didn't want to talk to him. But if he was calling because he wanted a second chance—She couldn't let herself dream. It hurt too much when dreams died.

"I wouldn't," Janetta said. "At least not now. Let him stew overnight. Let him wonder where you are, if you're out with someone. That'll set the hook. Then all you have to do is reel him in tomorrow."

Anne sighed. "Hope you're right."

**

When the phone rang at seven-thirty the next morning, Anne jumped out of bed wearing a big smile. If Gerry was calling this early, he was desperate.

"Hello," she said cheerfully. Then she reminded herself to play it cool.

"Anne?"

Her smile faded when she heard the panic in Peg's voice.

"Anne, oh dear God."

"What is it, Peg? Are you sick?"

"It's Gerry."

Anne could hear her gulping air.

"What about him?"

"He's been hurt."

Anne's eyes were open, but she saw nothing. She felt as if she were being sucked into another dimension. "Hurt? How?"

"Oh, Anne," Peg said, "come quickly. He's been stabbed."

Chapter 35

When Anne arrived, she found three squad cars, their blood-red lights flashing, parked haphazardly in front of Mac's Place. In the frosty morning air, a small crowd had gathered on the sidewalk. She pulled into the first available spot, shut off the car, and ran up the street, her pulse pumping in her ears, her mouth dry with fear.

A patrolwoman intercepted her at the door to the apartment. After Anne explained who she was and the officer radioed the beat cop who was upstairs with Peg, she was finally let into the building.

Anne flew up the stairs, down the hall, and found Peg sitting on the sofa, nervously fingering the crystal rosary beads Anne had given her for her birthday. Irma, her arm around a tearful Bernie, sat between him and Peg on the sofa, and a portly, gray-haired officer was sitting on the edge of the recliner, his notebook out.

"Oh, Anne," Peg cried. "Thank God you're here."

"Where's Gerry? What happened?"

Peg looked pale. She nodded to the policeman. "This is Fred Baranowski."

He dipped his head respectfully to Anne and rose. "I'll leave you now, Mrs. McMaster. If you need anything, give me a call."

Peg took his hand and held it. "Thanks, Fred."

When she released it, he touched her shoulder. "No problem. I promise you we'll find who did this to Mac." Then he hitched up his blue uniform pants and lumbered out of the room.

"Fred's been patrolling this neighborhood since Hector was a pup," Peg explained. "He thinks some dope head broke into the bar looking for cash, and Gerry must have surprised him. On the way to early Mass this morning, Bernie saw lights on in the bar and the door

293

ajar. He went inside and found Gerry lying on the floor in a pool of blood."

Bernie sniffled loudly. "He's hurt real bad, Anne."

Anne knelt beside Peg and took the old woman's hands. They were cold and trembling. "The ambulance just pulled out. Fred called Dave for me because he lives the closest, and he came over to ride with him because I'm not up to it."

"When they were loading him inside, he opened his eyes briefly and asked for you, Anne," Irma said softly.

Touched, Anne stood. She shook all over and asked, "How badly is he hurt?" She wanted to be strong for Peg, but she started to cry.

Irma came and put her chubby arm around Anne. "We don't know, Honey. Would you go to the hospital? I'll take care of Peg. They went to Presby. You understand all that medical stuff."

Peg reached out for Anne's hand. "You'll make sure they take good care of my boy, won't you?"

Anne took her hand and squeezed it firmly. "Do you even have to ask?"

***

Anne found Dave seated in the crowded Emergency Room, bent over, cradling his head in his hands.

"Dave," Anne said as she gently touched his shoulder.

Startled, he looked up. "Anne, you're here." He rose and wrapped her in a hug.

"Where's Gerry?" she asked. "How is he? Where have they taken him?"

He released her and pointed to a set of double door. "We just arrived. They wheeled him through there."

"How bad is he?"

She couldn't recall Dave ever looking concerned before; he was always happy go-lucky. That alarmed her.

"I don't know anything."

"Was he conscious?"

"In and out. He called for you though."

She went to the nurse's station and asked a woman with too much eyeliner and too little chin where they had taken Gerry and was told he was back in one of the exam rooms. They refused to let her in to see him. She argued with the woman, told her she was a nurse, stamped her foot, and threatened her. Finally, she began to cry. "But you don't understand," she sniffled. "He's asking for me."

"I'm sorry. You can't go back there."

Undeterred, Anne shot through the double door. She heard Dave distracting the nurse by asking where the restrooms were because he felt sick.

Anne looked into three exam cubicles before she found Gerry and a team of emergency personnel clustered around him.

"Gerry, I'm here," she called.

A heavy nurse stepped beside her. "You can't come in here."

"I'm a nurse." Anne pushed past her and went to his side. An attendant was cutting off his bloody clothing. There wasn't a mark on his lovely face, although his complexion was deathly white, making his dark whiskers more vivid in contrast. He needed a shave, and it struck her that his hair could be growing while he was in the process of dying. Instinctively, she glanced at the blood pressure monitor. Too low. Her heart wrenched in fear. No, he can't die. *Dear St. Anne, this can't be your plan!*

The right side of his head was bloody. The attendant removed his shirt, revealing a grisly wound where his left arm met his chest. There was so much blood Anne couldn't tell if he'd suffered any other wounds. As a nurse she'd seen hundreds of horrific scenes but never one involving someone she loved. She felt faint but knew she must be strong for him. Elbowing her way closer, she gently touched his cheek. It was cool under her fingertips. "Gerry. It's Anne. I'm here."

His head lolled toward the sound of her voice. His eyes fluttered open for a moment. "Anne," he rasped, then closed them.

Encouraged, Anne clasped his hand, patting it reassuringly. "Yes. Yes, it's Anne. I'm here."

A second nurse came and grabbed her by the arm and tried to lead her away.

"No. You don't understand. I promised his mother I'd take care of him. I have to stay."

"We've got to prep him for surgery."

"But I'm a nurse too. I can stay."

This nurse looked kindly at Anne and put an arm around her waist. "Then you know, Dear, that for his sake you must leave so we can take care of him."

Firmly but gently, the nurse began to move Anne away. She felt Gerry's cold, lifeless fingers slipping from her grasp. "Wait. Let me say good bye to him." Anne bent close to his ear and whispered, "I'll be right outside waiting for you, Gerry. I won't leave." She kissed his forehead and looked over her shoulder at him as the nurse led her away. Gerry lay pale while medical personnel swarmed around him. She could feel her heart splitting in two as tears swam before her eyes, blurring the image of him. "Is he going to be OK?"

The kind nurse made no reply; she only tightened her arm around Anne's waist and escorted her back to the waiting room.

Dave came to Anne, and she collapsed sobbing into his arms.

"Is he . . . ?"

"We're prepping him for surgery," the nurse said. "There'll be someone out to speak with you shortly."

Dave nodded. "Good."

Anne raised her head. "Oh, Dave, he said my name."

He smoothed Anne's red hair. "Honey, that's a good sign. Hold on to that." His deep, rich voice soothed her.

"Excuse me," a petite Asian woman dressed in green scrubs said softly with a slight accent. "I'm Dr. Park. Are you Mr. McMaster's family?"

Anne turned around and, wiping her eyes. "Yes."

"I'm his attending physician and from our initial examinations, it appears that he's suffered a blow to the head, but we have reason to believe that injury is not serious."

Anne felt herself go limp with relief.

"He has sustained two stab wounds—one to his left shoulder and one to his chest," said the doctor, "which we will address during surgery. Our first priority is to stabilize him, stop the bleeding. We're not sure how serious the chest wound is, if there is any lung involvement or damage to the heart. Our next priority is to save his arm and minimize loss of function in it."

"Will he be OK?" Anne asked.

"We will do our very best. I can assure you." She turned and left them.

Anne sank into a chair, the shock of it all catching up to her. Suddenly, she, too, felt as if she'd lost all her blood as chills shook her and made her teeth chatter when she spoke. "I-I-I promised I'd c-c-call Peg."

Dave patted her shoulder. "I'll do it."

"But I p-p-promised her."

"Listen, Anne. You need to sit here and calm yourself. Peg will understand." She was relieved. Anne wasn't sure she would be able to compose herself enough to talk to Peg without breaking down. With Peg's delicate health, Anne didn't want to further alarm her by falling apart with her on the phone. Dave took out his cell phone and headed for the exit.

There were other people in the waiting room with her, but she barely noticed them. So consumed by concern for Gerry, they appeared like paper dolls to her—each person reduced to a two-dimensional being. The tension was unbearable; she wanted to scream. *How do I calm yourself when the only man you've ever loved is on the O.R. table?*

She picked up a magazine, but couldn't concentrate. *Oh why didn't I call him last night? Maybe he was injured then. What had he wanted to tell her?* Even if he called to tell her that he hated her, she didn't care. She just wanted him to live.

Feeling as if ants were crawling over her, she walked to the window. The morning was dawning in full autumn splendor, orange, crimson, and gold trees against an azure sky. She heard the faint peal of church bells. Then she remembered. It was All Saints' Day. Anne began to pray, offering up her own litany, calling on every saint she could think of to intercede for Gerry.

Dave returned with a cup of hot chocolate. Glancing around at the others in the waiting room, the anxiety torturing their faces, he said, "I can't stand sitting in here. Let's walk."

Together, they paced the hallway, never straying too far in case there was word from the O.R.

"How was Peg?" she asked.

"As good as can be expected."

They were silent for a moment. Anne took a sip and looked into the cup. "He called me last night."

"He did?" Dave sounded genuinely surprised. "Finally, he's come to his senses."

She stopped. "What do you mean?"

"Oh, come on, Anne. It's obvious you two love each other."

She chuckled sarcastically. "I'm glad you're so sure."

"Well, what did he say last night?"

"Nothing. I was out. He left me a message. I was going to call him this morning." She gazed at Dave anxiously. "You wouldn't know what he wanted, would you?"

"All I know is that ever since you left, he's been miserable. That's not like Gerry. You've really done a number on him."

Chapter 36

Anne watched the clock's hands slowly make their way around the dial. She and Dave had run out of things to say.

A little after noon, Dr. Park appeared in the doorway. Anne and Dave walked over to her, Anne holding her breath.

"He's doing fine," she said.

Anne let herself breathe again.

"We've sutured the head wound. Fortunately, there was no skull fracture. He probably has a concussion though. As for the arm, he has suffered quite a bit of damage. But we managed to save it."

Save it? Anne reeled.

"I'm not sure what range of motion he'll have, but that's a bridge to cross on another day."

"What about the chest wound?" Anne asked.

"He is one lucky man. Another few centimeters and it would have struck his heart. He's stable now, but he lost a considerable amount of blood. Had he not been found when he was, we wouldn't even be here discussing his outcome."

Anne offered a silent prayer of thanks that his life had been spared. "Can we see him?"

"He's in recovery. As soon as he wakes up, we'll call you."

Anne and Dave both thanked Dr. Park. After she left, they hugged each other.

"I'll call Mrs. Mac," Dave said, rooting in his pocket for his cell phone.

***

A few hours later, Gerry was moved into his own room, and they were allowed in to see him. As they entered, Dave touched

Anne's arm. "I'm just going to say hello, then leave you two alone. Mrs. Mac and Irma probably need me."

They stood on either side of Gerry's bed. He looked so pale, Anne's heart ached. His head had been shaved where he'd been stitched. Only one arm of his hospital gown had been pulled up. His left side of his chest was covered in gauze. Her nursing instincts took over, and she ran a mental check on his condition.

Dave bent over the bed, "Mac, it's Dave. Don't worry about anything. We'll take care of it all. I'm going to go now. You get better, Buddy."

Gerry only moaned.

Dave kissed Anne on the cheek.

"Tell Peg. I'll stay here with him," Anne said. "And not to worry. I'll make sure they take good care of her boy."

When they were alone, Anne moved closer to Gerry's head. She stroked his cheek. It was warmer than before, and the stubble was coarse under her fingers.

"Gerry," she whispered. "It's Anne."

From the way his eyes shifted underneath his lids and the slight twitches in his face, she knew he was hearing her.

"You're going to be fine."

He slowly raised his eyes, peering at her with a glazed look. "Peg?" he murmured. "Did he get to Peg?"

"No, Peg's safe. She's fine."

The corners of his mouth rose in a weak smile.

She kissed his forehead. "Sleep, Handsome. I won't leave you."

He needed no coaxing and drifted off.

She pulled a chair up to his bed. With Gerry out of imminent danger, the heightened sense of alarm that had kept her on edge quieted. Suddenly she felt exhausted. Anne lowered the rail, and rested her head next to him on the bed.

**

Someone was playing with her curls. Startled, Anne sat up. She didn't remember where she was. Her neck ached. Then she remembered. Gerry had been stabbed. Quickly, she glanced back at him. He lay there his eyes open, a slight smile on his face.

"I always knew I'd get you to sleep with me," he whispered, his voice raspy.

"It's a pretty drastic way to con me into it."

She stood and stretched, her neck and back stiff. "How are you feeling?"

He closed his eyes. "What happened?"

She rubbed his right arm, the muscles firm and functioning. Anne hoped his other would be that way again soon. "An intruder stabbed you twice and gave you a concussion."

He moved and winced.

"They operated on your arm and your chest. That's where you were stabbed."

"Stitches?" he asked.

She smiled. "Or staples. I haven't looked under the bandages."

His lips moved slowly over his teeth as he spoke. "Glad I was knocked out."

She sat next to him and told him all that she knew about what had happened to him, what the doctor had said. "The police think it was some addict trying to get some money for a fix. If Bernie hadn't found you, you most likely would have died. You were very fortunate."

"I know." He patted her hand and grimaced. "I was afraid he'd get upstairs to Peg. She's OK?"

"Yes, she's fine. Does it hurt?"

He closed his eyes and nodded. With his good arm, he reached up and felt his head. He looked at Anne.

"Do you have a headache?"

"Yes," he said softly.

"They gave you a morphine pump for the pain." She handed him the trigger. "Press this button when you need it, and it'll give you more medication. You can't o.d. It'll only give you a little at a time, but you can push it frequently. It just won't release any if it's too soon."

Gerry pressed it a few times, and after a while, he seemed to be more relaxed. He looked at Anne, his eyelids drooping. "I called you."

"I know."

"Have to talk. Want to tell you . . . " He drifted off to sleep.

She covered him and kissed his forehead. "Yes, we do have to talk, but there's time, Gerry," she whispered, her lips lingering on his flesh. "I'm not going anywhere."

***

While he slept, Anne made several phone calls. She called Peg to tell her how Gerry was doing. She called her mother to inquire after Patsy and the babies and to tell her that if anyone was looking for her, not to be concerned because she was with Gerry at the hospital. Finally, she called Janetta and asked her to bring her a change of clothes and some toiletries.

Near seven o'clock, Janetta arrived with an overnight bag and a Subway hoagie. She crept into the room and gave Anne a hug. She stood over the bed sizing up Gerry who was still dozing. She widened her black eyes. "Talk about Sleeping Beauty. Even battered, he's gorgeous."

"I told you the first time I saw him," Anne whispered, "I thought my legs were going to give out he was so handsome."

Janetta touched the edge of his sheet and raised it a little. "Have you taken a peek?"

"Janetta!" Anne slapped her hand away.

"Come on. I want to know if he's gorgeous all over. You're a nurse. Can't you check his catheter or something?"

"No!"

"You're no fun. That's about as close as I'll be getting for a long while."

"Thanks for bringing this stuff," Anne said, tucking the covers around Gerry.

"So you're going to stay all night?"

"He might need me."

"You just want to stick around in case he needs a sponge bath."

***

"Anne?"

"I'm here," she said, rousing from a light sleep. She looked at her watch's luminous dial. It was two-thirteen. "Is it the pain again?" She put the recliner into an upright position and came to his bedside.

"No. I can't sleep."

She turned the light above his bed on its dimmest setting. "How are you feeling?"

"OK I guess for being shish-ka-bobbed." He looked up at her, and he seemed so much like a little boy. "Will you sit up with me for a while?"

"Sure. Would you like me to clean you up a bit?"

"Is than an invitation for a sponge bath?" He smiled weakly.

"I think that'll have to wait a bit." Anne filled a basin of warm water and wiped his face. She helped him to brush his teeth.

"Thanks," he said.

The hospital was quiet now. Only faint noises from the nurses' station drifted into the room.

"I called you," he said, reaching for her hand.

"I know you did," Anne said as she held it firmly, thrilled to touch him again. "I was going to call you back in the morning. Then this happened."

He licked his lips. She gave him an ice chip. "You know what I wanted?"

She sat back down. "No. Why don't you tell me."

He paused for a while, seeming to marshal his strength before he spoke. "Did Peg ever tell you that I was with my dad when he died?"

"No."

His voice became very soft. "I was nearly five. She left me home with him while she went shopping and to get her hair done. He had a massive heart attack and died in front of me."

The intimacy and quiet of the night enveloped them and seemed to strip Gerry down to his emotional core. He paused a moment while he tried to blink back tears.

Anne took a tissue and wiped them away. "Oh, Gerry, how awful."

"I never told anyone, but it scared the daylights out of me. I've had nightmares about it all my life. I've always been afraid I'd die that way too. Everyone has always said that I looked and acted just like him." He took her hand. "Slugger, that night on your couch. I wanted to tell you I loved you, but I couldn't." His eyes were as soft as the night. "You know why?"

She shook her head, the lump in her throat making it too difficult to speak.

"I was afraid. I made a pledge to myself when I was very young that I'd never work in the bar and never settle down because I was sure that if I did, I'd die just like my dad." He kissed her knuckles. "What an idiot I am. I almost died anyway. I'd rather die having loved you for one day than live a hundred years without you."

"Oh, Gerry!" She kissed his forehead, her broken heart filling with love for him. "You're not your father, and you're not going to die." I won't let him die, she thought. After losing him once, I'll never let him go again. And then she realized precisely what was tormenting her and causing all her anger. She had loved her baby, and she hadn't fought for it. The anger which she should have channeled to fight for her baby's life she had been unleashing on anyone who dared to come too close. She would not make that same mistake with Gerry. She would fight for him. Even if that meant confronting her past.

She sighed. "There's something I have to tell you, too. Something I'm ashamed of and have regretted every day of my life since it happened. I hope that after I tell you, you'll still love me because sometimes I hate myself because of it."

He squeezed her hand. "What is it, Slugger?"

She told Gerry all about Zach and the abortion.

"No wonder you were so angry with me after the wedding. But I swear to you, Anne, I'm not like Zach. Beneath all the b.s., I do have a heart because I can feel it breaking for you and what you've been through."

She looked sheepishly at him. "So you think you can still love me?"

"Think. I know." He pulled her close and kissed her.

She was surprised by the passion in his lips. "Wow," she said as she pulled away and rubbed his chest. "What are you going to be like when you get better?"

He reached up and pulled her close, giving her another kiss that left her lightheaded.

"Listen, Slugger," he said with fire in his voice, "I could make love to you right now, one hand tied behind my back."

"Take it easy, Stud Boy, there's plenty of time for that."

"OK, but maybe I could interest you in checking my catheter?"

She grabbed his cheek and tweaked it. "You are so awful."

"Janetta said she would do it."

Her mouth fell open. "You were listening!"

"So you did find me irresistible that first day when you came into the bar?"

Anne picked up the sheet, crawled in next to his warm body, and tucked herself under his good arm. She whispered into his ear, "And every day since."

He winced.

Alarmed, she looked into his mischievous blue eyes. "Is it the pain?"

"No," he smiled and pulled her closer to nuzzle her neck. "I think you better call the nurse. I need more slack in my catheter."

Chapter 37

"Sponge baths," Gerry said. "I didn't hear you mention anything about sponge baths."

Anne kicked his foot.

The discharge nurse looked up from her paperwork. "You don't need sponge baths. You're ambulatory. You can take showers as long as you take care to keep your incisions covered."

"But what if I get dizzy in the shower? I lost a lot of blood, you know. Why don't you just write in there that my nurse has to get in the shower with me?"

Anne blushed, leaned on her elbow, and covered her face with her hands.

The nurse peered over her half glasses. "If you're concerned, I'm sure you can work something out with whoever is assigned to you."

Gerry grinned and nudged Anne, knocking her elbow out from under her head. "See, she said it's fine."

It was Friday, five days since the attack, and Gerry was definitely feeling much better.

Anne glared at him.

He whispered, "I'll scrub your back, if you scrub mine."

The discharge nurse handed him his papers. She looked at Anne. "If you need a prescription for cimetidine, I'd be happy to arrange for it."

She and the discharge nurse chuckled at the inside joke. One of the little-known side effects of that drug was impotence.

***

When Gerry walked into the kitchen holding Anne's hand, Peg practically annihilated him with kisses. Irma, Bernie, Vera, and Luis were there too. Dave and Bob were at school. Irma and Vera also kissed and hugged him gingerly not wanting to hurt his arm that was now in a sling.

"Jeez, all these hot babes kissing me," he said basking in the attention, "I feel like Hugh Hefner."

Irma waved a hand at him. "You're so full of baloney."

Luis went to plant his lips on Gerry's cheek. "Knock that Latin kissy-face stuff off," Gerry said, offering him his left hand instead. Luis kissed it. Everyone laughed while Gerry groaned.

They'd all visited him in the hospital except Bernie. Irma thought it would upset him too much. So when Bernie saw his friend, he rushed toward Gerry, gently squeezing him around the middle. "I thought you were going die," Bernie said tearfully.

Gerry rubbed the little man's crew cut. "If it wasn't for you, the doctor said I would have. You're a real hero."

"And your best buddy?"

Gerry's lip began to quiver as he looked down at his lifelong companion. The person he'd always protected growing up had saved his life. "The best buddy any guy has ever had."

Irma handed Bernie a handkerchief, and he blew his nose loudly.

"Look," Peg said, sweeping her hand toward the kitchen table, "we made you a welcome home lunch."

He took his seat at the table. Peg kissed the top of his head. "It's so nice to have my Gerry back."

***

On Sunday, Anne drove Peg and Gerry to Mass. She took vacation the following week so that she could accompany him to therapy. By the next week he was able to drive the few blocks to the hospital using just his good arm, and she went back to work, taking care of Mr. Dunmire.

That Saturday, because Anne knew Gerry was going crazy sitting in the house, she took him to Patsy's to visit the twins and to her mother's for lunch.

He and her father talked about different brands of beer and how Rolling Rock, once only a local brew, could now be ordered all over the nation while her mother gushed and fussed over him. Before they left, she took Anne aside. "Is he serious?" she asked.

"Not often," Anne said, letting her hang about the status of their relationship.

In fact, Anne felt as if she were hanging too. Gerry had told her everyday since that night in the hospital that he loved her, but their relationship had not progressed any further. He never spoke about a future.

She told herself to be patient with him. It had only been two weeks, and he was still recovering.

***

Early the next Sunday morning, Anne woke to pounding on the door. She and Janetta met each other coming out of their bedrooms, each wearing puzzled looks. Janetta put an eye to the peephole then turned to Anne, her dark brows raised. "It's Gerry."

"Gerry? What the . . . ?" Anne opened the door.

He stepped inside wearing black dress slacks, charcoal crewneck shirt, and herringbone jacket, his arm in a sling, and whistled. "Wow, two beauties in sexy lingerie. Every man's fantasy!"

It was nearing Thanksgiving and the weather had turned cold. Anne was wearing red plaid flannel pajamas and Janetta sweatpants and a thermal T-shirt.

"Save it," Janetta said. "I'm in therapy. I don't fall for flattery anymore." She headed toward her room. "I was just going out for breakfast. I'll leave you two alone."

"No," Gerry said. "Go back to bed. I'm whisking Anne away."

"You are?" Anne asked.

"I are," he said.

Janetta yawned and gave a small wave. "Then goodnight."

Anne grabbed the shoulders of her pajama top. "But I'm not even dressed. And I need to take a shower."

He looked at his watch. "We have time."

"OK, but what shall I wear?"

"A dress." He pushed her tousled rust-colored curls away and kissed her neck. "Underwear optional."

"Is that anyway for someone who went to Confession and church for the first time in years last night to talk?"

He ran a hand up her pajama top. "It is if he's madly in love." His fingers were cold; she squirmed away. He caught her hand and pulled her to his chest. Running his thumb across her lower lip, he said, "I just said that about you and Janetta being my fantasy to make her feel good. You're the only one I ever dream about." Her lips puckered around his the tip of his thumb for an instant. Then she dashed into her room.

A moment later, she emerged wearing a thick bathrobe and ran into the bathroom. He knocked on the door. Anne pulled it open a crack. "What?"

He tried to peek in at her naked body. "Just wondering if you needed anyone to scrub your back?"

"Nice try," she said, closing the door in his face.

"Get a room," Janetta called. "I'm trying to sleep."

Twenty minutes later, Anne opened the door. She was wearing her bathrobe and her wet hair hung in bronze ringlets. "I'll be ready in a few minutes." She dashed into her bedroom.

Anne dried her hair and quickly dressed in a chocolate stretch velvet dress that hugged her every curve and a pair of brown suede heels. She didn't know why, but she was shaking when she put on her makeup. Perhaps it was because he had surprised her. What else did Gerry have in store for her?

She came into the living room. "Is this OK for whatever we're doing?"

He clicked off ESPN and rose.

He turned off sports? I must look good!

A broad smile appeared on his face. "More than OK."

"Let me get my coat." She took her faux sable from the closet, and he helped her on with it.

He caught her eye and the look he gave her just about melted her bones.

She stepped back, her hands on her hips, laughing. "What are you up to?"

"Well, Slugger, you've been such a wonderful friend, nurse, and girlfriend, I wanted to express my appreciation."

He picked up her hand and kissed it. "Come, My Dear."

Gerry led her out of the apartment to the lobby. Outside Anne could see a shiny, black limousine idling in front of the building. She gasped. He turned to her. "Anne Lyons, this is your day."

My day?

She put a hand on her chest to still her galloping heart. *My day. Thank you, St. Anne. It's finally come!*

Chapter 38

Gerry took her hand and helped her into the limousine. She sank into the cushioned leather seats. Gerry climbed in beside her and the limousine pulled out. He pushed a button, a compartment opened, and reaching inside it, he pulled out a red rose, and handed it to her.

"Thank you," she said, inhaling the fragrance. "I love red roses."

"I know. I asked Janetta."

"She's in on this?"

"How else would I have gotten into your building?"

She had been so excited when he arrived this morning it had never occurred to that she hadn't admitted him into the building.

He pressed another button and Michael Crawford's voice singing "Love Changes Everything" filled the air. Leave it to Janetta to tell him that I love that song.

Anne closed her eyes, immersing herself in the celestial sounds. "I'm truly flattered."

"I'm hoping for loved and appreciated."

She touched his cheek and smiled. "I'm that too."

The limousine pulled into Station Square and stopped in front of the Grand Concourse Restaurant. A stiff November wind blew, sending leaves scurrying along the curb. They stepped inside, and the maitre d' led them to a cozy table, which Gerry had reserved for them. It overlooked the Pittsburgh cityscape.

There was an elaborate buffet and piano player. Not wanting to be bothered with making excursions to the buffet table, and not being able to manage with his arm, he'd also arranged for a waiter to keep filling their plates. They ordered Mimosas and feasted on melon with prosciutto, Eggs Benedict, and mini cheesecakes. Gerry even fed her one. When she reciprocated, he held her wrist then seductively licked all her fingertips. She thought she'd slide under the table with desire.

After three Mimosas she was giddy. They left the restaurant and entered the waiting limousine.

She snuggled next to him. "Where are you taking me now?"

"You'll see."

She kissed him from the time they pulled out until the limousine stopped. When the chauffeur opened the door, Anne was surprised to see they were in front of Mac's Place. "What are we doing here?"

"Another surprise."

He unlocked the door to the bar, entered, and pushed the code number for the new security system. Inside, it was dark and quiet, like it had been the first time she'd come here, Anne thought. That day seemed so long ago now.

Gerry flipped a switch and turned on the Tiffany-style lamps.

"Have a seat," he said, guiding her to a table in the middle of the floor.

He took a chair, moved it so that it faced her, then sat. Unhooking the sling, he whipped it off. "I don't need this anymore."

"Oh, Gerry, that's wonderful."

"I wanted to surprise you, show you how much my range of motion has improved." He slowly raised his arm to shoulder height in front of him. "I can also move it behind me." He gingerly shifted his arm backward.

"You've really made great progress."

"Look, I don't even need you to reach into my pocket anymore." When he removed his hand from his pants pocket, he was holding a small blue velvet box.

Anne was too overcome to speak or move.

Gerry dropped to one knee, and she held her breath. He gazed up at her with eyes as blue as the velvet box and said, "Anne Lyons,

314

the day you walked into this bar and took a swing at me, you landed a knockout." Her heart leapt in her chest as the tears began to fall.

He picked up her hand. "I love you more than I ever dreamed I could love anyone. And there's nothing more I want in life than to marry you."

This truly is my day, she thought, bursting with joy.

"Yes," she squealed and threw her arms around his neck. Caught off balance, Gerry toppled backwards, taking Anne along with him.

"Did I hurt you?" she cried, grasping his shoulders, hoping she hadn't injured his arm.

"No," he laughed, wrapping his arms around her as she lay atop him.

She kissed him all over.

"Jeez, Anne," he said coming up for air, "had I known you preferred to be on top, maybe you wouldn't have thrown me out of your apartment that night."

Laughing and crying at the same time, she rolled off him and sat on the floor. She stayed there because she wasn't sure if she could stand. She helped Gerry sit up. Then he kissed her so hotly, she was afraid the spandex in her dress would disintegrate.

Finally, he stood and helped her up. "Where's the chair," she said. "I can't stand. You have literally knocked me off my feet."

"And you haven't even seen the ring."

He picked the box up and opened it, revealing a large emerald cut diamond. "Janetta said size 5."

At this point, she couldn't remember her name let alone her ring size. Her hand trembled as he slipped the platinum band onto her finger.

"Oh, it's magnificent," she said holding her hand up in front of her eyes. "More than I could have ever hoped for."

While she admired the way it sparkled under the lamplight, he walked behind the bar and brought out a bottle of champagne. He removed the cork with a loud pop.

On cue, Peg, Irma, Bernie, Dave, Vera, Bob, Luis, and Janetta came rushing out of the kitchen and swarmed around Anne and Gerry.

"You were all in on it?" Anne cried, clutching her blushing cheeks.

Anne had never been kissed and hugged so many times before.

After the champagne flutes were passed around and Anne and Gerry's happiness toasted, Luis served a luscious chocolate-hazelnut congratulatory cake he'd baked especially for the occasion. While Gerry showed off to the crowd how much progress he'd made in therapy, Peg toddled over and took a seat next to Anne, who was alone at the table gazing at her ring.

She picked up Anne's hand and examined it.

"Isn't it beautiful, Peg?"

"Yes, but after what he put you through, you deserve one the size of the Rock of Gibraltar."

"Sometimes I don't feel like I'm worthy of so much happiness."

Peg squeezed her fingers. "Honey, the past is the past. Leave it there. What did the good Lord say? See, I make all things new again. You're a new person. Gerry's a new person, and I'm a new person. I even have new heart."

Peg is right. We are all new people. Love does that to a person. It is the ultimate makeover. Anne looked at Gerry who was near the bar, showing Dave how far he could raise his arm. She smiled. "Oh, Peg, I'm so happy."

Peg slapped her arm and winked, "You should be happy, Annie Banannie. Not every girl gets to be my daughter-in-law!"

Epilogue

Three days after Gerry and Anne returned home from their honeymoon, Gerry kissed Anne goodbye as she lounged in their bed at their place on Washington's Landing. She had a few more days off before beginning her new position at the crisis pregnancy center and planned to spend this day putting away all their wedding gifts and writing thank you cards.

Gerry drove the few short miles to the bar, parked in back, and let himself in. When the new security system beeped, he quickly disarmed it, thinking that Peg must have slept in since she usually shut it off when she awoke.

When he went into her room to see if she was stirring and wanted a cup of coffee, he found her lying motionless in bed. Sometime during the night she had passed away.

The sick feeling that he experienced when he'd found his father washed over him but quickly ebbed. This time he was not frightened, but grateful. Peg had died peacefully in the home that she loved above the establishment where she'd devoted most of her well-lived life.

The sad news of Peg's death traveled quickly up and down Butler Street and throughout all of Lawrenceville. Anyone who knew Peg presumed that her bad heart had been the cause of her death.

Anne and Gerry, however, knew better.

After making arrangements for Peg's viewing, funeral Mass, and burial, Anne and Gerry left the funeral home and went back to Peg's apartment.

Gerry poured glasses of wine for himself and Anne. With salty tears and fruity wine, they sat at the kitchen table and toasted the life of Peg McMaster.

His glass drained, Gerry rose and sighed. "No use putting it off."

Anne took his hand. It pained her to see him so sad. "Want me to do it?"

"No, I'll do it," he said, giving her hand a gentle squeeze. "Why don't you call Irma and give her the details of the arrangements. I'm sure the Christian Mothers will want to know the viewing hours, so they can come and say the rosary."

Gerry dreaded going back into Peg's room, but he had to pick out a dress for her burial. As he passed the Sacred Heart statue in the hallway, he made the sign of the cross.

His eyes were drawn to the empty bed. The linens, like Christ's burial shroud, lay rumpled on it. Only he knew Peg wouldn't be coming back to him in three days.

Gerry, with his heart feeling like a wedge had been driven into it, moved to the closet. He saw Peg's war chest on the top shelf, and he felt his heart cleave in two. He hoped that all Peg had believed in was true; she deserved an eternity of bliss.

He pulled out a few dresses, but his overwhelming grief had sapped his ability to make a decision. What did he know about dresses? Tossing them onto the bed, he pinched the corners of his eyes to staunch the tears.

As if she sensed Gerry's distress, Anne walked into the room and put a hand on his shoulder.

"I don't know what to pick," he said, sounding like a little lost boy.

"How about this?" Anne said, pulling out the dress Peg had worn to Maeve's wedding. "I'll never forget how her eyes sparkled when she told us about the night you were conceived."

Gerry shook his head, laughing. Then he sat on the bed and covered his face and began to weep. Anne sat next to him, put her arm around him, and stroked his black hair while he sobbed.

"I know you're going to miss her terribly," she said, feeling her own tears sliding down her cheeks. "I already do. But I like to think she's in heaven now with your father dancing and watching over us."

He looked up at Anne, his blues eyes swimming in tears and kissed her on the forehead. "I don't know what I'd do if I didn't have you."

She touched his cheek reassuringly. His skin was damp from tears. "I'm going to pick some jewelry," Anne said. She rose and went to Peg's jewelry box and began searching for an appropriate pair of earrings. "Oh," Anne said, turning to look at Gerry. "Don't forget. We need her glasses."

Gerry went to the nightstand by the bed. Peg's glasses were there along with the rosary beads Anne had given her on her birthday. He decided he'd lay her out with them too. He was glad he'd thrown her the party, and despite the sorrow, a smile came to his lips when he thought of her basking in the party guests' attention.

Then Gerry noticed something lying on the floor. He bent and picked up two pieces of paper. One was a check in the amount of twenty dollars, that from the way the pen had scrolled off the paper, he assumed she'd been in the process of writing when she'd died. He turned the other paper over and read it.

"Anne, look at this," Gerry said, calling her over and handing her the paper.

"It's a prayer request card addressed to the Shrine of St. Anne," she said.

"Read the intention line," Gerry said.

Anne read Peg's shaky script aloud: "With gratitude for favors granted."

Anne's lips began to tremble and tears filled her eyes. Gerry hugged her. "She was always praying to St. Anne, asking that she find you a good wife."

It was then that Anne and Gerry knew. Peg hadn't died from a bad heart, but from a thoroughly contented one.

Excerpt from *A Shepherd's Song*

Read an excerpt from Janice's next release a Christmas novel: *A Shepherd's Song.*

Chapter 1-1992

I didn't belong here, but if I were truthful, I didn't belong anywhere. But I wanted the money. So I inched along Perry Highway, which bisected the heart of Perrysville, a small suburban community north of Pittsburgh, straining to read addresses through my Sentra's steamy windows. The heater has been broken for two years; the bomb was a meat locker on wheels.

This last Sunday in November, the four-block business district was deserted: everyone was either indoors watching the Steelers or at Ross Park Mall Christmas shopping. Through the condensation, I made out the address on the The Nuts and Bolts Hardware store across the street. It said 999 Perry Highway. One-thousand had to be close so I wedged the car into the first parking space I found.

After shutting off the engine, I re-read the note my roommate, Rob Bubash, had left me, wondering what a graphologist would make of his handwriting. It spiked on the page like a printout from a Richter scale.

Tom—

Got to be at work by eight. Deliver a Sammy to G. Davidson at three, 1000 Perry Highway, Ross Township. The chick was desperate. Squeezed her for $150!!!

When my eyes saw that figure this morning, they bungeed out of their sockets. In a matter of days, the toy's price had skyrocketed.

I stretched across the seat, wiped a porthole on the foggy window, and squinted, hoping to make out a mall, but there wasn't any—not even a dinky strip mall or shopping plaza. Now what?

Rob and I'd made it a practice to meet buyers at public places because last year we were robbed in a parking lot during one of our deals.

The area looked safe, but hey, you can get killed anywhere these days. Why would Rob agree to making a delivery here? One hundred fifty dollars probably had something to do with it.

My hands were not only cold now, but also clammy.

I opened the car door, put a foot outside, and stood, looking over its roof. The sign stuck in the small, snow-dappled lawn beyond the sidewalk, stopped my heart.

It read: Holy Redeemer Church. 1000 Perry Highway. I jumped back into the car and locked the door.

Oh, this had to be a mistake! I scrambled for the note and compared the addresses again, and to my dismay, they still matched. Maybe this was Rob's idea of a joke. He knows how much I hate anything to do with religion.

The keys still hung in the ignition, and I quickly moved my fingers to them, ready to start the car and pull out. But I hesitated. What if it wasn't a joke? I'd lose $150.

My hands dropped into my lap. Holy Redeemer? It sounded like a congregation of coupon clippers. I snickered. Ah, this is ridiculous to be afraid of a place. It was only a church. What could happen to me?

Pushing up my fatigue jacket's sleeve, I glanced at my Timex— three twenty-five. I was late. I got out of the car, scanned the street, and wished I were an animal so I could sniff the air for the scent of danger.

The church, a red brick giant, was squeezed in among the smaller buildings. There was no one waiting in front of it.

I shoved the note and my keys into my pocket, grabbed the green garbage bag containing the Sammy from the back seat, and closed the door.

Snow flurries fell almost in slow motion from the dust-rag colored sky, but they were too sparse to freshen the mounds of old, gritty snow lining the curb, which was all that remained of the Thanksgiving eve blizzard four days ago.

Hanging in the air with the flurries was a palpable creepiness. Something was strange. Who at a church would want to buy a toy?

I tilted my head, looking to the top of it. There was no steeple or bell tower. Unless you saw the small crucifix at the roof's peak, you might have mistaken it for a VFW or some kind of rec hall.

I walked to the far side. No buyer. A driveway ran along it and led to a rear parking lot, which was filled with cars, but there wasn't anyone milling about, looking like they were waiting for me.

I hurried back to the front of the church and decided to give my buyer a few more minutes to show.

Then I had a thought. With this lousy weather, maybe my buyer had gone inside to wait.

I climbed the limestone steps and set the bag down. I pressed my nose to the glass doors, which were etched with religious symbols. It was dark inside the church. Cupping my hands around my eyes, I peered in. All I could make out were some flickering candles.

I pulled the door's handle. Damn, it was unlocked. I stuck a foot inside, but quickly withdrew it. No way was I going into a dark church alone. I released the handle; the pneumatic door closer let out a sinister hiss as the door slowly shut.

Glancing over my shoulder, I checked to make sure no one had sneaked up from behind. Then I looked at my watch—three twenty-eight. Two more minutes and I'd be out of there in a flash.

I watched the Timex's digital readout form the numbers three thirty. Time was up. No one was going to come now. If this wasn't a joke, Rob was going to go ballistic that I'd been late and botched the deal. I'd have to lie and make up an excuse.

Annoyed at the weather, that I was at a church, and that I may have screwed up a deal, I picked up the Sammy bag to leave.

"They're in the church hall," boomed a voice behind me.

"Jesus Christ!" I cried, nearly jumping out of my Doc Martens. Whirling around, I saw a chubby man in a Steelers jacket standing there. His face was as red and round as the bulb end of a thermometer, and thick, unruly white hair stuck out all over his head.

"Sorry, wrong guy," he said.

"Huh?"

"Jesus Christ? You called me— Get it?"

When I didn't laugh at his lame joke, he waved his hand. "Ah, never mind. Sorry to scare you." He patted my shoulder. "Come on, follow me."

And for some stupid reason, I did. Holding onto the plastic bag's drawstrings, I trailed after him as he walked around the side of the church.

Perhaps I followed him because he seemed so harmless. His jacket barely covered his gut, and he walked on the toes of his suede shoes, swinging his arms happily at his side, reminding me of one Snow White's dwarfs, you know, Fatso, going off to work.

Coming to a side door, he opened it for me. The door led to a staircase. He smiled a dopey grin.

Ignoring my instincts to run, I stupidly went in. As I passed through the doorway, I felt for the note inside my pocket.

The door closed behind us with a loud thud, like the sealing of a vault. Inside the stairwell, an odor of dust, coffee, and stale Coke lingered in the air while a droning, like the buzzing of a thousand bees, rose up the shaft.

Midway down, I pulled the note from my pocket and read the name on the paper. My hand was trembling. "I'm looking for a G. Davidson," I said to Fatso. I didn't want him misconstruing my reason for being there.

Fatso pulled open the door at the bottom, releasing a sonic boom of chattering voices. As he walked into the hall, he said something.

"What?" I yelled, stepping in after him. But if he answered, I didn't catch it. What I saw inside the room made my ears ring and sent my other senses into overload. Blood. It was everywhere.

My vision spun away as my legs turned to blubber. I wanted to run, but blubber legs don't respond well to terror. Feeling myself starting to sway, I dropped the bag, reached behind me for the wall, and braced myself against it preparing to black out.

As I waited to faint, the tidal wave of adrenaline pulsing in me ebbed, and my sight slowly returned. And then I felt like a complete ass.

A table to the right was draped with a huge banner that read: "Pittsburgh Metro Blood Bank." Two nurses were seated there, while a line, hundreds of people long, snaked away from it.

I straightened up and caught my breath. "It's a blood drive," I whispered repeatedly to keep from passing out.

In the back of the hall, donors reclined on hospital beds while bags filled with blood were arranged on a nearby cart. I looked around, and Fatso was gone. Obviously, he'd mistaken me for a donor. My legs gradually changed from liquid back into solid, and I picked up the bag to leave just as he reappeared.

"This is Ginny Davidson," he said, presenting a dark-haired woman.

Fantastic! I hadn't lost the sale.

The woman was petite and looked to be about thirty. I could tell she was young because her body still had that youthful snap—like a green twig has when you break it. But her face looked much older, and her dark, straight hair hung limply on either side of her cheeks.

Don't get me wrong, she wasn't ugly; she just seemed tired or worn out. Her brown eyes were fixed on me, and looking into them, they reminded me of burned out light sockets. They had no juice.

"Will you excuse me a moment," Fatso said, and he left us.

The woman continued to stare at me while I waited for her to say something. After all, she'd been the one who called to buy the toy. Then she arched her brows, opened her palms, and said, "Yes?"

"OK, hold on a sec . . ." Turning my back on the crowd, I loosened the bag's drawstrings. "It's in there," I whispered.

Puzzled, she glanced inside the bag and then her eyes shot to mine. Electrical service restored. Shock registered on her face then rapidly bloomed into a smile.

She looked into the bag a second time. "Oh, praise God," she said, covering her heart with her hands. When she raised her head, tears were glistening in her eyes. "I can't believe it. Oh, God bless you." She threw her arms around my neck, hugging me so tightly, I swear she knocked my spine out of alignment.

Man, the way she carried on, you'd have thought I was giving her the toy. For $150 bucks, I should have been crying and hugging her.

One of the nurses at the table rose and called, "Mrs. Davidson, is something wrong?"

She released my neck and turned around, wiping tears from her cheeks. "Wrong? Oh, good heavens no." She picked up the bag containing the toy. "You'll never believe it. This young man is here to give Christo a So Big Sammy!"

Give a Sammy? Is she out of her mind?

A murmur rippled through the crowd.

What should I do? I know. What I should have done when I first got to this creepy church—run. I'll rip the toy out of her hands and get the hell out of there.

As I was about to snatch it away, the mob suddenly burst into applause. Surprised, I halted. A collage of eyes focused on me nailing my feet to the spot. If I grabbed it and ran now, they'd nab me and kill me. My intestines coiled into a giant knot.

I wanted my money, and I wanted out of there. The woman clung to me, mindlessly mumbling, "Thank you! Thank you!"

"Excuse me, ma'am," I whispered, prying her arms from my neck. "I'm afraid there's been—"

A voice like a shovel scraping cement pierced the thunderous applause. "Quick, film this!"

Film? What the hell is going on?

"What's your name, young man?" That voice again.

I jerked my head so that my shoulder-length hair fell in front of my face. And through the screen of hair, I saw a woman in an expensive navy suit standing next to me. She was all made-up like those cosmetic counter ladies in Kaufmann's who spritz you with cologne, and her honey-colored hair was short and puffy and so heavily sprayed, her head looked like a shellacked walnut shell. She held a notebook, and for some reason, she looked familiar.

A man with a camera perched on his shoulder like a flamethrower was aiming a lens at me. Then I realized that Walnut Head was a reporter, and I was going to be filmed by the Channel 6 News crew. I wanted to puke.

Walnut-head called to a young woman in a Channel 6 News sweatshirt. "Melody," she commanded, "get the sick kid over here. Let's get a shot of him," Walnut Head was pointing at me and talking to the cameraman, "giving the kid the toy."

Why did everyone think I was giving the Sammy away? I've got to get out of here.

The crowd wandered out of the orderly line and surged toward the camera, hemming me in so I couldn't make a break for the door.

"What'd you say your name was?"

"Huh?" I mumbled.

"Push the hair out of your eyes and speak up," she commanded. Her tone scared me, and like an ass, I obeyed. When I pushed my hair behind my ears, I saw that she'd traded in the notebook for a microphone. Uh-huh, no way was she interviewing me. I pulled my arm away but her French-manicured nails dug into my flesh.

"I got the kid," Melody shouted as she threaded her way through the swarming crowd.

Ginny Davidson called out, "Someone please find Joe."

"I'm coming," yelled a husky, bearded man as he emerged from what appeared to be a kitchen on the left. In front of him, an apron-clad old lady walked carrying a tray of doughnuts. The man reached over her shoulder, plucked two from the tray, and strode toward us, licking jelly filling from his upper lip. When he saw the TV camera, he looked as confused as I felt.

He swallowed hard. "What's going on?"

The intern put her finger to her lips and shushed him. She took the bag with the Sammy from Ginny Davidson, and shoved a small boy forward.

When I saw the kid my heart deflated like a steamroller had run over it. The boy's hair looked like the campus lawn after it had been dethatched. Did he have the mange or something?

I tried to move away but the crowd was too thick. Trapped, I constricted my nostrils, so as not to breathe in too deeply. If this kid had something contagious, I didn't want to be sharing the same air.

Walnut Head stepped in front of us and her transformation as she morphed into her on-air persona stunned me. She threw her shoulders back, raised her head, and began to speak. The annoying voice was gone. Instead one as sweet and smooth as fudge flowed from her mouth.

"As you recall," she said, "yesterday during our six o'clock broadcast, we introduced you to four-year-old Christopher Davidson, who is battling leukemia."

Leukemia! Man, this kid is really sick.

"We're here at Holy Redeemer Church in Ross Township, where a blood drive and tissue typing is being held with the hopes that his Christmas wish of finding a bone marrow match will be fulfilled."

Bone marrow? I've walked into a frickin' nightmare.

"We also told you that Christopher had another item on his Christmas wish list—a So Big Sammy. He is hoping Santa will bring him one. His parents, Virginia and Joseph Davidson, told us yesterday that they cautioned Christopher not be too disappointed if

Santa doesn't bring him one as this toy has become quite popular. In fact, Channel 6 News at our noon broadcast reported that all the local stores have been sold out of the popular toy and that toy scalpers are demanding upwards of $50 for one."

Toy scalpers? That's what they're calling us? It sounds so . . . so criminal.

Walnut Head continued to gush into the microphone. "But we're happy to report that one of Christopher's wishes has come true." She paused for effect.

The intern nudged Ginny Davidson, who then moved in front of the camera, bent down, and put her arm around her kid's thin waist.

"Christo," she said, "this nice young man has something to give you." Her last few syllables were punctuated with a sob.

The intern kicked me in the shin, snapping me out of my disbelief. She handed me the Sammy, cueing me to give the kid the toy. As much as I wanted to run out with it, I couldn't. There was no way to escape. I had no choice but to give it to him.

"Here," I said, grudgingly handing it over to the boy and making sure I didn't touch him.

The package was nearly as tall as he, and Ginny Davidson helped him unveil the bag's contents. When he saw the toy, color filled his pale cheeks, and his eyes lit up like a neon sign. "It's Sammy!" he shrieked, grabbing for the box.

Quickly, his mother took his small hands and held them tightly while she looked into her son's face. "What do you say to this kind young man?"

The kid looked up at me, and smiled, revealing baby teeth no bigger than grains of rice. Then he wrapped his arms around my leg.

I flinched; I felt like shaking him off like you do a dog that's humping your leg, but I couldn't because everyone was watching.

"Fanks so much," he said, butchering the "th" sound. "Now all I need is a twanspwant."

329

A transplant? I felt a squeezing sensation in my chest and hoped I wasn't having a heart attack. What kind of world is it, I wondered, when a kid too young to pronounce transplant correctly needs to have one?

I stared down at the boy with hair like the fuzz on a peach. It was time for him to release me, but he hung on tightly, and it scared me that now he'd gotten hold of me, he'd never let go.

"Welcome," I squeaked. Finally, he relaxed his grip on my leg to inspect the toy. When Walnut Head knelt to get Christopher Davidson's reaction to his gift, I made a break for it.

Running to the door, I hit the handle, and shot out of the hall. A collective gasp followed me as I climbed the steps two at a time. When I burst through the door at the top of the stairs, frigid air hit my face.

While I'd been trapped in the church basement, the snow had intensified, covering the driveway. I slipped as I sprinted alongside the building, skidding the last ten feet to my car.

As I stuck the key in the lock, I heard Melody calling after me from the doorway, "Stop! We didn't get your name."

I hopped inside and fired up the Sentra's engine. My back-end fishtailed as I pulled out, and the snow covering the rear window blew off, trailing behind like a comet's tail. In the rearview mirror, I saw Melody run into the street, waving her arms like she was Gilligan trying to flag down a rescue plane.

Walnut Head came running up beside her in her pumps, skidded, and fell on her ass. I laughed as I floored the pedal.

The last thing I saw in the mirror as I sped away from Holy Redeemer was Walnut Head sitting on the snow-covered sidewalk scribbling something in her notebook.

Chapter 2

I headed south on I-279. Rounding a curve in the East Street Valley, I came upon a line of cars, strung bumper-to-bumper stretching all the way into downtown Pittsburgh. As soon as a snowflake falls, everybody panics and forgets how to drive. I pumped the brakes. My tires slipped some and then grabbed the road as the car slid to a stop.

The storm had intensified, obscuring the city's skyline, softening the hard lines of the USX Tower and completely erasing the turrets atop PPG Place.

I punched the buttons on the radio, searching for some music. Only warmed-over rock songs and blather from that idiot talk show host, Mark Thornton, poured out. After ten minutes of him, I switched off the radio and sat listening to the snow crunching under my wheels.

The earth's land area is 57 million square miles, and of all the places in the world I could've been, don't you know I had to show up at Holy Redeemer at precisely the wrong moment. But that's how my whole life has been. If I believed in that mystical garbage, I'd think I was born under a bad sign.

Lately though, I'd been convinced that maybe my luck was changing. Since Thanksgiving, I'd been happier and more optimistic than I could ever remember. See where that got me.

I'd spent a miserable Thanksgiving Day in the dorm. Rob had taken pity on me and invited me to his family's place in Mars, a small town about fifteen miles north of Pittsburgh, for dinner. But I declined. Last year, I went home with him, but it made me feel like a charity case.

So I spent this Thanksgiving hibernating in my room. Hardly anyone remained in Stephen Foster Hall; a handful of foreign students had gathered in the lounge to eat a meal of rice and lamb. They said I could eat with them if I wanted, but their menu sounded like something prepared by Purina, so I passed.

I spent the time studying and listening to the Detroit Lions lose to the Houston Oilers on the radio. Unlike the rest of the rich brats in this place, Rob and I were too poor to afford a TV. Periodically, I took breaks to watch the falling snow as it buried the campus.

My holiday feast consisted of two hotdogs and a carton of chocolate milk I'd picked up at the 7-11. Afterward, I settled back on my bunk to enjoy my après dinner liqueur—an Iron City beer.

As I popped the aluminum ring tab, the six o'clock news came on the radio. "Heavy snowfall across most of the country has stranded holiday travelers."

My Thanksgiving had been no Norman Rockwell painting, but I guess it could have been worse. I could be marooned in some airport. I took a gulp of beer and savored the way it stung my tongue before it slid down my throat. At least I had beer and a bed.

"And in financial news," the radio crackled, "industry analysts released their annual report forecasting this year's list of hot toys for the upcoming holiday shopping season."

At the word "toy," my ears pricked up.

"Topping this year's list is So Big Sammy, the purple plush monkey that plays the game 'So Big.'"

I hopped out of my bunk to turn up the volume and spilled beer down my chest.

"Seems analysts are on target with their prediction," said the newscaster, "because retailers all over the tri-state area are reporting they can't keep the So Big Sammys on their shelves."

The voice continued: "Gee Whiz Inc., the manufacturer, has gone into round-the-clock production in an attempt to keep up with the demand. Even so, a company official cautions that they still may not be able to satisfy all the orders for the toy in time for Christmas.

"Consumers are reportedly paying as much as $100 a piece on the black market for the toy—more than triple its retail price. Wall Street analysts are predicting that if current indications hold forth, So Big Sammy could be the next Cabbage Patch Kids, earning record profits."

"Yes!" I thrust my fist in the air. Finally, something has gone right in my life.

"In a related story . . . " I cocked my ear toward the radio, holding my celebration in check for a moment. "This morning, a Steubenville woman sustained a concussion and broken nose when frenzied shoppers stormed a Toys 'R Us. The store had just received thirty of the coveted purple primates, when a mob rushed security guards and broke into the shipment. State Police were called in to restore order." Disbelief colored the newscaster's voice.

"Turning to world news . . . In Somalia, the Red Cross reports that thousands of people starving in Mogadishu have—"

I shut off the radio and unleashed my joy, dancing around the room. "Martinique, here I come," I shouted. I unlocked the door, and screamed down the hall, my voice echoing off the institutional green tile walls.

One of the Asian students peeked out from his room, saw it was me carrying on, shook his head, and slammed his door. I ducked inside and laughing, collapsed onto the orange vinyl chair.

My eyes darted around the room. The decor was hideous—a cross between early psych ward and post-Brady Bunch. Splashes of orange, avocado, and harvest gold assaulted my eyes. And the furnishings—cheap metal bunks, Naugahyde and chrome couch and chairs, pop-art daisy curtains, and out-of-date lamps—offended good taste. But tonight this small, rectangular room, this decorator's nightmare, looked like a palace because every available square foot of it was crammed with boxes containing So Big Sammys. We'd snagged fifty of them.

Everywhere I turned, the frozen grins of the purple monkeys stared back at me from behind their cellophane windows, looking like a troop from a psychedelic rain forest.

I ran to the desk, ripped a sheet of paper from my notebook, and as I searched for a pencil, I grabbed Rob's dirty sock that had been sitting on the window sill for over a month, and mopped up the beer I'd spilled down the front of my shirt.

I loved this sweatshirt. Rob gave it to me last Christmas after dubbing our toy selling partnership Scrooge and Marley, Inc. On it was a picture of Tiny Tim sitting by a fire, his hands curled around a mug, his crutch propped beside him. The caption said: "Let's Get Drunk and Scrooge!"

God bless us everyone! I chuckled as I blotted the beer. This was going to be a great Christmas!

Tossing the wet sock back onto the sill, I took a seat at the desk, and began calculating. If we sold the toys for $100 a piece, we should have enough money to get to Martinique during spring break. I raised my head and looked out the large window above the desk. Martinique sounded pretty good right now.

Three Rivers University, home of the TRU Bluejays, clung to a ridge on Pittsburgh's North Side that overlooked the downtown area. From my window in Foster Hall, the silvery cityscape shivered in the night.

Since last evening, six inches of snow had fallen, draping everything in a bolt of white flannel. Late this afternoon, it had stopped. Now approaching six-thirty, it was cold, and I knew windy by the white caps curling on the black glass waters of the Allegheny and Ohio Rivers. Out of habit, I checked the sky—it was clear and starlit.

Grabbing a box, I took out the Sammy. Turning it over, I flipped on its switch. As I grasped the silly-looking simian by its hands, a cartoonish voice cried, "How big are you?" The toy paused then asked, "Are you soooo big?" Then it raised its arms like it was doing the wave. "I'm sooooo big toooo!" It giggled and lowered them.

Sammy repeated the game until I turned it off. As I laid it on the desk, I shook my head. What parent in their right mind would buy their kid one of these ugly, annoying toys for Christmas? But then again, what did I know about parents and Christmas?

The room was quiet now, and I hated to admit it, but I was lonely. Even though Rob sometimes gets on my nerves, I couldn't wait until he returned tomorrow so I could tell him the good news—that Scrooge and Marley were on their way to Martinique.

Neither Rob nor I was loaded. He worked part-time at the Toy Trunk, while I collected chump change from toiling in the campus bookstore. I survived on a small academic scholarship, loans, and the infrequent check from my father.

We've never been able to afford a trip at spring break. In October, we pooled our money and began making the rounds of area stores, buying toys to sell at inflated prices. At each, we bought two or three toys, stockpiling them in hopes of making a killing at Christmas.

The rest of Thanksgiving evening, I spent composing a classified for the Post-Gazette offering Sammys for sale and daydreaming of lying in the sun on the beaches of Martinique.

Late on Friday afternoon, Rob exploded through the door and slung his backpack on the chair. "Ebenezer, my boy," he called, crossing the room and pulling a small neon-printed cloth out of his jacket pocket. He twirled the swatch on his index finger. "While I was at home, I dug out my thong because, man, we are headed to Martinique."

I plucked the fabric from his finger. "This isn't a thong."

"It certainly is."

I held up the bathing suit. The back of it was nothing more than a string.

"You'll look like a praying mantis in a diaper."

Rob paid no attention as he took off his jacket. He's aerodynamically designed so that insults flow without resistance right over him. He bent his long legs, sat on the lower bunk, and leaned forward on his elbows, reminding me of an origami bird I'd once folded in Mrs. Osborne's fourth grade art class. At six feet, four inches, he was all angles and points from his beaky nose to his knobby knees that jutted out beneath his jeans.

"I swear I'm not going anywhere with you if you wear that thing." I shot the bathing suit at him slingshot style.

He snatched the suit out of the air and put it on his head. "You may jest, Thomas, but I've been doing my mother's 'Buns of Steel' video."

I've seen his mother. "Buns of Tapioca" was more like it.

He stood, turned his backside to me. "You must admit, mon derriere looks perkier all ready. Oh," he growled, "I'm going to be a babe magnet in Martinique."

I didn't want to look at his derriere let alone comment on it, so I changed the subject. "I take it then you've heard how hot our friend Sammy is?"

"Hot?" Rob cried, picking up the toy that I'd left on the desk last night. "Hot? He's sizzling! This dude should be classified as an alternative energy source. Forget nuclear, man. We got Sammy. Last night, Tommy, I watched the news, and people were killing each other for this guy." He stroked the toy's head. "He was the only bright spot in my Thanksgiving."

"Why? Something happen?"

"Nah, same old stuff."

"Was it Fat Head?"

Fat Head Michalski was Rob's mother, Chickie's, latest live-in. A long-distance trucker, he had a head the size of the Pirate Parrot's. Or at least his head used to be that big. See, Fat Head had asthma and one night after washing away the miles with some Wild Turkey in an Indiana Motel 6, he passed out. During the night, the weather changed and his asthma flared. In the darkness, Fat Head fumbled for his inhaler on the night stand, but in a drunken stupor, picked up the pistol he kept for protection by mistake and shot off his upper lip and the ridge of bone above his right eye. The bullet reduced the circumference of his head by a quarter.

"Who else?" Rob said. "The doofus insisted on making the gravy. Man, you know how he can't control his spit. Well, I looked over and his drool was dripping into the pan. I yelled, "'Hey, divot head, that pot ain't a spittoon.' But the moron didn't care. He just kept on stirring his spit into the gravy." Rob shook his head. "Be glad you weren't there."

Believe me, I was.

"What'd you do for Thanksgiving?"

"Ah, not much. Studied. Watched the snow pile up. Oh," I said, grabbing a paper off the desk, "and I wrote that classified. I phoned it into the Post-Gazette this morning. It'll be in tomorrow's paper."

Rob read it over then handed it back to me. "Looks great. Be prepared, Tommy. I'm warning you, the phone's going to be ringing off the hook."

I grinned. "Oh, I'm prepared—prepared to make a lot of money. I swear, when I saw that stupid monkey the first time, I thought you'd lost it. I thought it'd be a dud."

"No, Ebenezer, my boy," Rob said, thrusting the toy in my face, "Sammy's the man. He's your ticket to paradise."

Now, as my car inched along in the storm, I was mad at myself for ever thinking that things could change for me. My life is one giant game of Sorry. Just when I think I'm getting ahead, someone yells "sorry," and I'm sent back to square one.

Thinking about what happened back at Holy Redeemer, how I'd been swindled, how I'd been made a fool, how I'd have to invent some excuse for Rob on why I'd blown the sale, I wasn't so sure anymore about what he'd said about Sammy.

A headache was forming above my left eye. As it gathered fury, I had the sickening feeling that Sammy was not my ticket to paradise but more like my passport to hell.

Acknowledgements

I owe a debt of gratitude to Judith Burnett Schneider, Mary Patouillet and Julie Long. Without you, *St. Anne's Day* would never have been the same, and my life would never have been so deeply enriched. You are gems!

Follow Janice at: JaniceLanePalko.com

Book Club Guide

1. Peg's view of romance and courtship differs greatly from today's. Do you think it was easier to find a mate and fall in love in the decades prior to the sexual revolution when Peg was young or now?

2. Were you surprised by Peg's reaction when Anne reveals what happened to her pregnancy?

3. Have you ever heard of the St. Anne prayer? Have you ever used any "aids" to help you find romance?

4. In the book Peg acts as the "wise woman." Can you recall any other novels where a wise character influences the other characters in the story?

5. In the beginning of the book, Gerry states that women enjoy when he flirts with them. Do you think women enjoy flirting? What is the most flirtatious thing ever said to you?

6. Anne is a very angry person, and we come to know the reason for her anger. Do you know any angry people and do you have any idea why they are that way?

7. Janetta is depicted at the beginning of the novel as a *bon vivant*, directly rebelling against her mother's subservient life. Do you think that by being less sexually inhibited that it has made women more independent or has it reduced them to playthings for men?

8. Why do you think Anne and her mother clash? Is there a person in your life whom you love but with whom you often clash?

9. Bernie saves Gerry's life. Do you know any people with special needs? How have they made a difference in your life?

10. Anger is a dangerous emotion, but did you feel any pleasure when Anne insults her cousin at the shower or smashes the cake in Gerry's face?

11. Do you think Janetta will change or will she return to relationships with men who abuse her?

12. Faith is an undercurrent in the novel. Do you like to read stories about characters who grapple with their faith?

13. When Anne is angry with Gerry, she says he is not a "real man." What do you think a "real man" is like?

14. Gerry is always making jokes. Do you like that type of person, or do you find them annoying? Why?

15. Peg acts as the novel's conscience, pointing out right and wrong to Gerry and the others. Can you recall any other novel where there is a character that acts as the story's conscience?

16. Peg asks Anne if she believes in true love. Do you believe in true love? Why?

17. Anne's father is described as spineless. Do you see him that way or do you see him as a peacemaker?

18. Do you think Anne is shallow for not accompanying Craig to Guatemala?

19. Anne finds it difficult to forgive herself? Do you find it easier to forgive yourself or others?

20. Who was your favorite character in the novel? Why?

About the Author

Janice Lane Palko has been a writer for more than 15 years. She is currently the executive editor of *Northern Connection* and *Pittsburgh 55+* magazines, where she also pens a column and contributes regularly to the magazines' content. She has had numerous articles published in publications such as *The Reader's Digest, Guideposts for Teens, Woman's World, The Christian Science Monitor, The Pittsburgh Tribune-Review* and *The Pittsburgh Post-Gazette.* Her works have been featured in the books *A Cup of Comfort for Inspiration, A Cup of Comfort for Expectant Mothers,* and *Chicken Soup for the Single's Soul.* Janice has won several awards for her writing including the prestigious Amy Foundation Award of Merit. She is working on her second manuscript, a Christmas novel entitled *A Shepherd's Song,* which will be released in late fall.